BREAKING HER FALL

ALSO BY STEPHEN GOODWIN

Kin

The Blood of Paradise

BREAKING HER FALL

———

Stephen Goodwin

Harcourt, Inc.

Orlando   Austin   New York   San Diego   Toronto   London

Excerpt from "Running on Faith" by Jerry Lynn Williams.
Used by permission of BMG Songs, Inc. and Steve Weltman.

Excerpt from *Twenty Love Poems and a Song of Despair* by Pablo Neruda, translated
by W.S. Merwin, copyright © 1969 by W.S. Merwin. Used by permission of
Viking Penguin, a division of Penguin Group (USA) Inc. and Random House UK.

Excerpt from "But Not For Me" (from the Broadway musical *Girl Crazy*).
Music and lyrics by George Gershwin and Ira Gershwin © 1930 WB Music
Corp. (Renewed). Gershwin®, George Gershwin®, and Ira Gerswhin™ are
trademarks of Gershwin Enterprises. All rights reserved. Lyrics reprinted
by permission of Warner Bros. Publications.

Library of Congress Cataloging-in-Publication Data
Goodwin, Stephen.
Breaking her fall/by Stephen Goodwin.—1st ed.
p.   cm.
ISBN 0-15-100806-X
I. Title.
PS3557.O624B74 2003
813'.54—dc21   2003008878

Text set in Janson
Designed by Cathy Riggs

Printed in the United States of America

First edition
C E G I K J H F D B

For Robby, a true companion

ACKNOWLEDGMENTS

I am deeply grateful to the Virginia Center for the Creative Arts, where this book got started; to Timothy Seldes, whose virtues as an agent include patience and absolute loyalty; to Susan Shreve, Sam Dunn, Eleanor Dunn, and Andrea Hatfield, early readers whose suggestions were godsends; to Buck O'Leary and Timothy Junkin, who tutored me in the workings of the criminal justice system.

BREAKING HER FALL

CHAPTER

1

———

On an ordinary summer night in 1998, my daughter, Kathryn—
Kat, we all called her, a fourteen-year-old who still liked to wear
her blond hair in pigtails—told me that she was going to the movies
with Abby, her best friend, but they never got there. Instead, they
hooked up with some of the other counselors from Rockrapids, the
outdoor camp where both girls were working that summer, and decided to blow off the movie. It was a hot, dense Washington night, and
one of the boys—Jed Vandenberg—invited everybody back to his
house. He had a pool. His parents were away. The kids started drinking beer and vodka shooters, and before long some of them had peeled
off their clothes and jumped into the pool. They started playing Big
Dare, a drinking game. Just before eleven, when Kat was supposed to
phone to let me know that she was safe at Abby's house, I got a call
from a stranger, a man whose daughter had been at this same party.
He told me that Kat—*your daughter*, he said—had gone into the pool
house to perform oral sex on a parade of boys.

I wanted to kill that man. *Performed oral sex on a parade of boys.* I can
still remember his exact words and his exact tone of disgust and judgment. He might as well have said, *Your daughter is a slut*, and I felt as
though I had been shot. I felt a deep, burning fury, a heat and pressure
that originated in my chest and made it hard to breathe, hard to speak,
hard to see. Even my eyes felt burning and heavy, boiling in their

sockets. I felt shocked and furious, and I was standing in my bed-room—naked, as it happened, with Christine extending her hand to-ward me in sympathy and puzzlement, whispering, "Tucker, Tucker, what is it? What's wrong?" and I brushed her hand away simply be-cause she didn't know what had happened. She couldn't know. She was in her blue-and-white robe, stretched across the bed, fumbling with the remote to mute the sound on the VCR as she reached for me with her other hand, and I cannot forget the hurt, bewildered look that crossed her face when I batted her hand away. She hadn't heard what this man had told me, and even if she had, she couldn't have known that I had already crossed a line dividing one part of my life from an-other, dividing the past from the part that was to come. I was a single father and this was a moment I had dreaded, the moment when a child of mine slipped out of my safekeeping and walked straight into harm and grief. I'd been unable to protect her—*failed* to protect her, I thought—and I was ready to do anything, anything, to bring her back. My life was going to change. Had changed already.

That, of course, is how I now remember and interpret that mo-ment, the minute or so—it couldn't have been much more than a minute—that I was on the phone with a stranger, another parent whose words seared into me as an accusation. I have replayed that con-versation, that whole night, a thousand times, and I come back again and again to that moment when confusion and dread and rage lifted me from the bed and seemed to be propelling me toward the future.

In these pages I don't want to inflate or exaggerate my emotions, nor to wrap them up in cheesy images (*cheesy*, one of Kat's favorite words), but there are some images I can't shake. They've just locked in, and by now they seem to be as much a part of my experience as the events themselves. They seem to be the only way that I can understand the journey that began that night. *Journey*—even that word sounds grandiose, since I am still right here in Washington. But let it stand. This story, my story, is a love story, the story of my fierce, clumsy, painful attempts to connect with my daughter, Kat, and to accept and enter into the soul-shaking mysteries of love between men and women.

So: I write here that when I now think of my reaction to that phone call, I see a rocket rising into space, jets of orange flame lifting it toward the unknown, just as we have all seen innumerable times on TV and in the movies. Cheesy.

Nevertheless, I was the rocket and I was speeding toward places I had never imagined.

ALREADY I have gotten way ahead of myself, and I am going to back up and try to describe what happened on that summer day: Monday, July 13th, 1998. It was hot and sticky, the temperature up in the nineties, the air quality code orange, and my crews—I have a landscape business—were on a summer schedule, working seven to four. After checking the work sites that afternoon, I went home to the Hut, the brown-shingled bungalow in the Palisades where I lived with Kat and Will, my twelve-year-old son. It was Kat who named it the Hut—she was always word savvy—and the name seemed to fit the house with its dark brown shingles, the bungalow huddled in the shade of several huge old oaks and maples. I bought the place when the kids' mother, Trish, and I separated and she moved to New York. Back then it wasn't much more than a hut, but now it's been beefed up like the other houses in the neighborhood, a bungalow on steroids. I poured money into it and extended the back of the house by twenty feet—kitchen, bedrooms—and turned the double-door freestanding garage into a rec room that soon evolved into a music room. It's soundproof, and it had become the headquarters for my ragtag band, the Make Believes, a group of other parents who got together occasionally to pretend that we could still rock. I was the drummer, and even though I hadn't studied music since taking piano lessons as a kid, I'd played in bands in high school and college, and music has always been an escape and release. I have more skill than talent, but I can pick out a tune on the piano and my voice is a junior varsity baritone. When I soundproofed the garage, Will and Kat were still youngsters and I had the fantasy that we'd make music together, a trio, a tight little family combo.

But neither of the kids was really into music, and that summer Kat's thing was rock climbing. She'd been thrilled to get hired as a junior counselor at Rockrapids, the camp she'd attended since the age of eleven and where she'd discovered her talent for climbing. Several times I'd gone to watch her, and often to belay her, when she scampered up and down the cliffs at Carderock and in the Potomac Gorge, where the sheer rock faces drop straight into the river. God, she was fearless. I don't like heights, and it made my stomach churn to watch her hanging by her fingertips, grinning down at me, beaming and proud, all but crowing. Heights, she told me once—she must have been all of twelve—gave her a rush. Like any father, I was astonished and awed by this child who'd found a passion of her own, this girl who was discovering a skill and strength and daring I'd never suspected. By that summer, the summer of 1998, she'd reached her full height—five eight—and while she still had the slenderness of youth, she was lithe and limber and deceptively strong. The muscles in her forearms leaped and twitched when she made a fist, and her hands were grainy as sandpaper from all that scrabbling on the rocks. "Climber's hands," I'd tell her. "At least they're good for something," she'd say. Kat had always been self-conscious about her broad, bony, big-knuckled hands, which she inherited from me. For years Kat had been determined to beat me at thumb wrestling, and whenever our big hands touched, our fingers hooked together by sheer force of habit and I'd feel her thumb reaching for mine, trying to pin it. *One, two, three, four, I declare a thumb war.* Sometimes, if she'd drifted away—and more and more she did drift away, hiding behind a sweet, dreamy smile—I'd grab her hand to pull her back, to start a thumb war, to connect with her, to see the gleam in her dark eyes. They're brown but look deep and tawny, like chunks of amber with old fossil fires still flickering in them.

That night, when Kat got home after the long bus ride, she was in a hurry. The bus was late, as usual. Part of her job was to stay on the bus until the bitter end to make sure that all the campers had been met by their parents. It was after 5:30 when she walked through the door, grimed with dust and sweat, deeply tanned, long legged in her yellow climbing shorts. Her backpack was slung over one shoulder and there were smudges of lavender climbing powder—the stuff they use to keep their fingertips dry—on her arms and legs and cheeks. There was even a dusting of lavender in her hair, in the little damp curling tendrils of blond that had broken loose along her hairline. I am her father and I can say that she was exquisitely beautiful that summer, exquisite because—it seemed to me—she was still indifferent to her

beauty. Kat wasn't exactly a tomboy, but she attached far more importance to her climbing than she did to her looks.

"I'm late," she said, dropping her backpack in the front hall, pausing just long enough to look at me, to notice that I had on tennis
clothes. "You're playing tennis? Isn't it hot for tennis?"

"A plan's a plan," I said.

"Playing with Christine?" That was an odd question, asked in a
tone of false, bright cheerfulness. Kat had little use for Christine.

"Yes," I said.

"Coast is clear, huh?" said Kat, and she darted up the stairs to take
her shower.

Maybe it shouldn't have surprised me that she could see straight
through me, but it did. The kids were away—Will was on Long Island
with his mother, and Christine's kids had just left for their camps—
and since Kat was sleeping over at Abby's, Christine and I had planned
to spend the night together. We were going to have an Amish night.
Kat had met Christine, of course, but we had always tried to keep our
private, intimate life concealed from the children, all of them.

But Kat had just let me know, for the first time, that she not only
understood what went on between us but also the way we kept it hidden. Her disclosure was hasty and might even have been inadvertent,
but as I listened to Kat showering and banging around upstairs, I wondered if it was time to tell her more about Christine. But what? That
we had an arrangement? That I still wasn't sure, after almost two
years, where our relationship was going, or if it was going anywhere at
all? That ever since Trish left me I hadn't wanted to get attached to a
woman? I thought that I was trying to shield Kat and Will from the
grown-up world of disappointment and betrayal when I kept Christine
at a distance.

Kat was showering upstairs—Kat, Kat, Kat, my little one, my
Goldilocks—and I remember sitting in the kitchen and wondering exactly what she did think, not just about me and Christine, but about
boys. About sex. She was getting ready to go out with Abby, but I
knew they'd meet up with a group of boys. And I knew that her drift
away from me had started when she had her first crush on a boy, although so many other things were happening to her then, so many jets

of hormones had kicked in, that I never believed that it was the boy—a redheaded kid who couldn't stop fondling himself—who'd made her shy around me, unreachable sometimes, hidden behind the sweet smile that she summoned so easily. I had no doubt that she was still a virgin. There hadn't been any other boyfriends since the redhead, and while she and Abby, her absolute friend, talked about boys, they certainly didn't seem boy crazy. I knew that boys sometimes called Kat, who had her own phone line, and she had several boys on her computer buddy list, but she had limited patience for instant messaging. Stupid, she called it. In fact, she and Abby seemed to have set themselves apart from their classmates at Byrd-Adams, the girls they sometimes referred to, disdainfully, as girly-girls. As far as I could tell, they thought of themselves as climber jocks—or maybe climber chicks—and hung out mostly with other kids who also had an independent streak.

Kat and Abby liked some of the music that other teenagers did, and some of the movies, but they prided themselves on being retro, on listening to Van Morrison and Ry Cooder and Bonnie Raitt and Linda Ronstadt, whom they worshiped. They thought Madonna was totally cheesy but they were intrigued by Marilyn Monroe, and Kat had a poster in her room—alongside posters of Everest and Glacier National Park and a calendar showing women climbers on terrifying rock faces—of Warhol's photographs of Marilyn, the ultimate blond, the repeated images of Marilyn bathed in deathly hues of red and green. Kat had seen most of Marilyn's movies and liked to imitate her breathy, singsong voice, but her best piece of mimicry, the one she used to drive her brother crazy, was of Peter Sellers as Inspector Clouseau in the Pink Panther movies. She took French at Byrd-Adams and she couldn't get enough of his clotted, nasal, loopy accent. For at least a year she couldn't say *room* like a normal person. It was always *rrrrheummmm*.

But her favorite line—her slogan, her mantra, her signature—was *Duzz yerr dugg bite?* (She loved that corny joke: Clouseau enters a hotel lobby, sees a feisty little dog, and asks the clerk, "Does your dog bite?" The grumpy clerk says, "No." Clouseau reaches down to pet the dog, who turns into a blur of noise, fur, and teeth. With dignity, with disappointment, Clouseau says, "I thought you said your dog does not bite!" The clerk replies, "That is not my dog.") On some days that line was her answer to every question, another way of vanishing into her own world, a way of putting up a smoke screen. Finished your homework, Kat? *Does your dog bite?* Want tacos for dinner? *Does your dog bite?* Have you called your mother? *Does your dog bite?* When are you going to clean up your room? *Does your dog bite?*

I didn't know what was going on in her heart or in her mind, but I always thought that she seemed to have her own purposes, even if they took the form of annoying her brother and exasperating her teachers. She was an inconsistent student. She was word savvy, as I have said, and did effortlessly well in languages (she was almost fluent in Spanish, having picked it up from our housekeeper, Gladys Ochoa), but she had trouble with math and the only time she took an interest in science was when the subject was the destruction of the rain forest. Ever since then she had regarded herself as an environmentalist, and she could get outraged by reports of pollution or global warming, but the subject that shook her to the core was history. As a sixth-grader she made her first visit to the Holocaust Museum, and she never got over it. A month afterward she was still crying about what she had seen. A year afterward she was still staying up at night to read Holocaust books—*Anne Frank: The Dairy of a Young Girl, All but My Life, Night, Alicia: My Story*—by the little light of her pillow lamp. She was undone by the atrocities in Bosnia; she made Gladys tell her about the years of war in Guatemala; she had a heart that went out instantly to victims of violence and oppression and injustice.

I was proud of her, proud that she seemed to chart her own course and think for herself. That was one of the Big Rules in our household: Think for Yourself. I had Big Rules and Little Rules stuck under magnets on the refrigerator. I tried to keep things on track and in order. Both Kat and Will sometimes called me Heffy, their way of saying El Jefe, the boss, which is what the guys on my crews, mostly Latinos, called me. *Sí*, Heffy, they'd say when they wanted me to lighten up on the enforcement of the rules. But after we settled into the Hut, when we began our life without Trish, once Gladys had started to work for us—a sturdy, steady woman with onyx eyes and a gold tooth who not only did the cleaning but also the cooking, the shopping, the driving, the ironing, and everything else needed to take care of us and free me to run the business—I began to understand how much structure and organization it took to keep everyone on track and on schedule, and I laid down as much routine as I could. I didn't know how else to manage.

WE WERE running late that Monday night. My game was at 6:30 and it was a gnarly ride from the Palisades, our neighborhood, over to Cleveland Park, where the Moorefields lived. Traffic, stoplights. I asked Kat what movie she was going to see. "I don't know," she said. She was definitely in a mood.

"Come on, Kat. You know how this works."

The rule was that she had to specify the movie.

"I'm fourteen," Kat said. "What difference does it make what I see?"

"I don't want you to see trash."

"You think it's all trash."

"I liked *The Little Mermaid*," I said.

"Ha-ha."

"I did. I liked the sea witch the best."

Silence. She stared straight ahead through the window of the car, the Honda that we called the *real* car, as opposed to the Jimmy I drove to work. It was a champagne sedan (*champagne*—who gives colors these la-di-da names?) with leather seats, a CD player, and a moon roof, these being features the kids had required. They'd hounded me for years to get rid of the old and embarrassing Volvo wagon, which Kat had dubbed the Tackle Box.

"Kat, I hate to quiz you. I just want to know where you are."

Lift of her shoulders. "We'll probably go see *There's Something about Mary*."

"I thought that was R rated."

"It is."

"So? You're fourteen. You're not supposed to be allowed into those movies."

"They don't check."

"You're telling me you've been to other R movies?"

Then Kat said, "What is it? Are you worried I'll figure out what men are like?"

She slipped down in her seat then, evidently to signal that the conversation was over, but I said, "No, Kat. That's not what I'm worried about. I'm worried that you'll think that men are like the idiots in the movies."

And she said dreamily, almost to herself, "Does your dog bite?"

Duzz yerr dugg bite?

She hadn't said that for months and it made me laugh. She shot a sly glance my way—surprised, I think—and put her feet up on the dashboard. Testing me. She knew that she was breaking one of the car rules (No eating, No drinking, No limbs outside the car, No feet on the dashboard), but in this moment of laughter and goodwill I didn't say a word. I don't like to quarrel with my children. I decided to let the whole subject of the movie just drop, but I did make her show me that her cell phone was charged. Yet another rule: she had to keep the cell phone on when she was out at night, and she had to answer it. She didn't like to be reminded of the rules, and it was clear that she didn't want any stern warnings about the dangers of the city at night. I looked at my daughter's lovely profile, her hair still damp from the shower and simply combed back from her face, releasing a fragrance of shampoo, a scent like a flower garden, and then I noticed that her tan feet were tucked into a pair of yellow flip-flops, yellow with a bright rubber flower, a yellow daisy, attached where the thongs joined, and it struck me that she had found time to put polish on her toenails. They were a shade—this is the kind of thing a single father knows— called Malibu pink. There wasn't a speck of makeup on her face but she'd painted her toenails, and I thought that if this was how she going to fix herself up—her feet, not her face—she was still a girl, still a long way from trouble.

Abby wasn't ready when we got to the Moorefields' and her mother, Lily, skipped out of the house, barefoot, her dog Rosa about a foot from her side and barking, with a CD she wanted me to hear— *Songbird*, by Eva Cassidy. Lily was a songbird herself, the vocalist in the Make Believes, and the best musician, the only trained musician in the group. She was always turning up new music. "Stop blowing your horn. You've got to overcome your LRTs." Latent redneck tendencies.

I said, "Are you going to let Abby grow up like you? Always late."

"El Jefe, so sorry," she said. Mock salute.

"What's this? The latest fad?" I caught hold of her wrist to look at the colorful woven bracelets she'd tied on.

"Are they not permitted by the dress code?"

"I thought there was an age limit on those things. Nobody older than sixteen."

Lily was leaning at the window of the car and she grinned at Kat, who had a single woven bracelet tied around her wrist. "I think he could use one, don't you?"

"Who'd give it to him?" Kat said.

Lily looked at my tennis outfit. "Big game tonight?"

"I'm late," I said.

"Big date," Kat said to Lily.

Those two, Kat and Lily, had always seemed to be on each other's wavelength. It wasn't just that Lily had known Kat since she was an infant—the Moorefields were neighbors and great friends when Trish and I lived in Georgetown, and the kids had grown up in and out of our two houses—but they shared a slightly offbeat, nuanced way of talking, laced with puns and halftones and odd dustings of emphasis. Sometimes they seemed to be more like mother and daughter than Lily and Abby, who tended to be direct and blunt. Abby was a grade ahead of Kat in school, and a year and half older, and she'd always been the trailblazer in the pair. In fact, I'd thought at first that rock climbing was just another case of Kat wanting to keep up with Abby, who was an out-and-out risk taker. Still, the girls had always shared a sense of humor, and they could talk and giggle for hours. I remember driving them back from a ski trip to Snowshoe, five hours in the car, and they talked the whole way. As soon as we got home after dropping Abby off at her house, Kat was on the phone—to Abby. Girls.

But Abby didn't look like a girl that night, not as she crossed the porch and came down the steps, her slip-ons slapping against the soles of her feet. She looked, excuse me, like what would have been called jailbait when I was in high school. She was dressed in shorts and a tank top, and she wasn't as tall as Kat, but she had filled out and she was shapely and dead sexy. Her shorts were cinched in at the waist, and there was a stretch of smooth tanned skin between those shorts and the bottom of her black ribbed top. This is the Age of the Midriff, and there doesn't seem to be much that parents can do about it, not when girls are Abby's age. That tank top showed every ridge of Abby's rib cage and the exact shape and size of her breasts.

"So long, Mom," Abby said, kissing Lily on the cheek.

They looked so much like each other that it was almost eerie. Same broad, high cheekbones, same wide-spaced blue eyes, same thick brown hair—though Abby's was sun streaked and Lily's blond highlights were, as she often said, store-bought—same wide, mischievous mouth that curled up at the corners and made it seem like they were always smiling, a cat-that-ate-the-canary smile. I saw that smile on Lily's face as Abby piled into the back of the car, and she used it to put a little spin on her rueful compliment when she said, "My glamorous daughter."

I handed her the overnight bag that Kat had packed for herself and she handed me the CD. We'd been talking about it while we waited for Abby. "Listen to that CD," Lily said. "There's a cover of 'Somewhere Over the Rainbow.'"

"You're telling me somebody had the balls to sing that song *seriously?*"

"*Shhh*," Lily hushed me. "Little pitchers."

"Lit-tle pitchers have lit-tle bit-ty balls," Kat said in a baby voice, and Abby giggled, and Lily turned her palms up. I drove the last few blocks down to Connecticut Avenue, where I let the girls off at the corner near Pizzeria Uno. Before they got out of the car, I did ask Kat if I knew any of the boys they might be meeting.

Kat said, "Don't worry, Dad. I'll let you know when my prince comes along."

She gave me a small nudge, not a kiss, as she stepped out into the evening. I was stopped at a light and I watched them stroll across the street, laughing, looking happy, looking eager to meet whatever might be before them, looking radiant and unafraid and absolutely heartbreaking.

I PLAYED sloppy tennis that night. Arrived late—I hate to be late—and never got into the game. Never found a stroke, a groove, a rhythm. Christine, as usual, was dependable and efficient, but we kept dropping points to Ted and Joan Walker, a couple we normally thumped. There was no breeze on the courts, the hazy air was the color of wet cement and even smelled like cement, and Ted Walker's face was red as a tomato. I was dripping with sweat and effort, but I couldn't keep the ball between the lines. I hate to play badly and I hate to lose, especially to a gloater like Teddy, whom I've known since I lived in Georgetown with Trish. He made a little fist pump every time he hit a winner.

And it irked me that Christine kept sucking up to him. She was ordinarily reserved, a no-nonsense midwesterner, a lawyer who worked for one of the big environmental groups, Worldwatch, and she was aware of the degrees and gradations of the Washington hierarchy. She needed to be, I suppose. But she was impressed by rank and title, and in her eyes Teddy Walker, plump and jowly, an assistant secretary of the Interior, was a person worth pleasing. My own attitude toward the Teddy Walkers of the world is complicated, I know, since once upon a time we were social equals and now I'm the lawn guy—the lawn guy whose ex-wife has become a minor celebrity because of her marriage to a very rich man and whose children go to private schools and whose income depends on maintaining ties with people of money and privilege, people who can afford a landscaping service. It's not cheap. The business did flourish initially because I was able to sign up old friends and acquaintances, but now, because I have gone out and hustled my tail off, because I make sure that my crews do better work than any other crews, Twill Landscaping (Twill, a combination of Kat and Will) has grown into a company with sixty-plus employees and annual revenues of more than $2 million. This is a point of pride, and I don't like the condescension I sometimes feel from people who've never had to meet a payroll but who are, after all, my bread and butter.

In any case, Teddy and Joan were old chums—pre-Trish I had actually dated Joan once or twice—and they were beating us at tennis, and Christine was flouncing around cheerfully, animated and flirtatious. Whenever Teddy won a point, she sang out some compliment, though she had nothing to say to Joan. "Too good," she'd cry out to Teddy, and she started making an exclamation, a yelp, a squeal—*eeeyewww*, like that—as if his masterful strokes sent a shiver through her.

Maybe I was jealous that she was flirting with Teddy—who felt her attention, by the way, and couldn't keep the smirk off his face—but I was edgy. I was off. I like tennis because the game usually erases everything that has happened during the day, and the tennis court is a place where I expect to be in the moment, as the woo-woos say. But that night I couldn't shake off Kat's remark—*Coast is clear, huh?*—and I knew that my frustration wasn't merely about the tennis but about my whole relationship with Christine, our arrangement.

Arrangement. That's a cold word, but that's what it was—an arrangement, not a romance. Christine and I had been going out together, sleeping together, for almost two years. We'd hit it off right away, as my old friend Jay Vellines had predicted when he set me up with her—a tennis date, as a matter of fact. She was my type, he said, long stemmed and brainy (it was news to me that I even had a type). She is a tall woman, five ten, and she is often described as striking, meaning that she is noticeable but not conventionally attractive. She has lovely dark hair, full and fine with a few white hairs shooting through it; she dresses carefully and she is conservatively fashionable; she has pale gray eyes and a correctness of bearing that give her, sometimes, a look that can be icy and intimidating. We had never spoken, not once, about our future. Most of our dates were movie dates, though we took occasional weekend trips and every now and then we were invited out, to dinner or to parties, as a couple. We'd even entertained together a few times, at my house—Christine lived in a smaller place on Yuma Street—but for the most part we kept our lives carefully separated. She had, as I have mentioned, two children of her own, Robby and Victoria, and we'd agreed that it would be confusing for the children if our lives got tangled together. Moreover, she wanted the children to spend time with their father, her ex-husband, Robert, who still lived in town. Robert Jeschke was the love of her life, the man she'd met and married at law school, a brilliant guy, the star of their class, an idealist who was determined to come to Washington to improve the world. So they picked up and left the Midwest and started their careers here and had their babies, then Robert came out of the closet. He fell in love with a man. Now Robert worked for the World Bank, developing projects to promote the economic independence of women in India, Pakistan, and Bangladesh. I'd met him. He spoke with enthusiasm about his work, he wore faint but detectable makeup—rouge, eye liner, mascara, the whole works. Christine had dropped his name and reverted to her maiden name, O'Malley, but she'd had a bitter fight with her parents when she decided to remain in Washington. They insisted that she return to Michigan, to the prosperous suburb outside Detroit where they still lived, but she thought it would be harmful to the children and devastating to Robert.

She'd revealed her story to me cautiously, in bits and pieces, and it was easy to understand why she'd be slow to trust me, to trust any man, and perhaps that is what we had most deeply in common. We'd had our hearts broken, I say now, though I wouldn't have admitted it then. It sounds so trite and banal and just so *cheesy*, an excuse for bad songs and bad movies. We'd had our hearts broken, though, and the fact that heartbreak is commonplace does not make it any less painful, and I think we must have recognized in each other a stubborn, silent grief that resisted our efforts to heal, and even our efforts to hide this grief from the world and from ourselves. We were kind to each other. We talked on the phone every day, usually late at night, after the children were asleep, and we liked to think that we gave each other more real pleasure, in bed and out, than any married couple. Not that we talked about marriage, not that we explicitly compared our situation to marriage, but we did sometimes pick apart the marriages of couples we knew, the implication always being that our arrangement was to be preferred. After a party one night, a party at which we were the only unmarried couple, Christine—usually reserved, fair-minded, slow to judge—said bitterly, "That's what I call Death Valley." She meant the smugness and falseness of the married couples that had filled the room.

The Walkers beat us that night in straight sets, and red-faced Teddy, seated on the bench at courtside, poured water over his head like a dopey schoolboy. He invited us to come back to their place for a drink—to the big stone house in Spring Valley, bought with Joan's money—but it was almost dark by then, and Joan said, pointedly, "I'm sure these two have better things to do."

Fuck, she meant, and it was impossible to mistake her meaning. Teddy looked as though he'd been slapped.

"How'd she know I was in the mood?" Christine asked when we were back at the Hut, showering off. "Was it so obvious?"

"Absolutely." I was doing her back and shoulders with the loofah mitt.

"Tell me, really. I don't want it to show."

"Then don't keep putting your hand down my shorts."

"Stop teasing," she said, but she reached around behind her to grope for me.

"Sorry I let you down," I said. "I played terribly."

"Just don't let me down now," she said, leaning back into me, reaching with both arms to pull me close.

I held her there under the water, wishing that I could forget Kat, wishing that I didn't feel this distance from the woman in my arms. I held her tight, but she was soapy and slipped around so that she faced me. "Tonight I'm going to blow your doors right off," she said. Her dark hair was flat on her skull and her eyes were narrowed as she reached for my cock, caught hold of it, and stood tall to place the tip of it between her legs, letting me feel her heat and readiness. She said, "Amish night," and made a growling noise, a long *grrrr*.

"Does your dog bite?" I asked, and wished instantly that I could have those stupid words back. They just popped out. They'd made me laugh when Kat said them, and they must have been lying just beneath the surface of my consciousness. I suppose I must have wanted Christine to laugh, too, at her torrid sex queen act.

"What?" she said, pulling her face back, uncertainty wavering in her eyes.

"Nothing, nothing. I was just goofing." And I held her close, pressing against her so that she couldn't see my face.

I didn't want to spoil Amish night. It was our ritual, one of our only rituals, our name for the rare nights when the children were accounted for and we could attempt to recover the bliss of the weekend we'd spent together in Amish country in Pennsylvania. We were still new to each other then, and the room we took in a bed-and-breakfast turned out to have a high, ceremonial bed, a massive bed with a canopy, gauzy curtains, and even a small wooden staircase at the foot of it. Perhaps every couple has a night like ours, a perfect night, a wild night, one that remains as the ideal, the pattern of joy. It is not always possible for Christine to forget herself, not always possible for me, but that night she was unabashed in her passion. At one point she took the tangled Amish quilt and wrapped it around herself and paraded around the room, then climbed that small wooden staircase at the foot of the bed. "Call me Madame Butterfly," she said, and I understood, as she opened her arms, as she spread that quilt like wings, as she delighted in her own nakedness and sensuality, as she descended upon me, that she was flying in her imagination. She was a butterfly and she was soaring.

The next morning we went for a drive in Amish country, and we kept seeing signs, hand lettered and brightly colored, with directional arrows leading to Stoltzfuss Baked Goods. It was late August, a glorious summer day, and we followed the signs as if we were on a treasure hunt, gliding along the farm lanes through a landscape of checkerboard fields and red barns with hex signs until we finally reached the last lane, a gravel road that ran through high corn to a picture-book farmhouse. Huge zinnias, pink and purple, bloomed in a cutting garden, and a smallish dog, mostly beagle, came sniffing over to greet us. A moment later old Stoltzfuss himself popped out of the house, a tiny gnome of a man with bright blue eyes and snow-white hair and beard. He was in Amish dress, the baggy black trousers with red suspenders over a white shirt.

"He looks like one of the Seven Dwarfs," Christine whispered to me.

"Honeymooners?" Stoltzfuss bellowed. He had a big voice and a suggestive smile, a leer, but we took it as a compliment that he guessed what we'd been up to. I admired the zinnias. "A dollar a bunch," Stoltzfuss said, "and that's for a big bunch. You can have 'em all, the whole garden, for ten dollars. The whole garden."

It was late in the summer, and he must have thought we were the last customers for zinnias. The semibeagle sniffed around Christine's ankles and looked up at her mournfully. He was still puppyish, gangly and loose limbed, but he had a sad face. Christine doesn't really like dogs but she reached down to pet him. I said, "Why not? We'll take the zinnias."

By magic, it seemed, a barefoot Amish boy appeared and Stoltzfuss told him to cut all the flowers and bundle them up for us. He saw us as easy marks, and when he led us into the house to show us the baked goods—two women in bonnets sat silently in the kitchen—he began to reel off the prices of all the items for sale. Cookies? A dollar per bag. Honey? Three dollars a jar. Jams and jellies? Two dollars a jar. The beagle had followed us inside and every minute or so, with an expression of helpless longing, he stood on his hind legs and tried to hump Christine's ankle. Stoltzfuss's blue eyes twinkled. When I happened to glance at a wooden footstool, he said, "Made that myself! You want it? Twenty dollars." When Christine looked at a rag doll that obviously belonged to one of the children in the house, he said, "That's an antique doll. Ten dollars." The house had the wonderful fragrance of baking and the women never said a word. Christine kept trying to shoo away the beagle, and giggling, and Stoltzfuss had an inspiration. "Honeymooners," he said, "need a quilt."

He beamed at us and produced three quilts from a cabinet, all with those incandescent Amish colors, all beautiful. "Newlyweds," he said to the women, and we bought a quilt for three hundred dollars.

While Stoltzfuss was adding up our bill, the beagle made one last futile effort to hump Christine's ankle, and the old man saw me trying to hold back a laugh. "That's a very friendly dog," I said.

"You like him? You like him? I got too many dogs. But this one, this is a good one. You can have him for ten dollars."

He realized quickly that he had overreached, and he said, "Ah, I'll just throw him in free of charge. No charge for the dog!"

And that is how I got my dog and why I named him Romeo.

And that night, after we had toweled dry and gone into the bed-room, as Christine and I moved all over each other on top of the Amish quilt with its pattern of orange and purple and royal blue and brilliant aquamarine, getting slick and sweaty and salty a second time, I thought about Stoltzfuss and Romeo—who was sleeping down in the kitchen—and imagined that Christine was thinking of Madame Butterfly. The AC was working to suck the heat out of the room, and I am sure Christine sensed my distance, for we didn't talk much but coupled as though the goal was not pleasure, not even ecstasy, but something more elusive and urgent, something that could only be achieved with great exertion. The music on the CD player was Miles Davis, *Kind of Blue*, and I remember this because the music ended be-fore we were done and lay exhausted on the quilt.

Christine said, "Jeez Louise, we should have timed that. I think it was a personal best."

It's pitiful, really, how men seize upon any compliment to their sexual prowess.

We finally ate, still on top of the quilt. We ate the fancy picnic food that Christine had picked up earlier. Christine put on the robe she kept at my place, blue-and-white silk, Asian in design, blue cranes winging their way over fields of waving blue wheat, very elegant. And she went to the trouble, as she always did, of making sure that we ate off china, and drank from proper wineglasses, and wiped our mouths with cloth napkins. These items had all been gifts from Christine.

Inevitably we talked—this was the summer of 1998, remember—about Bill Clinton and Monica Lewinsky, and Christine, who'd voted for Clinton twice, got upset. She seemed to take Clinton's behavior as a personal betrayal, and she railed against an editorial she'd read that day. Then she asked me, out of the blue, "You're not screwing around, are you?"

"Why would you ask that?"

"Are you?"

"Why would I? I have a woman. A good woman."

"God, why can't you just answer the question? Are you screwing around or not?"

"No," I said, "I'm not."

I moved the plates aside then, and kissed her, and through the silk felt her turn into me and press her length against me.

"Darling, darling, darling," I said, because I couldn't say what I knew she wanted to hear. I hadn't told any woman I loved her since Trish left me.

"I'm sorry," she said. "I had no reason to ask you that."

"Let's make a rule," I said. "No talking about Clinton."

"You and your rules," she said, but she smiled gamely, and soon I clicked on the VCR. Our movie that night was *Out of Africa*. Somehow Christine had never seen it, and we both liked movies shot in beautiful, exotic, faraway places.

THE PHONE call came at 10:48. When the phone rang on the bedside table, I noted the time because I expected it to be Kat, telling me that she was at the Moorefields'. I said to Christine, "There's a minor miracle. Kat's ten minutes early."

The caller was John Fogarty. I didn't register his name immediately because his tone of voice—careful, official, drained of all emotion, sounding as if it came from far away, from the other side of bad news—made me brace immediately. He asked, "Am I speaking to Tucker Jones?"

"This is Tucker," I said, sitting up at once. "Who's this?"

He repeated his name. He told me that he had gotten my number from the Byrd-Adams school directory. His daughter, Alexa, went to Byrd-Adams. She was in Kat's class. He thought we'd met at a parents' function. He took painful care in dispensing his words, and I felt a tingling and tightening across my shoulders.

"Has anything happened to Kat?"

"I apologize for calling so late," he said, with maddening deliberation, pronouncing every word carefully. "You haven't spoken to your daughter tonight, have you?"

"No. She went to the movies. What happened?"

"She did not go to the movies, Mr. Tucker."

"Jones. My name is Tucker Jones."

"Excuse me, I am very upset here. Very. I am sorry that I have to be the one to make this call."

By then I was on my feet. "Please. Just tell me what happened."

"My daughter came home sobbing tonight, and I decided—I decided I had to call you. Had it been my daughter, I would want to know. Immediately."

His voice was stiffening with disapproval. I said, "Kat went to the movies."

"She did not go to the movies," he corrected me. "She was at the party."

"I know nothing about a party."

"Believe me," he said, almost scornfully, "there was a party."

"Where?"

"At the Vandenberg house."

"I didn't know anything about it," I repeated. "Kat would have called me if her plans had changed." Why couldn't this Fogarty just tell me what had happened? I asked, "Is Kat hurt?"

"I don't know whether she is *hurt*," he said, "but you might want to go find your daughter. She performed oral sex on a parade of boys."

Even now I cannot say for sure whether I believed him. Every cell in my body seemed to rise up in disbelief, in protest, in anger. My first reaction was that he had to be wrong, that Kat would never do such a thing, that for reasons I could not fathom this stranger had decided to slander my daughter. But some part of me must have known that there was truth and urgency in what he was telling me, for I had risen from the bed, and I felt trapped in that room, frantic as I attempted to understand what I must now do. My daughter was in danger, and I had to help her. I had to go to her.

That is when I saw Christine shifting her gaze from the video, saw her lean across the bed, saw her reach toward me. I brushed aside her hand. I was trying to listen to Fogarty, trying to concentrate. I made myself ask him where the party was, and he gave me the address of the Vandenbergs. At least he did that. Davenport Street. Then there was a silence. He seemed to expect me to thank him. I could not possibly say how the phone call ended, but it did, and I was standing far from the bed, near the closet. She was saying, "Tucker, Tucker, what is it? What's wrong?"

And I heard myself say, "Kat's in trouble." I heard myself make a strange snorting noise as though some reflex of laughter had died on my palate. I told Christine what Fogarty had told me, but not in his words. I said, "He claims Kat went to a party. He says she went down on a bunch of boys." I said, "I'm going to go find her."

I was pulling on my clothes, and Christine made as if to get up and get dressed herself. She opened her robe and stepped into her panties. "I'll go," I said. "You stay here in case she calls."

She didn't argue. No doubt she understood as well as I did—better, probably—that she was not the person Kat would want to see on this night. But she did walk to the door with me, her robe pulled tight around her, and I remember how she said with wide-eyed resolve, "I'm here, Tucker. I'm right here as long as you need me."

It is a short ride, only a couple of miles from my house over to the Moorefields', but I sped as though I was on a rescue mission. The traffic was light and I blew through the stoplights on Nebraska Avenue, imagining somehow that if I could just get there fast enough, if I could just get there on time, I could still save Kat. I could keep from happening what Fogarty said had already happened; I could protect Kat. I could save her.

Kat's cell number was on the speed dial of my cell phone, and I called her. No answer, of course.

I can't explain, even now, why I went first to the Moorefields'. I must have hoped I would find her there, sitting at the cluttered pine table in the kitchen with Abby and Lily. I hoped I would enter the Moorefields' house and find it filled, as usual, with the kids who were always wandering in and out. Lily never locked all her doors and the house had always been a gathering place, a house where the moms showed up for coffee and the kids came and went, putting their feet up on the furniture and hanging out in the back room, where there was a big TV and a sound system. *A clubhouse*, Lily would sometimes say despairingly, as she tried to keep it all in order, but it had always been a place where Kat felt at home, and I wanted to walk in and find her, to see her glance up at me with her weary tolerance, to find her exactly as I had last seen her.

At the Moorefields' I parked on the street and for a moment, when I heard the music of a piano—Lily was playing—I felt tears sting my eyes. It was so calm here, so completely familiar. How could anything tragic have taken place here when the piano was playing and Lily was singing "It's All Right with Me" and the sprinkler system—yes, I noticed even that, the half-assed sprinkler system I had been telling Lily she ought to replace—was sending up a fine, pulsing spray that sparkled in the streetlight and hissed onto the pachysandra banked on the slope? The house was on the high side of Lowell Street, big and broad, a blue house with a porch running the length of the front. The house was lit up and it looked bright and inviting, even festive, with the light pouring out through the three sets of porch doors, sending a volley of long shadows over the porch furniture and making longer, streaking shadows of the porch columns. When I climbed the stone steps up to the house, I caught sight of Lily at her baby grand, hammering away at the keys and singing for her own pleasure, toying with the words, just noodling around. She seemed to be by herself.

Rosa barked when I stepped onto the porch. The front door was ajar, and Lily was already up, making her way toward me.

"Are the girls back?" I asked.

Lily said, pretending to scold, "You know I don't like to let anyone hear me practice."

"I'm looking for Kat."

She'd reached me by then and looked at me closely. "They're not back yet. What's wrong?"

"I have to find Kat."

"It's not time for them to be back, is it? Tucker? Talk to me." Lily was tugging at my arm. "What are you doing here? Kat's going to spend the night."

"They didn't go to the movie," I said.

"Where did they go?" Lily said, still tugging. "Sit down. Come sit down."

"I have to find her. Lily, she's in trouble."

"What trouble? Is Abby with her?"

It was when she asked about Abby that I felt suddenly like sobbing. Abby. Of course, Abby. Until then I hadn't thought for a moment of Abby, who must have been there with Kat, and as I looked at Lily—her hair pinned up but falling around her face, her smile for once flattened out, her eyes fixed on me, fixed as though she had to study me to figure out what was going on—everything about this night took on a terrible actuality. The girls weren't there. Lily was frightened. Something *had* happened. Abby had been present. Other kids were there. Until then everything had seemed so unreal, so impossible, as if that phone call had to be some awful mistake—but now I was looking at Lily, and her child was missing, too. "Oh god, Lily," I said, "I am so sorry."

Then I told her what I could. I told her about the phone call and said I was going to go find her.

"Is Tony here?" I asked. Tony Moorefield, her husband.

"I thought I told you. He's in Chicago."

"I'm going to go find her," I repeated. I'd asked about Tony because I thought he'd want to come with me to find Abby, but I didn't want Lily to come.

"Should you? Shouldn't you call? I'm coming," she said.

"I don't think you should."

"Why? I'm coming."

"I don't think you should. I'll go. The girls will come here. They'll probably show up any minute." I don't know if I believed this, but somehow it seemed right for Lily to stay at home. "I'll go see if they're at the Vandenbergs' and bring them back here—if they're there. If they're not, I'll call you and we'll try to find them."

Was this a sensible plan? I don't know, but I thought so then. And Lily agreed. She'd stay there. She said, "Call the minute you know anything." She walked out to the car with me. She said, "Tucker, they're children. Remember that. They're still children."

THE ADDRESS on Davenport Street was in Forest Hills, an upper-bracket neighborhood that borders Rock Creek Park. The houses are substantial and expensive and self-important, not family houses but showplaces, mock Tudors and imitation Georgians and scaled-down French châteaus, a bunch of bastardized versions of Old World pomp and privilege that seemed to be inhabited by women who liked to dress up like Martha Stewart, in garden clogs and stonewashed jeans and hundred-dollar garden gloves, and to follow around the landscape crews, pointing at this or that with their gleaming designer garden tools, giving orders. Twill Landscaping had a few maintenance contracts in Forest Hills and every one of them was a headache. Kat didn't think much of this neighborhood, either. On one of her birthdays, I ordered up a cake that was divided like a map of the residential neighborhoods of D.C., showing Georgetown and the Palisades and Cleveland Park and Wesley Heights and Chevy Chase and all the others. The girls were thirteen years old, and they scarfed up the cake, every crumb of it, except for the piece that was Forest Hills.

But she was here tonight, she and Abby were here somewhere, and I tried to make myself think how they would have gotten here. I dialed her number again. No answer. There are no buses to Forest Hills, and the nearest Metro stop is a long walk, much too long for teenagers on a night like this one, a night swagging with heat, the heavy feel of summer heat bunched up before a storm. It was much too long a walk for Kat in her yellow flip-flops and Abby in her backless slip-ons. But maybe they took their shoes off. Maybe somebody had a car. Maybe the boys were older, old enough to drive. My brain seemed to be trying to escape from my skull as I wound through the streets, trying to understand what had happened, trying to take it all in and decide what I could believe, trying to understand what I had to do next.

My cell phone rang—incredibly loud, incredibly jolting. *Kat*, I thought with a shock of hope, but the display was lit, showing the name of the caller on the greenish screen: Lily. Maybe the girls had arrived at her house. But she wanted to know the name of the people who owned the house where the party had been. I thought I'd already told her. "Maybe you did," she said, "but I forgot." Then she asked me the address, and she said, "I don't think you should be by yourself."

"I'm almost there right now," I said. "Why don't I see if the girls are there, and I'll call you right back."

Calmly, calmly. I had to make an effort to speak to Lily calmly, for the moment I had left her house, the moment I headed toward Forest Hills, I had been imagining the obscene details of what must have happened. I tried not to. I had been trying to find some logical trail of cause and effect, trying to figure out why Kat would have come to this neighborhood at all, trying to foresee what I would have to do, but I kept imagining drunken boys staggering around, grunting and panting like half-wits as they hoisted their hard-ons, hoisted them proudly, all of them porn stars in their own minds now that it was actually about to happen, now that they were stumbling toward their first blow job—toward Kat, my daughter, my daughter whose mouth was the shape of a rosebud, whose lips tended always to part, just a little, showing the shadowy, glistening tips of her teeth.

This is a father's nightmare. I couldn't stop these images from flashing and bursting behind my eyes. I must have believed by then that it had actually happened, but I couldn't believe that Kat had *wanted* it to happen. But the boys, the boys—I knew for sure that they had wanted it, and they had pressed for it, they'd gotten the girls drunk, they'd made it happen. I thought of Kat's mouth and of boys putting their hands on her head, on her blond hair, and shoving her face toward them, shoving their hips toward her, and my rage seemed almost to have created a separate presence, a force outside me, a presence that was disjointed and scrambled like the images on TV when the pixels are rearranged to prevent recognition of a face or form.

Rape. This had been rape. I believed that my daughter had been raped and violated and dishonored.

I wanted to find the boys who had done this to her.

Yet I had no plan to harm them, no conscious plan at all when I arrived at Davenport Street. The number Fogarty had given me was all the way down at the end of a cul-de-sac, the last block before the private land met with the land of Rock Creek Park, the last block and therefore the choicest, with the largest and most ambitious houses. This one was a Tudor, much of it concealed by shrubs and black trees that had the dense shape of hollies and magnolias. There were only a few lights showing deep in the house and no lights at all upstairs, in the mullioned windows set into the pale stucco, illuminated only by the faint upward wash of the lamps at the door, the heavy wrought-iron lanterns. The house looked closed down for the night.

But after I had stepped out of the car and closed the door as quietly as I could, I heard a soft, low murmur of voices. I could feel my heart thudding in my chest, but I made myself stand there and listen. I tried to think clearly. I tried to decide what I was going to do. My

heart was thudding, but at the same time I felt an almost preternatu-
ral kind of tension and alertness, and I was acutely aware that I must
not make a mistake. It even seemed to me that I had an important advantage because the kids—the voices had to belong to kids—did not
know I was there.

I also had a distinct, almost bodily memory of the afternoon, years
earlier, when I stood inside the door of the Georgetown house where
I'd lived with Trish. I'd found the door slightly, suspiciously ajar, and
when I called Trish's name, I heard the thud of footsteps overhead. No
answer, just those heavy steps. There was an intruder in the house. No
one knows exactly what he will do at such a moment, but I picked up
a tennis racket, one of many that stood in the umbrella stand in our
small foyer. I waited, listened, went up the steps. A man wearing a
woolen watch cap and carrying a tote bag stood in the bedroom door
at the top of the stairs. He said, "I'm leaving now. Back off and everything will be cool."

But I said, "This is my house." The guy wasn't as big as I am, and
to this day I don't know what he held in the hand hidden behind his
back—a weapon, a heavy object of some sort. He hit me with it and
knocked me down the steps, and I was conscious enough to know that
he kicked me a couple of times as he stepped over me. My nose was reduced to rubble. The police told me I was lucky the guy didn't have
a gun.

Calm down, I told myself, *calm down.* I listened to the voices and
noted the cars—an open Jeep, an old Volvo wagon like the one I used
to drive, a fancy SUV—parked in the driveway of Belgian blocks. The
voices were coming from behind the house, where the pool had to be,
and it looked as though there should be a path through the high
shrubs on the side of the house with the garage. There was, a stone
path. The voices were clearer now—the voices of boys, mostly deep,
but rising with spooky laughter and excitement. I didn't hear any girls
speak or laugh. I reached an ivy-covered fence, head high, and stood
just outside the gate. The gate had a circular top and I could see over
it into the pool area where the outdoor lights were hidden among the
plantings, lighting up some shrubs like lanterns and backlighting the
boys seated at a poolside table. There were five of them, no girls. No

one came or went from the pool house. The boys were in silhouette, sitting at a black iron table covered with glasses and bottles and the metallic glitter of cans, and the water in the pool wavered with quicksilver reflections.

I stood and listened.

I thought they sounded drunk, but maybe that was because of the gusts of laughter that kept puffing out of them. A boom box was playing, not loud. They were talking about a TV show called *Jackass*. By Dickhead Productions, one of them kept saying. Dickhead Productions. They were describing the stunts performed on the show. Those fucking dudes are wack, a boy said. I like the wee man, another one said, the midget. Every time I see the show that little fucker is just flying through the air. Dickhead Productions, another one said. *Jackass*. A boy asked, How much fun do you think they have?

A shovel was standing beside the gate. A garden spade, short handled and straight bladed, and I picked it up. The boys still had no idea I was there, and I have no idea, even now, why I picked up the shovel. I had not decided to use it as a weapon. Perhaps I was still thinking of that housebreaker. Perhaps I thought I would need protection. Perhaps I simply picked it up as I would pick up any stray tool when I was on a work site. I don't know. In any case, I picked it up and stood there listening to the boys talking about *Jackass* and Dickhead Productions.

I eased the gate open and they still didn't notice me. I was in shorts and tennis shoes and I had reached the end of the pool before one of them said, "Oh shit," and a couple of them stood up. They were backing up, sliding away, looking as if they wanted to run, and I was close enough to recognize the faces of two of them, other counselors from Rockrapids. They'd recognized me, too.

"Kat's father," one said. "He's got a fucking shovel." But the one I seemed to see most clearly was the one who didn't get up, who seemed to be the leader of this group, the one who eyed me calmly and with a thick insolence that I could feel even before he opened his mouth. He wasn't budging from his chair. He was bare chested and his dark hair was cut close to his skull.

"I came to get my daughter," I said.

"She's not here."

"She was here. Kat. She was here with Abby."

"They left a little while ago."

"They're not home yet."

"Really." Heavy sarcasm.

"How did they leave?"

"I don't know, dude. They just split."

"Listen, I got a call about what's been going on here. About the drinking. The pool house."

"Yeah. So?"

"You're going to sit there and pretend nothing happened?"

"We had a party, OK? And it's over now."

"Where's my daughter?" I asked. "I'm looking for Kat."

"Jesus," the boy said, and I don't know why I had such a strong sensation that he was concealing something, but I did. I remember looking into the wild, frightened faces of the other boys, and I asked generally, "Where is she? Tell me, goddamn it. Tell me now."

The boy who was sitting—he was Jed Vandenberg—answered for all of them.

"I don't know what your deal is, man, but you're trespassing. Kat's not here. You're trespassing," he said, biting off the words, leaning forward to put the force of physical menace behind them. "So *sayonara*, OK? This is a private party."

As an adult I have only been in three fights. One was with that housebreaker, and the other two didn't amount to much since other people were around to step in. I'd had a shoving match with Will's soccer coach, a hotheaded, bug-eyed man who took Will out of a game after he'd made a mistake, yelled at him, and pushed him so that Will stumbled and almost fell; I'd also gotten into a scrap with a workman I fired for drinking on the job. I can remember, all three times, how the air seemed to stiffen and tighten, how every word and tiny gesture took on a huge significance, and how the hair on the back of my neck suddenly bristled. It was bristling again as I stood there, squared off with this boy-man who wasn't going to tell me a thing, this truculent, sneering kid who'd decided to treat me like some workman who'd gotten out of line. He couldn't even be bothered to stand up.

I swung the shovel and swept the bottle and cans off the table.

I am not sure what happened next. I hadn't meant to swing hard, but there was a dazzle of glass and aluminum and a noise like the explosion of a grenade. Jed Vandenberg leaped up from his black iron chair, bellowing, and I remember feeling that I was standing in the center of a swirl of violent activity, with all the boys wheeling and circling and roaring. Jed had a bottle in his hand, and he seemed huge in the backlight, bare chested and long armed, with this great roar pouring from his open mouth. He stepped toward me. My intent was to fend him off with the shovel, to use the shovel as a shield to keep him from hitting me with the bottle, but I was bumped or pushed from behind, and pitched forward, and the blade of the shovel hit Jed in the shoulder, hard enough to spin him and knock him off balance. His feet slipped on the pool paving, or maybe on a can or bottle, and he went down. He just went down. One moment he was standing and the next moment he was on the paving. It hadn't seemed to take any time at all, yet all of us had heard the thud—the heavy, heavy thud—of his head hitting the edge of that black iron table.

"Get up," I said. One of the boys who was there that night said that I sounded like a boxer who wants his opponent to rise so that he can slug him again. He said that I wouldn't allow them to get near Jed and that I threatened them all with the shovel. To the investigator he said that I seemed out of my mind and bent on violence.

I did say, "Get up," but I remember that moment differently. As I looked down at Jed Vandenberg, this big and helpless boy, half bare, with a beach towel wrapped around his waist, sprawled among the bottles and cans, I seemed to feel my rage leave me as suddenly and absolutely as it had come. It was just gone. When I said, "Get up, get up, get up," in a kind of frenzy, I was wild for him to hear me and obey, and it even seemed to me that if I insisted, he *would* hear me and he would get to his feet and none of this would be happening.

The blood was seeping into his short hair. It ran over his eyes in a sheet and began to drip onto the paving.

"Head cuts bleed a lot," I said, aware of my voice entering a stillness. The boom box was still going, but there was a hush. I had put the shovel aside and I was on my knees beside Jed. I picked up a towel and

I placed it above his eye where the blood just gushed out. He was sprawled on his side, not like someone sleeping, not at all, but with a slackness and looseness in his limbs and body, with his head twisted at an unnatural angle, as if he had fallen from a great height. At first he seemed completely motionless. I knew basic first aid—had taken a one-day course so that I could deal with emergencies with Kat and Will, and at work—and the few facts I remembered now seemed momentous. Head cuts bleed a lot. Stop the bleeding. Clear the airway. Do not move the victim. Check for signs of shock. I was holding the towel to the wound on his head and his mouth was open, but he did not seem to be breathing at all. He was not dead, I told myself. He couldn't be dead. Out loud I said, "Head cuts bleed a lot, but he's going to be all right."

Of course I had no idea whatsoever of the severity of his injury, but I felt I had to speak. The other boys were standing around me. Bare feet. Breathing. One of them saying, "Oh fuck, oh fuck." The music still coming out of the boom box, idiotically, as if nothing at all had happened. *Clear the airway*, I thought, and I stuck my fingers deep into his mouth where there was a gob of vomit. It all came loose at once as soon as I touched it. The vomit rushed out over my hand.

And then he twitched. A muscular spasm jerked across his back and the whole beam of his shoulders seemed to lift. He made a small puffing noise with his lips, and then a deep groan came from within him, a groan of solid pain, and his head readjusted itself under the towel. He was breathing. He was alive. His fingertips stirred and one of his hands fluttered upward—not high, but high enough. A vital spark was still there, and behind me one of the boys said, with a great whoosh of breath, "Oh Jesus," and all of a sudden there was a babble of voices, and it really did seem as though there was more oxygen in the air.

"We gotta call 911," one of the boys said. He seemed to be asking for permission to call.

"Let's wait for a minute," I said, thinking that Jed was about to sit up, thinking that I could just drive him over to Sibley Hospital. I knew the gash would have to be sewn up, but I thought I could get him there more quickly. I thought, somehow, that this would all be kept quiet.

"You asshole," one of the other boys shouted, and I could see his feet near me, could see other feet, and knew that someone was restraining him as he kept lurching toward me, making a hissing, threatening noise, like a goose, as if he meant to attack.

"OK, OK," I said. Still on my knees, still holding the towel to Jed's head, I fished the cell phone out of my pocket, punched in 911, and talked to a woman whose precise voice somehow surprised me as she moved this event, this crisis and confusion, into a realm of fact. Yes, there'd been a head injury—that was a category, clearly, a known category, and I imagined her at a computer, touching a keyboard to bring up the screen that would direct her questions and advice—and she needed an address. Names. A phone number. There was static as she talked into another phone, and she told me that an ambulance was on its way. The boys stood by and listened quietly now.

"You say a boy fell?" the dispatcher asked.

"Yes."

"And it's a head injury."

"Yes."

"Is he conscious?"

"Yes. Well, I guess. He's moving. He's out of it, though."

"How long ago did you say this happened?"

"Just now. Five minutes ago."

"Are you the victim's father?"

"No, no. I'm just a parent."

"How old is the boy?"

"Fifteen. I don't know, maybe sixteen."

"His name?"

That's when I found out he was Jed Vandenberg. I had to ask the other boys who he was.

A short silence as the dispatcher considered. "And your name? Who are you?"

"Tucker Jones."

"Are you responsible for the boy?"

"I'm a parent," I said. "I had just arrived to pick up my daughter here."

"Are the boys' parents there?"

"No."

"Is there anyone else there? Anyone authorized to admit this boy to the hospital for care?"

"I don't think so. I just came to pick up my daughter."

"Do you know where his parents are?"

"No, I don't."

"Is there any way you can locate them?"

"I'll see. Somebody here might know."

"What is your home number and address please, Mr. Jones?"

I told her. Without inflection or haste or panic, she said that the victim should not be moved, that he should remain still, that I should make sure that nothing obstructed his air passage. Had he been drinking? He might become nauseous. She said the ambulance would be there in a few minutes and asked that someone please turn on any lights that could help the EMTs find their way to the victim.

When I hung up, the angry boy said, "This was no accident. You hit him with a shovel."

"OK, OK," another one said, "let's go in the house, OK? The ambulance is coming. Let's just go up to the house."

I asked him to turn on the lights, and they left, and the other two stayed behind, watching quietly as Jed struggled up through layers of unconsciousness, groaning, muttering, each degree of alertness seeming to bring more pain, for he kept trying to raise his knees and bring his arms to his chest, seeking a fetal position. When the lights came on—bright spotlights, burglar lights—they illuminated the pool area with an unforgiving brilliance, revealing all the sad waste and confusion of the night. There were cans and broken glass and blotches of black blood on the slate. The towel in my hand turned out to be white and it was saturated with blood. The pool furniture was heavy black iron cast into fantastic, hideous shapes.

I raised the towel to see if the bleeding had stopped or slowed down. His eye looked as if it had slid down into his cheek.

The two boys with me moved the chairs back and started, carefully, to remove the cans and broken glass nearest to Jed. One of them kept talking softly to Jed, touching his back or shoulder gently—"Hey, Jed, hey, bro, it's gonna be OK, they're coming for you, it's gonna be OK"—and they told me that Jed's parents were on Nantucket, where they had a house, and that his older sister, Vanessa, should be back at any moment. She was older than Jed, a college student, and she'd been left in charge for the week. It occurred to me that I was going to have to call his parents to tell them what had happened, and I could feel the magnitude of this disaster spiraling out, out, out beyond anything that could be controlled or contained.

Break it down, I have often told my children when they face a problem, *break it down. You can't solve it in a single stroke. You have to solve one piece of it at a time.* I have tried to make that approach a habit, but the pieces of this problem were as strewn and scattered as the cans and bits of glass. Jed still hadn't said a word. The ambulance was on its way. It wasn't clear whether he could be admitted to the hospital—but they would have to admit him, wouldn't they? I had an authorization form for Kat and Will on the refrigerator at our house in case they were hurt when I wasn't present, but what happened without a form? I asked one of the boys to look around in the house for some kind of authorization, and he couldn't understand what I meant, and I know our voices began to rise as I attempted to explain. I wanted to call Lily and find out if the girls, Kat and Abby, had shown up at her house. I had to call Christine. One of the boys had tried to call Vanessa on her cell phone but couldn't get her. From inside the house I heard a kid talking, maybe to his parents, but I couldn't make out the words.

What would I tell Jed's parents?

A boy came out the house, whistling. The boom box had been shut off, I realized, and this boy was whistling, nervously and puffily, "Hail to the Redskins." He brought me a Post-it with the phone numbers of Jed's parents, the Nantucket number and their cell phones, and Vanessa's cell phone. He said, "He's gonna be OK, isn't he?"

I didn't ask them what had happened with Kat. Couldn't, just couldn't, because now, with the lights on bright and the fear and tenderness in their voices, they weren't the boys who'd enraged me. They were just scared kids. And I wasn't just Kat's dad but the man who'd hurt their buddy.

When we heard the siren, the lights somehow seemed to get brighter, and I have a distinct memory of the stretcher gleaming, glistening white and chrome, as the medics came through the gate—the same gate where I had entered—and looped around the pool. I remember it almost as though it floated in by itself, a magical apparatus that promised deliverance, that would bear Jed away and take him to a place where someone would know what to do to fix him. The boys seemed to dance around, and I felt a hand on my shoulder, then felt it slide under my arm as one of the medics helped me stand. He was lean and hatchet faced, a young man with a widow's peak and a jutting Adam's apple, and he seemed sympathetic. His partner was a woman, a black woman, and they were both young, both in shorts and orange shirts, both wearing what looked like tool belts, black web belts loaded with stuff. I felt dizzy and light-headed as I stood back and watched them work over Jed, the man putting the stethoscope against his chest, the woman feeling his pulse as she held up the towel, looking at the wound, the side of his face that had collapsed. They talked to each other and to Jed, determining that he could hear them. "Keep still, keep still," the man said when he asked Jed to wiggle his fingers, then his toes. They explained each step as they rolled him over and straightened him out to put him on the litter, the board with all the restraining straps. The thick hunk of gauze they fastened to the side of his head seeped through slowly with blood.

"Big guy," the woman said as they lifted him onto the stretcher, lowered now, only a few inches above the paving.

She was looking at the bottles and broken glass.

"You responsible for this boy?"

"I'm not his father," I said.

She cocked her head and waited.

"My daughter was here earlier," I said. "How badly is he hurt?"

"What'd he do? Just fall?"

"He hit his head on that table." I pointed at the iron table.

"Party got out of hand," she said to no one in particular. "We'll take him to Sibley. I don't think he has a fractured skull, maybe a concussion, but what we gotta worry about is the eye. It's already badly swollen. They'll be able to tell you more at the hospital." A pause, and then she said, "You're going to the hospital, right?"

Without even waiting for me to answer, she clicked on her walkie-talkie to tell the dispatcher that she was leaving Davenport with the victim, a white male juvenile, possible eye injury, possible skull fracture, possible concussion, arriving Sibley Hospital in ten minutes. His condition was stabilized. The man pushed the stretcher, and she walked alongside, helping to maneuver it through the gate and smooth the ride over the Belgian block of the driveway.

I followed them—we all followed them—out to the ambulance, and I must have looked as though I expected to ride with them. "You'll have to go by separate vehicle," she said. "We can take only the victim and family members. Insurance regulations."

They slid Jed into the back of the ambulance and the doors closed on him. As the ambulance pulled away, in a whirl of orange-and-yellow lights, I became aware of people from other houses who'd drifted out to the street. I saw the four boys watching me, waiting for some word. "They'll take care of him," I said, and gave them my cell phone number. "Call me if Kat comes here, OK? Please call me."

A few blocks away, as the ambulance neared the busier streets, the driver turned on the siren, and the metallic wail ripped the summer night to shreds.

ON THE way over to Sibley, I felt as helpless as I have ever felt in my life. I wasn't far behind the ambulance, but there certainly wasn't anything I could do for Jed Vandenberg. I hit the speed dial on the cell phone to try Kat again, but I didn't expect an answer. By then I'd realized that she and Abby would show up only when they were good and ready to show up, and that it was absurd for me to have imagined that I would somehow track them down by driving through these dark streets where the houses were black and the trees even blacker. The girls could vanish completely if they felt like it. All I could do at the hospital, really, was wait for Jed's sister to arrive, or maybe some of the friends. He wasn't going to want to see me, and I had no reason to go there at all except to seek reassurance that he could recover from his injury.

I called Lily.

"Where are you?" she wanted to know. "Have you found them?"

I told her I was on my way to Sibley.

"Sibley? Who's hurt? Are you hurt? Good god, what happened? Are the girls all right?"

"I just lost it," I said. "I completely lost it."

Perhaps I expected Lily to be sympathetic, but she was too frightened. There were too many things she didn't know, and her urgent questions poured out. How badly was Jed hurt? How had it happened? Where were his parents? Did they know yet? Where were the girls? Did anyone know where the girls were? She has the sort of voice that shoots right through a phone, even a cell phone, and the questions seemed to buzz around me like hornets. I couldn't help Lily, either, except to promise her that I'd call again as soon as I knew anything more about Jed's condition.

The ambulance was at the emergency room doors when I arrived, and the lean-faced medic was seated in the cab, filling out his report. He told me that Jed had gone right in. I entered the hospital and headed past the receptionist and toward the wide door where patients are taken, intending to say whatever needed to be said to the doctors, but a nurse stopped me.

Jed had been taken to the trauma unit, she told me. Was I his father? No. Then I couldn't go back. Only immediate family was allowed back. Was I a friend? She was looking at me severely, and I realized for the first time that I had bloodstains all over my shorts and shirt.

I said I was the father of a friend, but all she could tell me was that an ophthalmologist had been called. She took my arm and firmly ushered me out into the reception area.

There was nothing to do except wait. I wanted to leave, but it seemed impossible to depart while Jed was there alone, and I kept expecting his sister to turn up at any moment, his sister or one of the other boys who'd been at the house—someone, anyone who knew him. I did talk to the reception clerk, but of course I wasn't able to give her any information beyond what the medics had already passed along to her, and I tried to sit still in the beige alcove, where a young couple waited, red eyed, arms around each other, and an elderly woman sat with her eyes closed, her hands clasped on the bars of her walker.

I was there for almost an hour. It was after one o'clock by then, and it felt as though time had stopped and the next thing—whatever it was—was never going to happen. I just waited. Every time the nurse came through the doors of the treatment area, I got to my feet and asked her about Jed, and she said that he was stable and that they were still waiting for the ophthalmologist. Why do these emergency rooms take forever to administer treatment? Then I'd step outside the building and try to reach Vanessa Vandenberg on the cell phone to see what was keeping her. I still wasn't ready to talk to the parents. I wanted to be able to tell them that their son was going to be all right, so I had decided to wait until the eye doctor showed up. I did call Christine, and I remember how incredible it felt to explain to her what had happened. I picked up a shovel. I had a fight with one of the boys. He was in the emergency room, in the trauma unit, but he did not appear to have a fractured skull.

How could I be talking about myself? How could I have done those things?

But I had. Christine said, "I'm coming to the hospital."

I told her to stay at the house. Who knew when or where the girls would turn up? Or what phone call might come next? By then I had called the Vandenberg house, trying to reach one of the boys to see if they knew anything at all about the girls, reproaching myself for not finding out exactly when they'd left and where they were headed. No one picked up at the Vandenbergs'.

I kept the cell phone in my hand, and it felt like a live bird when it finally rang—but it was not Kat. The display showed a number and area code I didn't recognize. I answered as I answer my business calls. I said, "This is Tucker."

"This is Richard Vandenberg." The voice was deep and heavy and thick with rage and the effort to control it, the effort to make me feel it. "That's Vandenberg. V-A-N-D-E-N-B-E-R-G."

I did not know that spelling could be an act of such aggression. All along I had thought that my first words to this man would be an apology, but I was too taken aback to say anything.

"Remember that, asshole," he said. "You're going to be hearing my name."

I told him that I was at Sibley and that I had intended to call as soon as I knew more about Jed's condition.

"I am aware of my son's condition," he said. "I've spoken to the doctor there. I do not need your fucking report. But maybe you'd like to explain why you took him to Sibley. Jesus Christ, Sibley. He should be at Georgetown, not at a neighborhood hospital."

"This is where the ambulance brought him."

"Are you a complete idiot? Ambulances go where you tell them to go. You could have called to find out where our doctors are. The numbers are all over the house. It is not your decision to take my son to Sibley."

"Is there a doctor you want me to call?"

"I've already called our doctors, and I do not want you to do anything, not one more fucking outrageous thing. Do you understand that? Not one more thing. I don't know who you are or what you think you're doing, but you have committed a crime and I want you arrested. All I want is for you to stay right where you are until the police come for you. I've already filed a complaint."

Until that moment it hadn't occurred to me that I could be arrested for what I had done. I remember sitting in that waiting alcove, listening to Vandenberg's voice, not really hearing his next words, just the sound of his voice, and realizing that the young couple was looking at me, and that the elderly woman had opened her eyes and seemed to be trying to figure out her whereabouts. Perhaps they'd heard the whole conversation.

I stood up and as I walked toward the door, I said, "I don't think you know what happened at your house tonight."

"I don't think *you* know what happened," Richard Vandenberg said. "You entered my property and you attacked my son. That's a crime and you're going to pay for it."

"My daughter was at your house," I said. "I went to your house to pick up my daughter."

"With a shovel in your hand. That is not how most people arrive to pick up their children. What kind of father do you call yourself? You could have killed him."

Then the connection ended. Vandenberg clicked off. I was standing outside the glass doors of the hospital, looking back toward the waiting area, where I saw a doctor in scrubs approach the young couple, saw them rise, and saw even at that distance how they slumped into each other. I stood there, thinking I should go, wondering if it would be considered an attempt to evade arrest if I did go, when the squad car rolled right up to the doors. No lights, no siren. The young cop in the passenger seat looked at me with surprise, taking in the bloodstains on my shorts and shirt, and I could see him thinking, *Arrest made easy.*

But it was his partner who did the talking. He got out of the car slowly and walked around the front of it, through the beam of the headlights, hitching at his belt, a youngish black man in a white shirt, not big but imposing somehow, giving off an air of authority and pride. He, too, looked at the bloodstains, and looked so that I would see him looking. He was hatless and had a shaven head and a neat mustache.

"You Tucker Jones," he said, not a question. "They said you might still be here. We need to take you into custody."

"So I heard," I said. I think I tried to sound wryly ironic.

"You were in a fight," he said, nodding at my clothes. "We got a complaint from the father."

"I just talked to him myself."

The cop nodded. He kept one hand on the heel of his holster and the name tag on his white shirt read Ellis. "You came here with the ambulance?" he asked.

"They wouldn't let me ride in the ambulance. I came in my own car."

"You just been waiting here?"

"I wanted to see how Jed was. And nobody else showed up."

"We already talked to the boys there, two of them. I'm going to need to arrest you and take you in. You know you have the right to remain silent. You have the right to an attorney. Anything you say may be used against you in a court of law."

Ellis had somehow grown threatening as he recited my Miranda rights, or maybe it was the familiarity of the words that struck home. In any case, they angered me as though Vandenberg himself had been standing there with a badge on.

"This is bullshit," I said.

"I need to take you in," Ellis said, and he slipped a pair of handcuffs onto my wrist. It happened so smoothly, so unobtrusively, that it felt like a magic trick. I still had my cell phone in my hand and Ellis said, as he took it away from me, "You mind? You can't be calling anybody now."

FROM THE backseat of the police cruiser, I watched Ellis go into the hospital and talk to a nurse before disappearing, presumably into the treatment area. The younger cop, also a black man, was standing by the car, holding my door open. He was light skinned and sleepy eyed, and he asked me how bad the boy was hurt.

I told him. I'd been read my Miranda rights, but I didn't think I had anything to hide, and I told him that Jed seemed to be in stable condition. "He must be hurt pretty bad, he needed to come here," this younger cop said, and then I told him how Jed had fallen, how he'd seemed to slip on the paving and how he banged his head against the metal table. The blow had knocked him out, but they didn't seem all that worried in the emergency room, not worried enough to get an eye doctor to come right away. This cop seemed not much older than a kid, and he seemed sympathetic, and I ended up telling him—in the two or three minutes we had while waiting for Ellis—that I'd gone there looking for my daughter and lost my temper when Jed wouldn't tell me where she was.

When Ellis returned, we drove over to the Second Precinct on Idaho Avenue, and maybe it was the familiarity of the place—I'd been there dozens of times to get parking permits for the landscaping trucks—or the fact that it was a quiet night, and everyone seemed worn out and weary, or that I was bone tired by then, but the process of getting booked seemed like a dull bureaucratic routine. It was not particularly degrading. I held a number in front of my face when a female officer took a mug shot, but the setup with the light shining in my eyes and the gray backdrop was the same setup they used for driver's license photos. Then I had to wait for a different officer to show up to take my fingerprints, a process that needs no particular explanation, though I will say that the ink is difficult to remove from one's fingertips. I thought I'd gotten all of it, but when I was sent into a bathroom to give a urine sample—so I could be tested for drugs—I noticed that I left faint fingerprints on my pecker and on my shorts, around my zipper. The cop who took the plastic cup from me looked at my clothes with their various blood- and ink stains and said, "You probably shouldn't be wearing white."

By then they'd taken my possessions away from me—my phone, my watch, my keys, my wallet—and put them in a Ziploc bag and asked me to sign a form stating that I had been advised of my Miranda rights. The officer who seemed to be in charge of the booking process told me that I could call my lawyer, but instead I called Lily. She could track down a lawyer for me and I wanted to ask one last time about Kat and Abby.

"I'm talking to them right now," she said.

"Are they all right?"

"No, they are not all right. Where are you? I've been trying you on the cell phone for hours."

"I'm in jail. Vandenberg has filed a complaint."

The officer could hear me and he seemed willing to cut me a little slack, just a little, enough for me to tell Lily that she should try to get hold of Brian Collinsworth, the lawyer who'd handled my divorce. And if he wasn't around, I wanted her to call around and find a lawyer who'd know what to do. And since I seemed to have only this one phone call, I asked her to phone Christine and tell her what was going on.

Then they took me to one of the holding cells. It contained only one other prisoner, a man whose hair was red and thin and whose face was as pink as if parboiled. He didn't say a word, just looked at me as though I were vermin, and then lay down on his bench and seemed to go to sleep. I was in that holding cell for an hour or so before Brian Collinsworth showed up—rather, before I was taken from the cell and led to an interview room to talk to him. Brian is a man about my age, somewhere in his midforties, but he has a boyish face and ringlets of curly sandy hair. I thanked him for coming out in the middle of the night.

"If you're ever arrested again, keep your mouth shut, OK? That's why they read you your Miranda rights. So you'll know you don't have to talk to anybody. Jesus, Tucker, don't you have better sense than spilling your guts to the cops?"

He'd obviously talked to them already, and he brushed aside my claim that I wanted them to know what had happened. "I'm sure you think you're innocent, but you have no idea about what you're saying. Of course it's too late now. You've already made your statement."

"I talked to one of the cops for a couple of minutes."

"After you'd been Miranda-ed?"

I had to think for a second. "Yes."

"And you still blabbed."

"I didn't see how it could hurt."

Brian calmed down a little then, but he was annoyed and impatient as he questioned me, making me describe the events of the night. He scribbled notes on a legal pad and we must have talked for nearly half an hour. He told me that he was trying to get me out that night, on a citation, instead of having me hauled down to superior court for an arraignment in the morning, and he explained the difference between felony assault and simple assault, which was a misdemeanor, but I know I couldn't grasp it all, not when he told me that a felony assault could lead to a prison term. Prison. My brain just shut down.

But I do remember Brian rubbing his temples with his fingertips and saying, "This is a tragic fucking mess."

Then I was taken back to the holding cell for at least another hour. It was after five o'clock when they came to get me, and I met Brian in the same place where I'd first been booked, and I signed more papers. I was being released on a citation and I had to agree to appear in superior court on August 5th to be arraigned. They gave me back the Ziploc bag with my stuff in it, and the display on the cell phone was blinking to tell me that a message was waiting.

Brian and I walked out of the precinct headquarters together and got into his car. He offered to drive me home, but my car was still at Sibley, so he took me there. I was lucky, he said, to be released on my own recognizance, but Ellis had decided to write up the incident as a misdemeanor.

"He did us a favor," Brian said. "I worked hard on him not to write up for a felony. What in Christ's name were you thinking?"

"I was thinking that my daughter was in trouble."

"I don't know about her," he said. "I hope she's all right. But you're in trouble. You understand that, don't you? Even if this stands as a misdemeanor charge, you're still going to be sued by this boy's family. This is going to cost you, and it could cost you big."

"I didn't injure Jed. He hit his head on the table."

"You just don't get it," he said, and by then he was too tired to do anything but lay it out for me. "You went after this kid with a shovel in your hand, and he ended up in the hospital. It doesn't matter what you had in mind when you picked up the shovel. You had it in your hand. You swung it at Jed Vandenberg—don't say anything, OK? Just listen for a minute. You got a phone call from stranger, a man you'd never met or talked to, who gave you a report about what Kat had done. You believed this story. Not only believed it, you were convinced that it had happened and that the boys had gotten Kat drunk and taken advantage of her. You didn't check it out, not with anyone. This guy who called you knew what he knew from his hysterical daughter, so it was already secondhand, and the girl herself—had she seen anything? What kind of girl is she? A gullible kid somebody decided to spook by telling her this? Probably not, but you didn't know. You had no way of knowing. And still you went to the Vandenbergs'—"

"I went to see if Kat was still there."

"You went to the Vandenbergs', picked up a shovel, and walked up to the boys who you thought had done terrible things to your daughter. Did you even ask about her, by the way? You didn't mention that."

"I did ask if she was there."

"And when they said no, did you ask anything else? Did you ask them where she'd gone? Did they give you any reason, any reason at all, to think that they had done anything out of order? Anything to hurt Kat? Did you ask them what had happened there at the party? No. You already told me you didn't. They were sitting there around a table, and they didn't do anything to make you believe that they were going to hurt you, did they? To make you think you needed to defend yourself?"

"Jed swung at me with a bottle."

"After you'd already knocked all the bottles off the table. You took the first swing, and you've already told the police about it."

"I didn't swing to hit him."

"But you walked in there as though you were on a mission. Don't you see that? You show up, and without any provocation, without any evidence that these kids have actually done anything to harm your daughter, you start swinging a shovel. And a kid ends up in the hospital."

We'd reached Sibley by then and Brian stopped his car in the parking lot. "I'm sorry, Tucker. I have a daughter, and I would have been out of my head if I'd gotten the phone call you got. But you can't go after a kid with a shovel. You just can't. Even if it's as bad as you imagined, you can't take matters into your own hands. You can't fix it by attacking a kid. Let's just hope this turns out to be nothing more than a bad cut. I called the hospital, by the way, but they couldn't tell me anything. He's still in the ER."

He looked at me and patted my shoulder. "Goddamn it," he said, "I am really sorry. Are you all right to drive? You look beat."

I told him I could make it home. As I got into the car, the day was just starting to brighten with silvery light and I saw that the parking lot was slick and puddled—so there'd been a downpour during the night. It must have happened while I was in the holding cell, deep inside the precinct building, for I hadn't heard it at all. A pair of crows was hopping around the edge of the asphalt, squawking, and off in the trees the first sparrows were singing their one-note songs.

I drove to Lily's house and tried all the doors on the porch until I found one that opened. Then I went up the stairs and into Abby's room.

There she was. Kat, my girl, dead to the world. The room was light enough so that I could see Abby's darkish head in one bed, Kat's blond head in the other. The sheet was down around her waist, and the hem of her T-shirt had ridden up so that I could see the small of her back, the shadowy line of her spine. She was on her side, and sometime during the night she'd put her hair up in a single braid that curved out on the pillow behind her. Her hands, both of them, were tucked under her cheek, and her mouth was slightly open, showing the glistening tips of her teeth.

She looked like a child.

I had imagined that I would find her awake, that I would find them all awake and sitting around the kitchen table, and I didn't really know what to do except to pull the sheet up over her bare back. She stirred when I touched her, and she felt warm. It seemed amazing that she could be so deeply at rest, and I decided to let her sleep, to let them all sleep for now. I walked back out of the house and saw that the sky overhead was cloudless and blue, catching the first bright bolts of sunlight. The air smelled fresh, and on the bank running down to Lowell Street, Lily's stand of lilies—masses of them, yellow and cream, her namesake flowers—stood upright with their trumpets open and dewy. A pair of early joggers, a man and woman, ran by and smiled at me.

It's time to go to work, I thought.

Work! The idea was so ludicrous that I couldn't make myself move. I could make no sense of what had happened that night, but it was daybreak, time for work! *Never fear, El Jefe is on the job!* As I stood there on the steps of the Moorefields' house, one of the black-and-white tuxedo cats appeared, stretched, then sat down on the porch steps and yawned, switching its tail and studying the pachysandra to see if any tasty rodents were up and about.

CHAPTER

2
———

"I want to take Kat back to New York with me," Trish said. "I've always wanted her with me and now, obviously, this has become an untenable situation."

"Kat's not going to New York," I said.

"This discussion will be moot," she said, "if you end up in prison."

We were at my house, my ex-wife and I, standing in the entry, and Trish spoke in the composed, reasonable, relentless tone of voice that had become familiar to me after years of divorce but still made me feel as if I'd been cuffed by the back of her hand. She'd removed her sunglasses so that she could look at me directly, her face conveying sadness and determination and a deep disappointment, as though she'd known all along that I was bound to fuck things up and she'd been powerless to prevent it.

It was just after noon. That morning, when I phoned Trish to tell her what had happened, a call I hated to make, she began immediately to plan her departure, figuring out how to get Will to his tennis lesson, what invitations and appointments her assistant might have to cancel for her, how to get the plane—her husband's company plane—from its hangar in Connecticut to Islip, where she would board it, and so on. That has always been her way of taking charge of a situation, a crisis. She makes elaborate plans, and she makes them aloud. When we were married, I used to try to kid her about manufacturing crises, about her preference for a world in a constant state of crisis, but she didn't want to hear it. And that morning, as I heard her urgency translate into a plan to get herself to Washington, as I imagined her scribbling notes on a pad, I had to acknowledge that, this time, she did not have to manufacture anything at all. This was a crisis.

When I phoned Trish, not long after eight, I was at home, having showered and changed, having already called Max, my second-in-command at Twill, to tell him that I wouldn't be coming in, having already called Christine at her office. She didn't pick up and I left a message. I'd missed her that morning. By the time I got home, she'd already gone to work at Worldwatch, leaving the bed straightened and a note on the kitchen table: *Tuck, I am so sorry. Call me when you can. Love, C.* My other call that morning was from Lily, who phoned to say that she thought she'd heard someone in the house. "I hope it was you," she said. "I was so worried. Are you out now? What happened? Why didn't you wake me up?" I tried to answer some of her questions, but we were both sleepy headed, for she'd been up with the girls till four o'clock.

"Does Kat know about me?" I asked.

"She knows," Lily said. "There were lots of phone calls all night long. They think you *attacked* that boy."

She paused to give me a chance to deny it, and I did, but I think I realized even then that I would be called on to repeat my version of the story over and over again. "That poor boy," Lily kept saying, and I could hear that she was trying not to cry. She cannot see or contemplate the physical pain of others without wishing to relieve it. I could barely form words to explain myself, and in the end we agreed that we'd let the girls sleep a bit longer, since everyone was so exhausted and these weren't things to talk about on the phone. I couldn't remember the last time I'd tried to sleep during the day, but I turned off the ringer on the phone and lay down on my bed, on top of the quilt, and looked out the window at the treetops in full summer leaf, at the blue sky beyond, and hours later I woke up to the sound of Romeo barking—that high wailing *rooroooroo* of the beagle in him—to let me know that Trish had arrived.

She'd pushed open the unlocked front door and she was standing in the entry, scratching Romeo's ears, and I could see her puzzlement at the empty house and at my appearance when I came down the stairs. I was wearing gym shorts and a T-shirt and I hadn't even splashed water on my face. It was clear that I'd been sleeping, and Trish had no doubt expected all the stir and activity of an emergency. "Did I wake you up?" she asked.

"I didn't sleep last night."

Behind the sunglasses she seemed to be peering into the house, looking for Kat. In a low voice, she said, "I haven't said anything to Will, but of course he's going to have to know something soon. He just knows that I've come to Washington. I had to tell him that much. Is Kat asleep?"

"Yes. I think she's still asleep."

"Think? You think?"

"She's not here. She's still at Lily's. She was going to spend the night with Abby last night, and, anyway, that's where she ended up. She didn't get to sleep until pretty late."

A pause as Trish processed my answer. "Have you talked to her?"

"No. I was in jail most of the night."

"You haven't spoken to her at all?"

"No."

"You left her at Lily's house." A statement.

"She's talked to Lily. She and Abby talked to Lily when they got back last night."

"And what did they tell her?"

"I'm not sure. Trish, please try to remember that there was a lot going on last night. There really wasn't much time to sit down and chat."

"So I fly down here and Kat's at Lily's house. And you haven't talked to her. You don't know what happened to her last night."

"I thought the best thing might be just to let her sleep for a while. The damage has been done. I'm sure she feels horrible."

"This is unbelievable," Trish said, "absolutely unbelievable."

"It was a long night."

"She's not Lily's daughter," Trish said. "She's my daughter. Our daughter. This is not Lily's problem."

"Trish, we should sit down. Let's sit down and talk about this."

"You may be prepared to let Lily handle this, but I'm not."

And that is when she told me that she wanted to take Kat back to New York. We were standing in the Hut's small front entry—not a hall, not a foyer, just a space off to the side of the living room, a place marked as an entry by a rose-colored Turkish carpet, a magic carpet, and a huge old hall tree, an oak monster with a bench and mirror and dozens of brass hooks, all of them covered with the caps that we all seemed to collect—and the small space was jammed with tension. Outside at the curb, looking ridiculously official on a sun-dappled neighborhood street, stood the black Lincoln that Trish had hired, the mustachioed Indian driver standing, arms folded, and watching curiously as his passenger stood in the open doorway of a modest brown-shingled house, a woman who'd arrived in a private jet and carried herself as the embodiment of wealth and privilege and was now, obviously, at odds with a man in workout clothes. The princess comes to the peasant's cottage.

When Trish took off her sunglasses and reminded me that I might be in prison soon, I said, "I'm not behind bars yet."

And I stepped past her to close the door. "I'm sorry, Trish. I didn't expect to be asleep when you got here. Can we sit down? We should talk before we see Kat."

"So that we can present a united front? I don't think it's possible for us to agree this time."

She looked into my house, her children's house, letting her eyes adjust to the dim rooms, standing there rigidly and angrily, a very rich woman whose appearance, every single detail of it, bespoke her station in life. She could dress simply, as she was dressed that day—in a white top and gray pants that reached to her calf, sandals on her feet—and no one could have looked at her without seeing that her clothes were stylishly cut and perfectly fit, made of the most expensive materials, or that her short blond hair (blonder than ever) was beautifully shaped in a Princess Di swirl, or that her milky skin had the smoothness that comes from the salon, or that her left hand moved with the flash of gems, the diamonds of her wedding band and engagement ring (the small one; she had another, much more opulent engagement ring that she wore when she wanted to take part in the rock derby). Every inch of her, in short, was buffed and burnished, tended and groomed, and it was impossible for me, who had married a small-breasted and weak-chinned Trish, not to notice that her breasts were larger now and stood firmly forward underneath the silk of her top, and that some surgical sleight of hand had sharpened her jawline and enabled her to wear her hair short, much shorter than when she was my wife, when her hair was a darkish ash blond and fell loosely about her face to conceal the short chin.

At forty, Trish was more attractive than she'd ever been, and it was hard to believe that she had once been my wife, the woman with whom I had shared an intimate life.

She no longer even called herself Trish. She'd become Patricia Timlin, the socialite, the wife of Ray Timlin, the owner of an apartment on upper Fifth Avenue (it had been photographed for a couple of magazines) and a big house on Long Island, in the Hamptons, a hostess whose parties were reported in various society rags and even sometimes mentioned on Page Six of the *New York Post*, the holy writ of gossip. She was a "major" collector of contemporary photographs, a generous contributor to a number of charities, and of course sat on their boards; she was a pal of several genuine celebrities, entertainers and movie stars and artists; she was a busy and formidable woman who'd taken to this role as though she'd been born to it and carried it off in style. No doubt she had to work at it, and work hard, but she'd taken to it the way Kat took to climbing, discovering something powerful within herself that had always been there, waiting to be expressed. She was now an established figure in that moneyed world and a darling of the gossip columnists who'd had their fun with her when she first married Ray Timlin, the king of hostile takeovers, a guy who made boatloads of money for himself and his investors when he bought ailing companies and streamlined them, putting thousands of people out of their jobs. Ray was twenty years older than Trish. His divorce had been public and bitter, and Trish, on Page Six, had been described as "the chippy" who'd come between him and his wife. By the time they were finally married, Trish was pregnant with their first child, a boy named Cameron. Their second child, Lindsay, soon followed. From the little I had seen of Trish and Ray together, I could believe that her husband appreciated her skill in giving him precisely the high-profile life that he wanted and felt he deserved. Over their bed in the Long Island house—this I knew from Kat—hung a life-size nude portrait of Trish. Or, I should say, of Patricia.

She looked at me as if seeing me, really seeing me, for the first time that day. "You look like hell," she said.

We'd moved into the alcove just off the kitchen, the place where the kids did their homework, and Trish perched on the reading chair, the ratty old wing chair where Romeo likes to curl up. She sniffed and made a sour face. That chair is permeated with the fragrance of beagle.

Trish said, "It's obvious that Kat needs a change of environment."

"It's not obvious to me," I said, "and in any case, that's not your decision to make. That's a court decision, and it has been made."

"It can be unmade."

I'd taken my seat opposite Trish, on the small sofa, and I became aware that I kept raising my hand to my brow, a gesture that the kids have often mimicked. My woe-is-me gesture. "Let's try to talk ourselves, can we? Before we drag the lawyers in. Again."

"Kat's fourteen," Trish said.

"I'm aware of that."

"I think she's ready to make up her own mind about where she lives."

In our custody agreement, we had left open the possibility that the children, at age sixteen, could decide which one of us they would live with.

"She's not ready," I said. "After last night, how can you possibly say that? How can you think she's ready to make her mind up about anything?"

"Last night was a cry for help."

A cry for help. Trish uses language with care and force and she has no sense of irony whatsoever when it comes to psychobabble. She had read countless books on parenting, and she said things like this—*a cry for help*—as though they were self-evident, as though they had the force of higher authority and anyone who dared to disagree with her was a complete fool.

"How would it help her to go live in New York?"

"She'd live in a stable family environment, for one thing. She'd have a mother to talk to every day, her own mother and not the mother of a friend, not someone who wants to be her pal. Lily has never been able to set limits on anyone, and Kat's at an age when she needs a mother, an adult role model. She has plenty of pals her own age. She needs a mother and she needs to see a functional married couple live their lives, instead of what she sees here."

"Which is?"

"A series of affairs, as far as I can tell, without any commitment."

"I've been seeing Christine for two years. I'm not sure it's an affair."

"Is there a commitment? Is there going to be? Tucker, I don't ask the children questions about what goes on here, and I don't intend to pry, but my impression is that they have no idea what to make of this woman who's in your life, and therefore in theirs. How do you expect them to form any concept of what a marriage can actually look like?"

I crossed my arms to keep my hand from rising to my brow. "I think I won't comment on your marriage," I said.

"Big of you," she said.

"I'll only say that I'm not sure it's the model I'd like Kat and Will to have."

"That is a comment," Trish said. She sat very straight, her legs tightly crossed, her open sandal dangling from her raised foot, slapping softly against the sole of her foot. She'd always found it impossible to keep that foot still.

"Kat hates New York," I said.

"*You* hate New York. Kat doesn't. If she tells you she does, it's to please you."

"I don't think so. I don't think she's faking when she comes back and tells me how out of place she feels. How she feels like a hick among the city slickers. How glitzy it is."

"Did she ever really say that? Glitzy? Or are you putting words in her mouth? When she's on Long Island, or in the city, there's nothing glitzy about it—it's just kids hanging out. She has friends now, friends she's known for years. It would be an easy transition for her now. She has a life waiting for her."

"Her life is here."

"I don't think she could have done anything to signal more clearly that she's finished here. Done. In any case, would you really want her to deal with this here? I grew up here. I know what a small town Washington is and what her reputation is going to be. You know, too. She's going to be the girl who went down on a gang of boys."

The way she said that, the way she stated it as inalterable fact, sucked the air right out of my lungs. Trish doesn't really look all that much like Kat, but they have the same full rosebud mouth and the same way of twisting it at one side. Kat does it when she's uncertain, and Trish does it when she's feeling victorious. "It is what it is. Isn't that the slogan around here? Call a spade a spade."

It is what it is. That was one of the Big Rules, one of the phrases I liked to repeat, a way to get the kids to look at problems or troubles head-on, and Trish was watching closely as she turned the words against me.

"You think it's better for her to run? Better to move away than stay here and deal with it? She's going to have to deal with it no matter where she lives."

"Of course she is. I'm not suggesting that she won't. But I am saying that she'd get branded here, and somewhere else—in New York—she'd be able to deal with it on her own terms. Not to mention the fact that she'd get better help in New York."

Trish believes that the best doctors are in New York. To hear her on the subject, you'd think that every doctor in Washington was a quack.

"You're ignoring the fact that she's been at Byrd-Adams since the third grade."

"All the more reason to leave," Trish said. "It's a small school, and I know exactly how incestuous those relationships get to be. It's time for her to spread her wings. It's a tiny world she's in."

"As opposed to the huge world of New York? Where she can ride in the subway and eat in expensive restaurants? Kat wants to climb rocks. She hasn't been complaining about all she's missing here."

"Can we please not make this ridiculous? This is a serious conversation."

"What's ridiculous is the idea that she should leave. This is her home. This is where she grew up. Besides, it's July. I can't believe there's a school she could even get into at this date."

Trish's mouth twisted up again at the corner. She'd anticipated this. "I made some calls this morning," she said, and added, "from the plane." She knew someone, of course, a trustee of a private school, the Burden School, not the best school, not the school she'd really like Trish to attend, but a decent school. There was a good chance she could get in.

"How much will that cost Ray?" I said.

"That's a shitty remark," Trish said, and she was right. I didn't apologize but I lifted my hand to my brow again.

I wasn't looking at Trish, just listening to her voice, and it seemed to soften when she said, "Tucker, sometimes people need to make a change but they don't know how to do it. So they do something extreme. They drop a grenade. They're so desperate to change that they're willing to risk hurting themselves and anybody who happens to be standing close by. I know something about this, Tucker. I'm not an expert, but I spent years trying to understand it."

She was evidently referring to herself and the way she'd left me and the children. She sounded almost vulnerable, and she seemed to be making an appeal.

"When we talk to Kat," I said, "let's ask her and see what she thinks."

"Let's ask her," Trish said, and I realized that this was exactly the outcome she had wanted. She stood up and stretched her back. She was ready to go find Kat.

THE GRENADE theory was one I'd never heard, though Trish had offered several explanations at the time she left me, explanations that usually came down to the same slogan: *Follow your bliss.* She left me and neglected her children because she fell in love with another man, Blaine Baker, the handsome cowboy.

He was a hunk. That was the first thing I heard about him, the way Trish had described him when she came back from her initial meeting with him in Dallas, where she had gone to look at the photographs that were to be included in his show at the Corcoran and to put together a strategy to kick what she called the fame machine into high gear. She was a flak, not the chief of publicity at the Corcoran but the one who handled the PR for all the photography exhibits—the Corcoran Gallery of Art, a stone's throw from the White House, is known as one of the country's top showcases for photography—and it was apparent from the start that she saw Blaine Baker as her opportunity to create a star. The man was gorgeous and his photographs were sexy. "Erotic," Trish said, repeatedly in those days, "erotic, not pornographic." The exhibit was called "Adam and Eve," and the pictures traced the sexual awakening of a boy and girl just past the age of puberty as they discovered their bodies, their own and each other's. The children were achingly beautiful, the setting was Texas—rusty and dusty, no horses but a couple of pickup trucks, lots of wide-open spaces with sagebrush and a couple of kids getting it on, all the right elements for what Trish in her press releases called an "intensely American authenticity"—and the photographs gave me the creeps. I have never liked to find myself on the side of the censors, the moralists and sanctimonious prigs, the prurient and righteous crusaders who wear their outrage as a badge of honor and virtue, but I cringed when I saw the catalog for the exhibit. I thought Blaine Baker's photographs were scandalous.

They weren't as graphic as the Mapplethorpe photographs—and this was 1990, just a year after the Mapplethorpe provided such a feast for the censors—but they were even more disturbing. These were kids, and I couldn't look at the photographs without wondering how they had come to be taken, how Blaine Baker had secured their trust and prevailed upon them to act out, if they were acting, the motions and gestures of love. And if they weren't acting, why would they have permitted him to violate their intimacy with a camera? I wasn't the only one to whom these questions had occurred, for the exhibit had already been shown in Dallas, and Blaine Baker had refused to answer questions about the kids and how he had come to shoot the pictures. Refused in order to protect the kids, he had said.

Protect them. After taking pictures that revealed their private moments to anyone who walked into the gallery or bought a catalog, he wanted to protect them? I thought Blaine Baker was full of shit.

But I kept my opinion to myself. I could see that Trish was in overdrive, and we lived in Georgetown then and moved in circles that would surely be called sophisticated, and I didn't want to be disloyal to my wife. Didn't want to seem like a censor. Kept my mouth shut in the months leading up to the exhibit, the late winter and early spring of 1990, as Trish kept telling me about Blaine Baker and the fame machine and the way that this story seemed to be breaking just right. Trish was tireless. At this point she was thirty-two years old, she'd been at the Corcoran for six years, she knew her job, and she seemed to know as much about contemporary photography as any critic or curator. I'd heard her talk to them, and she easily held her own. As I watched and listened to her tout Blaine Baker and his photographs, I wasn't blind to her excitement and I winced inwardly at the references to his looks and the cynical calculation that was so much a part of her effort, the awareness that she was trying to catch a ride on the coattails of the Mapplethorpe controversy, though she always insisted that she was taking the high road. These photographs deserved serious artistic consideration, she'd say, and I think she really believed it. By then she had her own strong opinions about American photography, and she was dead certain that Blaine Baker was a major talent. Her words, repeated tirelessly. A major talent.

The exhibit was in May, and Blaine came to Washington not merely for the opening, as all artists did; he came to stay. Trish set him up in a suite at the Willard, within walking distance of the Corcoran. This was his moment, his apotheosis, and he wasn't going to miss one second of it. He was my age, thirty-six, and he really was the handsome cowpoke. He had the broad shoulders, the broad jaw, the wavy hair, the mean but lonely baby blues. He had the boots and the big brass belt buckles and the tight jeans that revealed the nature of his religion. It didn't seem to make a bit of difference that the image was bogus, that Blaine actually grew up in Dallas, attended Southern Methodist University, and had hands as smooth and soft as baby gerbils. Who cared if he was just a dime-store cowboy? That isn't how the fame machine works. He was from Texas, he had the twang, he took the pictures, and he was ready for his close-up. In my memory of him, he is always standing in the center of a group of women, his head cocked as he listens, cocked as though he is straining to hear the un-spoken messages of desire, his face grave as though he does indeed hear them and understands their weight and sadness, his lonely eyes shuttered as though the power of contact, of direct exchange, might be more than anyone could stand.

Trish was never far from his side. He was her charge, and she made catty remarks about the women who couldn't stop swooning. Perhaps it was her way of putting me off the trail. Of course I could see that she was attracted to him, but we were a solid couple with careers, a house in Georgetown, a couple of kids. Kat was six years old, Will four. We had a nanny, a busy social schedule, and the kind of marriage that might glide along for weeks or months without much connection or passion, but then, with a glance or a gesture, the distance would vanish and we'd fall right back into each others' arms. Trish liked to talk when we made love and liked me to talk—not sweet nothings, not romantic whispers, but bawdy talk that right now, as I write this, I re-call with astonishment, almost disbelief, wondering if I could really have exchanged those private moments, those words, with a woman who betrayed me. But perhaps our only intimacy was physical. I don't know what Trish was thinking that spring, but her campaign to make Blaine famous was working, and we often made love late at night, after the receptions and parties, when she still glistened with energy, and my elegant wife would say, "Fuck me, stud, fuck the living day-lights out of me."

She must have been thinking of Blaine by then, and it happened just as it always seems to happen: I was the last to know. To everyone else who knew her, who knew us, who saw Trish with Blaine, the signs were bright as neon. I saw them, too, but just didn't believe them. Couldn't believe them. Couldn't believe that she would fall for this dubious character who seemed so unscrupulous and self-infatuated. By then I'd seen enough of Blaine behind the scenes, after all the func-tions when the group shrank down to a handful, to know that he was shrewd and wickedly funny, and even to understand how he'd put in his time, years and years, drudging away and waiting for his break, and how the fact that it was finally happening, that the spotlight was finally on him, that he was moving up to the bigs, as he said, going to the big show—I understood all that. I saw that the excitement came off him like waves of heat off a radiator. I saw and heard how he schemed with Trish every day about how to make the most of the joyride they were having on the fame machine. All the little artsy papers and magazines had covered the show and raved about it, and then Trish got the big one—the *New York Times*. The Washington papers, even the *Post*, were just hometown papers in her opinion, but the *Times* was the maximum paper for anything having to do with the arts, and when the *Times* anointed Blaine Baker—first with a review of "Adam and Eve," a piece that placed him in the company of Diane Arbus and Richard Avedon, and then a long profile, a puff piece, a Valentine—the fame machine became a runaway train.

Trish was exhilarated and all my resentments—my jealousy, I suppose, though I didn't recognize it as jealousy—finally exploded one night after yet another private dinner in Blaine's honor, one to which I had not been invited and which kept Trish out till well past midnight. I waited up for her. When she came home, I took her wrist and led her to Kat's bedroom and said, "This one? Her name is Kathryn. Kat for short. She's six years old. She's your daughter. I don't want you to forget in your moment of glory."

She pulled free of my grasp and rubbed her wrist as if to remove all traces of my touch. "I don't deserve this," she said.

"She doesn't deserve this," I said. "She deserves a mother."

Trish left the bedroom and I followed her. She smelled like wine and she was wearing her hair, long in those days, pulled back over one ear. She had a big flower, a goddamn camellia, pinned to her hair over that ear. I said, "You've done enough for this guy. This smut merchant. He can take care of himself now."

"Smut merchant? What are you talking about?"

I ranted about the show then and about the exploitation of the two kids. I said that it was kiddy porn, and Trish—poised, collected, not allowing herself to be drawn into my tirade—told me that the work was powerful, that Blaine had a vision, that it wasn't in the least bit obscene but, on the contrary, an effort to make people like me—like me—understand that teenage sexuality had its own beauty and integrity and dignity. "You can't really look at those pictures and think they're dirty," she said.

"I think they're filthy," I said.

"Well, a picture is like a mirror. If a jackass looks in, you can't expect a jackrabbit to look out."

This was Blaine's line, oft repeated, one of his Texas truisms, and Trish knew that I would recognize it. I said, "Would you let Kat pose for those pictures?"

"She's six, Tucker."

"Say she's thirteen or fourteen. Would you let him photograph her? To capture her beauty?"

"Can we please decide then, and not now? This is an absurd discussion."

"I wouldn't," I said. "I'd tar and feather the son of a bitch if he tried."

"Very old-fashioned," Trish said, and she went downstairs and slept in the grungy room in the basement.

We never made up after that, never made love again, and hardly spoke between that night and the night that Trish really left. Is it strange that we didn't argue, not directly, about her attraction to Blaine but instead about his pictures? That I didn't even know that what I was really trying to do was keep my wife, the mother of my children, from leaving me? Leaving us?

For I knew absolutely what was happening when she called a few nights later from a bar—the boozy laughter in the background made it sound like a bar—to say that she'd be home late. In retrospect, it is surprising that she even bothered to call and to make herself sound as though she were annoyed to be kept out. And it is surprising that I said, *Don't sweat it.* I remember those words: *Don't sweat it.* I knew that my wife was about to commit adultery and I said, *Don't sweat it.*

Anyone who has ever spent a night like the night I spent then will not need to be reminded of how it goes, or how it doesn't go. It lasts forever. You lie in your bed wide awake, hearing every creak and tremor of the house, feeling the strangeness of the heart beating in your chest, hearing the stirring of your children, feeling the blood moving like hot molasses through your veins, remembering—oh god, remembering—the tenderness you have shared with the woman who is gone. You weep and rage and lie awake for what seems like hours and look at the clock and see that minutes have passed, only minutes, and realize that this night will be a night you remember forever, a night that your life changed, a night that seems to swallow up all the nights of joy as though they had never existed.

It was May, and the leafy, earthy smell of a spring night came in through the open window. I got in and out my bed. I spent part of the night in a chair by the window at the front of our house, and I hoped that the next car in the empty street, the cobbled street with the old trolley tracks down the middle, would be Trish's car, bringing her home. I listened to Van Morrison, to the *Moondance* album, her favorite album, playing it over and over again, absurdly, sending out a call as animals do, the call of the male primate who wishes to attract a female, imagining somehow that it would bring her home, but recognizing that the moon was almost full and the words of the title song—*"It's a marvelous night for a moondance"*—made a mockery of me and my tears, me and my woes. I felt small in the midst of that vast and endless night that spread out in all directions like a black and silent ocean. The music played, the tears washed over me, just seemed to shower down out of the blackness, and I'd go check the little ones and stand over their sleeping forms, and kiss them, and straighten their covers, and the time wouldn't budge. Then I'd stand at the window again and I remember laughing, laughing, laughing like a maniac when a black man on a unicycle pedaled down the street, all by himself, singing "That's Amore," the old Dean Martin song, singing and pedaling in time with the song, almost dancing to the song as he started and stopped, jigged and jagged, crooning, *"When the moon hits your eye like a big pizza pie, / That's amore..."*

Trish came home at daybreak. She said, "You're still up." She looked at me without flinching, without shame, the corner of her mouth turned up tightly.

"Where've you been?" I asked.

"On Bourbon Street," she said, her face breaking into a smile and her mouth expressing victory.

I knocked over a lamp and broke it, and I said more, but not much more. I knew it was useless. Bourbon Street. They were not only lovers but already had their own code, their own private language, their own passionate geography.

I moved out that morning. Moved out, though the stages that led up to our separation and divorce were drawn out and costly and crushing. In fact, I spent many more nights in that Georgetown house, nights when Trish was away, in New York, with Blaine. Washington was nowhere near big enough for the handsome cowboy. And Trish couldn't bear to be parted from him. "You have to follow your bliss," she told me once, more than once, when she packed up to fly off to New York, leaving the children with me. Sometimes she went unexpectedly, or failed to come home when she was supposed to, and she'd call me, or her mother, to take care of the kids. Even her loyal mother saw what was happening and reproached her, but Trish was simply on fire. She was in love and tormented by it, and the power of it was stronger than shame, stronger than loyalty, stronger than ambition or duty or reason. She managed to keep her job at the Corcoran, but she started to look for other jobs in New York, as I learned by accident when I answered a phone call from a gallery owner who wanted to interview her.

That is when I went to Brian Collinsworth, my lawyer. The separation papers were already in place, and I had originally intended to let the process run its course, getting the standard no-fault decree with joint custody. But I was not letting her take the children to New York. By that time nearly a year had passed, and Brian thought that if I really wanted custody, I could probably get it. I was angry and heartbroken and I wanted to hurt Trish. Brian filed the request, and we met with Trish and her lawyer, an intense woman who wore purple, whose eye liner was purple, whose lips were purple, and whose voice made me think of a coyote who'd just smashed his nuts on a rock. This woman professed to be amazed and outraged at my demands. Brian looked at her in his earnest choirboy way and said, "I'm not saying that she's neglected her children, and I'm not trying to say that she's a tramp, but I am saying that we certainly believe that we could make a strong case to that effect. I don't think we want to go there, do we?"

Then he stood up. I am no lawyer, but I do understand winning and losing, and somehow it was clear, absolutely clear, that we were going to win. The moment Brian stood, all four of us in that room understood. I know I was grinning, but I will never forget the look that I saw cross Trish's face then as the awareness of her defeat, of the magnitude of her defeat, rushed through her.

She changed lawyers and we worked out the divorce agreement with a minimum of savagery. I got custody, Trish moved to New York, and soon thereafter Blaine Baker left her and took up with a model, age nineteen.

So Trish had had her heartbreak, too, though she never spoke of it, not to me. I do know that she spent years with a shrink. I have sometimes suspected that her marriage to Ray Timlin was the purest calculation. Only now and then, in unexpected asides, like her comment about the grenade, has she given me the slightest glimpse of the pain she must have carried. I no longer had any idea, and maybe I had never really known, what went on inside this woman. Still, as much as I differed with her and distrusted her, as excruciating at it was for us to talk about anything more complex than the children's travel arrangements—and even those could stir up a blood bitterness—I did not doubt that she loved her children fiercely, or that she would go to any lengths to take Kat away from me.

I CALLED Lily before we left for her house, to let her know that we were on our way, and then we went separately. I offered to drive Trish. In fact, I assumed that we would go together and asked her to wait while I changed. She looked at me with disdain and said, "I have a car."

When she left the Hut, walking swiftly in her pitched-forward gait, Kat's gait, I saw the driver snap to and open the door for her. Then I pulled on a pair of khakis and a clean shirt, let Romeo out into the backyard to clear his jets, and arrived at Lily's in time to find the women seated at the kitchen table, already at odds with each other.

It is hard for me to say whether Trish and Lily were ever close friends, even though we had known the Moorefields so long and so well back when the kids were toddlers. We had lived on O Street, and Lily and Tony lived just around the corner on Thirty-fifth, and we could get to each other's houses the back way, via the alley. That alley was a whole jungle world to the kids. The women had spent hours together, but Lily was the stay-at-home mom and Trish had her career, and when Tony was around and we spent time together as couples—we must have had hundreds of meals together—Trish often seemed to pair off with Tony. Tony is a lobbyist, and the two of them were always eager to talk about the insider stories, the latest scoop on who was in and who was out, the tales of ambition and treachery and intrigue that are the grist for Washington's mill. Both of them, young as they were, regarded themselves as players in that big game. As for me, I was an editor at Time-Life Books, with an office in Alexandria, which might as well have been a million miles away. Lily, the would-be singer, was out of the loop, too. When we were at the Moorefields', we'd often end up around the piano, sometimes the four of us, sometimes just Lily and I, while Tony and Trish sat in the kitchen or, on summer nights, outside under the big magnolia tree, yakking away. When Trish moved to New York and Kat kept spending so much time with Abby and Lily was the mother on the watch, the jealousies and run-ins were probably inevitable.

Trish announced as I entered Lily's kitchen, "The girls are still upstairs."

"Not still asleep?" I asked.

Trish turned to Lily with a flashing look of impatience.

Lily looked tired. She is normally quick moving and full of animation, but that day she was subdued. "They came down for lunch"—she gestured with her hand at the two plates still on the table, plates with half-eaten sandwiches and half-plucked bunches of grapes—"but they scooted back upstairs when I told them that you were coming over. I think this is still pretty overwhelming for Kat. For both of them."

"It's overwhelming for all of us," Trish said.

"Having you both here, I mean," Lily said. "Facing you both." Then, to Trish: "I don't think she was expecting you to come."

"I'm her mother," Trish said. "God, this is like dealing with a press secretary. Kat locks herself in a room and sends word to us through you."

Lily has long eyebrows and they lifted fractionally. "I'm just telling you that she's scared to death. She's terrified."

"I'm not here to punish her," Trish said. "I'm here to help. I'm here to help my daughter get through this." That, too, was stated as an announcement, and Trish stood up from the table and actually shuddered, as though shaking off the forces that kept pushing circumstances into a configuration she didn't like or accept.

"I'm going to talk to her," she said, seeming to dare Lily to stop her.

She left the room and clattered down the hallway, then up the stairs.

"Coffee?" Lily asked. "You look beat."

I did want coffee but I asked first about Jed.

"His surgery is scheduled for this afternoon," Lily said, standing, rolling her shoulders, stretching for a moment before clearing the plates from the table, taking them over to the sink. Her kitchen is a big, open, airy space extending out from the work counters into the area where the table stands, and beyond that to a pair of green sofas overhung by big potted plants, ficus and hibiscus, and beyond that to the many-paned windows that give onto the overgrown backyard with its dense and dark green stand of bamboo. The room has a northern exposure, but it still seems bright, and Lily has photographs everywhere, most of them big black-and-white enlargements of her three children—Abby, Sophy, and Rafe—and there are more photographs, snapshots, on the refrigerator, and still more in frames on the bookshelves. To sit in that room is to feel that you have wandered into a family album.

"It's eye surgery," Lily said, fiddling with the coffeemaker, the kind with a plunger. She put a kettle on the stove to boil water. She had to be listening, as I was, to the sounds from overhead—to Trish's voice, crisp and imperative, and Kat's fluty, liquid voice. I couldn't make out the words. Lily told me that Jed's parents had arrived early that morning on a chartered plane, and Jed had been moved from Sibley to Georgetown University Hospital. He was fully conscious. He'd had a severe concussion and some short-term memory loss, but, as Lily understood it, there was no longer any concern about a skull fracture or brain damage. At some later date, he would need reconstructive surgery for the bones that had been broken in his cheek and brow. Right now they were concerned about his eye.

Lily was moving about as she spoke and she passed close enough to me to pat me on the shoulder. "Sorry," she said, and managed a small smile.

I asked Lily how she'd found out about Jed.

"It turns out Abby knows him." She straightened the items on the table—the newspaper, the two wooden candlesticks shaped like little monkeys, the napkins the girls hadn't even unfolded, the wooden slab that had been carved and painted to look like a luscious red slice of watermelon and had somehow become the permanent centerpiece.

There had been a drifting insinuation in her voice, and I asked, "Knows him well?"

"As of last night, it seems." The kettle was starting to hiss, and she asked, "You want it hot? Or would you rather have it iced?"

"Hot's fine. So you know what happened last night?"

"Not everything. I have a rough idea."

Now I heard Kat's voice rising, her voice but not the words.

"Trish wants to take Kat to New York," I said, "to live with her."

"She told me."

Lily knows how I take my coffee, of course, and she got out the milk and sugar.

"She's even got her lined up at a school. The Burden School. She called from the plane."

"She doesn't waste time," Lily said.

Lily gave me my mug and Trish was on her way back down the steps. When she entered the kitchen, she stood in the doorway and waited to speak until Lily looked up at her. She said, "I've been sent down to get the story from you. You really are the press secretary, I guess. Kat says you know the whole story. 'the whole *fucking* story' is what she said. Where does she get that mouth? As if I have to ask."

She glared at me, of course, and Lily said, "I really don't want to be in the middle of this, you know?"

"Kat wants you to be," Trish said, making a noticeable effort to take the edge off her voice. "I want to know what happened."

"It's so hard for them to talk about," Lily said. "Maybe it's best if it comes from me first. Do you want any coffee, Trish? I can ice it."

Trish didn't want any, but she sat down at the table. Lily sat down, and I could see that she wanted to talk as though this were an ordinary kitchen conversation, as though she were just recounting the events of a summer night, as though her calmness could neutralize the crisis. Yes, the girls had talked to her when they finally came home last night, and a little more that morning, or really that afternoon, when they woke up, but it hadn't been easy to get it out of them. Abby seemed to have decided that we—adults, that is—were the enemy and had no right to know anything.

"Kat seems to have reached the same conclusion," Trish said.

"She's just frightened," Lily said, but I could see that Trish didn't want anyone, and certainly not Lily, correcting her perceptions of her daughter.

As Lily pieced the story together, the girls had met up with some other counselors from Rockrapids at Pizzeria Uno, as they planned. Jed Vandenberg had turned up, too, with some of his friends. That, apparently, was also by design, since Jed and Abby had taken a shine to one another. *A shine*, Lily said, using a word that sounded innocent, making an expression that let us know it wasn't. Jed wasn't a counselor but he and Abby had been in touch, and she, Lily, hadn't known a thing about it. Hadn't even heard Abby mention his name. The girls swore they didn't know anything about the party until they were sitting there eating their pizza. They started making phone calls while they ate and soon the party was on. Some of the boys had cars, and they went to the Vandenbergs', where, as we knew, the parents were away.

The boys started drinking beer and playing the game Big Dare. Lily couldn't really explain it, and it didn't sound like much of a game, just a way for kids to spur each other on. It seemed that they drew cards, and the Jack of diamonds was the Daremaster, and he got to challenge the players. To lay down the dares. I dare you to strip off and jump in the pool. I dare you to chug a beer. I dare you to knock back another shot of vodka.

"Not all of them played," Lily said quietly. "Some of them went inside. Abby wasn't at the pool, she says. She was in the house with Jed."

She gave me a short, mournful smile. Bad luck, it seemed to say. The worst luck. The boy who got hurt, the boy who was about to go into surgery, had been inside with Abby all night. He hadn't been involved with Kat.

"Oh god," I said.

Even Trish looked at me with something like pity.

"Other couples were inside, too," Lily said, "in the bedrooms. Abby said she kept her shorts on. She didn't mention her top." She made that same smile. "She didn't really know what was happening out at the pool. And Kat doesn't remember much."

"She blacked out?" Trish said.

Lily spread her hands, palms up. "She knows she drank several shots of vodka and she doesn't remember anything after that. But she did take her clothes off. Abby had to help her dress when they left. She was sick, too."

Trish's shoe was slapping against the sole of her foot. "So she doesn't know what happened with the boys?"

"No."

"Do you?"

"I know what I've heard—well, what Abby heard. She's talked to some of the boys."

"And it happened? Kat gave them all blow jobs?"

I covered my face with my hands then. I couldn't bear to look at Trish and didn't want to hear Lily's answer, but I did hear it. I heard her say that there seemed to have been several of them. I heard Trish say, "I want their names," and Lily trying to put her off, saying that Abby wouldn't tell her the names and Kat didn't know them. I remember imagining, as I had the previous night, the details of this scene, how Kat, naked and drunk, her hair wet from the pool, her eyes unseeing as she waited for one boy after another to come to her in that pool house, gagging on the nausea that must have been rising in her throat, choking on their semen.

"That's all it was?" Trish asked. "She gave them blow jobs? They didn't fuck her?"

Lily shook her head. "I don't think so. Abby says they didn't."

"Bastards," Trish said. "Was this a dare? Somebody dared her to do it?"

"I don't really know. I think it started there, somehow. Apparently quite a few of them had taken their clothes off, and there was a lot of drinking. That much Kat does remember. And then the Fogarty girl—Alexa, the one whose father called you, Tucker—she got spooked and ran off, according to Abby. She was talking about calling the police, and the kids who weren't drinking decided they'd better clean things up. From what Abby says, it sounds as though Jed directed the plan to try to sober up everybody who'd been drinking. He got one of the boys with a car to drive her and Kat down to Georgetown, to an apartment that belongs to one of the boys' brother. All the kids who'd had too much to drink went somewhere."

"The ones who were there when I got there hadn't been playing the game," I said.

"Maybe not," Lily said.

"What time did Abby and Kat get back here?" Trish asked.

"About three," Lily said.

"She was sober then?"

"She was sobbing."

"She was younger than most of the others, wasn't she?" Trish said. "She had to be quite a bit younger if some of them were already driving."

Trish brushed the tears from her eyes. "She must have felt that she had to prove herself. They were all so much older," she repeated, and tears kept seeping into her eyes, a porcelain blue much intensified by the contacts she wore. She looked back and forth from Lily to me, as though bewildered by her emotion. "I'm sure she wanted to prove herself. I know I did when I was her age. On the way down here this morning, I thought of all the stupid stuff I used to do—god, it seems like a million years ago. You know what I couldn't get out of my mind? Grace Kelly. Princess Grace. My father was completely smitten with her, and when he called me his princess, I knew that's what he meant. Grace Kelly. I hadn't seen a single one of her movies, but that's what I wanted to be."

Trish was babbling, but she couldn't stop herself. Her eyes were wet and a few streaks of black liner dribbled from her lashes. Lily reached across the table to put a hand on her arm, and Trish clutched at it. "What's happening to them?" Trish said. "What's happening to them?"

"She'll be OK," Lily said.

Trish dabbed at her eyes and said, "I've got to do something. I've just got to get her away from here. I'm going to take her back to New York with me."

Lily kept saying that she would be OK, and I sat there at that table, listening to them trying to comfort each other, unable to think of anything but my naked daughter shivering in the darkness of a pool house, waiting for the door to open and the next boy to walk in.

I AM NOT much of a churchgoer, and my only prayers are those that escape from me when I am beset by fear and confusion and remorse. Old habit, I suppose. Until I was twelve or thirteen, my mother, a social Episcopalian, used to drag me to church. I'm not sure that she was a great believer, either, but she liked the music and she would sometimes urge me to leave my troubles with God. "I just shred mine into little pieces," she'd tell me, "and poof! I let God take care of them." She'd make a shredding motion and then blow at her fingertips, as if blowing a kiss, to show me and my sister how to accomplish this.

I don't often pray, and maybe the wish for forgiveness that had come to me as I sat there at the kitchen table doesn't really count as a prayer, but I know that I was ashamed of myself. I was bone weary that day, soul weary, and I remember now, as I write, how much effort it took to speak, or even to look at Trish or Lily. It took all my strength, more than all my strength, just to hold my head up. I was ashamed of myself. It wasn't a fiery, burning sensation but more like a paralysis, the kind of paralysis—here's another cheesy image—that overtakes the wasps and hornets and bees when the landscape crews have to spray them, and the spray turns into frothy, sticky stuff that attacks their nervous system and doubles them up, and their little bug legs twitch helplessly.

It is not easy for me to describe the emotions of that day.

Of course I thought that I had failed Kat, and I knew that because of what I had done, a boy was undergoing surgery. He could lose an eye, and I was ashamed of myself and realized that all my rules, the rules I had tried to live by and tried to teach the children, hadn't worked. Hadn't kept Kat from harm and hadn't kept me from doing harm. As practical and limited as they were, I had always regarded them as a basis for right behavior, for justice and self-respect. The Big Rules had evolved over time and were now printed out, fancy computer printing with a frame around them, held to the refrigerator by a guitar-shaped magnet, sometimes covered up by other refrigerator items, photos and schedules, but nevertheless the rules of our household.

 1. *It is what it is.*
 2. *Think for yourself.*
 3. *Show up (on time).*
 4. *Finish what you start.*
 5. *Play hard, play fair.*
 6. *Clear your desk every day.*
 7. *Don't complain.*
 8. *Be brave, be bold, let not your heart grow cold.*

That last rule was Kat's, added in her angular, slanted handwriting, the refrain of "The Gate Girl," one of her favorite fairy tales, added because she had grumbled that my rules were just army rules and I had challenged her to come up with a rule of her own. I'd offered Will the same challenge, but his only addition was to the Little Rules (tie your shoelaces, take your hat off in the house, and so on), which were handwritten on another sheet of paper, a sheet that had been much scribbled upon. His addition: "No fair making up rules whenever you feel like it." I didn't mind—was pleased, in fact—that the kids could tease me about the rules, for it seemed that we were all in it together, all involved in the effort to keep ourselves on a true course. The house rules weren't absolute, and I was not a die-hard disciplinarian, meting out punishments for all infractions. What mattered the most was not strict obedience to the rules but talking about them, carrying on a conversation, a family conversation, about the way to live a principled life, and helping the children to discover that there must be order within or all is chaos and confusion.

I see now how limited these rules were, and no doubt they meant more to me than I was able to express to the children. I wanted to be a good father to them, and I wanted them to be proud of me. I wanted them to be able to take pride in themselves, and my own understanding of pride was expressed in a scrap remembered from a tale I read in a college lit class: "Pride is the belief that God had some purpose in mind when He made you." The words had stuck with me, an essential piece of my flypaper philosophy, and I would have said with certainty that my purpose was to raise my two children, to care for them and protect them, and to help them find their purpose and their pride.

But I sat in a friends' house on a summer afternoon, barely able to speak to my ex-wife, unready to face my daughter, waiting for a report from a hospital, ashamed of what I had done.

And I realized that Kat was probably feeling much the same.

THE WOMEN were making plans for the girls. Lily said that she'd spoken to Tony, who'd be home that afternoon, and they were thinking that Abby probably shouldn't finish out the summer at Rockrapids. They'd all but decided to send her to Tupper, up in the Adirondacks, where Tony's family had a place, and where she could simply spend time with her cousins, who were there now. The whole family was going up in August, but Lily had already talked to Abby about going early.

"I want to take Kat back with me this afternoon," Trish said. "She might as well come now. She only has three more weeks at the camp anyway. And we've juggled the schedule already."

This was a reminder that Kat's time with Trish had been broken up the last few summers because of Rockrapids. Her first years there Kat went only for two weeks right after school was out, but the last two years she had wanted to spend longer and climb more. That summer, as a junior counselor, she'd signed on for eight weeks. Trish had offered to get her into other outdoor camps, fancier camps out west, but Kat had chosen to stay here, to be with Abby and other friends.

"I think she should finish out her commitment," I said. "And I don't think she should just vanish. She can't run away."

I insisted on that. I argued that Kat should remain in Washington, or return soon if she did go to New York. I said I didn't want her to slink out of town as if she were in disgrace.

Trish said, "Disgrace? What are you talking about? This isn't *The Scarlet Letter.*"

"That's my point," I said. "It makes it seem worse if she leaves."

"It gives her a chance to pull herself together. Tucker, she's only fourteen. She can't be expected to sort all this out in one day or one week. Right now she's up there"—Trish lifted her face toward the ceiling, toward the bedroom upstairs—"and she's furious at herself. She's furious at everyone. At me and you. And I can't say that I blame her. We have work to do, too."

"I'm sure we do," I said, "but this is absurd. I want to see Kat."

I must have sounded abrupt, and the feeling had come abruptly, but I suddenly couldn't wait another moment to see her. I heard Lily say "Tucker" in a cautionary voice, but I was on my feet and out the door, and I took the stairs two at a time.

Abby's door was closed and there was music playing in Abby's room, some kind of hip-hop, playing softly, when I knocked. Noises inside the room, the sound of scurrying. I had to knock again before Abby said, "We want to chill for a while."

"Abs, it's Tucker. I want to talk to Kat."

"Not now."

"Kat? Kat? We don't have to hash everything out right now, but I really want to talk to you."

No answer.

"Kat? Is something wrong?"

"She doesn't want to talk, OK?"

Abby again.

"Kat? Say something to me, Kat."

Silence, except for the hip-hop.

"All right, Abby. What's going on?"

"We've already said everything to Mom."

I rapped hard on the door.

No answer. I said, "Abby, I'm going to open the door. I'm coming in."

"The door's locked," Abby said, and it was.

"This is not acceptable," I said.

"It is to me," Abby said.

"I'm coming in."

"Stay out of my room."

"Kat? Come out now, Kat. Enough of this."

The doors in the Moorefields' house are old and loose and the locks no longer fit snugly, and when I shook the door hard, it opened.

"This is my room," Abby said, "and I told you to stay out."

She was in her room alone, sitting straight on one of the twin beds, facing the door, and she looked defiant. She is the oldest of Lily's children, and the most independent and stubborn, the most willful. Though Abby had no curls, Lily sometimes referred to her as the girl with the curl in the middle of her forehead, the nursery rhyme girl who when she was good was very, very good, and when she was bad she was horrid.

Abby was now prepared to be horrid.

"Where's Kat?"

"You broke the door."

"Where's Kat?"

"Not here."

"I see that."

"I don't know where she is."

"I think you do."

"I have no fucking clue."

"She was here a minute ago."

"What are you going to do? Hit me with a shovel?"

I've known Abby since she was two years old. I've seen her temper and had it directed at me only once, years before, when I took all the kids biking on the towpath along the C&O Canal. Abby got fed up with biking and refused to go any farther. I told her she had to keep going, at least long enough to get back to the car. She threw her bike into the canal, I fished it out, and we all walked back.

"I'm very sorry. I'm very sorry Jed is hurt."

"Get out of my room," she said.

"He fell. I don't know what you heard, but that's what happened. He hit his head when he fell."

"Just shut up and leave."

Footsteps downstairs, Lily's voice calling, both women coming up the stairs.

"I didn't mean to hurt anyone," I said.

"Oh sure," Abby said.

Then Trish and Lily were there. They didn't want to believe that Kat had actually left, but there was no mystery about her departure. Abby's bedroom is at the front of the house, and her front window opens out onto the porch roof. The gutter is sturdy copper, and it wouldn't have been any problem at all for Kat to slide down it to make her escape. More than once, Lily had told me, Abby had used that gutter to disappear from the house, and I thought that she must have put Kat up to leaving. It did not seem possible that Kat, obedient even when she wanted to be otherwise, could have decided on her own to leave the house. She would have needed encouragement, and I felt anger toward Abby and toward Kat, too. How dare she run off when she knew that we were downstairs trying to understand what to do about *her*. When she was the one whose behavior had plunged us into this tangled mess.

But Lily kept asking Abby where Kat was, asking and looking around the room, peering into the closets. She even looked under the beds. "Good thinking," Abby said. "You might want to check the bureau drawers, too."

"Don't you talk to me like that," Lily said.

"She left. Can't you get that through your head?"

"You are going to Tupper, young lady," Lily said.

Young lady. That must have been an echo from Lily's own past, the way her mother had reproached her, and Abby didn't miss her chance.

"I'm not going anywhere, *old* lady," she said, curling her face into an ugly sneer.

"You're going to Tupper," Lily repeated, but the threat had no force. It just made Abby sneer harder.

"Try to send me, *old* lady."

Lily put her hands on her daughter then, put her hands on Abby's shoulders and shook her, and Abby growled—the kind of low growl a dog makes before a fight. Then they pushed at each other, those two women who looked so much alike, neither of them giving an inch of ground, until Trish and I were able to separate them. Abby looked wildly at us, seeing three adults ganged up against her, and said, "Get away from me. Just get away."

Outside Abby's door, once she had slammed it closed, Lily kept apologizing to us. "She is not like that," she said over and over again, and she was shaking. She was shaking and she kept adjusting the way she stood, changing the attitude of her head and the position of her arms and the distribution of her weight, as though she did not know how to carry herself at such a moment. Trish was trying to console her, and—as the seconds ticked away—we came up with a half-cocked plan about pursuing Kat. Lily wanted to go, but she was afraid that Abby would run off, too, and Trish insisted that she stay home. She, Trish, was going to go down to Connecticut Avenue in the Lincoln because the parking was always so impossible and the driver could just double-park while she checked the shops and eating places where Kat might have gone.

I went by foot. Somehow I didn't think that Kat would go far, and I looked first at the Macomb Street playground, just a block away from the Moorefields'. No sign of Kat. A group of boys was playing basketball, boys younger than Kat. I asked, but they hadn't seen anyone who looked like her.

So I walked over to the grounds of the National Cathedral. This was the most likely place for Kat to go, for she had once attended Beauvoir, the little school that is literally in the shadow of the cathedral. Will had gone there, too, and moved on to St. Albans, another school on the cathedral property. On the grassy slopes around Beauvoir, the kids had played hide-and-seek and Mother may I? and other games, and in the winter this was their sledding hill. If there was a place Kat knew, this was surely it, and I felt certain, somehow, that she was there—but she might have concealed herself anywhere on the hilly, wooded grounds with their walls and nooks and gardens, and she could have vanished in the mazes of all the dependent buildings, the residences and school buildings and maintenance buildings, scattered over the several acres of property.

I didn't have a deliberate plan as I hurried along, moving at a half-jog, half-walk up the hill past the tennis courts, past the greenhouse and the school, then along the mulched path to the play areas. Still no sign of her. The grounds seemed to stretch on forever, and on impulse I decided to look in the National Cathedral itself, a faithful replica of the great English cathedrals, a marvel of flying buttresses and angel-goosing spires, the place of worship where I have most often taken the children. A place of worship, I say, though the Cathedral has become a tourist site, and on weekdays, when no services are under way and the docents are leading the tour groups about, it can feel more like a museum than a church, just another one of Washington's much-visited public buildings.

I entered the Cathedral through the south portal and paused for a moment to let my eyes adjust to the dimness. The vast, vaulted space is always dim, of course, and I have always thought that it is the light—the light falling from the high windows of the Gothic clerestory, light that seems suspended and serene and profound—that gives the Cathedral its majesty. Two or three tourist groups were in the nave, peering up at the flags of the states, and a couple of workmen were running their industrial buffers on the patterned marble floor.

Kat was in the Children's Chapel.

I caught sight of her, of her blond head, through the ornate grill-work that separates this little chapel from the apse. She was seated near the door, on one of the chairs—a child's chair, too small for her now—seeming to study the needlepoint on the kneeling cushion in front of her. The chapel contained an elaborate gilt altarpiece, and a statue of the boy Jesus (who looked very much like a well-bred English schoolboy) stood just outside the grillwork, but it was the scale of the place that had always drawn Kat to it, the dollhouse scale and those needlepoint cushions with their representations of lions, tigers, ele-phants, and leopards.

She didn't see me until I'd reached the entrance, and she said, in a whisper, "Stay away from me. Just stay away."

"You can't do this, Kat. You can't run away."

She'd stood up, and I saw that she was wearing shorts and a T-shirt that weren't hers. They must have been Abby's. They were loose, in any case, and somehow made her look forlorn.

She was moving carefully, her back pressed against the metal, trying to slide past me in that entry. Amazing. I caught hold of her arm, but she was far more determined than I was, much clearer about what should happen, and she easily twisted loose. She ran a few steps, enough to put space between us, and then walked as fast as she could in her squeaky running shoes, walking away from me.

"Kat. Kat, wait."

She ignored me. She understood that I wasn't going to run after her, not in that place, and she walked swiftly and purposefully toward the nearest group of tourists. They were standard American tourists, wearing sandals and shirts that hung outside their shorts, clutching their guidebooks and cameras, listening politely and dutifully to the docent as they tilted their faces upward toward the stained-glass windows at the rear of the Cathedral. They were all middle-aged, but Kat—wild and feral and forlorn—joined herself to the group as though she belonged to it. She craned her neck and looked upward where they were looking.

My cunning daughter.

I hung back a few steps, then approached her.

"You can't do this," I whispered.

No answer. A few heads turned. The group started to move slowly away and Kat moved with them. I reached for her arm.

"Let go of me!" she said loudly. "Let go!"

Her voice boomed through the hushed space of the Cathedral, echoing as it traveled. Now everyone looked at her, at us.

A large man with close-cropped white hair, a man who looked like a coach, loomed up beside her.

"Is there a problem here?" the man asked Kat.

"She's my daughter," I said.

She looked up at me in that way she has, her face bent shyly down, her amber eyes peering up through her lashes. She was making up her mind what to do. I think she was completely aware of her power.

"It's all right," Kat said in a tiny voice, letting her gaze fall toward the floor.

"You sure, sugar?" the man asked.

She nodded, and the man looked at me doubtfully.

"She's Kathryn," I said. "She's my daughter."

The group moved away then, and Kat started to walk, not looking at me but not fleeing, either, toward the main doors. I followed her at a slight distance, watching her move, watching that stride like a lope, aware of the eyes of God-fearing people upon us, more conscious than ever that she was a mystery to me.

"How did you find me?" she said when we were outside, her eyes blazing. She'd look at me and then look away, as if she was once again considering flight.

"Why don't you explain what this is all about. What do you think you're doing?"

"I don't want to talk about anything. I'm sick of talking."

"You haven't said a word to me."

"I'm sick of it. Sick, sick, *sick*. I don't want to hear how bad I am, OK? How many fucking rules I broke."

"I don't want to have to go looking for you again."

She waited, wary and angry, trapped.

"You're my daughter," I said, not knowing what else to say, not wanting to let my anger flash out.

"So what?"

"So I want to know what's going on."

"Like you have a right."

Her voice was all disdain. Where was *her* anger coming from? I remember how hard I tried to keep my voice level when I said, "I don't know who you are when you're like this."

"You don't care who I am," Kat said.

She snorted and started to walk away, and that is how we returned to the Moorefields', without speaking, with Kat several paces ahead of me.

I GET HEADACHES. Not migraines, the doctors have told me, but standard stress headaches, and it is not surprising that I felt one coming on that afternoon as we sat there—Trish, Kat, and I—in Lily's kitchen, trying to talk reasonably about what to do next. Trish had evidently reconsidered her strategy while patroling Connecticut Avenue, for she opened her arms wide to Kat when we entered the house—opened them theatrically, I thought, and stood there in Lily's kitchen with her arms outstretched and her face twisted with relief, leaving poor Kat no choice but to rebuff her completely or slink across the floor and lean against her, which she reluctantly did. Nevertheless, that seemed to make it a done deal that Kat was flying back to Long Island that afternoon, for Trish simply assumed that she needed and wanted a few days away from Washington, and discussed the arrangements so that any suggestion to the contrary would have led to an argument. We were seated at the kitchen table, and with the phone ringing every minute, with Lily carrying the cordless into other rooms so that we wouldn't be interrupted—and wouldn't overhear her end of the conversations—I had to acknowledge that it might be a good idea for Kat to leave.

The news about what had occurred was obviously ripping through the parental network. So Kat slouched in her chair while Trish and I talked about how long she'd stay, and when she'd return, and how all this would affect the rest of the summer and Will's return to Washington and our annual boys' trip, and so on. In this kind of conversation, I am no match for Trish, and she knows it. She grinds me into dust.

The only time that Kat seemed to take much interest was when Trish asked me when I had to be in court. Trish caught the lift of Kat's eyes and explained, "Your father has to be here for his arraignment. He was arrested last night."

"Lily told me," Kat said, and shrugged. She did ask, "How come you're already out? Don't they keep people in jail?"

"He was released on his own recognizance," Trish said.

"I'd prefer to explain this," I said to Trish, "not you."

"Explain then. She asked a question and you just sat there."

"It doesn't matter," Kat muttered.

"It does matter," I said. "I want you to know that I didn't mean to hurt anybody. I went there to try to find you."

"Whatever."

"I want you to understand this, Kat."

"Is this necessary?" Trish asked.

"Yes," I said. "This is between me and Kat. You can leave if you want."

"There is no point in attacking me." Trish didn't budge from her chair.

"Kat," I said, taking a breath, trying to push aside everything but what was most essential. "I know that Jed was badly hurt. I don't know what you've heard, but I didn't attack him or anything like that. I didn't hit him with that shovel, but when he wouldn't tell me where you were—I lost it. I lost my temper. I knocked the bottles off the table and Jed thought I was trying to hit him. He got up and took a swing at me, but I still didn't try to hit him."

Kat, looking down, not looking at me, asked, "So how did he get hurt?"

"He fell. He took a swing at me and fell against that metal table."

My daughter flashed her dark eyes upward long enough to meet mine, long enough to let me know that she would like to believe me. My ex-wife said, "He *fell?* I certainly hope there's more to this story, for your sake."

"He fell," I repeated, talking to Kat, trying to ignore Trish. "He swung at me and he fell. That's what happened. I shouldn't have provoked him. I shouldn't have smashed those bottles—god, I made so many mistakes. I know that. I made so many awful mistakes, and I'm sorry. I've made this a hundred times worse for you, for everybody, and I'm sorry. We both made awful mistakes last night, Kat, but it is what it is. The only way to fix it is to face it."

Kat had heard those last words before, and so had Trish, who gave me the look that was the visual equivalent of a snort, the look that said I had yet again ignored her advice, and yet again managed to make things worse. She said, "I'm sure you're concerned about how people might perceive you, but it's Kat's situation we have to put first, and we're going to have to finish this discussion later. Right now I think we should get out to the airport. The plane has to be back before five o'clock."

I wanted Kat to say something, and I asked, "You're coming back, right? You're going to finish out your last week at Rockrapids?"

Trish got to her feet. "She can make that decision later," she said. "You have got to stop badgering her."

"Stop it," Kat cried, and pulled that woven bracelet from her wrist and held it across her mouth like a gag.

Defeated. I felt completely defeated, and there is no other way to put it. While they were gathering up what few things needed to be gathered—Kat had as much stuff up in New York as she had here—I went outside, out onto the porch, just to breathe different air, and I was standing there when the cab stopped at the curb to drop Tony Moorefield.

He was arriving from the airport, and I'm sure he didn't expect to see me there. I hadn't expected to see him, either, though Lily had said she'd reached him by phone, and he was taking the first plane he could back to Washington. He didn't notice me until he'd paid the driver and stepped out of the cab, and then, visibly, he hesitated. He did the double take I would see often in the next weeks and months. Tony Moorefield is outgoing and confident, smooth and worldly and not easily disconcerted, but he did a double take and tried to figure out what to say to me.

What *do* you say to a man who's no longer what you thought he was?

He was wearing business clothes, the jacket of his dark suit folded over his arm, and he took the stone steps in his long stride, two at a time. Tony has physical grace and energy, and I remember thinking, as he set his duffel bag down and shook my hand, squeezing it, that he wanted to erase that double take and assure me that he was in my corner. "This is outrageous," he said, referring to my arrest, and he carried on for a few moments about Vandenberg, whom he knew slightly. Major asshole, he said, major asshole, and he offered to put me in touch with some top lawyers, top litigators who'd know how to handle things if Vandenberg decided to press charges. There was no way this should get to the courts, Tony said, no way it was anything more than a case of teenagers getting into the booze, and I have to admit that I wanted to believe him, wanted to believe that he could take over and this whole mess would just vanish, even though I knew that Tony was bullish by nature and even though he was already looking past me, looking into his own house, looking for his wife.

Rosa was barking by then, and pushed out through the screen door to jump up on Tony, frantic with excitement, and in a moment Lily was on the porch, too, embracing her husband while he held his jacket out to the side like a scarecrow. There was an urgent neediness in the way she held him, and he kept murmuring what she wanted to hear. It will all be fine, he said, fine, fine, fine, and I think Tony always believes that for him things really will turn out fine. He believes that he has a charmed life, and he is grateful for it, and he told me once that whenever he conducts a job interview, he regards one question as crucial: *Are you lucky?* He owns a firm that does lobbying and public relations, and he won't hire anyone who doesn't have the right answer to that question, or anyone who has to think for even one second before answering it.

"Where's Abs?" Tony wanted to know.

"In her room," Lily said. "I told her to stay there. She's been impossible."

"She's going to Tupper," Tony said, an announcement, and right away Lily started trying to tone down his anger. Tony and his oldest daughter had a stubborn, long-standing conflict that flared up easily and often. He was a disciplinarian and Abby had never taken to discipline, and, beyond that, there was the tension that always comes when a father can't conceal a preference. The Moorefields had three children—Abby, Sophy, and Rafe—and it was an open secret that Rafe, age eight, had come into this world because Tony was determined to have a son. Lily hadn't wanted another child after their third girl, Julia, died a crib death. But she had given in to Tony and conceived a fourth time, and though Tony had always tried not to show his partiality for Rafe in any obvious way, the girls knew where they stood. Children always know.

"How long has she been seeing this Vandenberg kid?" Tony asked Lily, speaking in a low voice, and I moved farther away to give them privacy, stepping off the porch and meeting the gaze of Trish's driver, the man with the luxuriant mustache, leaning against the fender of the car and not missing a thing. He was having a fucking field day.

Behind me there was the scuffle of departure. Kat and Trish were at the door, ready to go, and Abby had come downstairs, too, and there were kisses and hugs of farewell. The whole scene was awkward and miserable, and I ended up following Trish and Kat out to the Lincoln, hoping that I could get some kind of word from Kat, some exchange, anything that seemed to connect us. But her face was tear-stained and she just slid into the backseat and across it and stared out the far window, and Trish lowered the window to take one last smug look at me. She was taking Kat back to New York.

The Lincoln pulled away and I watched until it turned onto Reno

Road. I must have stood there for a minute or two, not knowing what to do next. In any case, I was still at the curb when I saw Lily come through the front door and walk to the front of the porch, where she stopped. From the slow and deliberate way she had moved, from the stiffness of her stance, from the terrible expression on her face, I knew that the call had come.

"Jed's out of surgery," she said. "Abby just got a call from one of her friends."

I waited.

"He lost his eye."

Beside the steps there was a concrete planter, a big urn mounded high with white impatiens, and I had to catch hold of it to steady myself. To keep from staggering.

I TOOK a Percodan when I got home that afternoon. At the Moorefields' I'd taken a couple of Advil, but over-the-counter drugs don't touch my worst headaches, and this one was a killer. I don't like taking drugs of any kind, and I keep the Percodan, an old prescription, hidden away at the back of a bathroom cabinet so the kids won't find it, not that I have ever suspected them of any interest in experimenting with chemical substances.

Here's a curious fact: my headaches tend to settle in behind my left eye. When I was married to Trish and worked at Time-Life, I used to get headaches a couple of times a week, almost always behind that eye. The headaches had become far less frequent since the divorce, and since I'd escaped from the corporate, commuting life I had despised, but they still occurred along that fault line, for I had come to imagine my brain as a geological structure and those headaches as my internal earthquakes, disturbances that took place every time the pressure built and the plates shifted.

Jed Vandenberg had lost his left eye.

I am no New Ager. I do not read horoscopes, I have to bite my tongue when I hear intelligent women—including my mother and sister and ex-wife—blather on about their yogis and their chakras and about *feng shui*, and I do not believe that all pain is psychosomatic or that all coincidences are meaningful, but still.

I couldn't stop thinking of that boy. It felt as though my own eye was being squeezed out of my skull as I waited for the Percodan to kick in and listened to the phone messages echo in my empty house. On the cell phone there were a dozen work messages, mostly from clients who wanted something done immediately, and a couple of messages from Christine, who'd also left a message on the home answering machine. Jay had called, too—Jay, my old fraternity brother, my housemate when I first moved to Washington, my lifetime friendly rival in tennis, my best man when I married Trish. His message had all his usual squawky gusto: *Hey, boy, what's this I'm hearing? You been busted? Attacking teenagers? The news travels fast. People've been calling me all morning. Tell me what I need to say to 'em. Over and out.*

There were a couple of messages from Max to reassure me that everything was OK at work. One from Will: *Hey, Dad, what's going on? Mom acted weird this morning. Is she still there? Anyway, you should see how much topspin I'm getting on my forehand. I guess that's it.*

And there was one message that made my pulse race, a message from a boy whose voice I'd never heard before, a teenage croak. He asked for Kat, but the boys who knew her and called regularly knew that she had her own line. He mumbled and swallowed his words, and I had to replay the message a couple of time to catch his name: Luke Childs. There was such a long silence at the start of the tape that I had been ready to hit the delete button before he started to talk. *Hey, Kat, this is Luke Childs.* Pause. *I guess this is the right number. Anyway, I got it from the school directory.* Pause. *I was just calling to make sure you were OK and everything.* Pause. *I'm sorry about what happened and that's what I wanted to say.*

There was another long pause before he clicked off as if he'd wanted to say more, but he couldn't squeeze out another word.

My copy of the school directory was in the open file beside the phone, and Luke Childs was listed as a tenth-grader. I placed the call.

Luke Childs answered.

"This is Tucker," I said, "Kat's dad. She's not here right now, but I know she'll be glad you called. I don't think we've met."

The boy was too taken aback to speak.

I was able to keep my voice even and calm. I said, "Kat's with her mother now, but I wanted to tell you how much I appreciate your call. I know she will, too."

"I was just calling to, you know, apologize and all."

"Thank you," I said, "thank you. You weren't there when I got there, were you?"

He placed his hand over the receiver and spoke to someone with him, words not intended for me to hear. "It's her dad."

Soft thuds as the handset was passed, and a woman said, "Mr. Jones? This is Audrey Childs, Luke's mother."

I identified myself again. I asked her to call me Tucker.

"Luke and I decided he should call, but he wasn't expecting to speak to you. I'm sorry. I mean, he's sorry, but he thought he was going to speak to your daughter. This has to be just so terrible for her. For both of you."

"Kat went to New York," I said, "with her mother."

"You're separated?"

"We're divorced."

In a small, shaky voice Audrey Childs told me that she was a single parent, too, and she seemed to cry a little when she told me how scared she was every time Luke went out at night, scared that something like this would happen because they all grew up so quickly now. I think she babbled because she'd expected me to be angry, and I was, but above all else I felt an absolute need to hold my emotion in check until I found out everything I could from this distraught woman who wanted me to know that her son had never done anything like this before, never. He was an athlete. He was in training. He never drank. Last night he'd told her what Kat told me, that he was going to the movies, and she didn't let him go to anyone's house unless she cleared it first with the parents, so she had no idea that he'd been at the Vandenbergs' until that morning when she was already at work and she heard about Jed.

"Luke didn't say anything last night?" I asked.

He hadn't come home. He'd spent the night with a friend, Danny Owens, and she'd talked to Danny's mother. She had no idea, she repeated, and when the phone calls started to pour in this morning, she was shocked. "Luke has never done anything like this," she said.

"Neither has Kat," I said.

"I am so, so sorry," she said.

"Audrey, I don't know much about what happened last night. Kat doesn't remember anything. All I know is that she went into the pool house with some boys."

It wasn't easy for her to say that Luke was one of them, but she said it. "They were playing some game," she told me. "None of them knew what they were doing."

"Was it oral sex?" I asked her. "I'm sorry to ask, but I don't know. I'm hoping that's all it was."

Audrey Childs wept freely then. "That's all it was," she said when she had control of her voice. "Luke swears there was nothing more."

"Do you know how many boys there were? Was Danny Owens one of them?"

"Yes. There were three, I think. Yes, three. I know your daughter got sick."

In the background I heard her son speak sharply to her.

"Who was the other boy?"

"I'm humiliated," she said, "but Luke knows what he's done, I promise you that. He wasn't raised that way."

I asked again for the name of the other boy, but she was talking to her son, and when she came back on the line, she said in a tight voice that she had to get off.

"Who was the other boy?"

"I think they should call themselves," she said.

"You're the only one who's called, and I can't tell you how grateful I am. I've imagined so many awful things that it's a relief to know."

"They should call themselves," she said again.

"Who was the other boy?" I asked.

"Matt Wyckoff," she said, "and that's all I can say."

A loud voice, another thud, blank air. I don't know whether Audrey Childs or her son broke the connection.

Luke Childs. Danny Owens. Matt Wyckoff.

The three names burned into my brain as though they'd been put there with a branding iron, and I groaned loudly enough to make Romeo, lounging in the wing chair, lift his muzzle and let loose a sympathetic wail. I called to him to stop, and when he came to me, I lay down on the rug in the alcove. I have always gone to the floor when my headaches come, and Romeo licked my face a few times before settling down beside me.

THERE was still one call I had to make: Christine. I lay there pinching myself from time to time to check the degree of numbness in my arm, to see how the Percodan was working, and soon I began trying to rally myself with the slogans I use on the kids—no time like the present, et cetera—but it took a good long while for me to sit up and reach for the phone. It wasn't so much that I didn't want to talk to Christine but that I wanted not to talk, period, not to anyone, not about the events of the last night and day. I didn't want to think about them. I lay there and tried to visualize a blue triangle in which I could store all the pain, a cockamamy scheme I had picked up in some book about samurai. You try to gather all the pain and contain it in your imaginary blue triangle.

It didn't work but eventually the Percodan did, and I made the call. Christine picked up right away, and the warmth in her voice shot through the handset. "Are you all right? I've been sick with worry. I got the message you left this morning—oh, Tuck, what you've been through. Are you OK? Where are you?"

With a sort of bubbly, foolish chuckle, I said, "I'm at home. Not in jail, anyway. I'm sorry I didn't have a chance to call you earlier, but Trish came down. Flew down to take over. She was here all day."

"And Kat? How's Kat?"

"She went back to New York with Trish."

"She went with Trish?"

"Yes."

A short silence, and I could imagine Christine at her desk, letting this information sink in, waiting for me to complete my answer. But I didn't. I said, "They operated on the boy today. Jed. The boy who was hurt." I had to force the words out, but I wanted to get through the miserable report as quickly as I could.

"They had to operate? Why?"

There was so much I hadn't told her. "He lost his eye," I said.

"Oh no. Oh no." In the next short silence I could hear her trying to control her breath so that she could ask, "Are you alone? Can I come over? This is just so awful. I'll stop on the way and get something to eat. Should I come? I'm going to leave right now. Oh, I love you, Tucker, and I want to hold you."

That wasn't the first time Christine had said she loved me, but the words had never before come so spontaneously, and I wanted her to come—though she would expect a full account, and I couldn't imagine how I was going to tell her. She certainly had every right to know how I'd behaved. We'd been lovers for two years, and despite the boundaries we had carefully kept in place, our lives had braided themselves together. Lovers. I think Christine was secretly proud of the wicked sophistication that was implied by the words *lover* and *mistress*, words she rarely used, and never in public, but liked to say every now and then when she was, as she would put it, in the mood. "I've never been a mistress before," she'd say when we were in bed and she wanted to express gratification or desire, or she'd say, "Can we get naughty?" Naughty. She was a midwesterner, as I have said, and had been raised in a solidly middle-class, prosperous, Catholic family, and both she and her husband, Robert, came to Washington in search of a worldliness that would enable them to shake off the strictures of their upbringing. They'd bought a condo in one of the made-over mansions near Dupont Circle and lived, even with their young children, what they considered a sizzling metropolitan life.

Christine. It pains me now to remember how I thought of her that afternoon, how I reminded myself of every small difference and disconnect between us. Who was I to find fault with her? But I had never been able to get used to her self-consciousness, to the way she constantly seemed to remind herself to keep her back straight, her shoulders square, her chin up. She wanted to turn her height into a virtue. She'd been one of those girls who'd shot up at an early age and been teased about it (the teasing that stung most came from her father, who called her Olive Oyl) and spent years trying to get over it. I'd always had the impression that for her even the most fundamental movements and gestures were not instinctual but had to be acquired—how to stand, how to walk, how to speak, how to present herself. She dressed with care, in the conservative fashion of most professional women in Washington, wearing tailored suits, discreet jewelry, and quiet colors, mostly grays and blacks. Her style and manner seemed intended not just to make her fit in but to conceal most traces of individuality and sensuality, though she could never completely discipline her fine dark hair, which she wore long and usually pinned up in loose coils, lifting the mass of it free of her long neck. It gave her an elegant, old-fashioned look, and there were always stray locks drifting about her temples and forehead, softening the features of her face, her strong brow and Roman nose. When we were alone, she liked to make a ceremony of letting let her hair down, her way of signaling that the cautious public woman was ready to play the part of the mistress.

"Let me draw the veil," Christine would say when she went down on me, and she often did, letting her hair fall like curtains around my midsection, using her hair—along with her fingers and tongue and teeth and lips—to give me intense pleasure. She was practiced and skilled at oral sex (and I couldn't prevent myself from suspecting that Robert had carefully coached her); she was proud of her skill and excited by the act that awakened an old taboo, and as I awaited her that afternoon, I could only imagine that such private moments now belonged to the past. Less than twenty-four hours ago I had been in bed with Christine, but our intimacy seemed almost as far away, as *unthinkable*, as my marriage to Trish.

She arrived carrying a couple of green-and-white Sutton Place bags, with a bouquet of flowers and a loaf of bread sticking out of the corner. She put her arms around me and kissed me with tenderness. She busied herself in the kitchen for a bit, long enough to put the flowers in a vase and to set out some nibbly things in small colorful dishes (gifts from her, as were nearly all the attractive items in my kitchen). She joined me on the small sofa in the alcove and put a glass of wine in my hand.

"You need taking care of," she said.

"I'm not an invalid yet."

She still had office clothes on, a black skirt and silvery silk blouse that buttoned high around her throat. Her hair was pinned up as I have described. She had never seemed so forward as she did that afternoon, so ready to share my life. Her eyes are pale gray and they looked expectant, almost transparent.

"I want you to let everything go."

"That's exactly what the Percodan has been saying to me."

"I want to take care of you," she said. "Sometimes you should let someone take care of you."

She was leaning against me, with her long legs tucked underneath her, and I was aware of a loosening in her body and her gaze, of the way that she let her body adjust itself to mine, and I cannot express, even now, how kind she seemed at that moment. When she stroked my cheek, tears came to my eyes and I said, "I am so ashamed of myself."

"Let it go," she said, "just let it all go."

We kissed and she reached up to take the tortoiseshell pins out of her hair. She looked lovely and vulnerable, and she lowered her head so that her face rested against my shoulder and her hair spread like a fan across my chest. At that moment I think she accepted me completely and wanted only to give herself to me, and I talked about Brian Collinsworth and Richard Vandenberg and what I understood of the charges against me.

She tried to listen, but of course she knew what was happening. She knew that I was keeping her at a distance. She sat and let me talk for a while. She stroked my cheek again and said, "Poor Tucker."

"This Percodan is making me woozy," I said. "I probably shouldn't drink on top of it. This is a killer headache."

A headache—could anything be more commonplace? Any excuse to avoid intimacy? Christine smiled and stood up and set about preparing the meal she'd brought. I talked about my arrest, and when we sat at the table, I reached for her hand and brought it to my lips.

I had just tried to explain why I'd called Lily from the precinct headquarters and why I hadn't called her.

"I'm sorry," I said. "I was hoping to hear that Kat had shown up."

"I understand."

"And today—it just turned into such a nightmare. I'm sorry I didn't call. I just didn't have a chance."

"I understand," Christine said, but she drew her hand away. She tucked her lips together as she does when she has something to say, something difficult. "I know that you had other things to deal with today. I wasn't going to say this, but last night it did hurt when Lily called. It makes perfect sense that you would have called her. But today, when I was wondering where you were and what was happening, I realized that I wanted to be the person you turned to. The one you called first."

I apologized.

She stood up and said, "Oh, Tucker, I'm sorry. I shouldn't have said that. You don't need anything more heaped on you right now. You don't need to know about my hurt feelings."

She straightened her shoulders and tucked her lips together, and I would have given anything to be able to love her.

CHAPTER

3

___

On the scales of misfortune and suffering, the sexual trials of an American teenage girl do not register, not in milligrams, not in millionths of milligrams, or so I tried to tell myself during those midsummer days of 1998 when Kat was with her mother on Long Island and I was alone in Washington. Christine came by several times, and we played tennis or went out to eat or to the movies. There were no Amish nights. There was no sex at all. I went to work every day and did everything in my power to lead an outwardly normal life, but there was scarcely a moment when I was able to escape or even mute my obsessive thoughts about Kat and Jed Vandenberg and that one night that had changed my life beyond recognition. I could go to prison. I could lose Kat, I could lose Will, I could lose the business. Richard Vandenberg could and probably would sue me for every penny I had. I could lose everything that I had worked for and valued, and my mental state was a riot of dread and confusion that kept me awake at night and gnawed at me throughout the day, as though the very composition of my mind had been altered.

I staggered through the hot, hellish days with a sense of foreboding, and I know that I sometimes talked to myself, and what I talked about most was Richard Vandenberg. I know, I know, I know that this man had every reason to despise me and it was understandable that he would wish to punish me for what had happened to his son, but I couldn't get the hateful sound of his voice out of my mind, and every time I talked to Brian Collinsworth about the charges that could be brought against me, I felt the anxiety surge through me in waves. Vandenberg wanted to destroy me. I'd been arrested for simple assault, a misdemeanor, but he was hounding the AUSA—the assistant United States attorney, as prosecutors are called in the District of Columbia—to go to the grand jury to seek an indictment for assault with a deadly weapon, a felony that could carry a sentence of five years' imprisonment. Furthermore, as Brian had learned from John Briggs, the AUSA in charge of the case, Vandenberg had already hired a private investigator to gather evidence about what had taken place, and about me. No matter what happened in the criminal case, Brian expected Vandenberg to come after me with a civil suit, and he warned me that it wouldn't be an easy defense.

My knowledge of the law was based mostly on what I'd seen in the movies and a few high-profile lawsuits, and so I understood, thanks to O.J. Simpson, that the rules were different in civil cases. A charge did not have to be proven beyond a reasonable doubt, and the whole question of my intention was almost beside the point. In a criminal case, Brian told me, I would have to be shown to have acted "knowingly and deliberately" to inflict an injury upon Jed, but in a civil case the mere fact that I had shown up with a shovel in my hand and set in motion a sequence of events leading to his injury was probably enough to establish my guilt.

My conversations with Brian—usually brief, usually on the phone— made my head ache and tied my gut in knots. I fixated on Richard Vandenberg, my enemy, a man I'd never seen but imagined, who knows why, as a hairy black spider, fat and patient and fatally spinning, spinning, spinning out the filaments of the lawsuits that were intended to ruin me, and sometimes I felt as though I were already caught in his web, kicking and helplessly fluttering. At one point I asked Brian why he couldn't arrange a meeting with Vandenberg so that we could talk face-to-face and I could tell him that I had never intended to hurt Jed and had, in fact, only tried to block his swing at me. Brian made a muffled sound, a sawed-off laugh, and pointed out that most people accused of a crime were eager to proclaim their innocence, but they weren't always their own best witness. It might do us more good, he said, to start our own investigation. *Our own,* he said, and I was glad to have someone on my side, but his suggestion opened up a future of days and weeks and months of legal maneuvering. He had someone in mind, a law student interning in his office, a young woman who might be able to relate to the kids, he said. He thought she could talk to them in their own language.

"She's going to talk to the kids who were there?"

"They're the only ones who saw what happened."

"What do you expect her to find out?"

"I don't know," Brian said, "but right now we know next to nothing."

"There were three of them," I said. "I know that much."

He seemed surprised—astonished, even—that Luke Childs had called to apologize and wanted to know exactly what he and his mother had said, and it was my turn to be astonished when Brian said there might be grounds for charges of sexual misconduct against the boys. I hadn't thought about that. Couldn't think about it. I obsessed about those three boys (god help me, I'd combed through Kat's Byrd-Adams yearbooks, looking for pictures of them, studying their thumbnail faces in class pictures and team pictures, for they were all jocks, searching for clues about what to do next and how to regard them, this trio of Luke Childs, Danny Owens, and Matt Wyckoff, searching for ways not to hate them), but I knew I didn't want this case, this fucking nightmare, to keep growing and spreading and sucking more people into its vortex. I didn't want to be a Richard Vandenberg.

But I told Brian to go ahead and start an investigation. I agreed to pay a retainer of ten thousand dollars. He warned me that the legal fees could easily go as high as seventy-five thousand. All of this happened within days of July 13th, the date that divided my life into Before and After, and I was falling to pieces. I ranted about those boys. I railed against Vandenberg in the privacy of the truck, and Romeo, on the passenger seat, would look at me as though he'd seen a ghost. I know I talked about Kat, too, and spent hours trying to convince myself that it didn't matter what Kat had done, didn't matter whether she'd been drunk or sober, didn't matter whether she'd gone down on one boy or a dozen, didn't matter whether she could remember a single instant or whether everything had been obliterated from her memory. It didn't matter because she was still a child and she had her whole life ahead of her and it would not be marred forever by this one night.

But if it didn't matter, what had possessed me that night? And still possessed me? What had made me so crazy with rage? Or set off like a knight-errant to save Kat? To save her from *what*? Why had I instantly concluded that she had been raped? What had made my fears so powerful that a sixteen-year-old boy who'd been making out with another girl ended up half-blind? What did I think those boys had taken from my daughter?

What had possessed me? I'd never been the kind of father who felt the need to drive away any boy who showed an interest in his daughter. It is an age-old story, fathers trying to protect their daughters from sex, but this was 1998 and like most fathers I knew, I wanted my daughter to have all the liberties and opportunities that boys had. The double standard no longer applied, not in the classroom, not on the playing field, and not in the bedroom. Every now and then, a father would make a joke—a bad joke, a nervous joke—about chastity belts or tower rooms where the girls could be locked up, but I suppose we all regarded ourselves as too enlightened or too highly evolved to admit how frightening it was to watch our daughters come of age, to develop hips and breasts and turn into young women at a time when the juggernaut of popular culture seemed to bear down on them with the relentless message that they could fulfill themselves as dopey sex kittens with glitter on their eyelids and rings in their belly buttons. We were urbane private school dads, and perhaps we even thought that, somehow, our privileged daughters would find ways to protect themselves from the torrents of smut and pornography that jammed magazines and songs and movies and the airwaves. In any case, no one wanted to be the kind of laughingstock we could all remember from our own childhoods—to be, for instance, like Mr. Prunty, the father of Libby Prunty, a girl I knew when I was a freshman at Granby High School in Norfolk, Virginia. I had a crush on Libby, and one night when I went over to her house to watch TV, Mr. Prunty wandered into the room and joined us for a while. He was drinking a beer, and he burped and excused himself and went into the bathroom just off the TV room, separated from it only by a hollow-core door, a door that actually seemed to amplify the groans he made when he voided his bowels, groans and grunts that began as a low rumble but swelled in volume and urgency as he laid a mighty woofer, producing a squishing, sputtering, stupendous flatulence that sounded as though a drunken elephant was attempting to play the bagpipe. When the noise finally ended in a Niagara of flushing, Mr. Prunty returned to his chair and asked, "Did I miss anything?"

What makes fathers behave that way? I didn't know, but I remember wishing that I had been merely ridiculous like Mr. Prunty, who never harmed anyone. It had been years since I had thought of him, but, as I have said, my thoughts and emotions were strange to me that summer, and I was no longer sure what kind of man I was, or what kind of father.

THE HEADQUARTERS of Twill Landscaping is off River Road in Maryland, just beyond the District line. Our building is cinder block, painted a weird orangy pink by some previous tenant, and I leased it because the office space is attached to a garage and the twelve-foot doors and big bays are the right size for trucks. The company owns five trucks, including the Jimmy, and leases eleven more. Before moving to this location, I spent a damn fortune having them serviced, but now I have my own mechanic, a Peruvian named Hugo who takes care of all the equipment, the trucks and mowers and saws and blowers. He can fix anything. He has Popeye forearms and hands that can bust a bolt loose from years of rust. My hands are strong but I once thumb-wrestled Hugo and felt as though my thumb was trapped in the door of a bank vault.

We have a big parking lot, of course, surrounded by the usual hideous chain-link fence, where the trucks are parked at night, and the plant stock—along with mulch and fertilizer—is kept in another open lot at the back of the complex, behind the odd agglomeration of cheap, ugly buildings that sprouted before the zoning authorities got serious about building codes. There are a few more cinder-block garages, a couple of small tin-sided warehouses, and a pair of Quonset huts. Two other smaller landscaping outfits have their headquarters down here, but a cheerful Greek named George—he drives an old El Dorado and wears a toupee that couldn't have cost more than twenty bucks—rents most of the buildings for his body-shop operation, and when the air is still and heavy, the whole area reeks with the fumes of auto paint.

Still, I have always liked starting my days with the arriving workmen, most of them Hispanic, most of them carpooling over from Silver Spring in their little cars, the ten-year-old Nissan Sentras and Toyota Celicas that they somehow keep running and gussied up with new chrome, grill bras, tinted windows, fancy mirrors, and bright bumper stickers attesting to their personal relationship with Jesus. They are religious, these hardworking men from Nicaragua and Guatemala and El Salvador. In fact, nearly all of them belong to the same church, the Church of the Glorious Miracle, and they are always pestering Max—Max, my second-in-command, a handsome Cuban with a neat goatee—to hire some friend or relative. We have never had to recruit actively. My original partner, Carlos Fuentes, was a member of the church, and even though I bought him out (he started a Latino grocery store, which has prospered), the men of the Glorious Miracle have continued to look upon Twill as a good employer. I pay ten bucks an hour for unskilled labor, a little more than most other landscapers, and I move the pay scale up quickly when guys show me they are willing to work. I keep several people on the payroll year-round—Tomás Ochoa, Gladys's husband, has been one of my top crew chiefs for years, and he makes, with overtime, almost forty thousand a year—and generally try to take care of them, recognizing that I am a lucky gringo to have a workforce made up of these skilled, sober, reliable immigrants who aren't afraid to hump it all day long and know how to make plants grow. When I watch them mill around in the yard, waiting for Max to step out with his clipboard and dispatch them, wearing their green duck pants and white T-shirts—yes, I require that all employees wear a uniform and insist that it be clean every morning—I take pride in the way the business has grown and wonder about these men, sipping their coffee and talking quietly to one another, accepting the fate that has carried them so far from their homelands and their villages of palm and oleander and piled them into Nissans to go zooming around the Beltway of the capital of the free world.

On early summer mornings I have sometimes fantasized that I, El Jefe, am a general moving among his troops. It is Romeo who inspires this fantasy, for he seems to stand taller when we are at the yard and to look the men over carefully, as if inspecting them. He doesn't exactly strut, but he has sensed that I am a figure of some importance in this milieu, and he takes it upon himself to be a worthy sidekick. Every now and then the men actually salute him, and I swear that he understands the gesture and returns it with a lift of his muzzle. This is endlessly amusing to them, and to me, and it is also endlessly strange that I should have arrived at such a place in life—a white guy in short pants, accompanied by a self-important semibeagle, a landscape contractor whose contribution to society is to employ men who have left behind everything familiar in order to make better lives for themselves and their families in the land of opportunity, where they joined the Church of the Glorious Miracle and tried to save enough money to buy a condo.

Does any life ever turn out as expected?

I doubt it, and it might be simply another measure of my state of mind during that summer that I found myself looking at familiar scenes in such a strange way. Normally, I would have been content to arrive at the lot as day was breaking, while the night's coolness still drifted through the air, while the busy, shameless crows congratulated each other for having achieved complete dominance of the dawn (every now and then some other birds would peep, but the crows ruled at daybreak), and I would have talked to some of the workmen, joked with them, giving them a chance to laugh at my meager Spanish. I freely admit that I looked forward to most days, I liked being El Jefe, and I liked all the little routines in the office, where, besides Max, there was Dee, Wee Dee—the tiny, ideal receptionist with her bleached hair and camouflage outfits and sexy voice—and Don and Randy, who did all the buying and estimating and the simple designs, the ones that didn't require Barbara, the pro, a trained landscape architect, a lovely, quiet woman who went everywhere with her dog, a black-and-tan mutt she had saved one day out on Rockville Pike and whose eyes never left her. Our bookkeeper was Jackie, the office mom, who wore cat's-eye glasses and always had a ten-gallon jar of trail mix for us to dip into, and except for Dee and Randy, everyone had been at Twill for at least three years, and nobody complained about the lack of privacy or the sawhorse desks or the single bathroom (there were two more bathrooms out in the garage area, built at large expense to satisfy federal regulations), where the toilet was so high that Dee's feet didn't touch the floor.

As a rule, I spent the first few hours of the day in the office, talking to the staff, trying to stay on top of the contracts and bids and the progress of different jobs, and then I'd get into the Jimmy and drive around to the sites, or meet with clients, most often the builders in Montgomery County, the guys who accounted for over half of the company's volume, the easy half. They wanted sod and foundation planting around their town houses or McMansions, and they were usually in a rush and willing to pay top dollar and not too fussy about the results. Once the day was well launched, the cell phone rang constantly and I slipped into the familiar speedy feeling as I drove around, barreling ahead, checking things off the list I kept on a yellow legal pad, solving problems. That's what I did all day long. I barreled ahead, solving problems. It was like crossing a stream on a log: slow down and you lose your balance. I tried to figure out how to get another truckload of sod to a site in a hurry, without getting gouged by the supplier, or how to get eight tons of gravel into a fenced backyard, or how to calm down the woman who thought the crews had trampled her yarrow and coreopsis, and so forth and so on. I was El Jefe, the guy in the short pants and hiking boots, the guy who made sure his crews met their deadlines and left the sites clean and tidy, the guy who tried to be reliable and fair and forthright in a business not known for those qualities, the guy who solved problems.

But I wasn't myself that summer. I pulled a crew off a big job in Potomac because the developer kept griping about the size of the hollies we put in. They were exactly the size specified in the contract, but he kept griping and I told him to get his head out of his ass. I blew up at another crew when they sliced three irrigation lines while they were putting in new plants. I had words with Jackie about a mistake, a minor mistake, she made on a weekly income statement. And I lit into Max one morning when I overheard him telling Randy about one of his stocks. We all knew that Max watched the market throughout the day, checking quotes on the computer, and that he was riding the boom in tech stocks, but that morning I just didn't want to hear him gloat. "This isn't a goddamn brokerage house," I told him. "You want to trade stocks, fine, but don't do it on my time. I'm not paying you for that."

The office is small, and everyone heard me. I saw Max, who has that goatee, a man in his midthirties who always had too much mousse in his hair and more than a touch of vanity, look at me with surprise and deep offense. It is a lousy boss who disciplines employees in public, and Max was more than just another employee. He was my right hand.

"My mistake," he said quite formally, with a slight ironic bow of his head, after a silence that felt long and dangerous, "my mistake."

When I apologized to him at the end of the day, he said, "Forget it. *No importa*. We know how things are. Maybe you need to take some time?"

Maybe I did, but I wouldn't have known what to do with myself.

THERE were many other moments like that, moments when I realized that people were looking at me in a different light. Of course the news had spread like a brushfire, and of course the reports had been exaggerated and inaccurate. When I played my usual Thursday night tennis with Jay, he told me that he'd heard that Trish had taken Kat to New York and was refusing to let me see her. He'd heard that I'd only stopped beating Jed when the other boys pulled me away from him, and that Vandenberg was going to sue for $5 million. In the small world in which I mostly conducted my personal life—just a couple of zip codes, really, a few neighborhoods in Northwest Washington—I kept running into people who looked curious or alarmed or stricken when they saw me. Clients whom I hardly knew lowered their eyes when we talked, and some acquaintances turned their backs on me in the movie line and at the grocery store. At a Starbucks one morning,

I was standing behind two mothers from Byrd-Adams, women I knew slightly, and after their first reaction of panic—honestly, their eyes bugged out and their cheeks flushed pink and their heads swiveled and they gave every other indication of being terrified to find themselves face-to-face with the Shovel Fiend—one of them, a chubby-cheeked woman who sold real estate and blabbed readily about her own private life and everyone else's, told me how sorry she'd been to hear about Kat. Not how sorry she was *for* Kat, but how sorry she'd been to hear about it. "It probably had to happen," she said, and caught herself, realizing that I could think she meant to blame me. Perhaps she did. But she added, "I mean, things like this are going on everywhere. Now that the whole world knows about Clinton and the BJs in the Oval Office. It's like a new fad. Is Kat going to stay at Byrd-Adams? I heard she might be going to New York."

"No, she'll be staying here."

"Oh." The realtor sounded dubious, and it ticked me off to realize that I had turned into a kind of local figure, someone whose life was now the subject of all sorts of gossip, and it galled me to no end that busybodies like Chubby Cheeks were speculating about Kat, but I had decided that I would be as polite and patient, as *normal*, as I could be. I wasn't going to avoid anyone, I wasn't going to tuck my tail between my legs and cringe every time I ran into someone who knew what had happened, I wasn't going to hole up in the Hut and just hope the whole thing would blow over. In fact, in those first few days after Kat had left, I made myself get on the phone and talk to people who'd called and left sympathetic messages (I was disproportionately grateful for these messages, even when I suspected that they were just feelers, motivated by a desire to worm some juicy detail out of me). I called my sister, Emily, who now lives in a sweet bungalow in Croton-on-Hudson, about thirty miles north of New York City, and has three kids of her own. She's a year older than I am, a quiet, thoughtful, somewhat shy woman who teaches fourth grade at a private school so that her children can get free tuition. "It's going to be all right," she kept saying in the soothing voice that she uses to talk to little ones.

I also called my mother, Mary Carter, who didn't sound particularly surprised or upset even though she adores Kat. She said instantly,

"I saw a program about that. I forget which one. There's always one on when I'm at the gym, one of those talk programs with a fat lady. It must make everyone feel more comfortable if the hostess is chubby. Now that I think of it, I believe I've seen more than one program about blow jobs and how so many young girls are doing it now. They think it's safe sex. Some of the girls don't think it's sex at all."

Gulls, she said, not *girls*. My mother is almost seventy years old, and she has not lost one soft syllable of her Tidewater accent. She has lived on the Isle of Palms, in South Carolina, ever since my father died (during my junior year in college, in an automobile accident) and she "set up housekeeping," as she puts it, with Larry Vickery, her high school sweetheart. They are not married. By remaining single they enjoy some financial advantages, but I think Mary Carter likes to shock people by declaring that she and Larry live in sin. In any case, they seem to dote on each other, and I have to say that she is as high-spirited and effervescent as ever. I know far more about her sex life than I have ever wished to know. She'd always been an outspoken character, and people in Norfolk often told me what a charming, great-looking couple my parents made, but I thought they were miserable. My father was a hard-drinking country clubber, one of those Jekyll-and-Hyde drinkers who was all sweetness and light in a social setting, all darkness and gloom at home. He hated working for his father, who owned the Cadillac-Oldsmobile dealership in Norfolk, and my mother's kookiness sometimes seemed like her way of protecting herself, and Emily and me, from his black moods, her way of creating a make-believe world where his misery couldn't touch us, though I now realize that she is naturally and irrepressibly kooky. She seems to work out for several hours a day, either at the gym or at home, where she often talks to me on the speaker phone while she does her yoga in front of the television. Yoga clears her mind, she says. Her yogi tells her it is important to keep her ass above her head, and when I talk to her, I think of her upside down, wearing her outfit of white spandex as she moves gracefully through the poses she has demonstrated for me and Kat and Will, her buns of steel above her snow-white head.

"What I don't understand about Bill Clinton," she said, "is why they never *did* it," and she was off and running about the impeachment. This was the summer of 1998, remember, and it was impossible to listen to the radio or read a newspaper or enter a coffee shop without being caught up in the frenzy and fascination of the scandal of the president and the intern. That summer the whole country was consumed by what was happening in Washington, riveted by the mortifying and grotesquely precise details, ranging from the fabric of the semen-stained dress to the number and date and duration and exact location of the eleven blow jobs, and the method of washing up thereafter, and the procedures and protocol of impeachment, and the hilarious spectacle of the Republican leaders, who kept solemnly proclaiming that it was "not about sex," which, as every child in the Republic knew, was the biggest fib of all.

Yes, yes, I know that Clinton told plenty of fibs of his own, including a couple of in-your-face whoppers ("I did not have sexual relations with that woman") and evasions that have come to stand as classics of hairsplitting ("It depends on what the meaning of *is* is"). I have no interest whatsoever in defending the man or apologizing for him, but I felt almost sorry for him when I heard my mother carrying on. I could understand how it felt to have strangers raking over the details of your private life.

My mother headed into a digression on the history of oral sex, tracing it back to Cleopatra and lipstick—this, too, she had learned from TV—and gradually I saw that she was making a point in her own roundabout way. "Those people on TV always act as if it's a brand-new day. They were saying how girls these days just have to try all these different things, the sparkly makeup and the little bitty shorts and the thongs and all that, as if every girl before now was pure as the driven snow. But girls have always wanted to do what makes boys like them. It makes them feel good. It's not as complicated as they make it out to be."

She paused and asked, "Do you understand?"

"I think so."

"I mean, Kat's just a girl."

"I know that, Mom."

"Girls are entitled to a few mistakes, too."

"I know."

"It's better to make them now than later."

"I know."

"Well, just don't be too hard on her. You can be hard."

"What makes you think I'm being too hard?" I asked.

"I just know you," my mother said. "I know how you can get when something worries you. You can't let go. But, Tucker honey, this time you have to. You've just got to forgive her, really and truly forgive her."

Fahgivuh.

When I heard the careful emphasis in my mother's voice, I realized that she had forgiven Kat instantly, unconsciously, and completely, without a second's hesitation. And I knew that I hadn't.

That's when I told her about Jed. She was silent while she listened to the story, and she hesitated before she said, "I love you, Tucker darling."

I was forty-four years old and it still mattered to hear her say that. It is almost embarrassing to admit how much it mattered as I sat in the empty house on that summer night, a middle-aged man holding a buzzing phone and clinging to his mother's words, a father without his children.

ON IMPULSE, I drove to Carderock to search out Abby Moorefield. It was late on Friday morning and I was in the Jimmy, headed out on River Road toward a work site, and the thought of Kat slipping away from me, just slipping away, was a needle in my heart. She'd been gone for three days, and I'd spoken to her on the phone—the rule was that we'd talk every day when she was at Trish's—but her voice had sounded small, faint, and vanishing. It was as if we no longer knew how to talk to each other, as if I was losing her, and I missed her so sharply that I pointed the truck toward Carderock, thinking that if anyone knew what Kat was going through, it would be Abby.

The green Rockrapids van was parked in the far lot, and Romeo pranced along in front of me as I followed the trail down through the woods to the cliffs along the river. Except for the gliding sound of the river, the park was quiet that morning, and I heard Abby's voice before I saw her. The trail of beaten clay winds along between the foot of the cliffs and the riverbank, and she was coaxing a young climber, her voice patient and encouraging. I slowed down, advancing cautiously, not wanting to startle her, and caught sight of her as I rounded a shoulder of granite—Abby in a red helmet and black climbing harness, standing back from the rock face, belaying a skinny boy who was high above her, telling him where to place his hands and feet, reminding him not to hug the wall, calling him Spider-Man, urging him upward, playing out the safety rope to keep just the right degree of tension. She had on shorts and a black sports bra and she was the only one standing, though there must have been at least fifteen other kids scattered about on the rocks, some watching the climb, others just chatting. With the sunlight dappling down through the canopies of beech and poplar, and the broad, slow river rustling by, the whole scene had a sweet tranquillity and Abby seemed to be the one in charge.

Abby. She hadn't noticed me yet, and as I watched her, I had one of those moments when a child—your own or someone else's, but a child you've known for years—suddenly appears in a different light, almost a different dimension, when she seems to have grown up in the blink of an eye. Here Abby wasn't Lily's daughter, wasn't anybody's kid, wasn't a junior counselor or a junior *anything*. She was the boss. Dusty and half bare, almost dancing as she stepped about, intently watching her young Spider-Man up on the rock, the muscles in her arms and shoulders rippling with each slight movement, her voice clear and calm, she had presence and substance. She had an air of complete confidence.

I considered leaving before she saw me. This was not the Abby I had expected to find, but before I could turn away, Romeo scooted ahead and Abby glanced down. She recognized him, of course, and a curious expression—surprise, irritation, suspicion—crossed her face when she saw me hovering on the trail. One by one the other kids noticed Romeo and sensed my arrival, and it occurred to me that at least some of them would identify me as Kat's father, and thus as the man who'd injured Jed Vandenberg, Abby's boyfriend, and they fell silent, watching me approach as if they expected some kind of showdown.

Abby looked upward again, focusing on the climber, ignoring me for the moment. I stepped forward and called to Romeo to keep him from trying to greet Abby and tangling himself up in her feet. Up on the rock the boy sensed a change in the tension and glanced down, breaking the spell of his effort; he relaxed his body and let go, giving his weight to the rope, to Abby, who played out the line smoothly as he walked backward in a slow-motion rappel, descending.

"What do you want?" she asked me, helping the boy out of his harness, not bothering to lower her voice or disguise her hostility.

What had I been thinking? In my distress I'd been so preoccupied that I had somehow expected Abby to defer to me as Kat's father, even to sympathize with me, overlooking everything that had happened the night of July 13th. I know how ridiculous and lame I must have sounded when I said I wanted to talk to her, and she thought it over, wrapping the climbing rope into a neat coil before she spoke—not to me but to an older boy, the senior counselor, who was seated in a folding canvas chair, a Walkman in his lap, holding the earphones he'd just removed. She told him to take over. She said she'd be right back.

Then she walked past me and led me back along the trail, her short ponytail extending from the back of the red helmet and swaying on the nape of her neck, until we were out of sight and hearing of the others. Her wide-spaced eyes were filled with mistrust when she turned to face me.

I apologized. I apologized for showing up without warning, and I apologized, clumsily, for what had happened to Jed. She watched me without blinking, and I felt as though our roles had been reversed, as though she was the stern parent and I was the guilty child attempting to explain my behavior. I said I was sorry about his eye.

"You should tell him," she said, "not me."

"You're right. I should. I will tell him," I said, trying to collect myself, trying not to let all the wild feelings within me run loose, trying to remember what I'd come for.

"Abs," I said, calling her by that familiar name, pleading, "I came here to ask you about Kat. I need your help."

She waited, swatting the air to disperse the tiny gnats that swarmed about us both.

I told her that I didn't know what to do. I told her that Trish wanted Kat to remain in New York and go to school up there.

"I know," Abby said.

I asked if she'd talked to Kat.

"A couple of times," she said in a voice that gave nothing away.

"I don't want to force her to do anything. I want to do what's best for her, obviously. But I don't know what's best. I don't know what she wants. It's been hard to talk to her. I don't know what's going on with her."

I hadn't intended for my voice to waver but it did, and there in the wooded, shady silence, the words seemed to break up and clatter on the rocks.

"Ask her," Abby said.

"I do ask her."

What a hard, pitiless look Abby had, the look of a gunslinger. "She says you don't. She says you don't talk about anything important. She says you act as though nothing has changed when you call her. She says you talk about regular stuff like, hi, it's just another day."

I had to look away. "I know this must be strange," I said, "your friend's dad asking you to tell him about her. I don't want you to betray any confidence."

"I wouldn't," Abby said. "She'd tell you this if you asked her."

"It's hard for me to talk on the phone. It's hard to get started." Then I blurted out, "Why is she so angry?"

That look. Abby let the moments pass before she said, "You really have to ask?"

"I don't know. She never seemed angry, but now..."

Hopeless.

"She doesn't like the way you fight over her," Abby said. "It's like you don't care about her, just about sticking it to each other."

"Does she want to stay in New York?" I asked. "Is that what she wants?"

"She doesn't know," Abby said in a tone that made me understand that Kat was considering it. She waved her hand before her face, shooing away the gnats.

I asked her what would happen if Kat returned to Byrd-Adams. I asked whether the kids would make it hard on her, and Abby said, "It's not like she's totally different because of what happened. She didn't turn into a freak or anything. She's still Kat."

She sounded almost indignant, as though that question had been particularly uncomprehending, and she had reached the end of her patience with me, her willingness to take part in this conversation. Perhaps she felt she had already said more than she should have. "I have to get back," she said.

I thanked her and then, as she moved to pass me on the narrow trail, I did that awkward side-to-side jig, trying to get out of her way.

I must have had some inkling of how desperate I had become, for when we reached the truck, I heard myself saying to Romeo, "It's time for me to see a head doctor. It is definitely that time."

MONDAY morning I took the Metro downtown to see Brian Collinsworth. It had been a week since I'd been arrested, and I'd talked frequently to Brian on the phone, but this was to be our first face-to-face meeting and I was jittery. I'd hardly slept the night before and the simple matter of getting dressed that morning, of putting on real clothes, long pants and leather shoes and a shirt with buttons, immediately brought home the fact that I was about to enter into the realm of Law and Order, where people dressed differently and where the lines of my life would be redrawn. Guys in suits were now going to square off and wrangle with each other to determine whether or not I went to jail and whether or not Vandenberg was going to wipe me out.

Brian's office is on L Street in the center of downtown Washington, and I felt all my old discomfort when I rode the Metro at rush hour, the old unwillingness to be wedged like a sardine into an underground railcar, smelling other people's underarm deodorant and aftershave lotion, the old reluctance to travel as a flunky. At that hour the Metro was packed with lawyers and bureaucrats and office workers, with clerks and flunkies, and the trip reminded me of how I'd felt all those years I'd worked at Time-Life Books, shuttling to Alexandria on the Orange Line, grinding out work to meet rigorous standards of blandness and banality, kissing asses and dancing to a corporate tune and wearing the official nine-to-five uniform, the badge of which was the necktie—the utterly useless necktie, as much a sign of meekness and obedience as a monk's tonsure, the collar and leash of the flunky, his noose. The only time I wear one nowadays is when I go to a wedding or funeral.

And maybe a trial.

It was a stinking hot morning and I was sweaty by the time I entered the sleek, cool, marble lobby of Brian's building, took the elevator to the twelfth floor, and followed the receptionist to his corner office. I was glad to see that he'd already loosened his tie and rolled up his sleeves. He'd obviously done well. Seven years ago his office was in a town house near Dupont Circle, but this was a corner office with a view of McPherson Square, an expensive office with a big cherrywood desk, leather easy chairs, and a bay with a conference table. At first Brian attempted to be low-key and informal, to make small talk, to laugh a little about the patch of green carpet he'd put down in the corner of the office, his putting green. There were several balls on the carpet and a couple of putters leaning against the wall. He'd caught the golf bug, he said, and told me he'd finally gotten into Congo— Congressional Country Club—after years on the waiting list. He didn't brag but seemed to be mocking himself slightly, bemused by his need to convey his social success to the likes of me. I don't really know Brian all that well, and I don't know jack about golf, but I told him about my father's annual effort to win the club tournament down in Norfolk, and we chatted, I suppose, as though we knew we had better get to know each other since we were looking at a long haul.

Brian said, "I'm afraid this guy is really on the warpath. This case isn't going to go gently into that good night."

We were sitting in the leather easy chairs in front of his desk, and Brian already looked slightly rumpled and rueful, his sandy ringlets breaking loose from the comb tracks in his hair. He had a golfer's tan, and he was sitting forward in his chair, holding a putter, looking down at the putter blade, as he talked me once more through the legal situation with the thorough, slightly irritated manner of a doctor conveying bad news to a patient, repeating himself to give the patient time to let it sink in. Most of it I had already learned in bits and pieces over the course of the week, but on that morning in that office the information acquired a different significance, a gravity that nearly immobilized me as the silly putter swung to and fro.

First, there was the criminal charge. Brian had worried all along that the original misdemeanor charge might be challenged, and now that the extent of Jed's injuries was known, we had to expect Briggs, the AUSA, to go to a grand jury to have the charge bumped up to a felony. He had almost no leeway, not even enough to listen to a pre-indictment plea. They charge first and bargain later, Brian said, but I was still trying to take in the fact that he'd already been negotiating my guilt with this guy Briggs. "You discussed this with him? You talked about how I'd plead?" Brian said they'd never gotten that far, never gotten past the point where Briggs told him flatly that he couldn't let this slide by as a misdemeanor. The mind-set at the U.S. Attorney's office was to indict, he said, to make sure that the public record was accurate and complete, but it didn't mean they wouldn't negotiate later. It didn't mean we'd go trial, he said. "That's the case we'll try to make to him," Brian said. "He has to charge you, but I don't think he'll want to try the case. You don't have any record. You're not a career criminal. You're a middle-aged white guy who runs a business and who went a little nuts when he heard about his daughter. We'll tell him he's got real crime to deal with in the District—does he want to bother with you? Does he really want to tie up his office to put away a guy who went off the deep end because he was worried about his daughter? But he's going to hear from Vandenberg that he can't let people run around smashing up kids just because they're being kids."

"Being kids doesn't mean getting girls drunk and taking them into a pool house for oral sex," I said with more heat than I intended.

Putt, putt. Brian knocked a ball toward the hole in the carpet and said, "Listen, Tucker, I'm sorry to ask but I have to: that investigator isn't going to come up with anything on you, is he?"

"What do you mean?"

"I didn't check, but you don't have a record, do you? No previous convictions? No fights, nothing that's going to make you look like a hothead?"

"I don't have a record," I said, but I did tell him about the house-breaker who'd broken my nose and the two other fights I'd had.

Brian studied my nose—it's broad but not quite a boxer's nose—and said he'd represent me if I wanted to bring charges against the plastic surgeon who'd fixed it.

He wanted details about the fights and listened carefully when I told him about the coach I pushed and the workman who got drunk on the job. He said, "Let's hope their investigator doesn't find out about them. I found out who they hired, by the way—a retired D.C. cop, a guy who's been around the courts for years. I doubt he'll call you, but you'll know when he starts poking around. He'll probably try to talk to your friends, people who work for you, people you do business with, just trying to turn up whatever he can."

"He works for the U.S. Attorney? For the government?"

"No, no. He's been hired by Vandenberg. The idea is to prepare evidence for a civil suit, but they'll share whatever they find with the AUSA."

I made myself keep quiet.

"Our girl's already been out," Brian said, "our investigator. I sent her out last week, and she managed to make contact with a couple of the kids who were at the party. You can see the report if you want."

I said I'd like to. From Brian's expression, from his air of complete neutrality, I gathered that this report was significant. He said he'd prefer that I didn't read it until we'd gone through our own Q-and-A so that it wouldn't influence any of my responses. In just a moment, he said, he'd call Ian—Ian Bricker, whose name I'd heard a couple of times, a litigator who was going to work on the case.

"We're going to try to keep this from getting to trial," Brian said. "I want to make sure that we're in agreement about our strategy. I'm assuming you don't want a trial."

"Of course I don't."

"And you want the investigation to be handled as discreetly as possible, I assume."

"What are you getting at?"

"I just don't want to be too passive. Vandenberg is a fairly big cheese—I've done some asking around about him. I expect him to go after you with guns blazing, and I don't want to be unprepared."

"Besides an investigation, what else is there to do?"

"We could consider countercharges."

"Against the boys?"

"Possibly. Against Jed, possibly."

"No," I said emphatically, "I don't want those kids dragged into it like that."

"OK," Brian said. Then he told me that he'd asked Ian to join him because he knew his way around the criminal courts. A smart, smart guy, Brian told me. He himself would stay in touch with the case and handle the civil action when it came, but they were turning into specialists these days. Sometimes he felt like Dr. Divorce, he said as he smacked a ball with his putter. He didn't mean to hit it as hard as he did, and as it rolled past the hole in his carpet, he said in the bland manner of a TV announcer, "Looks like he still has some work to do."

IAN BRICKER first struck me as eager young beaver, a whiz kid. He must have been standing by for Brian's call, for within seconds he was breezing into the office, looking fresh and showered and starched and crisp. His dark hair was neatly combed and he had wire-rimmed glasses and bright blue eyes and he could have passed for a college student even though he was dressed like a lawyer: dark trousers, white shirt, patterned suspenders, yellow bow tie. He was slightly built and had a head several sizes too large for his body, but it was the bow tie—the bow tie, the fashion statement of the straight arrow—that made him look almost cartoonish. This was the guy who was going to save my hide?

When we shook hands, he said in a voice that was unexpectedly deep and mellifluous, "You're more presentable than I thought. I was imagining someone with his name on his shirt. A hairball with maybe a boil on his neck."

I had to laugh, and a smile flickered in Ian's blue eyes. He somehow made it seem that he was surprised at the effect of his cheeky remark. Brian grinned broadly. He was standing and remained standing when Ian and I sat down at the round conference table and Ian arranged his legal pads. He was left-handed, I noticed, and I saw that one of the pads already had swollen pages that had been covered with writing. He sat primly in his chair, regarding me with that bright, droll look, as though what we were about to do ought to be fun. Brian said that he wanted to go over the events of that night while they were still fresh in my mind. As though I was likely to forget them. There were too many holes in the record he'd put together, he said. Was I up for a few questions?

"Am I under oath?" I asked, trying to sound cool and witty but coming across as a nervous jerk.

Ian noted that, of course. I think he took in every nuance of my tension as he began with a series of lazy, low-key questions that must have been intended to put me at ease.

"Could I start by confirming a few things?" he asked. "My esteemed colleague was a little sketchy about the early part of the evening. Blank, as a matter of fact. So some of this is my conjecture. Forgive me if I get it wrong."

He looked at his notes, but I had the sense then, and later, that this was mostly for the sake of appearances, and he had already committed the facts to memory.

"Kathryn—you call her Kat, don't you? Do you mind if I call her Kat? We'll keep it all in the family." Enigmatic smile.

"I don't mind at all."

"Kat was planning to go see a movie and spend the night with her friend Abby. Right?"

"Yes."

"She was planning to spend the night with Abby, but she didn't say anything about a party, did she?"

"She didn't know anything about a party."

"So as far as you were concerned, this was just an ordinary weeknight. You'd spoken to Abby's mother, to Lily, and you were satisfied that everything was in order."

"It was in order."

"What movie were they going to see?"

"I'm not really sure."

"You're not?" Ian's eyes widened the tiniest fraction, just enough to convey that this could be seen as a dereliction of parental responsibility. "You let her see what she wants to see? You give her that latitude?"

"She can go to PG-13 movies. Sometimes when they get to the Cineplex, if there's a gang of them, they change their minds about what to see."

"So she does have some latitude."

"Within limits, yes."

"You trust her to make good decisions."

"Completely. She's not a kid who looks for trouble."

He nodded, letting me know that he'd caught the edge in my voice. His own voice sounded neutral but it was rippling with insinuations.

"She'd never run off without telling you where she was going."

"No."

"Not even for an hour or two."

"She never has, not that I can remember."

"You'd say that she was an obedient child."

"Yes."

Ian said almost absentmindedly, "But Kat didn't always tell you everything."

"She's fourteen. No teenager tells her father everything."

Glasses down, sympathetic smile. "Fourteen—a notoriously tough age. Tucker, how would you characterize your relationship with your daughter? In broad terms. Are you close?"

"I'd say so, but she is a teenager. She's moody sometimes. We're not as close as we once were."

He scribbled on the pad. He asked, "Is she sexually active? Have you ever discussed that?"

A reasonable question. I did not want to talk to Ian Bricker about my daughter's intimate behavior, but I knew I had to. "I'm sure she's made out a few times."

"You discussed it?"

"No."

"You just inferred it. Suspected it."

"That's right."

"Nothing more than that? No intercourse? No previous fellatio?"

He tone was so casual. He could just as easily have said, *No milk? No cookies?*

"Not that I know of," I said, hoping that my voice remained level.

"And she wouldn't necessarily have told you. Almost certainly wouldn't have told you," he said as though thinking out loud.

"I'm sure she's a virgin," I blurted out, wanting to correct the impression I was giving of a man who knew too little about his daughter. "Nothing like this, remotely like this, had ever happened before."

Brian spoke up then, evidently to help me settle down, telling me that if we went to trial, the matter of Kat's sexual experience would probably come up. "You have to excuse us," he said, "but we don't know her at all. We simply have to ask these questions. At some point she could be asked."

And so we talked for hours, it seemed, about Kat's sexual education, her school, her friends, her relationship to her mother, and my status as a single father. Having been through a divorce, I knew that these questions would be asked and that they would feel like violations, for so many private matters get dragged into any legal inquiry. Ian and Brian were as considerate as they could have been, but their questions cast a harsh light on me as a man who was at odds with his ex-wife, who'd had a series of sexual relationships and didn't always conceal them from his children, who had mostly avoided the frank and difficult discussions about sex with those children, who had not provided them with any systematic religious training, who had not turned off the car radio during a raunchy skit about Bill Clinton and Monica Lewinsky, who had in fact laughed with the kids about it, and who attempted to defend himself as the kind of parent who wants to teach his children how to deal with the real world, not shield them from it.

"Ah," said Ian, not disapprovingly, but the whole process felt like a vivisection, and I realized over and over again the extent to which I had steered clear of this whole part of Kat's life, leaving her to figure it out on her own.

When he'd finished asking me about Kat, Ian asked how I was holding up. Brian brought me a cup of coffee. Ian showed me a picture of his two sons, both toddlers. He asked if I'd mind going through what had happened when I arrived at the Vandenbergs' on the night of July 13th, and his first questions was about that shovel.

"I can't explain the shovel," I said. "I have no idea why I picked the damn thing up. I can't tell you how much I wish it hadn't been standing there."

"You didn't have any intention of using it as a weapon?"

"No, I didn't. The shovel was there by the gate and I picked it up. That's all."

"You stood there outside the gate for a moment, didn't you? What did you see from where you were standing?"

"A group of boys sitting around a table."

"No girls?"

"No girls."

"Did you think Kat was still there?"

"I assumed she was."

"You thought she was still there. But you didn't see her. Could you see the pool house from where you were?"

"I could see that it looked empty."

"So when you went in through the gate, you didn't go to the pool house to check it out. You went straight to the boys at the table."

"Yes."

"Why was that?"

"I thought they'd tell me where Kat was."

Ian looked down at his notes, but that meant only that he wasn't happy with that answer.

"Had you been able to hear them talking?"

"Yes. They were talking about a TV show called *Jackass.*"

"Not about Kat?"

"No."

"Did they sound drunk to you? Were they still playing the game? Big Dare? Is that what it's called?"

"I thought they sounded drunk but no, they weren't playing the game."

"So they weren't talking about Kat, and they weren't playing the game. But you thought she was still there, in the pool house or somewhere else. You thought you were catching them in the act. Is that right?"

"I suppose so."

"Did you think you had caught them in the act?" He didn't raise his voice, but he made it clear that this was a significant question.

"Yes," I said. "I mean, they might have finished doing what they'd been doing, but I thought they were the ones."

"So you regarded this as an explosive situation, is that fair to say? You were walking into a situation that was potentially dangerous, a situation in which your daughter was being violated, or had just been violated. Is that right?"

"Yes."

"It was a situation from which you might have to extricate her. You were surprising these boys and you didn't know how they'd respond. Is that accurate?"

Was he coaching me? Was that how I'd felt? The room had gone quiet and I was aware of Brian, of both of them, watching me closely. "I just don't know," I said. "I wasn't sure how they'd react to me, but I can't say that I thought they'd attack. I don't think I had any idea of what they'd do."

Ian drew a breath that didn't hide his disappointment.

"All right. You walk up to the boys and what happens then?"

"I asked where Kat was."

"That was your first question."

"I think so. Yes. I said I'd come to get her."

"And they said she'd already left."

"Yes, but they wouldn't say when. They didn't say how she'd left."

"At this point you were talking to Jed Vandenberg?"

"Yes, but I didn't know him. I didn't know who he was."

"Why were you talking to him?"

"He was the one who spoke up."

"The only one?"

"The others said a few things, but he was the main one."

"The leader of the pack. And how would you describe his attitude?"

"Surly. He told me to leave. He told me I was trespassing."

"How long did you talk to him? Before swinging the shovel."

"Not long. Just a minute or two."

"Do you remember what he said that made you swing?"

"He told me to leave."

"And?"

"I had come to get my daughter and he was being completely hostile."

"Did you say anything threatening? Did you threaten to harm him?"

"No, not that I can remember."

"You told Brian that the table was covered with bottles and cans. How big was it? About as big as this table?"

"About."

"Do you mind standing up for a moment? Brian, give him a putter. I'll be Jed Vandenberg. I want to understand how this happened."

Brian handed me a golf club.

"No one else is at the table, right? Are you about the right distance away? Is that the right angle? And the putter is about the same length as the shovel, isn't it? It was just a garden spade."

"It's about the same length."

"So you have to be pretty close to swing it in such a way that you clear the table."

I was standing right next to the table.

Ian asked, "How hard did you swing?"

"Hard enough. Harder than I meant to."

"You didn't just push the stuff off into Jed's lap?"

"No."

"Swing. Show me how hard you swung."

"Jed was sitting back from the table," I said. "Farther back than you are."

Ian pushed his chair back.

"This far? Like this?"

"About there."

And then, at his command, I swung, but it was a controlled swing. I could easily have hit him with the putter. In the daylight of that office, it was clear that I could easily have hit Jed Vandenberg with that shovel and that the bottles and cans would have flown up into Jed's face.

"All right," Ian said. "So now I spring to my feet, and somehow I have a bottle in my hand. I come after you. *Grrrr.* Show me what happens next."

And he was moving toward me, this lawyer in his white shirt and suspenders and bow tie, brandishing an imaginary bottle, asking me to show him how I had tried to protect myself, how I'd used the shovel as a shield, how hard I'd been pushed, whether I'd seen the boy who pushed me, getting me to push at him with the putter, trying to feel how hard a shove it would have to be to make him spin and fall. "I get it, I get it," he said as he spun in slow motion, twisting away from me and turning, flailing at the table and trying to catch it to break his fall.

He didn't fall, but he did take off his glasses and scrunched closed his left eye. "I think I get it. I hope we never have to reenact this moment. But I think I get it."

He put his glasses back on and said, "You may now put the putter down."

I hadn't realized that I was still holding it high.

We all three sat down at the table then. I didn't ask how I'd done, but I had the sense that I had not fared well on the test they'd just given me. They seemed vaguely embarrassed for me as we went over the next steps, and Ian repeated some of what Brian had already told me about Briggs, the AUSA, and assured me that my arraignment on August 5th would be a nonevent. Briggs would tell the judge that he was going to ask for a felony indictment, the judge would set a date for a status report, and that would be that. We'd have plenty of time to get our ducks in a row.

"So," Brian asked, "you had enough for one day? Or do you want to see the file Corinne has put together?"

Corinne was the young woman he'd sent out as an investigator, and of course I wanted to see it. When Brian dialed Corinne and asked her to come to his office, Ian took his leave. He shook my hand and said that he'd see me at the courthouse on August 5th. He gave a fruity wave and said, "Toodle-oo."

CORINNE SAVINO was a second-year law student who looked about twenty years old. She was a petite woman with a long face and dark liquid eyes that conveyed immediate warmth and sympathy, and when she entered his office, clutching a slender folder in her arms, I could see exactly why Brian thought she'd be able to win the trust of the kids she'd be talking to. When Brian praised her for getting started so quickly, she glanced at me almost apologetically, perhaps because she already knew so many damaging things about me. The sooner you got to work on discovery, Brian said, the more likely you were to get an accurate picture. Wait too long and the cement started to harden. Corinne had already interviewed Alexa Fogarty, the girl who left the party, the girl whose father had called me, and Colin Fletcher, one of the boys who was there when I'd arrived.

"They were willing to talk to you?" I asked her.

"Alexa was eager to talk about it," Corinne said. Even her voice, soft and modest, conveyed a quality of sincerity. "I think she wanted some kind of closure. It was an awful experience for her. I can't begin to imagine what it must be for you."

"This won't be easy reading," Brian said. "You're sure you're up for it?"

Was I as fragile as they seemed to think? I said again that I wanted to read the file, and Brian showed me to an empty conference room so that I could read in private and without disturbance.

The table was bare and the folder was brown. My hands shook when I opened it. The pages were typed, double spaced, and legal sized, clamped at the top with one of those old-fashioned fasteners. The top page noted the date and place of the interview, and the first page consisted of several preliminary questions that established Alexa's age and address and so on. Her account of the party started on the second page.

Q. When did you first start to worry about what was happening?

A. As soon as we went out to the pool. I mean, the guys started talking about skinny-dipping. Matt and Danny did.

Q. I'm sorry, but could you tell me their full names? I'm just starting to put all this together so I'm hearing about this for the first time.

A. Matt Wyckoff and Danny Owens.

Q. OK, thanks. Now this is before you started to play the game, before you started to play Big Dare.

A. Yeah.

Q. Did anybody go in the water? Tell me what happened.

A. Matt and Danny and a couple of other guys jumped in. They still had their clothes on, but they started stripping, you know, like it was a big turn-on. They'd peel off their T-shirts like they were strippers and then throw them at us.

Q. People were already drinking at this point?

A. Yeah. There was stuff to drink.

Q. But at first it was just the boys who went in the pool.

A. And Judy Walsh. She went in.

Q. Dressed?

A. You could say so. I mean, she kept on her bra and she was wearing this thong. You could see everything when she got wet.

Q. She was the only one who went in with them?

A. Trey went in, too.

Q. Trey? Who's Trey?

A. Her boyfriend.

Q. I have to ask you his name, too.

A. I think it's Altschuler, something like that. He doesn't go to BA.

Q. BA? That's Byrd-Adams?

A. Yeah.

Q. Where were you exactly? Just sitting by the pool?

A. I went inside a couple of times. People were coming and going. Moving around.

Q. And you were with friends.

A. I was mostly with Lizzy Warner. I went there with her but, yeah, I was with other friends.

Q. You knew most of the people there?

A. Most of them.

Q. They were all from Byrd-Adams?

A. Not all of them. Most.

Q. How well did you know Kat Jones?

A. Not well, really. She's a grade behind me. I knew her to say hello, that's about it.

Q. But she was at the pool? Was she with anyone in particular?

A. She was like lost. I mean, I knew she came there with Abby, but Abby went off with Jed and she was just sort of by herself. I think that's why the guys started paying attention to her.

Q. What kind of attention?

A. Just talking to her, you know. Hitting on her.

Q. Did you hear what they were saying?

A. One thing I heard, they were mentioning Abby, like, "I wonder what she's doing," stuff like that. It was like everybody knew what Abby was doing except Kat.

Q. Sorry to be dense, but what did everybody know?

A. Well, everybody knew they were sort of a couple. That's what people were saying that night, yeah. They were saying that they were going to do it. Before it even got dark, they went upstairs in the house. That was like the whole purpose of the party, for them to hook up.

Q. They were going to have sex?

A. That's what I heard, yeah. Judy and Trey went in the house, too, so the other guys were like, "Hey, why don't we all do it?"

Q. Did this upset you?

A. I don't know. I wasn't all that surprised or anything, not about Abby and Jed.

Q. But you were upset by what was going on with Kat?

A. All the guys were coming on to her and she seemed, I don't know, confused. But like I said, I didn't really know her.

Q. She was drinking, right?

A. Everybody was drinking, but yeah, Danny kept trying to get her to chug beers. I saw that. He acted like it was some great skill to chugalug.

Q. Kat tried it?

A. She tried. She got wasted pretty fast.

Q. So what are you doing all this time? You're just sitting by the pool talking to your girlfriends?

A. Not sitting, but yeah, I was mostly out at the pool, and it was weird, like the guys had decided to ignore everybody but Kat. They were totally coming on to her, you know, like coyotes or wolves or something. It was like, "Are we going to get her?"

Q. Did you do anything about it?

A. I did. I did. I told Pete Wicker and some of the others to leave her

alone. I told them to tell Danny and Matt to leave her alone because you could feel it, you know? Once it got dark and they
started playing Big Dare, you could feel it, this weird vibe. They
were totally concentrating on Kat, saying all kinds of stuff.

Q. What kind of stuff?

A. Like tonight's the big night, that kind of stuff. Tonight's Abby's
night, it could be your night, too.

Q. You weren't playing the game?

A. No.

Q. Just a few people played?

A. It's a stupid game. It's not really a game at all, just a way to make
people act stupid.

Q. You were drinking, though.

A. I drank some beer. It's not like everybody there was drunk.

Q. Was Kat drunk?

A. She was wrecked.

Q. How did you know that?

A. I saw her try to walk to the house. I guess she had to go to the
bathroom or something, and she could hardly stand up. I think she
would have fallen but Danny was practically carrying her. That's
when he got her to take her clothes off. He said she should just go
in the bushes, it would be OK.

Q. And she did?

A. I heard her say it would be like camp. They just went in the bushes
at camp. So she went, and then she went in the pool.

Q. She was naked then?

A. Yeah.

Q. She took her clothes off herself?

A. I don't know. I didn't really see what happened. They went in the
bushes. Danny went in the bushes with her. Then he went in the
pool, too.

Q. Was he dressed?

A. No. He was skinny-dipping. Then some of the other guys went in.

Q. Just boys?

A. Yeah.

Q. Then what happened?

A. That's when they started talking about the pool house, the pool house.

Q. They weren't playing the game anymore?

A. No. They were just saying, the pool house, the pool house.

Q. Did you know what they meant?

A. It wasn't that hard to figure out.

Q. What did you do?

A. I told them to stop. I told Pete.

Q. Was he in the pool?

A. He was watching, but he's friends with those guys. He said, "Hey, come on, guys, she's out of it, don't do this."

Q. And what did they say? Anything?

A. They said don't worry, she's cool with it.

Q. She's cool with it? What did that mean to you?

A. I guess she said OK she'd do whatever.

Q. And she went in the pool house then? Did you see her go into the pool house?

A. It was dark, but I saw her, yeah. I saw her go in there. The guys were all around her, kind of holding her up.

Q. She was so intoxicated she needed to be held up?

A. She was wasted.

Q. What did you think they were going to do?

A. I knew what they were going to do. I knew they wanted, you know, blow jobs.

Q. Did you hear anyone say that?

A. Yeah.

Q. I'm sorry I have to ask you this, but was that all? Did they talk about anything else?

A. What do you mean?

Q. Did they mention any other sexual acts? Did they talk about intercourse?

A. I don't remember. I didn't hear that.

Q. OK, I know this is tough and you're doing great. It has to be tough to remember all this.

A. I didn't know Kat, that was the thing. She wasn't part of our crowd. Nobody really knew her. I think that's why nobody stopped it, you know?

Q. But you tried. You did what you could. Do you remember how many boys went into the pool house? Take your time.

A. Danny and Matt, they went. And Luke Childs. They were the main ones. A couple of others were over there, but they were more on the edges. They were hanging around outside the pool house.

Q. Is this when you went inside?

A. Yeah, I went in the house.

Q. Why?

A. I was going to find Abby. I thought, she's Kat's friend, she can do something about it. Plus, it was Jed's house and those were his friends, so he could have done something.

Q. Did you speak to Abby?

A. Not really.

Q. Not really?

A. I knocked on the door—

Q. What door?

A. A bedroom door. I went upstairs and there were a couple of bedrooms where people were. Where the doors were closed. So I knocked and Abby said something. Then Jed said, "Later." Then I was like freaking, you know? It was happening out in the pool house and I tried to open the door, but it was locked. So that's when I decided I had to go. That's when I decided I had to leave and tell somebody who would do something. I was going to call the police but I went home instead. There was a taxi dropping somebody at their house and I got in it and went home. I told my mom and dad and they called her dad and, well, that was it. That was all I saw. I just heard about what happened later, when her dad got there. I guess everybody has heard about that.

My breath was coming in snatches when I finished reading.

Kat.

She was like lost, Alexa Fogarty said, and I kept imagining how she must have looked and felt as she stumbled through that night, losing her way with every step. I remembered how she'd looked when I drove her to the movies, so tanned and healthy, so glowing. I thought of how we'd kidded around in the car, with Kat talking in that silly accent. *Does your dog bite?* I remembered how I had watched her and Abby cross Connecticut Avenue, imagining that they were two young girls eager to discover what the world had in store for them, never dreaming that everything could go so wrong on that one night. Hundreds of other images roared through my mind, and my chest felt like a cave full of sick, frightened bats, but there was the one unbearable image.

Kat. Kat unable to stand by herself, my helpless, naked child staggering into that pool house.

I had to leave that office. I couldn't read another word. I left the folder with the receptionist and called Brian that afternoon to leave an apology on his voice mail for taking off without saying anything. I told him this was turning out to be tougher than I thought.

I COULDN'T sleep that night, but that was nothing new. All my life I've had trouble sleeping, as has Kat. We're just wired that way. I once went to a sleep clinic where a grave-looking, slow-talking doctor named Mars listened to my story and told me that I was an ideal candidate for treatment, which consisted of spending the night at the clinic, with sixteen electrodes attached to various parts of my body, and sleeping while one of the technicians monitored the biofeedback screens and observed me. Dr. Mars explained the purpose of the electrodes and the kind of observations that the technician would chart while I slept. Slept! How could any insomniac fall asleep with sixteen electrodes attached to his body and a guy with a clipboard sitting there taking notes on his eye movements and erections?

So I just live with my insomnia. I do crossword puzzles, or wander out to the music room and fool around on the piano, or read. Those late hours when the world is completely still, when the only sound is the rustle of the air in the vents and the wind visiting the trees outside, when the darkness is tucked tight around the house and you feel as life itself the movements of your own consciousness—these are wonderful hours to read. There is no interruption, and I can get lost in the great sagas of history, the stories of battles won and lost and of empires that have come and gone. In college I was a history major, and I used to think that I had drifted into it to avoid majoring in English, but it has turned out that I have a lasting albeit somewhat haphazard curiosity about the past. Mostly I seem to read about the American past, and I try to keep up with the endless stream of books about Thomas Jefferson—founder of my alma mater, the University of Virginia—and about the Civil War, but I read biographies, too, and nonfiction thrillers about shipwrecks and mountain climbing and medical marvels, and in the deep, dreaming hours I am easily moved by the stories of the real men and women who have lived out their passions on a scale so much greater than my own. It is at night, with a book open and these noble ghosts rising from the page, that I believe most strongly in the grandeur of life and feel most alone.

That night I was trying and failing to read a book about the explorations of Lewis and Clark. In August I was planning to go to Montana with Will for our annual trip, and we were going to follow the Lewis and Clark Trail for a few days. It was the sort of book that usually absorbs me, but I couldn't forget my hours with the lawyers, and couldn't shake my forebodings, and most of all couldn't get Kat out of my mind. I had talked to Trish that evening, and she'd brought me up-to-date on Kat's tests, for of course she'd had to be tested to make sure she hadn't picked up any sexually transmitted diseases. I had talked to Kat, too, but I hadn't told her what I'd read in the folder, and she had sounded especially listless and distant. She had nothing much to tell me about her day, and I'd tried to get her to laugh with the kind of story that usually amused her, a story about a Mexican guy on one of the crews who'd been asking me about Romeo. He was thinking of getting a puppy, he said. "But then I would have to eat the dog," he told me.

"That isn't required in this country," I told him.

"No?" he said.

"No," I told him. "In fact, it might be against the law to eat the dog."

"No, no," he said. "You have to eat the dog."

"No, you don't," I said.

"Yes, yes."

"No, no."

"Yes yes, have to eat the dog."

"No no, bad idea to eat the dog." It went on like this, and the other guys on the crew started to lose it, they were laughing so hard. They knew he meant to say *feed* the dog.

Kat didn't laugh.

And long after midnight I was still thinking of her. The light was on in my room, and the book was beside me, and the thought of her was so intense that she could have been one of those ghosts. Everyone must have moments like that, shuddering moments when the memory of someone you love is almost physical, when a tremor stirs your soul like a breeze sailing across a surface of water. For a split second I actually believed that Kat was in her room, tossing in her sleep, and that I could walk in and put my hand on her, that I could touch her brow and it would feel warm as a biscuit, that her big dark eyes would open and take me in and remind me of who I am.

I knew she was hundreds of miles away, but the sensation was so electric that I stood up and walked to her door. The hallway was dim and I could just make out the shape of the twin beds with their comforters folded up at the foot and the big mounds of pillows at the head. All her life Kat has liked to sleep sunk down deep, sometimes completely hidden, in great fluffy things. It makes her feel safe, she says, and I suppose that I must be frightened of sleep, too, of dropping down into the black well of dreams. When she was little, after Trish had left, Kat would make me sing her a lullaby over and over again, and she'd cling to keep me from leaving the room before she went to sleep. I sang her all the usual lullabies, but the song she came to prefer wasn't a lullaby at all but an old torch song, "All the Things You Are," and the line she always wanted to hear was "You are the angel glow that lights a star." Sometimes she'd ask me just to hum until I came to that line, and then she'd whisper the words as I sang them, and her eyes would search my face as I sang the next line, "The dearest things I know are what you are."

There were such longings in that girl, and my own longings that night were so real that I entered her room and sat down on her bed, the one farthest from the door, and started humming that song. I imagined that she was there, and that she was a child again, and that our love was as absolute as it once had been. I pretended that there was no distance between us, and I stretched out on the bed and imagined that I was cradling her, my daughter, my little one, just holding her while she fell asleep and lit the stars.

How could I not forgive her?

WHEN THE sun came up the next morning, I was already close to Baltimore, on I-95 on my way to Long Island. I'd left the house in the dark and called the office from the road to ask Max to make sure that somebody went by the house to let Romeo out. Sometime in the small hours of the night it had become clear that I had to see my children, not just Kat but both of them. I had to see them. I had to connect with them.

Confession: I knew that Trish would be in the city that day. It was one of the few bits of information that Kat had passed along in our conversation the previous night, and I had definitely factored it into my decision. I don't think I would have gone if she'd been there. I would have expected her to bar the door or find some other way to defeat the purpose of the trip.

I hadn't called the kids to warn them. I didn't want to give them a chance to discourage me, and you'd think that by the end of the six-hour drive up the New Jersey Turnpike and out through the snarl of the Long Island roads, I would have known exactly what I'd say to them. I didn't. In fact, the closer I got to Trish's house, after getting directions from a gas station attendant who looked like a retired tycoon, the more I doubted that I should have come at all. This was a strange world to me, this posh part of Long Island, and I had imagined it as a place of in-your-face ostentation and glitz, but the road on which Trish lived wound through low, green hills where most of the houses were tucked discreetly away in the scruffy woods. Near the ocean the road straightened out, and through the open windows of the car I could hear the boom of surf and smell the salt air and every now and then, when the road rose to a low crest, I saw the midday glint of the Atlantic, vast and brilliant, just on the other side of the oceanfront houses. Cottages, they are called, but they are multimillion dollar mansions, and I admit that I was dazzled.

I was also bewildered. How could my children be *here?* It was as if they had a secret life, or a double life, a life with their mother that was hidden from me, a life in which I was not welcome—but perhaps every divorced parent feels this. I know that Kat and Will were instinctively reluctant to talk much about Trish, though Will—a lover of expensive toys and a techno freak—was always babbling about the cars and gadgets at this place and in the city apartment. As to their inmost experience with their mother, however, the children were silent, and it seemed to me that it had to affect them, this effort to keep the two halves of their lives in balance. I thought they must have adapted like the trees along the shore road, the stunted oaks and willows that had grown lopsided in the prevailing wind.

Trish's drive was marked by a pair of huge upright stones, Stonehenge sized, and it curved through thick stands of beach plum and multiflora rose covered with small pinkish blossoms until, nearer the house, the wild vegetation blended almost imperceptibly into a more orderly arrangement of succulents and grasses. As a landscaper, I was impressed, and the house—I didn't want to like it, but the fucking house was beautiful, a rambling, gray-shingled place with white trim, with outbuildings, with pink roses climbing all over it.

Sandra answered my ring. That's Sandra, pronounced *Sondra*, Trish's personal assistant, to whom I had often spoken on the phone. We'd never met. She has a New York accent sprinkled with small pretensions, and she turned out to be a woman of about thirty, skinny as an X ray, with short dark hair longer in front than in back, and she looked at me suspiciously.

"I'm Tucker," I said, and she drew a blank.

"I'm the kids' father. Kat and Will's father."

"Oh."

She was still suspicious, and alarmed, but she let me enter. "Out of context," she muttered. "They didn't say you were coming."

"They didn't know. This is a surprise visit."

I probably looked exhausted. I was wearing a decent pair of shorts and a tennis shirt, but I'd been driving for hours, and Sandra obviously didn't know what to make of me. "You drove up from Washington?"

"Yes," I said. "Are they here?"

They were, both of them. Sandra glided off to find them and left me standing in the entryway, a hall that cut straight through the house. On either side, on tables, stood enormous bouquets of fresh flowers, and through the open doors at the back of the house I saw a sliver of the sea. The rugs were Chinese, I think, plum and orange, and the walls were hung with black-and-white photographs from Trish's collection. The one that caught my eye was of a dark woman, maybe Arabic, in a harsh mountain landscape, breast-feeding a lamb.

"Dad," Will said, sauntering in, forcing his voice down into the low register that he'd just discovered. I hadn't seen him for nearly a month, and he seemed to have grown a foot. It was only inches, I know, but he'd had a spurt for sure, and for the first time ever he looked like a teenager—slouched, bored, lazy, his baggy shorts pulled down low on his hip bones. He was wearing a visor with the bill upside down, and neither of us knew how to greet the other. A couple of years earlier, Will, then a fifth-grader, had asked me to stop hugging him.

I did put my arm around his shoulders. I squeezed him whether he liked it or not. I told him he'd grown. He said, "Yeah, I'm almost as tall as Kat." That had been a sore spot for years, since Kat got her growth early, and Will had lagged behind, one of the smaller kids in his class.

"You look like a surfer," I said. Will has my dark coloring and tans easily and deeply. His skin was almost as dark as his hair, a walnut brown—the color mine used to be before it turned gray. But he doesn't really look much like me, and I don't know where he got his water-off-a-duck's-back personality. He is not easily fazed, but I thought he was unnaturally tense in that hallway. I know I was.

There'd been pretty good surf, he said. Killer waves. He was working hard on his tennis, he assured me. He usually went to the club in the morning, but today he'd decided to sleep in. He shrugged as though he expected me to reproach him. He knows I have opinions about slugabeds.

"Mom didn't say you were coming or anything," he said.

"She didn't know. I just decided to come this morning. I missed you guys. I didn't want you to think that I'd turned into a monster with all this stuff going on."

I made a strangled sort of chortle and Will looked away. "Yeah, well. What is going on?"

I hadn't told him much. I said, "Legal hassles. I spent all day yesterday with the lawyers."

"So I guess you're in trouble."

"Nothing that changes anything important," I said. "I was reading about Montana last night. About the Lewis and Clark Trail."

"We're still going?"

"Absolutely."

Why couldn't I say more? I hadn't driven all that way just to reassure him about our trip, but I didn't know how to talk to him, not there.

"I don't know where Kat is," he said vaguely. "I guess you want to talk to her."

"I wanted to see you both. I've been missing you both. It's quiet at the Hut."

"So when do you go to jail?"

He meant it as a joke, his kind of cool joke, but he caught me so off guard that I didn't know how to answer, and I was just starting to explain about the lawyers when Sandra came into the hallway with a phone in her hand.

"Trish," she said, glaring, pointing to the handset. "She'd like a word with you."

The loyal assistant had wasted no time getting in touch with her employer. Trish was furious and went into a catalog of reasons why I should never have come. Will wandered off but Sandra hovered in the hallway as I walked to the back of the house and stared out over the dunes toward that slice of shining sea. Didn't I understand that Kat was at a turning point? Didn't I realize that she was at a sensitive age? Didn't I see that she needed a safe, secure environment to recuperate in? That she certainly did not need the upset of my arriving unannounced and plunging her back into a crisis she was already having trouble managing?

"I'm her father," I said. "I don't think that will threaten her security."

"Tucker, she is so vulnerable right now. She's trying to decide what's right for her, and it's not going to help to have you putting pressure on her."

"I have no intention of putting any pressure on her. I just wanted to see her and Will, for god's sake. I felt the need to see my children."

"Don't you think I feel that same need? I do, often. But I don't show up in Washington when you're not there. I don't indulge myself."

"Trish, I'm here."

"I know exactly where you are, and it's disruptive. You've never done anything like this."

"I'm here, and I'm going to talk to Kat. I've talked to Will. I didn't come here to talk to her about next year."

"How can you say that? Just by being there you're trying to influence her decision. It's almost worse if you don't say anything."

"Trish. I'm going to talk to Kat. I'm not going to stay long. I'm going to talk to Kat and then I'm going to leave."

Trish asked to speak to Sandra.

"It's for you," I said, holding out the phone. "I hope it's not bad news."

Sandra was not amused, and I wasn't trying to be funny, but Trish knew how to piss me off. For the next half hour, we all—Sandra, Will, Kat, and I—staged an awkward shuffling in the kitchen, with Sandra now tight-lipped and Will seemingly eager to make a getaway to the club and Kat, still sleepy eyed, pouring herself an enormous cup of diet Coke with shaved ice.

She'd drifted into the kitchen after the rest of us, and she looked as though she'd just awakened. Could she really have slept this late? I forced myself not to ask. She'd ducked her head when I hugged her, and she padded about barefoot while she and Will tried to work out a schedule that wouldn't have Sandra driving back and forth to the club all afternoon. "How long are you going to be here?" Kat asked me.

How long was I going to be there. Maybe she meant it to sound as though my presence confronted her with a pesky inconvenience. It certainly didn't seem as though she wanted to spend any time with me. She found it hard to look at me. Her hair was loose and unbrushed and she kept crunching ice between her teeth.

"OK," Will said, after changing into clean tennis clothes, "I gotta ride."

I said we'd play when he got back home. Sure, my son said, giving me a high five, and then he was gone.

Kat and I were alone in the spacious, airy room that smelled faintly of herbs, and she gazed studiously into her diet Coke. She sat at a table of pale pine, and the chairs, I noticed, had all been brightly hand-painted with scenes from the life of the occupant. She was not sitting in her own chair, which showed a blond girl climbing a rock face under the moon, sun, and stars.

I sat down in that chair. I told her I'd missed her. I told her I'd spent a long night missing her after a day at the lawyer's office. I told her I'd read the investigator's report about what had happened on the 13th.

"Investigator? What investigator?"

I tried to explain why Brian had wanted to have an investigator.

"So they're going to talk to everybody who was there that night?"

"Not everybody, but enough of them to find out what happened."

"Why didn't you tell me? Why didn't you *ask* me?"

"I guess it didn't occur to me," I said, taken aback by her sudden anger.

"I'm the one they're going to be talking about," she said, "and I don't want people talking about me."

"It's not just about you, Kat," I said as gently as I could, and reminded her that I was the one who'd been arrested and could go to trial. I told her the investigator was a young woman, as if that might make some difference.

"So who'd she talk to?"

"Alexa Fogarty."

Kat looked out the sunny window toward a white pergola, and the light made her face pale and her eyes orange.

"I know what happened," I said.

"That's why you drove up here? Because you couldn't wait to tell me? I already know I fucked up."

She was taking short, sharp breaths, and she turned toward me as if daring me to contradict her.

"I came up here because I missed you. Because I love you."

"Oh sure, like that's what you're thinking. 'I love her, my daughter the slut.'"

"You're not a slut. Stop it."

"That's what everybody thinks."

"It's not what everybody thinks."

"What do they think, then? How would you know?"

"I talked to Abby."

"To Abby? Why?"

"I asked her about you."

"You went behind my back? I can't believe you'd talk to Abby."

"I wanted help, Kat. I didn't know what to do."

"She didn't say anything, did she? Abby wouldn't. She wouldn't."

"She didn't say anything."

Kat looked away again, jut jawed, and I knew from the set of her face that she was near tears. She doesn't like to let herself cry, and I don't know why I couldn't just reach out to hold her, but I couldn't. I was afraid she'd push me away again.

"It was a mistake," I said. "Maybe it was a mistake coming here, too. But I read the stuff. I read what Alexa had to say, and it doesn't change anything."

"It changes everything," Kat said.

"It doesn't have to. Don't let it, Kat. That's one thing Abby did say—you're still the same Kat. You have to believe that."

"Maybe that's the problem. I'm still the same. Maybe I'd like to be different."

For just a moment she cast her eyes at me, then quickly away. She wanted me to say something, I think, but I could think only of the kind of encouraging things she'd heard over and over again. Pep talks. They weren't what she wanted to hear, or what I felt in my heart.

All I said was, "I still like the old Kat, and I want her back. I just told your mother that I wouldn't talk to you about schools, and I won't, but I want to ask you to come back to finish out your last week at Rockrapids. Will you do that? Will you, Kat? It's just one week."

She sat completely still.

"I miss you," I said, reaching for her hand, hoping to get her into a thumb war, and she let our hands couple but tucked her thumb inside her fist.

She said, "Not that game."

"Please," I said.

She tried to detach her hand but I said, "I'm not letting go until you agree."

She tossed her hair back but let her hand rest for a moment in mine.

"I felt that," I said. "I'm taking it as a yes."

She shrugged but didn't argue, and I thought that was as much as I could hope for. I was so afraid that one wrong move could be fatal. I stood up, bent and kissed the crown of her head, and left.

What I couldn't get out of my mind on the long drive home was how she'd bristled when I said I loved her, how quickly she'd dismissed the words as empty. *Forgive her*, my mother said, and Kat must have known that I still hadn't.

CHAPTER

4

A fter that trip to New York, I didn't know what to do. I hadn't felt so helpless, so down and desperate, since Trish ran off with the handsome cowboy. Back then I'd quit my job at Time-Life, sold the Georgetown house, bought the Hut, and started the landscape business—in short, changed my life, but all along I had been driven by a sense of necessity and purpose. My wife had taken up with another man, and I knew that my job was to take care of my children.

Now they were teenagers, and I was no longer sure what my job was. All those earlier rearrangements—moving to the Hut, fixing it up, building the business, making the rules—no longer seemed to apply. Suddenly, impossibly, the kids had outgrown the small, safe world I had tried to create for them, or so I felt, though I know that such changes do not take place in the blink of an eye. Kat and Will must have been quietly plotting their escape for years, and I'd been so intent on making sure that their homework was done and their desks were tidy and their shoelaces tied that I'd missed all the signs. All along I'd taken a certain pride in the way we operated as a family, believing that the mostly good-humored kidding and banter was proof of our ability to understand and accommodate each other, confident that it reflected a deeper trust and intimacy. That summer, and especially after seeing Will and Kat in Trish's house, I began to think that my adaptable children had become so skillful at going along with my schemes and rituals and rules that I had failed to notice the ways in which they were detaching themselves. Not that I'd been completely blind—no one could have failed to notice Kat's moodiness or Will's inability to walk past a mirror without stopping to check himself out. But I kept thinking that such behavior was merely age appropriate, a term that seems to apply to nearly all teenage behavior, a handy catchall that lulled me into believing that as long as their small (I thought) snits and vanities and discontents could be labeled and categorized, as long as I could check them off the age-appropriate master list, they were still right on track, doing exactly what they should be doing as they struggled toward adolescence.

And then Kat went to a party, got drunk, took her clothes off, jumped into a pool naked, went into a pool house, and got down on her knees.

What had happened? What had I missed? How had she gotten so far away from me? So lost? *My* Kat was the last girl in the world who'd do such things. She was not rebellious or unhappy or wild for boys. *My* Kat had never seemed even slightly tempted to drink, she didn't climb out windows and run away from me, she didn't embarrass me in public shrines, she didn't say *fuck*, she didn't even talk back, and she didn't sleep till noon or flash out at me with anger and resentment. As much as I blamed myself, and Trish, for the problems we had passed along to the children, I was disappointed in Kat and hurt by the way she had turned from me, and I was not able to rise above the feeling that everything she had done that night, July 13th, had been directed at me as a statement of defiance and repudiation. Sometimes, god forgive me, I'd lie awake and think that she was just like her mother and deserved whatever misery she had to endure, and then I'd remember Trish's grenade theory, her idea that unhappiness builds and builds until you can't take it any longer and *boom!* You pull the pin. You're so crazy to make a change that you don't care what happens to anyone nearby.

Night thoughts. I couldn't quiet them, and they were sometimes dark and mean, and I knew that Kat was suffering, and when I couldn't sleep and couldn't keep the violent, bitter images out of my head, I'd turn on the bedside lamp and open one of the books I had bought about teenage girls. I'd try to find my daughter in the statistics and case histories of the girls who spoke of the transformation that came over them as they felt the change in their bodies and the expectations of maturity. "Everything good in me died in eighth grade," one said, and they all tried to describe the way that their sense of self, of wholeness, of hope and joy, began to vanish. They talked about suicide, and some did kill themselves (usually with pills, which of course made me tremble, thinking of Kat's poster of Marilyn Monroe). Girls killed themselves, or maimed themselves, or starved themselves, or fought terrible depressions, and as I read I kept telling myself that Kat wasn't as badly off as most of the girls in the book, and I kept splicing the stories together with all the other information that I was collecting, for this was now my subject.

Reports about adolescent girls were everywhere. I couldn't turn on the radio in the Jimmy without hearing a talk show about the presidential blow jobs, and how this was symptomatic of what was happening all over the country, how teenage girls called blow jobs lollipops or Popsicles, how they gave them on the school bus or in school hallways, between classes, because the guys liked them and it kept them from having to fuck all the time. I learned about the studies that charted the rise of teenage promiscuity—34 percent of all teens have sexual intercourse by the ninth grade—and the general teen indifference to the risk of STDs and AIDS despite the enormous efforts to teach them about safe sex. From my sister, Emily, who knows her way around the Internet, I received regular e-mails, alerting me to the trend of blow job parties, usually arranged by the girls themselves. No doubt Emily wanted me to take some comfort in knowing that Kat wasn't alone, that my daughter was subject to the same prevailing winds as the girls in the articles she downloaded for me, but I was not comforted. I was appalled, and I was afraid that it was only a matter of time before Kat's story, and mine—the story of July 13th—found its way onto the Internet and into the dismal annals of lost girls and clueless parents.

Buffalo jumps. I'd been reading about Montana, and I kept thinking about the buffalo jumps, the cliffs over which the Plains Indians drove the herds of buffalo, slaughtering them in great numbers. That was happening to the girls. As I say, my imagination was drawn to violent

images, but when I saw knots of girls on the street in their summer outfits, their tiny shorts and halters, with their spangly makeup and paste-
on tattoos, when I saw them acting out the roles defined for them in
the thousands of commercials and TV shows and popular songs and
movies, when I put all this together with the case studies I was reading
of the girls who cut themselves or couldn't eat or simply couldn't function, when I thought of what was happening to Kat—when I tried to
make sense of it all, it seemed to me that the girls were as helpless and
confused and panicky as the buffalo must have been as they stampeded
over the edge of the precipice, that in all the noise and din they had lost
their bearings, that they had no idea of the dangers of the plunge they
were about to make.

Girls, buffaloes. Absurd. I realize now how skewed my thoughts
were, and even at the time I recognized them as the twists and turns of
a guilty, troubled, disordered, sleep-deprived man, a parent who
wanted to save his daughter and didn't know how. And who, for that
matter, didn't know how to save himself.

One night I woke up in the empty house, scared and sweaty, sitting
bolt upright in my bed, muttering, "I can't take this."

I needed help. I needed a head doctor, and I even had one in
mind—Joe Jarvis, a client of mine—but I kept putting off the call.

WHAT KEPT me going was the daily routine, the familiar pattern of my
days, starting with the first light and first sounds—the thud of the
newspaper hitting the walk, the caw of the crows, the whir of the traffic helicopters heading up the Potomac to make their rush hour reports. I was glad to have the exhausting nights come to an end, glad to
rise, to shower and shave, to slip on my cargo shorts and Twill polo
shirt and lace up my hiking boots (lightweight Gore-Tex jobs with
air-cushion soles, ugly as sin but astoundingly comfortable) and let
Romeo out for his shit-and-sniff and climb into the Jimmy. I was glad
to get under way, glad to have the list working, even if I was short
fused and tense, even if I did mutter to myself and flinch every time
the cell phone rang, afraid that there would be more bad news.

And it wasn't always bad news. Christine called a couple of times a
day, just to check in, and so did Jay and Lily, and I was grateful to

them. Depended on them, I suppose, in the same way that I depended on my mother's occasional calls and Emily's e-mails and the way that Jackie, the office mom, fussed over me. Christine tried to make sure that we always had a plan in place, and Jay usually asked for legal updates. He has two daughters of his own, younger than Kat, but whenever I began to say anything about the books I was reading, or anything generally about adolescent girls, he grew quiet. He didn't want to hear, and I understood perfectly. I wouldn't have wanted to hear two years ago, when Kat was twelve and I couldn't have imagined that anything like this would happen. With Lily, the phone calls were longer, often sequential, interrupted when I went to a work site or she got involved with her own chores, resumed later, a continuation of our long-running conversation about our daughters. She was having her own troubles with Abby, of course, but wanted to know every detail of Kat's behavior, what she said and how she said it, and I felt reassured that we were partners, a couple of parents in the same boat as we tried to deal with our teenage daughters.

I know I counted on Lily's loyalty, and I was shocked when I realized that she had spoken to the investigator—not Corinne but the investigator hired by Vandenberg. And Lily didn't even tell me about it herself. I found out inadvertently when Christine called me on the cell phone to say that the investigator had just called her. "He called me here, Tucker, at the office. How'd he find me? How did he even know about me?"

I had no answer for her. I was dumbfounded. I was on my way to a site in Rockville, and I pulled off on the side of the road to talk to her and tried to remember if I'd mentioned her name to anybody besides Brian and Ian. I didn't think I'd said anything to Ellis, the police officer. I tried to get my mind around the fact that this investigator, whoever he was, was now prying into the private corners of my life.

"He gave me the creeps," Christine said, and I could hear her effort to compose herself. "At first he tried to make it sound as though he knew you. 'I know you're a friend of Tucker's,' he said, all chummy. Not Tucker Jones, just Tucker. He said he was trying to get a better picture of what happened that night. He knew I was at your house. Then he said it could help *you* if I talked to him. He wanted me to tell him about your state of mind when you got the phone call. Tucker, what's going on?"

I must have sat there for fifteen minutes, pulled off on the shoulder of Seven Locks Road, going over every word of Christine's conversation with this man who hadn't even given her his name. He hadn't mentioned Vandenberg, either. He wanted to make it sound as though his purpose was to help out the U.S. Attorney—to help, he kept saying—by gathering statements from people who might be able to clear up all the questions about what had happened that night.

"He's not working for the U.S. Attorney," I told Christine. "He's working for Richard Vandenberg. Did you tell him anything?"

"I told him to get a subpoena if he wanted to talk to me," Christine said. "I'm a lawyer, you know, not that it would have taken a lawyer to know that he was fishy. How could he have known that I was at your house?"

I didn't have a guess, not while Christine was on the line, but after we'd hung up, after I'd made a lame joke that Amish nights would have to be indefinitely suspended while this character was slinking around with his Spycam, it occurred to me that there was only one person who could possibly have told him.

Lily.

Lily was the only one, besides Kat and my own lawyers, who knew that Christine had been at the Hut that night.

Lily. She was open and trusting and could have been taken in, I suppose, but to believe that she had knowingly talked to this man, that she had given him Christine's name and place of work, felt like a betrayal. I did not want to believe it. It was the only conclusion I could reach, but I kept telling myself that it just couldn't be so, that he must have gotten his information elsewhere. For years, Lily and I had been carrying on our conversation about how to rear the girls, and I believed that we were like brother and sister, fixtures in each other's lives, long past the point of wondering how we'd slipped into such a familiarity, and loyal to one another as a first principle.

And she had talked to this investigator and hadn't even mentioned it to me.

I didn't phone Lily right away. Couldn't bring myself to phone her. I wanted to give her the benefit of the doubt. I wanted to give myself a chance to find out that I was wrong, and that somebody else had told this investigator about Christine, or else give Lily a chance to tell me about it. For two days I put off calling her and didn't hear from her.

And so, the next day, a Friday, I swung by the Moorefields' house. It was midafternoon and I was in her neighborhood to look at the thirty-foot cypress trees we had just put in, with a crane, for a couple who wanted their garden to remind them of Tuscany. Another case of money to burn (eight cypress trees, thirty-two hunded dollars a pop). This was an older couple and they seemed thrilled, and who am I to say that a Tuscan garden behind a white clapboard house on a small lot in Washington, D.C., is a tacky idea? I told them it was not an ideal time to plant mature trees, not in the midsummer heat, and showed them how to use the water bags that fit like big, fat bagels around the tree stems.

The Moorefields' house was only a few blocks away, and in the solid glare of that July afternoon, it looked intensely blue. That particular shade of blue, Lily claimed, was a mistake. She said she'd never meant to offend the Taste Police—her Cleveland Park neighbors who grumbled because her house wasn't white or yellow or beige or taupe or some other unobtrusive hue. Her house was bluebird blue and it looked gaudy on Lowell Street, and I think it was precisely the color and effect Lily had wanted. She liked bright, bold colors.

Her car, a Cherokee, fire engine red, wasn't parked in its usual spot at the curb. I thought of driving on by, but it could have been around back, in the alley, and I parked the Jimmy. I walked up the stone steps and right through the front door—unlocked, as usual—and into the house and called out a greeting. One of the cats sauntered into the hall and raked its furry black flank against the top of my boots, but there was no sign of Lily or of Rosa, who usually began barking as soon as a visitor crossed the porch. I went into the kitchen and I was looking around for a notepad when I heard a noise, a soft thump that seemed to come from the back room that juts out into the bamboo, the room with a monster TV and a couple of big beat-up sofas. "That you,

Lily?" I called, moving toward the sound, expecting to find the occasional Filipino cleaning woman, or maybe one of the workmen who always seemed to be hanging around the Moorefields', doing the odd jobs that Lily came up with.

Instead, I found Abby. She'd obviously heard me coming. She was standing beside one of the sofas, facing me, looking frantic, with both hands plunged into her thick sun-streaked hair as though she was trying to smooth it out. Tan as she was, I could see the flush in her cheeks and the wavering in her eyes as she looked away from me, down toward the sofa where I saw a boy's dark hair and his shoulder. The rest of him was hidden by the back of the sofa, and I cannot tell you exactly what made me realize that he was trying to close his shorts, but he was. He was trying get his prick zipped back into his pants. It took a second, maybe less than a second, for me to realize that I had walked in on the scene I had expected to find at the pool house.

But the girl was Abby, not Kat. And when he looked over his shoulder, over the back of the sofa, I saw the white gauze bandage over his left eye, over the socket where his eye had been, and realized that the boy was Jed Vandenberg.

Someone had to say something, and I said, "I was looking for Lily."

"She's not here," Abby said.

Jed stood up then, and we were all too stunned to move or speak. We just stood there, the black sofa between us, caught in a force field, trying to get our bearings, trying to let the tensions settle. Abby kept lifting her hair, the color racing in her neck and cheeks and her halter top showing the smooth skin of her belly. Jed had that glistening patch of white above his eye socket, but his other eye was fixed on me, and when he moved his hand to rearrange himself, his small mouth twisted at the corner in a sneer. He wanted me to see the front of his shorts bulging with his erection.

My jaw was shaking and I had to try hard to keep my teeth from clicking together. I made myself say, "I didn't know you'd be home. I thought all of you were at camp during the day." I meant all of the Moorefield children. I knew that Sophy was going to a dance camp and Rafe was at an all-day baseball camp.

"I left early," Abby said.

We had both spoken in ordinary voices, somehow able to maintain the pretense that this was an ordinary encounter. Abby lowered her hands and pulled at the waistband of her shorts in an odd impulse of modesty.

"Well, I'm sorry," I said. "I was just looking for your mom. Tell her I stopped by."

"OK," Abby said.

And that seemed to be that. I felt a grimace twist itself onto my face as I turned and walked back toward the kitchen. I wanted to be out of that house, but when I reached the porch, I stopped. I felt dazed, really, but I knew that I couldn't leave, not like that, not without trying to speak my mind to Jed Vandenberg.

And so I went back. This time I rapped on the glass of the main door as I opened it, and I called Abby's name. I kept calling it as I walked back toward the TV room where Jed and Abby were still standing, closer together now. Jed had put his arm around her. He, too, had had time to think of what he should have done, and he was angry. He stepped away from Abby as if to signal that he needed room for his anger and this was now between me and him. "What is your deal?" he said. "What the fuck is your deal?"

I said I wanted to talk.

"Did you come back to get my other eye?" The sneering schoolboy sarcasm came readily to him. He was a big kid, at least six three or four, and he stood with a slouching, twitching arrogance, as though he was tuning and directing the currents of anger moving through his body. His chin was covered with the stubble of a beard, and his right eye was dark and deep-set under a ledge of bristling eyebrow. The patch of gauze over his left eye was attached with tape that was supposed to be transparent but had the lifeless blue sheen of ice.

"I had no idea you were here," I said as calmly as I could, "but I want to talk to you. I want to apologize."

"Fuck you," he said.

"I want to apologize," I repeated, and I wish I could say that the words had more conviction behind them, but I couldn't get past his fury. "I never meant to hurt you. I don't know why I picked up that shovel."

"Bullshit."

"I did not intend to hurt you," I said slowly.

"So what was the shovel for? You just stopped by to dig a hole?"

"I don't know why I picked it up."

"That's total bullshit. You picked it up to use it."

"I didn't know what I was going to do with it."

"Jesus," he said with disgust. "You're just trying to cover your ass. My dad is right about you."

"I was there to pick up Kat. I thought she was in trouble. If you'd told me where she was, none of this would have happened."

"She was long gone. I told you that, and I had nothing to do with what happened with her. Nothing."

"I know you were in the house with Abby. I didn't know it at the time."

"You should have found out what was going on before you went psycho. Nobody made Kat do anything."

"She was drunk. Somebody got her drunk."

"She decided to drink. Nobody made her drink anything. I wasn't drunk. Abby wasn't drunk. You better figure out what's up with her."

"She's fourteen. She can't handle alcohol. That's what's up with her."

"Listen, I was in my house, OK? I tried to take care of her. I wanted her to have time to sober up before she went home. You had no fucking right to come in swinging that shovel."

"I had a right to come get my daughter. I had a right to know where she was. And you wouldn't tell me."

Jed took a step toward me then, and when Abby put a hand on his arm, he shook it off. "I didn't know where she was, OK?" He held his left hand up to the patch over his eyeless socket, almost touching it, leaning as much toward me as he could with that couch between us. "You're saying you had a right to do this? You're saying you had a right to put my eye out?"

"I didn't put your eye out."

"Then who the fuck did?"

"Come on," I said, trying to be reasonable, trying to keep my own anger from rising. "We both know what happened. You hit the table when you fell."

"The table put my eye out? That's what you're saying?"

"I'm saying you fell when you tried to hit me with a bottle. You fell and hit the table. That's what happened."

"And you just happened to be standing there. Like you had nothing to do with it."

"I'm not saying that."

He kicked the sofa then, hard. "Fucking loser," he said. "I can't believe I'm standing here talking to you."

He was so furious that I felt forced back, driven from the room. I know that I took a step away from Jed, retreating back into the passageway that connects that room to the kitchen, for I became aware of Lily's presence. She must have just arrived, for she was still holding a bag of groceries. Her head was cocked a little to the side, quizzically, and what I remember most vividly is that her shadowy smile lifted the corners of her mouth. It seemed so preposterous, that smile, given what had just been said.

"Tucker? What's going on?" she asked, but she must have heard our voices. I spread my arm toward the kids.

She set her bag down on the kitchen table and moved down the passageway, still smiling as though she was curious to discover what kind of surprise awaited her. She must have been coming from some sort of lunch, for she was more dressed up than usual, wearing a skirt and a proper blouse, and she looked only perplexed when she saw Abby and Jed.

"Abby? You're not supposed to be home."

"This is perfect," Abby said, "just perfect."

"Why are you here?" Lily looked at Abby, then at me, seeming at last to pick up on the tension in that room. "Why aren't you at camp?"

"I left early," Abby said. Then she said, "Nothing happened, OK? I don't know what he's going to tell you, but nothing happened."

"What are you talking about?"

"We were making out, but that's it."

"I walked in on them," I said to Lily.

"You didn't walk in on anything," Abby said. "Nothing happened. We were just sitting on the sofa. We were mostly talking."

"You knew I was going to be out most of the day," Lily said. "What are you doing here?"

"I just came home early. A bunch of people left early today because it's Friday. And so I called Jed to see how he was doing."

Abby spoke defiantly, and Jed had moved closer to her again, almost as though he intended to protect her. "It's my fault, Lily," he said in a conciliatory voice. "Abby didn't ask me to come over. I just decided to come."

Lily? Since when did he call her Lily? And what was all this contrition?

"You know better than this," Lily said to Abby. "I want you to go up to your room. And you, Jed, you have to leave."

"I'm not going to my room," Abby said. "I'm not going to let you punish me because he happened to walk in."

He was me.

"I'll go," I said to Lily, to all of them. "I'm the one who shouldn't be here."

"Go to your room," Lily said, a command, but it was spoken with frustration, for she knew that Abby would never obey her.

"If you make Jed leave, I'm leaving, too. You can't make me not see him."

"You can see him but not here, and not by yourselves," Lily said.

"I know I shouldn't have come by," Jed said. "Lily, I'm really sorry."

Lily looked at me helplessly, and I left.

I left the house and got into the Jimmy and gunned the engine and drove away. I'd left the windows open for Romeo but the cabin was oven hot and I felt scalded. I felt mortified. What kind of idiot would surprise a kid making out, a kid who already had every reason to be defensive and distrustful, and think that this was the moment to achieve understanding? Why had I not imagined, not for a single moment, that Abby would still be seeing Jed? What kind of stupid, stubborn faith kept making me believe that this whole nightmare would end if I just had the right opportunity to tell my story?

And why hadn't Lily told me anything about Jed and Abby? How could she allow Abby to keep seeing Jed? How could she have befriended him? And never mentioned it, not once in all our conversations when she seemed to be so concerned and forthcoming about Abby? Was she so ruled by her need to be liked by all the kids, to be a cool mom, that she was afraid to set any sort of limits on her daughter? Didn't she realize what was at stake here?

I no longer had any doubt whether she'd talked to the investigator. She couldn't say no to anybody.

IT WAS STILL early in the afternoon, but I couldn't go back to work. Instead, I went home and did something I hadn't done for years: I took my feelings out on the drums. Picking out a tune on the piano sometimes calms me down, but that afternoon the piano seemed far too delicate and dainty, and so I moved over to the throne, picked up a pair of drumsticks, and started banging the way I used to when I was a teenager. Back then I didn't know what I was doing, but when I got home from school I'd go down into our basement in Norfolk and whale away until I was carried off in a cyclone of noise and crazy energy. It was all about release, and I loved the frenzy of it, the way that my chaotic emotions turned into movement and the movement turned into a storm and blast of sound. When I was down there rattling the snare and pounding the toms and banging the high hat and stomping the kick drum, I felt lifted up, whirled away in my own private tornado.

But I didn't fly anywhere that afternoon. Couldn't get airborne. I hadn't tried to cut loose like that for years. My drumming had become more orderly and disciplined, and mostly I just laid down a solid rhythm when the Make Believes got together—nothing too fancy, nothing tumultuous. In any case, after a couple of bursts of noise, I found myself just sitting there in the music room, looking around at the stuff I had accumulated over the years—the guitars I played badly and infrequently, the scaled-down starter drum set I had bought for Will and he'd barely touched, the recorders and pennywhistles Kat had ignored, the beautiful African and Caribbean drums I was always intending to master, the dozen cymbals of different shapes and sizes and tones, the scatter of CDs and sheet music everywhere, the mikes and music stands and amps and mixing boards that we used when the Make Believes practiced. The musical equipment was my one extravagance, really, and this was my favorite room anywhere, the room I had soundproofed and fitted out for my pleasure, the room I regarded as my refuge, the place I came to escape.

That day I couldn't. I couldn't get away from my troubles, and I sat there, feeling the silence fill the room and thinking about my mother and her yogi. Every time we talked on the phone, she urged me to try yoga to clear my mind. I thought maybe I should get down on the floor and get my ass up in the air somehow, get it higher than my head, as Mary Carter recommended, and see if I could just stop thinking and let my mind go blank.

But of course I didn't get on the floor, and when I left the music room and walked the few steps to the house, the phone was ringing. Lily's name was on the display.

"Tucker?" She acted surprised when I answered. "How's a girl supposed to know who she's talking to?"

A weary old joke. During business hours I normally answer, *This is Tucker*, and for some reason this has always struck Lily as laughable. But that afternoon I had merely said hello and her kidding was flimsy and forced. I said nothing.

Lily said, "Just tell me one thing: Did Abby have her clothes on?"

"She had her clothes on."

"Maybe that should be the rule: She has to keep all her clothes on. Or I'll make her stick by the old rule. One foot on the floor at all times. Remember that one? I never really understood it. You can get into a lot of trouble with one foot on the floor."

I agreed.

"You're going to make me ask you what they were doing, aren't you? Let me ask you this first. Do I really want to know?"

"I doubt it."

"They weren't just talking, were they?"

Her habit of downplaying everything annoyed me, and I said, "He had his shorts unzipped. That shouldn't come as any surprise. They're sexually active, Lily. You know that, don't you? Why are you trying to pretend they're not?"

There was a silence before Lily finally said in a small voice, "I know. I know, but I don't know what to do about it. These last few weeks Abby has shut me out of her life, as much as she can. I don't know what to do with her."

"Maybe you should start by telling her she can't see Jed."

"She ignores me, Tucker. You heard her."

"Why should she pay any attention? She knows you're not going to do anything if she disobeys."

"That's not fair."

"You can do whatever you want with Abby," I said. "It's none of my business. But I would like to know why you're letting her see Jed Vandenberg."

Another pause, then Lily said, "I was going to tell you what was going on with those two, but I just didn't know how. Everything is so complicated right now."

"It's not that complicated. There are only two sides in a lawsuit."

"There's no lawsuit yet."

"Lily, I was arrested—you remember that, don't you? I was charged with a crime and I have a court date. There is going to be a lawsuit."

"Don't talk to me like that."

"I'm tired of pretending that everything is *all right*. I don't see how you can keep pretending when you know it is *not* all right. Why didn't you tell me about Abby and Jed? Why didn't you even mention it? God, Lily, how many times have we talked these last couple of weeks? Did you think you were sparing my feelings? What did you think? How could you not tell me that you and Jed were pals?"

"Pals? We're not pals."

"He calls you Lily. The way he talked to you it's obvious that you two aren't strangers."

"I don't know a thing about him except that he just had a terrible injury and he's mad for my daughter. And she's mad for him. I'd like to keep them apart, but I don't know how. You know how Abby can get."

"Forget it," I said, "just forget it."

"No, I'm not going to forget it. You know I'm on your side, but when Jed calls up, I talk to him. I say hello. I ask how he's doing. I want to know something about the boy my daughter is crazy about. And I have to say that he's more polite and communicative than she is."

Everything she said was reasonable, and yet I couldn't stop myself from saying, "So why didn't you mention him? And why did you talk to the investigator that Vandenberg hired? You didn't mention that, either."

She hesitated again. "That man was hired by Vandenberg?"

"What did you think?"

"He said he was from the U.S. Attorney's office."

"Maybe he made it sound that way. But why would you talk to somebody from the U.S. Attorney's office? They're the prosecutors. They're the ones who will try to send me to jail."

"Well, why wouldn't I talk to them? I only talked to him for a few minutes. I don't think there's anything to hide from them."

"Do you not understand that they are trying to put together a case against me? Do you not understand that?"

"Nothing I said could possibly have hurt you."

"Anything could hurt me. Tell me one thing: Did you mention Christine? Did you tell them that she was at my house that night?"

Silence. "I might have. I must have. I can't remember everything I said."

"Why can't you admit it straight out. Say 'yes.' Say 'yes, I told them.'"

"Don't yell at me."

"I want you to realize what you're doing here. This isn't a playground feud. It's not going to blow over because you smile at everybody and give them a hug and a kiss and tell them to make up and be friends."

"Don't talk to me as if I'm a child," Lily said, although she sounded like a child on the verge of tears.

The phone went dead.

I listened to the blank air on the handset for a few seconds, then set it back in its cradle. Before I went upstairs to take a shower, I played the messages on the answering machine—one from Lily that had come while I was in the music room, and one of Trish's endless messages, telling me that she was completely opposed to the plan for Kat's return on Sunday, that it seemed like cruel and unusual punishment—her exact words—when Kat was so obviously depressed and ashamed of herself, but since I was insisting on it, the least I could do was recognize her sensitivity and not force her to talk about it. No interrogations, Trish said, though it took her a few thousand words to say it. My machine accepts only two-minute messages, and it cut Trish off twice. She called back each time. Her final advice to me was to sign up for one of the answering services and get rid of my crappy little machine.

There was also a message from Phyllis Friedel, the assistant headmaster at Byrd-Adams school. She'd heard about the unfortunate incident, she said in a velvety voice, and asked me to call to set up an appointment so that we could discuss the effect this might have on Kat's academic year.

THAT EVENING Christine and I had planned to meet for drinks on the roof terrace at the Hotel Washington and go to dinner at Palena, her favorite restaurant. We were meeting downtown so that she could stay late at her office and wrap up everything before leaving the next morning to pick up her kids, Robby and Victoria, at their camp. Then they were all going to Bethany for two weeks, where they'd share a beach house with another single mother and her children. Christine and I had tried to approach the evening as a festive occasion, and I left the Hut early to give myself time to stop in Georgetown and buy some sort of gift for her. She loves presents, loves intricate bows and beautiful paper and elegant cards, and her excitement when she receives a gift is sweet and genuine and moving. But the traffic was heavy on Friday afternoon, and it took me half an hour just to beat my way the few miles from the Hut down to Georgetown, and by the time I was finally standing in Trumbull's, a gift shop, one of Christine's favorite shops, I was feeling harried. Worse, I realized that I not only had no idea what to buy for her but that any gift at all would have been an attempt to disguise the distance that had become so palpable between us in these last weeks. I stood there until I finally picked up a giraffe, a wooden giraffe about a foot high. It had been carved in Zimbabwe and cost eighty dollars. I remember standing there for minutes and looking at that giraffe as though it had some important but difficult message to convey to me, a message I simply couldn't receive, and I finally put it down and left the shop empty-handed and heavyhearted.

Christine was on the packed roof terrace by the time I arrived, a few minutes late, her *kir* in front of her, my rum-and-tonic waiting for me, pleased with herself for having secured a table near the front railing where we could look directly over the roofs of the Treasury Department and the White House at the setting orange sun. One of her sayings is that it doesn't matter where you go; it only matters where you sit. She smiled, and I would have bent to kiss her, but for some reason she raised her hand, and I took it and put it to my lips. Courtly. "Some days I really love Washington," she said when we clicked our glasses together. "I always feel that way when we come here and see this view. It makes me feel that I'm *somewhere.*"

Christine's smile is lovely, but tentative, as though she is not quite sure that she should risk it. "I'm glad we came here," she said, "and I don't care if we are the oldest couple."

We'd laughed about that when we made our plans. It's mostly a young crowd that fills the terrace in the evening, well-heeled and well-dressed singles who do a lot of gazing into each other's eyes. On summer evenings, with the panorama of the white city streaked with the long shadows of sunset, that roof terrace is thick with romance.

"You can see right into Bill's bedroom," Christine said, nodding toward the back of the White House.

"Not much to see in there now," I said, "not since Clinton became suddenly celibate."

How do such things get said? Christine and I exchanged a strange look, as though I had referred to our own moratorium on sex.

I asked her if she'd gotten everything done at her office, trying to pretend that the exchange had never occurred.

"Clear," she said, drawing her hand across the surface of an imaginary desk. "I'm clear to go. I want to spend two weeks thinking about absolutely nothing."

"You and Mary Carter," I said.

Christine has met my mother and knows that she does yoga. I thought she had even heard me talk about the yogi and the principle of keeping one's ass above one's head. But perhaps not. She looked puzzled and asked, "Mary Carter?"

"That's her goal, too. To think about nothing. She recommended it for me. And I admit, it sounds wonderful." I did not mention my drumming failure that afternoon, or my failure to empty my mind. I didn't want to get into the whole subject of Abby and Jed and Lily.

"I wish you could come down for a few days," Christine said.

"I wish I could, too," I said, and meant it, but with Kat returning for her last week at Rockrapids, with the Montana trip scheduled after that, I couldn't get away. I took hold of Christine's hand and interlaced our fingers.

"Rough day?" she asked. "You seem down."

I told her about the call from the school, and I tried to make it sound amusing. "'We have heard about Kathryn's un-for-tu-nate in-ci-dent,'" I said, reproducing the tone of velvet insincerity, "'and would like very much like to discuss the potential effects of this un-for-tu-nate in-ci-dent on the coming ac-a-dem-ic year.'"

She laughed a little but wanted to know what I thought it meant.

"It means that they are deep-ly con-cerned."

"You sound like Mr. Rogers," she said. "Are you concerned?"

I was and admitted it.

"They can't punish her, can they? It's not a school matter."

"I think they just want to slap me on the wrist. Give us some kind of warning. But it is slightly om-i-nous."

"What would you do if Kat was suspended? That would be outrageous."

"It would be," I said, but I wished that Christine would turn loose of the subject instead of pushing it toward a serious discussion.

"I've never heard of a school doing that," she said, "holding students accountable for what happened during a vacation."

"That's why I pay the big bucks," I said.

"Can they do that? Do they have a policy about off-campus behavior?"

"Parental behavior?"

"No," Christine said, ignoring my effort to divert her, releasing her hand from mine. I do not know why her seriousness, her *earnestness*, always turned me into a smart aleck. "Student behavior. It seems like a kind of double jeopardy."

"They do try to beat a sense of identity into them. They're always telling the kids that they're the school's best ambassadors to keep them on the straight and narrow when they're not at school."

"Well, of course, but that's not a policy."

"No," I said.

"What is their policy? Do they have a handbook? Can they punish Kat? You don't think they can suspend her, do you? Or expel her?"

"To tell the truth, I don't know. And I don't want to think about it tonight, all right? I really don't want to think about it."

I spoke far more sharply than I had intended and saw at once that I had stung Christine. She tucked her lips together, then took a sip of her drink, and after a terrible pause I tried to tell her that I was worried about the school, and it had been a long day, and I was sorry for snapping at her, and I really just wanted to spend these last few hours thinking about the sunset and the beach and the meal that we were going to eat—tried, in short, to save the moment.

"I can't talk about Kat, can I?" Christine said. "I am not permitted."

"Of course you can."

"No, I can't. I can't. This happens every time I mention her name. You don't want to hear what I have to say. It's never the right time. You always close the door. I am not permitted to know her and not permitted to speak about her. Or Will. Or anything else that matters to you."

I said that wasn't true. I said we had talked for hours about my legal situation, and we had.

"We talked about the lawyers, and we talked about legal strategy. We talked about everything except what happened, and why it happened, and how you feel about it. I don't want to be your lawyer. I want to be your lover. I want you to love me."

She spoke deliberately, in an even voice, looking toward the sun, but I think those words took her by surprise. They certainly surprised me. Then she lifted her hand, as if to shade her eyes from the light, and waited for a moment to see if I would answer.

There was only one possible answer and I could not make it.

"I was afraid this would be our last night," she said, her hand shielding her face. "It just felt that way. I'm not sure why. Maybe because we didn't talk about Amish night. That got ruined, didn't it? But that was almost the only thing that I felt I could talk about without the wall coming up. I loved Amish night, Tucker, but you've put everything else off-limits, and now that. There's nothing left. Don't say anything, please. I actually rehearsed this today, this speech. So I suppose I was more than afraid it would be our last night. I must have decided. But there's too much that's not permitted, just not permitted. That's the speech, really. It's not a time when I want to say good-bye, but I'm not permitted to say much else. I don't feel as though I'm leaving you without a confidante. I'm not even sure I'm your friend. It's strange, isn't it, not to know that after so long? I know you don't love me, and I tried to figure out today if I loved you, and I didn't know the answer to that, either. All I know is that I wanted to, and I think I could have if you'd let me."

She stood up and put a hand on my shoulder to keep me from standing. "Stay," she said. "Stay long enough to let me get away. Good luck, Tucker."

She had to make her way carefully among the tables and chairs, her shoulders slightly raised, her dark hair swinging forward about her face. She did turn her head in my direction before she disappeared, but she did not wave and she did not slow down. I stayed on the terrace long enough to finish my drink, wondering why her dignity and courage were not enough for me.

KAT FLEW back to Washington that Sunday night on a commercial flight, and I drove out to meet her at National Airport after working all day since, on Saturday, a summer storm had ripped through the city, knocking out power lines and uprooting trees, and a few frantic clients had put in emergency calls. Most of these so-called emergencies were just clean-up jobs that could wait, but one family in Chevy Chase had the crown of an enormous locust tree in their kitchen, and I spent hours standing on a stepladder with a chain saw, bucking the limbs and trunk into bolts of wood that Hugo, my mechanic, stacked in the backyard. He was one of the few men who didn't belong to the Glorious Miracle and thus one of the few available to work on Sunday—for overtime pay, of course. It had been awhile since I'd handled a chain saw, though in the early days of Twill I did plenty of grunt work, and I still pitch in when extra hands are needed. That Sunday, in any case, I was glad to have useful occupation, for otherwise I would have done nothing but fret about Kat.

I was sick with worry. I'd spoken to her and Trish, and Kat hadn't changed her mind; she really was coming—so that was something. I wouldn't have been surprised if she'd decided to blow off the last week of camp. To blow off Washington, period. Why wouldn't she want a fresh start in a different place? It had been no picnic for me to keep showing my face in town. For Kat, at an age when all emotions are magnified, to return would mean facing judgment at every turn.

Maybe Trish was right. It pained me to think so, but that afternoon, as I put on clean clothes to go to the airport, I told myself I'd try to make the most of this week no matter what Kat decided. I would do nothing to make her feel she shouldn't go live with her mother. I showered and put on pressed pants (Gladys irons everything), and I kept changing shirts like a kid about to go on his first date until I finally remembered that Kat had given me a navy blue shirt. I wore that one. I took the real car, not the Jimmy, and put an Emmylou Harris CD in the player, a CD I knew Kat liked, and as I drove along the Parkway, the Potomac had the glint of pewter and the monuments glistened in the late light of a summer afternoon. It had been a rare day, crisp and sparkling, with cool northern air pouring in after the storm, and the Washington Monument—the Pencil, Kat had called it as a child—was so clear that I could see the knife-thin lines between the individual stones.

A summer afternoon. Kat, when she was about seven, had once put her hand on my neck and murmured those words over and over again. *"Summer afternoon, summer afternoon, summer afternoon,"* she said, drawing every bit of sweetness and music out of them. "They're the most beautiful words," she said, and her voice had sounded to me then like the very sound of bliss. She was seven, and we were alone on a beach on the Outer Banks, on our first vacation since Trish left. Will was playing at the edge of the surf, and I remember it as the end of a glorious day, a day when I knew somehow that we were going to make it, that she hadn't taken away our happiness. Kat, the nest maker, had fashioned a sort of shelter out of towels and blankets and other gear, and we were curled up together, the two of us. At that age she had chatted freely, her child's spirit equal to the sky and sand and ocean, but I cannot remember how her chant began. "*Summer afternoon, summer afternoon, summer afternoon,*" she said, a tiny hypnotist, looking straight at me with her flecked amber eyes, her warm hand on my neck, speaking as though she wanted to fix this moment in my memory, and hers. She even said, dreamily, "I want to stay here forever." And added, "Will can go. But we'll stay."

Kat. This child had thrilled me then, and the first glimpse of her at the airport thrilled me, too, as it always did after an absence. When her plane landed and she emerged, at last, from the gate, she showed me a faint, weary smile, not much more than a glance of recognition, but it was enough to make me stand tall. She had a dun-colored baseball cap pulled low over her eyes—*Maidstone*, it said—and trudged along with her hands tucked in the straps of her backpack, her T-shirt outside her shorts. She merely leaned her head against my cheek when I hugged her.

"Going somewhere?" she asked me, running her glance over my clothes.

I told her about the storm as we walked toward the airport doors, and how I'd spent the day as a logger, and how I'd decided I might as well get spruced up. I asked her if she wanted to get something to eat on the way home.

"Not really," she said. "You know Mom. She made me eat before I left."

We made conversation. We talked about tennis and the kids at the Maidstone Club. As always, she was careful to seem neutral about Long Island, but she did mention that the book in her hand, *The House on Mango Street*, was on the summer reading list for the Burden School. Had she already decided to go there? I didn't ask, but why would she mention it if she hadn't made up her mind? Why would she be doing the summer reading?

In the car, when I punched up the CD, she didn't say a word. There was hardly any traffic that Sunday night, and on impulse I headed up Independence Avenue after crossing Memorial Bridge. Kat said, "What's the deal? Aren't we going home?"

"It's a gorgeous night. When was the last time we looked at the monuments?"

"I've seen them like a thousand times," Kat said.

"You exaggerate," I said, for some reason sliding into a goofy French accent, the Pink Panther accent. Kat had in fact seen the Mall often, for we always came down to this public part of the city, the tourist part of the city with its museums and government buildings, its statues and memorials, when we had visitors. "Do you know"—I stuck with the broad, bad French accent—"who created zis city? Eet was a Frenchmon! 'Ees name was Pierre L'Enfant, wish mean Pete-air ze Child."

I thought I saw a trace of a smile on Kat's face.

"Yais, yais, a Frenchmon. 'E was young, but 'e was ze greatest city planner in ze world." Roll the *r*'s, *worrrrled*. "And 'e deed all zis in only seven days."

And then I couldn't stop. This was a kind of nonsense Kat had heard from me all her life, and once I started, I kept rolling on maniacally, adding in every feature of the city as we passed. "And on ze third day, Pierre made ze pond, and ze Mint, and ze road he called Seventeenth Street, and ze flowers by ze road, and ze crosswalks, and ze stoplights—no, I zink ze stoplights come later. He made ze temple with ze gold dome, and zen he go home and have a glass of *vin rouge* because for a Frenchmon a day wizzout wine is like a day wizzout sunshine."

And so on and so on as we went along Independence Avenue. This was, as I say, the kind of silliness that had entertained Kat hugely when she was little, and I kept glancing at her, and she kept listening with a tiny smile showing at the corner of her small mouth. She didn't say anything until we got near the Smithsonian, down around Fifth Street, where she saw a sign for L'Enfant Plaza, and she asked, "Was there really someone named L'Enfant?"

"What have I been zaying? O zay do not leesten, ze children."

"Seriously, Dad. Is this a real guy?"

"*Mais oui!*"

"Lose the accent, OK?"

She was suddenly impatient, just fed up, and I drove on toward the Capitol for a couple of blocks, past the Air and Space Museum and the Botanic Garden, before I said, "He didn't do it exactly as I described, but he was real. He laid out the city. And he was a young guy. But there were only two city planners in the world at the time."

No comment from Kat. She just nodded, looking ahead at the Capitol dome, great and gleaming that evening, brilliant white in the light of sunset. I almost hesitate to mention that "Together Again" was coming from the CD player—why is it that songs have such a way of marking moments in a life? In my life, anyway. That song about the sweetness of reconciliation sounded mocking as we drove along in silence, and I had to blink back the tears that started to my eyes.

For a few blocks I didn't trust myself to speak, but when we were doubling back on Constitution Avenue, I asked her if she was ready to go back to Rockrapids. I asked if she'd talked to Abby.

"Once or twice," she said.

Loaded question, loaded answer. I didn't think Abby would mention that I'd walked in on her and Jed, and didn't ask, but I did say, "What does she think about this? About your going back to Rockrapids?"

"We didn't talk that much about it," Kat replied, too dismissively, in a tone that let me know she wanted no more questions about Abby.

"But you feel all right about going back?"

"I'm here."

"I'm glad you're here, sweetheart. Be brave, be bold."

"Whatever," she said.

She closed down every attempt I made to get her talking, and I didn't bring up the phone call from Phyllis Friedel at Byrd-Adams until I'd turned onto Canal Road, where the trees overhang the pavement, the darkness gathered in the leaves, and the night seemed to fall all at once. I told Kat that I'd made an appointment on Tuesday morning at eight o'clock so that she could go straight from there to Rockrapids.

"Phyllis," she said carefully. "When did she call?"

"Just a few days ago."

"They're going to kick me out," she said.

"I don't think so."

"Why else would they ask us to come? Nobody's even there." Her hands lifted impatiently then, and she said, "Oh, this is just great. I'm so glad I came home for this."

"I think you're wrong. I think they just want to—I don't know. Give us a warning."

"Not us, Dad. Me. You're not in school. It's *me* they're going to kick out. Shit."

I asked her not to jump to any conclusions, but her head was turned and she looked out the window into the dark shadows. Perhaps I should have tried to say more, but I was afraid she was right and I didn't want to offer false hope. At the Hut, Romeo greeted Kat with his usual shameless glee, and when she went upstairs to her room, I was glad to hear, through the cracked door, that she was talking on her phone. It was a good sign, I thought. At least there was somebody here that she wanted to talk to.

That night, with Kat in it, the house seemed to breathe again.

ON TUESDAY morning, when we left for our meeting at Byrd-Adams, Kat was subdued, though she'd been almost cheerful the night before after returning from her first day back at Rockrapids. People had seemed glad to see her, maybe a little too glad. "It was like they went out of their way to be nice," she told me, "like I had just gotten out of the hospital." Then she did, with her whispery irony, the bit from the famous Academy Awards acceptance speech: "They like me. They really like me."

My daughter has always been able to make me laugh, and on the ride to the school, I tried to make a joke about the headmaster, a jolly, pink-faced sweetheart of a man, but Kat didn't smile. She said, "I wish we were seeing him." The students all knew that he was the softy and Phyllis Friedel, the assistant headmaster, was the enforcer at Byrd-Adams, a school that had a reputation as an "alternative," meaning that it wasn't quite as obsessed with SAT scores as the elite private schools in the city, the high-ambition, high-pressure, high-serotonin schools where the kids were prepped and packaged for Ivy League colleges. Will went to one of those schools, St. Albans, but he was a math whiz with a phenomenal memory and a temperament that seemed utterly immune to stress. Kat was far more high-strung, and we had looked at several schools, with Trish, before choosing Byrd-Adams, a place where her weaknesses in math and sciences wouldn't loom so large, and where her gifts for language and the visual arts would be encouraged and rewarded. She'd been at Byrd-Adams since the third grade and saw it as *her* school, the place where she belonged, and my heart went out to her that morning as we walked toward the administration building and she strode ahead of me in her long, leaning-forward gait, her shoulders hunched a little, her head down, as though she were fighting against a tight rein. She was wearing her climbing clothes since she was going to camp straight from the meeting, and her golden hair was pulled into a thick, ropy braid. Her arms were folded as though she felt some chill in the heavy summer air. There was no chill but she always folded her arms when she didn't know what to do with her hands.

The Byrd-Adams offices are in a handsome stone building that was once a rich man's house, and the only person in the front office that morning was Dawn, the woman who always seemed to be there. I am not sure what exactly her job was, but she knew everybody and usually had some banter for me, or some request, for my crews took care of the school's grounds (for a fraction of the fee anyone else would have charged). On this morning she looked at the wall clock—we were a few minutes early—and told us that Phyllis had just arrived. Phyllis. Byrd-Adams was the kind of school where everyone was on a first-name basis.

Phyllis Friedel was waiting for us at her neat desk, a heavyset woman with long dark hair and the kind of presence—soft, warm, powdery—that made her seem at first glance like a kindly aunt. Her blouse was of thick, striped Indian cotton and she wore a necklace of what looked like polished beach pebbles. She gave the impression of a flower child who'd grown up to be an earth mother until she opened her mouth and the smooth voice emerged, the lips pursed and the words carefully sculpted, the tone unmistakably official and scarily humorless. "You're a counselor at Rockrapids," she said to Kat, smiling a bogus smile, and every syllable seemed to have a tiny space around it.

Phyllis hadn't stood to greet us, or shake hands, but motioned us to take a seat in the black wooden chairs that were stationed in front of her desk. As they talked, Kat somehow came up with that sweet, dreamy smile I hadn't seen for weeks, and then Phyllis said, "Well. We all know why we're here. We have a set of extraordinary circumstances to consider. In fact, our administrative committee met last week, and we discussed the situation at considerable length. As you know, we regard our students as our patients here at Byrd-Adams and don't give up on them just because they're sick."

Sick? What was she saying? She nervously aligned the pencils and notepad on her desk, and it took me a moment to connect her remark with the story that the headmaster liked to tell, a story about a doctor who'd said, when his son was in trouble at school, that doctors don't turn away their ailing patients. Why should schools? The headmaster repeated the anecdote tirelessly, intending to convey the school's loyalty to its students, even the difficult students.

Phyllis had butchered the story. "We don't give up on our students," she said, "but there are circumstances in which we feel it would be to a student's benefit to consider alternatives."

Circumstances. Benefit. Alternatives. The dismal euphemisms of the bureaucrat, and Kat, I saw, knew exactly what the woman was saying. She had lowered her head to stare down at her hands in her lap. Phyllis turned the bogus smile on me, a smile of relief, it seemed, as though she was proud of herself for having broken the news with such grace and sensitivity.

"I don't get it," I said. I was in no frame of mind to make this easy for her. "What exactly are you saying?"

She swallowed, dropped the smile, and said, "In the best judgment of the administrative committee, Kat would have a better chance to flourish elsewhere. I can assure you that we have talked this over very carefully."

"Kat and I have talked this over ourselves," I said, though we hadn't talked much at all, "and in our best judgment she should stay here. She's been at Byrd-Adams since the third grade."

Kat spoke up then, and Phyllis looked at her gratefully when she said, talking to her hands, "I told you, Dad. They don't want me here."

She got to her feet and spread her palms in a show of helplessness. Her voice was mild but her eyes were flashing when she said to me, "They don't want me, OK? I'm gone."

And she left so quickly that she seemed almost to have vaporized.

Phyllis and I eyed each other as we listened to her shoes squeak in the hallway.

"Excuse me," I said. "I'll go talk to her."

"She's upset," Phyllis said, "and there's really no need to come back. I think we understand each other."

"We'll be back," I said.

Kat wasn't in the hall. Dawn was—she'd been eavesdropping—and she nodded her head toward the bathroom, the women's bathroom.

I went right in.

"You can't come in here," Kat said, standing at the sink counter, glaring at me. "Goddamn it, why won't you leave me alone?"

"We're not finished here," I said.

"What's not finished? They kicked me out. They've done it, OK? I told you that's what they were going to do." Her voice slammed around in that bare bathroom, echoing off the metal and tile.

"The least she owes us is an explanation."

"You're not supposed to be in here," Kat said, looking about wildly. If she'd found something on that counter, I think she would have thrown it at me.

"This isn't the way to leave, Kat."

"Why not? Why can't you hear what she's saying? I'm out. I'm a sicko. They don't want me here."

"I want to know why."

"I screwed up big-time. That's the explanation."

"No, it's not. What rule did you break?"

"Didn't you hear her? I screwed up and they kicked me out."

"I want to know how this is the school's business."

"Why? Why can't we just go?"

Her eyes looked huge and bright as if the tears had waxed them.

I said, "I don't want you to leave here thinking you deserve this."

"I do deserve it."

"No, you don't."

"I do. Even if there's no fucking rule about it, I deserve it, OK? It is what it is." She rubbed the back of her hand across her nose and tried to throw my slogans back at me. "Accept it. Live with it. Suck it up. It is what it is."

"She has to tell us why."

"It's obvious why."

"Not to me."

"Use your imagination, duh."

"Kat, they have no right to expel you. They haven't even given you a hearing."

"I'm a sicko. You heard her."

"You're not a sicko," I said, unable to keep my anger in check. "Listen to me: You're not sick. That woman doesn't get to tell you that. Do you hear me? She's not the one who decides what you are. You're the one."

Kat glared at me, but she seemed calmer. She was trying to get control of her breathing, and when she looked at herself in the mirror, she said, "Tears and snot, just tears and snot." I can't even remember how that phrase became the family shorthand for outbursts of crying, but Kat had always used it to bring herself back into line. She splashed water on her face.

"Let's go back and make her talk some more. I like the way she overpronounces all her words."

Kat switched her mouth, tempted to smile but holding it back, and Phyllis was not happy when we returned. She sighed with theatrical annoyance and made a small grudging motion to grant us permission to sit down. During the time we were gone, she appeared to have re-arranged her hair, and it now flowed back over her shoulders, revealing earrings that looked like birdcages. They should have contained little buzzards.

I said we'd like to understand how the committee had reached its decision.

"There is a provision in the school handbook for exceptional cases," she said, carving out each syllable of each word with her lips, tongue, and teeth. I tried not to stare at her mouth as she defended the school's authority to expel Kat. "Expulsion is at the discretion of the administrative committee," she stated as though she were quoting, "whose decisions are not open to appeal."

"I'm not appealing," I said. "I'd just like to understand your reasons. You yourself have said that the circumstances are extraordinary, and I think we have the right to some explanation."

By then, I suppose, she understood that we weren't leaving until she did explain, and she sighed again. "Surely you must realize how awkward it would be for Kathryn and Jed to be in the same student body. His injury would be a constant reminder—"

She waved her plump hand, indicating that any fool could draw a conclusion from what she'd said.

"Shouldn't that be left to Kat and Jed?" I asked. "Wouldn't you like to know how they feel about being in the same student body?"

"We've reached our decision."

"I'm not appealing that decision."

"They're not the only students who would be affected."

"No," I agreed, "they're not. Let me ask you about that. What about the others who were involved? What about the boys? Are they being asked to leave, too?"

Phyllis sat very straight and placed her hands on the desk, one upon the other. "You can't expect me to discuss other students."

"Did you consider them at your meeting? Is Kat the only one being kicked out?"

"What happened at our meeting is confidential. I assure you that we considered our options carefully. Exhaustively."

"How could you?" I asked. "How could you conduct an 'exhaustive' review without knowing what happened? And I can assure you that you don't know, not unless you have your own investigator."

"We didn't feel the need for an investigator."

"So you operated on hearsay? On rumor?"

"We're satisfied that we know all the pertinent facts."

"You can't possibly know," I said.

"Dad, let's just go," Kat said.

"What we do know," Phyllis Friedel said solemnly, "is that one of our students, Jed Vandenberg, was seriously injured. He was disfigured."

"He wasn't injured by Kat," I said.

She plowed right on. "Jed has been a student here since the sixth grade, and his sister graduated from Byrd-Adams. They're members of the Byrd-Adams family."

Was she telling me that she was punishing Kat on behalf of the Vandenbergs? I repeated, "Kat didn't injure Jed Vandenberg, and for that matter, neither did I. As you'd know if you'd bothered to consider any facts."

"We know that you attacked him," she said, "with a *shovel*. We know that you have been charged with a crime. Can you really *not* understand the effect that it would have on the school, the atmosphere of the school, if the parent of one student was on trial for harming another one? It would be disastrous."

"So this is not about Kat," I said. "She is not being kicked out for anything she did."

"These events are intertwined. What is the purpose of trying to separate them?"

"The purpose is to be logical," I said, "and to be fair. Apparently that's too much to expect, but at least you gave us an explanation. You're punishing Kat for what you think I did—and just for your information, I didn't *attack* anybody."

Kat said, "Come on, Dad."

"You get the picture?" I asked her. "They don't know what happened. They just want to make it look as though they have some kind of standards, but they obviously don't. There's no fairness here."

Phyllis Friedel stood up, and the little birdcages were shaking with her anger. "There is no need to be insulting and to impugn our motives," she said. "I'm asking you to leave, *now*. I assure you that we placed Kat's best interests first and foremost."

There were no formalities on the way out, though Dawn did wish Kat good luck as we went through the door. I told Dawn that the Twill account was now closed and she'd better start calling other landscape services. The parking lot was empty, and Kat didn't talk until we got to the car. "Satisfied?" she said in a voice thick with anger.

"No," I said, "and I won't be until I'm sure you understand what just happened in there."

"I do understand. I got kicked out."

"Kat, listen. They kicked you out because they want to wash their hands of this whole mess. They didn't know what else to do. If anybody should be kicked out, it's those goddams boys, not you, but there are too many of them. They probably sat around and figured out who gives them the most money each year. Did you hear what she said about the Vandenbergs? I bet he gives megabucks to the school."

"What difference does it make? They kicked me out. Period. So just shut up about it."

"There's a big difference. I don't want to hear any more of this stuff about being sick. What happened wasn't your fault, Kat. I know that."

Kat was reaching for the door of the Jimmy, but I put my hand out to keep her from opening it. "You hear me? It's a bullshit decision. They don't have a clue what really happened that night, and they don't care."

"You have it all figured out, don't you?" Kat said, stepping away, her face red and her voice a lash. "You're so right, Dad, so fucking right, and they're so wrong. You really showed her how wrong she was. Thanks for fucking *nothing*."

"Don't talk to me like that."

She looked at me with such rage that she was unable to talk at all, and she turned and began to stride across the parking lot. "Stop," I said, but she did not stop. I was not going to let her get away.

When I ran to her side, she kept saying, "Let me go." She kept pulling her arm away from me. She finally slowed down and braced herself and with all her strength tried to push me away, but I held on. Big sobs were breaking from her when I hugged her, and I made out the words "Now I don't have anywhere to go."

IN HINDSIGHT, I see clearly that I shouldn't have taken Kat to that meeting, certainly not without ascertaining beforehand what action the school intended to take. I'd been unable or unwilling to believe that the school would expel her, and when we returned to the Hut—Kat was too humiliated, too raw, to go to camp that morning—she said she just wanted to go up to her room and read. I stayed home, too, answering my work calls from the stone patio behind the house, seated at the shaded picnic table with my yellow pad in front of me. Gladys wouldn't be in till the afternoon, and I was afraid to leave Kat alone that morning (I went so far as to take my Percodan, the only prescription drug in the house, out of the bathroom cabinet and put it in my pocket). I had no idea what my daughter might do.

Around noon, though, she asked me to drive her out to Carderock. She told me she was bored and said she might as well get it over with. She'd told Abby and some of the other counselors that she was meeting with Phyllis. "I'm sorry I acted like such a baby," she said, with a hitch of her shoulders intended to demonstrate that she could shrug off small matters. She apologized from keeping me from going to work, but when I tried to make my own apologies, when I told her that her reaction was completely natural, she forced a smile and asked me if we could please not talk any more about this right now.

And we didn't. As soon as I left her at Carderock, after making sure she'd joined up with the Rockrapids group (I couldn't shake the idea that she was about to run away, and that afternoon I believed she was capable of throwing herself into the river), I called Lily on my cell phone. Who but Lily could I turn to, to talk about Kat? We hadn't spoken since our quarrel, and she asked instantly if I was calling to yell at her again, but there was a familiar welcome in her voice, and the apologies, hers and mine, tumbled out easily. I told her that I felt embarrassed and stupid, and Lily said, "Let's not yell at each other again, OK? I'm no good at being mad at people."

She sounded so present that when I started to tell her about that morning, everything gushed out—all of Kat's reactions and my own fears and mistakes and confusions. On River Road, not far from my office, I pulled into a parking lot so that I could keep talking. I didn't seem to be able to hold anything back, even the things I thought I should keep to myself—the confession that I'd always felt closer to Kat than to Will, always believed that we were attuned to each other in a way that Trish never grasped, always felt that Kat was *my* child, and I admitted that sometimes I was so hurt and angry by the way she separated herself from me that I *wanted* her to go live with Trish, that in my blackest moments I thought she deserved to live there and that I would be relieved to have her gone. But those were the night thoughts, and I knew that what I really couldn't take was this sense of alienation and distance from her, of not knowing her, of having lost her. I remember saying that I knew every child had to grow up and leave—"I think Abby did that when she was five," Lily said—but this was too far ahead of schedule and everything was happening in the wrong way. Kat was supposed to grow up and fall in love, not go to a party at age fourteen and get drunk and have oral sex with three boys. "I can't get that image out of my head," I told Lily. "I know it wasn't her fault, but I have this anger at her—Lily, I feel so guilty. They wouldn't have thrown her out of school if I hadn't gone in there that night with that goddamn shovel. That woman Phyllis said it straight out, that it was because of the lawsuit that Kat was being kicked out. She's being kicked out because of *me*. She doesn't have a chance to put this behind her because of what I did, and I feel so guilty about it, and about Jed. I've wrecked their lives, both of them."

Lily asked, "Where are you, Tucker?"

"In the American Plant Food parking lot."

"Why don't you come over here for a while. I want you to talk to me."

"Do I sound that bad?"

"You sound pretty bad."

I tried to keep my voice steady when I asked, "What should I do? Should I let her go? To New York, I mean. Should I just recognize how I've fucked things up and let her go up there with Trish?"

Lily said gently, "I don't think so. I think she wants to stay here—if she didn't, if she'd already made up her mind, she would have let you know. She probably would have let the school know, too, and she wouldn't have gone to that meeting today. I don't think Trish would have wasted any time telling Byrd-Adams if Kat was going to withdraw."

I told Lily that Kat had been reading a book from the Burden School summer list, but even as I spoke, I was allowing myself to believe that Lily was right and that Kat still had not made her own decision, and I realized that I was now in a fundamentally changed relationship with my daughter. She'd always been my child, my treasure, my darling—*mine*—but she didn't belong to me any longer, not in that absolute way.

Now I wanted her to choose me.

If I wanted her to stay in Washington, I had to find another school for her. I had to make it possible for her to stay. Even if Trish and I had put her in the terrible position of choosing, I was determined to give her a choice.

So Lily and I talked about schools, and she told me that she was leaving the next day for the Adirondacks, for the camp at Tupper Lake, driving up with Sophy and Rafe. Abby was going to stay until the end of the week, finishing out the session at camp, and then fly up with Tony. She needed a respite, Lily said. "They're in love," she said wanly, meaning Jed and Abby, "and you know how that goes. No power on earth can keep them apart, and I'm tired of trying. I'll let Tony deal with her for a few days. I'm just here trying to pack up the car—you sure you won't come by for a minute?"

I assured Lily that I'd be fine, and thanked her for listening to my troubles, and as soon as I got back to the office, I started making calls to private schools. I knew that Wilson, the public high school, wasn't a possibility, partly because I thought Kat could get lost in the size of the place, and also because I knew that Trish would never hear of it. At most schools I reached only the voice-mail system, but I did catch a few administrators who seemed used to handling these desperate last-minute calls. One of them, well-meaning, asked questions about Kat, and then suggested a boarding school in Colorado where the students went on hikes and climbing trips.

Then I called Joan Walker. I have never been one to seek special privileges or favors, but Joan was on the board of trustees at the Tandem School, and I asked if there might be a place for Kat. I'd known Joan for years, going all the way back to the days when we were both single, and we'd even dated a couple of times, movie dates that had made us friends, not lovers. After inheriting her fortune, Joan had been invited to sit on the boards of several organizations, and she'd been a generous donor to Tandem, the school that had taken in both her children when the more elite schools had turned them down. She was instantly on Kat's side. "Bastards," she said, meaning the people at Byrd-Adams. "As if it's not hard enough for Kat already."

She'd heard the story, of course, and not from me. She knew

Richard Vandenberg and his wife, Valerie. She said, "Teddy and I call them Ego and Egad." I'd always liked her bluntness, but she didn't think she'd be able to do anything for Kat. Like every other school in the city, Tandem had been turning applicants away, and she knew that there was a waiting list. She said, "It must be the same at every school. I'll check, but I don't see how I can do anything. I'm sorry, Tucker."

But I kept trying. I kept calling schools, and I mentioned this to Kat, casually, not wanting to initiate a conversation that would force her to make her decision. I simply said that I was waiting to hear from several places, and that seemed to suffice. Kat went to camp every day and also went out to the movies a couple of nights in a row. She took her cell phone and told me what movies she saw. Her manner toward me was polite and obedient. She mentioned that she'd seen Abby. And Jed. "He was nice," she said. "He wasn't weird or anything. I mean, we talked about it and he said he knew I didn't have anything to do with what you did. With your fight or whatever," she said, correcting herself, letting the event disappear into vagueness, wanting not to sound as though she held me accountable.

ON THURSDAY, when I played my regular late afternoon tennis game with Jay, Kat was alone at the Hut for a few hours, and she took a call from Joan Walker.

"What is this about Tandem School?" she asked me when I got home. "And who is Joan Walker? She talked as if she knew me."

Joan wouldn't have called back just to repeat the bleak message she'd already given me, and I tried not to let Kat hear my eagerness when I told her that I'd asked Joan about getting her into Tandem.

"Are you ever going to ask me what I want to do?"

"Sweetheart—"

"I feel like the rope in a tug-of-war," she said. "Mom puts me in a school I never even heard of, and then a strange woman calls up and tells me I'm going to Tandem, like I won the lottery or something."

"She said she got you in?"

"She said you still had to do the paperwork. She wants you call her. Do you care what I think about it? It's not even like a school. It's just those buildings, office buildings and that old grocery store. It's like some, I don't know, halfway house."

We were in the kitchen and she'd backed away from me, out into the open space of the alcove, as if she needed that distance and that space to move in. She was in her usual shorts and her bare feet kept moving on the rug of rose and green. "I mean, it's a geek school. That's all I know who goes there, geeks and losers. They don't even have grass or anything. I won't go there. I won't, won't, won't."

She caught a breath and looked at me fiercely.

"There's not much choice," I said.

"OK, OK, I know I put myself in this position. That's what you're going to tell me, right? How I messed up and now all the schools have waiting lists and blah, blah, blah. You and Mom, it's the same thing. She told me how she screwed up and gave me this whole big story about how sometimes you don't get what you want and you have to gut it out and show people what you are."

"She's right."

"I don't want to gut it out," Kat said. "Maybe you can do it, but I can't. Everything's screwed up, and you just go off and play tennis like nothing happened. It's like everything's fine and dandy, and you expect me to act that way, like woo-hoo. But it's not fine. Everybody in Washington thinks I'm a slut and I got kicked out of school and you put Jed's eye out. You could be put in jail and now you want me to go to some loser school and I'm supposed to be all hooray about it." She was glaring at me and she stamped her bare foot down, her hands balled into fists.

"I played tennis," I said, "but sometimes I need a break. I have to stop thinking about lawyers and schools and all the other things that are on my mind constantly, Kat, constantly. I can't think of anything except how to solve all these problems."

"Problems, problems, problems," Kat said, the words exploding in the room. "That's how you see the whole world, as a problem you have to solve. Like it's one of your stupid crossword puzzles and you have to fill in every stupid blank. Ta-da! Finished that one! And I'm just another problem, but you can't finish me. I'm too fucked up for that. You can't finish me."

She stomped out of the room then, and up the stairs, and slammed her door. I stayed in the kitchen, still at the counter, still in my sweaty tennis clothes, shaken by her outburst. I hadn't realized how much I'd clung to the slender hope that some school vacancy would occur and Kat would jump at it. It had taken her no time at all to reject Tandem. She wouldn't stay here. I'd been clutching at straws, postponing the moment when I would have to ask her to make up her mind, hoping that I could find a way to keep her here, but I could put it off no longer.

I stayed in the kitchen for what must have been ten or fifteen minutes, long enough for the house to grow quiet again, long enough for Kat to put a CD in her player. The music was nothing more than a far-off hum, but it meant she was calmer, and I wanted to apologize to her. For being unable to talk to her, for letting this turn into a contest between me and Trish. Christ, for all the ways I'd let her down.

She was upstairs in her room, stretched out on her bed. No lamps were lit, and the objects in the room seemed to be dissolved in the dimness. She had music on—a female vocalist, a voice I hadn't heard, a woman singing a torch song, a mesmerizing voice.

"Kat? Kat? Are you OK?"

"Yeah." A soft, smothered noise.

"Who's that you're listening to?"

Kat had to sniff, and in the low light I saw that she moved a hand to her cheek. I can't describe the sadness of her position, curled into a question mark, sunk down into her pillows and comforter. She'd been crying, and I heard the huskiness when she said, "Eva."

"Who?"

"Eva Cassidy."

I listened for a moment to one of the most glorious voices I had ever heard, even at the low volume, even on Kat's tiny speakers. No one could listen to this woman for a moment without feeling that the music poured straight from her soul.

"Who is she?"

"She died, Dad."

I heard Kat trying to get control of her voice, and her words seemed to stop my heart. *She died, Dad.* I waited, not wanting to move, not wanting to breathe, waiting to hear what my daughter would say.

"She lived here," Kat said, "in Washington. You really don't know who she is?"

"I never heard her before. She has an amazing voice."

"She even worked as a landscaper. She could have worked for you. You've had girls, right?"

"Eva Cassidy. She didn't work for me."

"It was like she knew she wouldn't live long."

What was my daughter telling me? "How do you mean?"

"She just knew. You can tell if you listen to her. The songs are so sad."

"Where did you get the CD?"

"It was in the car."

"I don't remember it."

"It's the one Lily gave you."

"When?"

"You know. That night."

Then I remembered that Lily had given me a CD on the night of the 13th. I must have put it in the console and forgotten about it.

"I never heard it before."

Kat sat up and looked at me, and I could make out the shine of her big dark eyes. "She never even made a CD while she was alive," she said. "There were just some recordings, but they put them all together, however they do that stuff. You probably know about that."

"Not much."

"She had a friend who made the CD. A friend and her dad. Her dad kept her tapes or whatever. And now there's a CD. It's all that's left of her."

Kat was pushing at her nose with the back of her hand, and we just listened for a moment to this woman's piercing voice.

"Why does somebody like that have to die?" Kat said, the words coming thick through her throat.

Then her head just sank and her shoulders shook with sobs. I went to her and put my hands on those shoulders.

"You want to know how I feel?" Kat said, but she didn't try to get away from my hands. "That's how I feel. I feel how she sings."

"What do you mean, Kat?"

"I mean I want to be someplace else. Not here."

Of course I thought she meant here in this house, in this city, with me. "Where do you want to be?" I asked.

"I don't know. Some place I've never been. Some place where I haven't screwed up yet."

I just rubbed her shoulders.

"I want you to listen to one song, OK? Don't make fun of it."

"I won't make fun of it."

"You did when Lily told you about it."

"What song?"

"Just don't make fun of it, OK? Promise me."

"I promise."

She slipped off the bed and went over to the CD player to hit search and move ahead to the track she wanted. "You're probably going to hate it," she said.

It has been given to me only three times in my life to hear a song as I heard that song in my daughter's room. It began with a few chords on the guitar, then that voice of transcendent purity, singing "Somewhere Over the Rainbow." This was a song that I would have said was beyond redemption, buried under layers of sentimentality and millions of bad renditions, but this woman Eva Cassidy made me feel that I had never heard it before and never recognized the longing in it. With Kat watching me, with my daughter opening her heart to me, I heard all the anguished longing in that song, the longing and the ache to turn it into something holy and beautiful.

I reached for Kat's hand.

"Let's dance," I said.

"Dance?"

"That way we used to dance. Step up on my feet."

"Dad."

"Please, Kat."

"It's not exactly dance music."

"Please."

She stepped toward me and put one of her bare feet on top of my foot. "This isn't going to work," she said. "I'm too old for this."

"Try it," I said. I had put my hand behind her waist, and she lifted her left hand and let it rest on my shoulder.

"It's beautiful, Kat, beautiful."

Then her other foot was on my tennis shoe. "Aren't I too heavy?"

I shuffled my feet, and we took a step or two, and I felt how easily Kat adjusted her weight and balance to mine, how—still—she could make herself as light as a child. This might have been her last dance as a child, and in that twilit room, as I danced with my daughter, her eyes searching mine, the two of us just floating, I felt something give way inside me. Maybe it was forgiveness, arriving at last, but I remember it now as though all our old love, every particle of it, had been restored to us by the music we were hearing.

I am old enough to understand that moments like that do not last, and when the song was over, I said, "Thank you, Kat," and made a slight bow.

She wiped at her nose. "That song gets me every time. Tears and snot. But you see what I mean about her? How she just knows?"

"I see. I think I really do see. I love you, Kat. You know that, don't you?"

"I know," she said.

"I'm sorry we've put you in such a horrible spot—about schools. About where to live. And I can understand why you wouldn't want to go to Tandem. I should have talked to you about it before saying anything to Joan."

The room was dead quiet and we stood with a little space between us.

"You've decided, haven't you?"

"Yeah," Kat said.

I could feel myself straighten as my body braced itself. "So you're going to live with your mom."

"I'm going to stay here," she said, nodding, looking around the room as if to confirm the decision. "Yeah, here. This is home."

"You sure?"

"Anyway," she said, dreamily, "you might go to jail, so I should probably see you while I can, right?"

How amazing it seems that we both stood there and laughed.

O utside my kitchen window stands a rose of Sharon, *Hibiscus syri-acus*, a healthy tree—a dense, shaggy shrub, really—that blooms profusely in August, attracting bees, butterflies, and the occasional hummingbird. I have a special fondness for all late summer bloomers since so many gardens, and all the fancy perennial gardens, have shot their wad by then. I have a hard time talking clients into making a place for the hardy, humble annuals—cosmos, cleome, zinnias—that can hold their heads up in the August heat, but I try. My affection for these plants goes back to my childhood in Norfolk, when I earned my allowance by working in my mother's garden. She loved that garden and didn't mind working in the heat, wearing a big straw hat and giving me my first instructions about how things grow. "I think it is a privilege," I remember her saying, "to get to know another species, don't you?"

I thought she was cuckoo, of course, but I realize now how many of her lessons stuck with me. About the rose of Sharon, for instance, I remember the biblical origin of the name, from the Song of Solomon: *I am the Rose of Sharon and the lily of the valleys. As the lily among thorns, so is my love among the daughters.* Admittedly, the fact that this scripture is on the tag wired to all the shrubs that come through Twill has helped fix the words in my memory, and I was thinking of them the day Kat finished her stint at Rockrapids, for she came home to find a thick letter from my mother awaiting her, and she read it, seated on the wing chair in the alcove, while I fixed our dinner.

That rose of Sharon came from my mother's garden. It's not hard to propagate *Hibiscus syriacus*, and Mary Carter brought a cutting up from Norfolk when Kat was born and planted it in our little Georgetown garden. Another of her principles was not to buy plants, not if she could help it; she preferred plants that were cuttings or seeds from someone else's garden so that they had a pedigree and a story. When she looked at her garden, she said, she wanted to be reminded of something other than a cash transaction. When we moved to the Hut, I transplanted that rose of Sharon, its blossoms cream colored with a crimson center, as well as the white dogwood that she had given us to mark Will's birth. The man who helped me was Carlos Fuentes, and that was when we agreed to start the business that became Twill Landscaping.

Everything happens for a reason, Mary Carter says. I'm not sure that I share her faith in the mysterious interconnectedness of all things, and I couldn't help wondering what she'd written to Kat, who was completely absorbed in the letter. Mary Carter doesn't write often, but when she does, she writes volumes, covering page after page with her big, open handwriting, throwing in plenty of smiley faces. I was making a Greek salad with heaping portions of briny Kalamata olives and salty feta cheese, two of Kat's favorite foods, and I saw her finish reading. I saw her looking out through the glass doors toward her rose of Sharon.

"What'd my mother have to say?" I asked. "She want you to take up yoga?"

"She mentioned yoga," Kat said, smiling a little. But she wasn't going to talk about the letter. She folded it carefully and replaced it in its envelope, then drew her knees up to her chest, checking out the various scratches and bruises and strawberries on her long legs. I sometimes kid her about the way she sits, folded up like a monkey, patiently inspecting herself. She clenched and unclenched her toes, picking at the chipped pink polish on her nails. "My toes are smooshed," she announced.

"You must have done some serious climbing today. You look more banged up than usual."

"Yeah," she said, "we all got to climb a lot since it was the last day. I did a 5.10," she said, glancing up at me slyly. Kat isn't one to boast, but all climbs are given a rating, and a 5.10 is a serious climb. "It was only tough in one place where there was like this nonexistent toehold."

"You know what ballerinas do, don't you? They use raw veal when their toes ache."

"Veal? Raw meat? No way."

"It's true. They wreck their feet and raw veal is the time-honored remedy."

"How do you know weird stuff like that? You're kidding, aren't you?"

"I have my sources," I said.

"Yeah? Did one of your ballerina pals let you in on the secret?"

I let the silence drift through the room. I'd already congratulated Kat for sticking out her commitment at Rockrapids, and I could tell that she was pleased, too. She had a right to be. Neither of us was in any great hurry to talk about Trish, who would be expecting the evening call. She was going to have to know that Kat had decided to stay in Washington.

"Tell me about the climb," I said. "Was it the first time?"

"Yeah," Kat said. "I'd tried it before but I couldn't do it. There's just the one place where you basically have to be a lizard."

"I don't know where you get this from. I can't take heights. A stepladder is too high for me."

She seemed to finish with her toes and started checking out the ends of her hair, still slightly damp from the shower. "Abby said Tandem isn't that bad."

"She did? So you told people about Tandem?"

"Yeah, a few. Today we were all together in one group since it was the last day for a lot of people. All the JCs got to do a climb with everybody watching—it was sort of like a recital or something. You know, Greg was there and he announced us and then described it like he was a sportscaster at some amazing event. *'Now watch as she dangles from the rock face by a single fingertip,*' like that. It was pretty fun, actually."

"So is Abs ready to go to Tupper?"

"She goes tomorrow," Kat said, and added, "I like Tupper. *Tuppah. Black buttah.*"

The Moorefields have a couple of powerboats on Lake Tupper, and on the days when the black water is smooth, and ideal for water skiing, they call it black butter. We'd visited them twice at Tupper and had a standing invitation to return, but there'd be no time this August for a trip to the Adirondacks. Kat was returning to Long Island on Sunday.

Kat looked across the counter at me. "Remember that time you fell? When you were trying to drop a ski? You just *bounced* across the water."

"I'm so glad you remember that."

"It was funny, Dad," she said, and cocked her head a little to the side, her lips slightly turned up in a pleading smile. "Will you tell Mom? I mean, I'll talk to her, but would you tell her—you know, that I'm going to go to Tandem?" She quickly caught hold of a couple of strands of her blond hair and studied the ends as though on the brink of some discovery. "She'll want to talk to you anyway. Please, Dad. You can explain it better than I can. I don't want her to think I'm mad at her or anything like that."

Of course I should be the one, not Kat, to break the news to Trish.

"Sure, I'll call her," I said, trying to sound as though it would be easy. "You want me to do it now?"

"No time like the present," Kat said, shooting me a glance that shimmered with an understanding of how much I disliked talking to Trish. As long as we've been divorced, the kids still pick right up on the strain in my voice when I talk to their mother. "No time like the present," Kat repeated, taking a certain pleasure in turning one of my sayings against me.

So I made the call on the kitchen phone, and Trish herself answered at once. My number would have been on her display, but she expected to hear Kat's voice, not mine. "Tucker?" she said sharply. "Hold on while I get rid of this other call."

Kat was dealing with her split ends, and I stepped toward the dining room, turning away from the kitchen. This was not going to be a conversation for her to overhear.

"What is it?" Trish said when she came back on the line. "There's nothing wrong, is there?"

"No, nothing wrong. I just wanted to touch base before Kat leaves. We have some planning to do."

"About what? She's flying up on Sunday, isn't she?"

"She'll come up Sunday, but we have to talk about the rest of the summer. And about the fall."

From the quality of the silence on the line, I knew that I had her full attention.

"Kat and I have been talking about schools," I said.

"What is there to talk about? She told me she was expelled."

"She was, but I've been asking around. Long story short, she's been admitted to Tandem."

"Tandem? When did this happen?"

"Joanie Walker is on the board," I said, and I tried not to rub it in that I, too, knew people of influence.

"Tandem is a joke of a school," said Trish, who must have seen where this was heading.

"It's a little unorthodox, but it might suit Kat. The kids get to take art classes at the Corcoran, your old stomping grounds—did you know that?"

"Tucker, we've always had an agreement that we'd make all educational decisions jointly. You can't put her at Tandem. Why are you springing this on me?"

"I'm trying to remember—did we discuss the Burden School *jointly?*"

"That was an emergency. It still is, and there's no point in being sarcastic."

I glanced back to see that Kat had put her face to her knees and pulled her shanks tightly against her chest, making herself even smaller, hearing the notes of discord even if she couldn't make out the words. I went into the dim part of the dining room. "The emergency is over, Trish. Kat has made up her mind. It hasn't been easy for her. It's been hell, as a matter of fact. We should never have put her in a position where she had to choose. But she has chosen and she's going to Tandem."

"Don't put that on me," Trish said. "*You've* made it hard. I would never have suggested that Kat change schools if you hadn't injured that boy and gotten yourself into such a mess."

I paused to let pass the urge to correct Trish and remind her of what had actually taken place. There was no point in arguing. I said, "She's made a decision, and I think we should respect it."

"This is a colossal mistake. Colossal."

"I disagree. It would be a colossal mistake for Kat to leave."

"I can't believe what I'm hearing. You're going to be arraigned when? Next week? You could be in jail. Is that your idea of a home environment?"

"It will be months before any case goes to trial. *If* any case goes to trial. I've told you that."

"But this scandal is going to be hanging over you until then, and it's—god, it's perverse. I wish you could think for one moment about your daughter's welfare instead of your own desire to get revenge on me."

She kept talking and I pretended to be listening thoughtfully. She told me how perfect the Burden School would be and how excited Kat had seemed (*excited*—I doubted that) and how sure she was that Kat was now simply trying to please me. She should have known that I would try to force the decision while Kat was in Washington, with her friends, and the Tandem School? It was a school for problem kids, and I couldn't be serious about letting Kat go there. When she finally paused for a breath, I said, "You should talk to Kat, but this subject is closed. Her mind is made up, and I repeat: We have to respect her decision."

"Do you think I don't respect it?"

"I'm not sure you do."

Silence again. I imagined Trish pacing about in her oceanfront house, struggling to accept this defeat, feeling her inability to make life conform to her wishes. "Is Kat right there?" she asked finally. "I hope she hasn't been listening to this."

Trish didn't miss many chances to put me in the wrong. "She hasn't heard anything," I said. "Do you want to talk to her?"

"OK," she said, and I heard that she'd given in.

After I'd passed the handset to Kat, I listened long enough to hear her trying to talk up her new school. "Yeah, Mom, they have pretty interesting-sounding classes. And it's not like a regular school the way they let you take classes all over the place. It's like some kind of drive-thru school." She was trying to make it sound acceptable while putting it down gently, and it occurred to me that this was why, at least one reason why, she was going to stay in Washington: I picked up the threads of her irony, and Trish usually didn't. With the phone against her ear, Kat stood up and wandered out into the hallway, needing privacy of her own.

I set the table and when she'd finished talking, and passed me the phone to replace on the charger, our hands coupled as if for a thumb war. Her heart wasn't in it. She gave me that look of hers, up through her dark lashes, and tried to smile, but her face just fell apart. "I wish we were a real family," she said.

IT HAS NEVER been easy to let others speak for me, and certainly not to think for me. I am the kind of person who hates, for instance, to sign my tax form without checking every computation that my accountant has made, and though I tried not to second-guess Brian and Ian, tried not to obsess endlessly about my legal predicament, I ended up spending hours at the neighborhood library with the black volumes of the District Code piled up in front of me, reading over and over again the pages relating to assault, attempting to understand the difference between simple assault—for which I had been arrested—and assault with a deadly weapon, which was a felony and carried a maximum sentence of five years. One of the guidelines for determining the kind of assault was the gravity of the injury, and there was no disputing the fact that Jed Vandenberg had lost an eye. But the other key consideration was *intent*, and as often and as searchingly as I put the question to myself, I always came up with the same answer: I had not intended to hurt that boy.

I wish I could have just left it at that. I wish I could have forgotten all about the case, about Richard Vandenberg, the spider-mastermind who was out to get me; and about Briggs, the prosecutor who didn't like the misdemeanor charge; and about Jed, who kept showing up in my dreams, a boy with a hole in his squarish, blocky face, a hole that opened up to what looked a whole universe of stars and black space. I wish I could have silenced all the tormenting speculations about how the case would turn out. But I couldn't.

I continued to go to work, of course, and on Tuesday morning, the day before the arraignment was scheduled, I was in the office early. Here's a silly, small confession: I wanted to get all the paperwork off my desk, wanted to have everything at the office shipshape in case I was thrown in jail. I was thinking like an old lady who wants to die in clean underwear. Ian had assured me, more than once, that the arraignment was just a formality and that the worst possible outcome was that I would have to post bond, but I got to the office before daybreak on Tuesday and beavered away as though it was my last day of freedom, and I was still there just before noon when a young woman turned up.

It is rare for us to get visitors. The Twill office is hard to find, tucked away behind several buildings that belong to George's bodyshop operation, and the few people who arrive unannounced are our regular vendors or job seekers. We do have a tiny reception area near Dee's desk, and my office opens off this area. My door—the only door in the place—was open and I got a glimpse of the woman and heard her ask if the boss was in. "Let me see if he's available," said Dee, in her coolest professional voice, impersonating some receptionist she'd seen in a movie. She was chewing gum and wearing cargoes but it amused her to pretend, brazenly, that she was the gatekeeper in a downtown glass tower. She stood just inside my door and pointed, mouthing, if I am not mistaken, "Some gal to see you."

I stood and went to the door. The woman standing at Dee's desk looked as though she might be a landscaper herself, for she was sturdily built and wore jeans, light boots, and a cotton shirt. She had darkframed glasses and her straight, clean hair was pulled back from her face and held in place with a pair of plastic barrettes. Everything about her, including the Pony Express briefcase she carried, an old leather satchel with accordion pleats, suggested that she was a woman used to working, and I imagined that she was carrying designs in her briefcase. More than that, I made a connection with Eva Cassidy, for this was only a few days since I'd first heard her voice, and I'd gone out and bought all of her CDs, and I'd been listening to her and reading about her, the doomed, brilliant Eva who had indeed worked for a landscaper in Washington, just as Kat had said. And so I was prepared to welcome this woman, and had she come looking for work, I would have hired her on the spot.

"I'm Tucker," I said. "How did you find us?"

"It wasn't that hard," she said, reaching into the worn leather satchel she carried. "I've found a lot tougher places, believe me."

She'd taken out a manila envelope. "Is this a delivery?" I asked, realizing that I must be mistaken about her.

"Actually, I'm a process server," she said, "and I've got a complaint and summons for you."

The envelope had a thick routing slip affixed to it, and she read, "William Tucker Jones, Twill Landscaping, that's you, right? I'm gonna need you to sign this."

"A process server," I said stupidly.

"Most people expect a guy," she said, "or else somebody disguised as a pizza delivery man. Too much TV. It's basically not much different from FedEx or UPS. I hand you the envelope, you sign the receipt, and that's it. You're served."

I did sign, and she removed the two copies of a triplicate form, leaving me with the envelope and the bottom copy with writing so faint as to be almost invisible. With a brisk shrug, she said, "Well, good luck," and she turned and made her way out.

I know that I was trying to keep my breathing level when I went back to my desk and sat down. The whole office was dead quiet. Everyone had heard the transaction—not just Dee, but Don and Randy and Jackie and Max—and I'm sure they knew that the envelope was the official beginning of the Vandenbergs' lawsuit against me. Brian and Ian had told me that the complaint might not arrive for months, not until all the medical bills could be tallied up, but obviously Richard Vandenberg had different ideas about the right timing. To file the civil action one day before the arraignment—a nice touch, eh?

I slit open the envelope and removed the complaint, the top page of which had been stamped with the date and the seal of the superior court. I want to write that my blood was boiling, though of course it was not. It merely felt that way. It felt as though the pilot had been ignited in a small explosion, a *whoosh* of flame, and all the emotions that had been simmering, simmering, simmering came to a full boil as I read the pages of that document.

In the Superior Court of the District of Columbia Civil Division

Jonathan C. Vandenberg
2217 Davenport Street N.W.
Washington, D.C. 20010

Vs.   Case No: 98-ca004534

Defendant:
William Tucker Jones
5440 Harding Place N.W.
Washington, D.C. 20016

SERVE: DEFENDANT

JURY DEMAND: SIX

COMPLAINT

Comes now the Plaintiff, Jonathan C. Vandenberg, having suffered grievous personal injury, unlawfully inflicted, and by and through his attorneys, Marsh, Paley, Rothman, and Mitchell, does hereby move for judgment against the Defendant on the grounds of Trespassing and Aggravated Assault and Battery, seeking damages in the amount of Seven Million Five Hundred Thousand Dollars ($7,500,000), for specific cause as hereinafter set forth.

This court has jurisdiction pursuant to Title 8, Section 114, and Title 12, Section 921, of the District of Columbia Code (1981 ed. as amended).

COUNT I: TRESPASSING

1. At all times relevant herein, the Plaintiff, Jonathan C. Vandenberg (hereinafter "Vandenberg") was a resident of the District of Columbia, residing at 2217 Davenport Street N.W.

2. At all times relevant herein, the Defendant, William T. Jones (hereinafter "Jones") was a resident of the District of Columbia, residing at 5440 Harding Place N.W.

3. On the night of July 13, 1998, at or about eleven o'clock, the Plaintiff was at his place of his residence, enjoying in a peaceful and law-abiding manner the company of four friends. They were seated outdoors in a lighted area adjacent to a swimming pool.

4. Suddenly, without warning or provocation, the Defendant, Jones, entered the premises brandishing a sharp-edged iron shovel and demanding in a belligerent, threatening fashion to know the whereabouts of his daughter, Kathryn A. Jones, who was not on the premises.

5. The Plaintiff remained seated as he repeatedly and calmly answered the Defendant's questions, declaring that he was unaware of Ms. Jones's whereabouts. The Plaintiff informed the Defendant that Ms. Jones had left the premises some time earlier and asserted that he was not aware of her intended destination.

6. These truthful declarations did not satisfy the Defendant. As his manner grew increasingly threatening, the Plaintiff requested that he leave the premises of 2217 Davenport Street N.W. The Plaintiff explicitly stated that Jones was trespassing.

7. Despite the repeated declarations and statements of the Plaintiff, made in the presence of witnesses and clearly indicating that the continued presence of the Defendant did constitute unlawful trespass, Jones refused to leave the premises.

COUNT II: ASSAULT WITH A DEADLY WEAPON

8. Upon reiteration of the fact that he was trespassing and the request that he leave 2217 Davenport Street N.W., Jones attacked the plaintiff with a

dangerous weapon, a sharp-edged shovel he had carried into the pool area.

9. The Plaintiff was seated at a table covered with various beverage containers of glass and metal. When the Defendant, standing, attempted to strike the Plaintiff with the shovel, he hit some of these beverage containers, effectively turning them into sharp projectiles. Medical records note contusions and abrasions that appear to have been caused by these projectiles.

10. Realizing that the Defendant was intent on causing bodily harm, the Plaintiff rose to his feet in an effort to defend himself.

11. The Defendant continued his attack with the shovel, striking the Plaintiff with sufficient force to cause him to fall against the iron table.

12. Severe trauma was the result of this fall caused by the blow that the Defendant delivered. The Plaintiff suffered a concussion and multiple fractures of the Orbit, the Temple, and Zygomatic Arch, these being the bones that surround and protect the eyeball.

13. The collapse of these bones created intense pressure on the eyeball, resulting in a massive rupture of the globe itself, as documented in the medical records which are attached as Exhibit A to this Complaint.

14. The Plaintiff's eyeball had to be removed after surgical efforts to repair the rupture had failed.

15. The Plaintiff had to undergo extensive reconstructive surgery to repair the fractures of the Orbit, Temple, and Zygomatic Arch.

16. These injuries, unlawfully inflicted by the Defendant, have resulted in the Plaintiff's loss of sight and permanent disfigurement, and to anxiety, mortification, depression, shame, and other grievous suffering in mind. The Plaintiff, a juvenile aged 16 years and 2 months at the time of this incident, can expect a lifetime of 73 years and 4 months according to data promulgated by the U.S. Census Bureau, wherefore these injuries can be assumed to have a duration of some 57 years and 2 months, working their insidious effects over nearly six decades.

17. These injuries also close to the Plaintiff many avenues of profit and pleasure, reducing in significant ways, for the remainder of his life, the scope and breadth of his activities, his professional opportunities, his lifetime earnings, his enjoyment of sport and athletics, his confidence, his self-esteem, and complicating and compounding the difficulties of innumerable daily tasks and duties so that his sense of competence and well-being shall be forever and profoundly impaired.

18. The Plaintiff seeks the award of damages in the amount of Five Hundred Thousand Dollars ($500,000) in compensation for present and contemplated medical expenses, including the expense for lifelong emotional counseling; Five Million Dollars ($5,000,000) in compensation for the mental suffering and lifelong loss of opportunity and enjoyment endured by the Plaintiff; and Two Million Dollars ($2,000,000) in punitive damages, assessed as a part of the judgment of the Defendant's brazenly unlawful behavior.

19. The Plaintiff therefore prays, for the relief of his pain in body and mind, for judgment in the total amount of Seven Million Five Hundred Thousand Dollars ($7,500,000).

RESPECTFULLY SUBMITTED,

Michael M. Paley
Marsh, Paley, Rothman, and Mitchell
818 17th Street N.W., Suite 799
Washington, D.C. 20036

JURY DEMAND:
The Plaintiff hereby demands a trial by a jury of six (6) as to all issues raised in the Complaint.

And that was it, the missive I had been anticipating and dreading. I felt, honestly, as though I'd been whacked in the head with a lead pipe, as though little lights were popping and exploding all around me. I didn't attempt to read, not then, the medical records that were attached to the complaint, though I did glance at the summons, a much-copied, tired-looking form stating that I had twenty days to file an answer to the complaint.

I think I must have been in a daze, but I was aware of the hush in the office. They were dying to know, of course. I went out to the reception area and I probably sounded demented when I announced, "He wants seven and a half million, folks. Seven point five million dollars, so we're going to have to pick up the pace. That's a lot of lawns to mow."

THE SUPERIOR COURT of the District of Columbia looks like something that Mussolini might have ordered over the telephone. It is unfathomably ugly, a squat and massive bunker of sooty concrete with columns of tinted windows that look, excuse me, like giant shit stains. On the morning of August 5th, 1998, as I waited for Ian Bricker in the plaza of the courthouse, I know that I saw that building through troubled eyes, but no one could mistake it for a temple of justice. It looks like a way station to the nearest penitentiary.

Yet the plaza with its empty concrete planters was thronged with people, the overflow and human spill of the courthouse. It was late morning when I got there, and the air was thick and hot and heavy with the fumes of summer, the stench of traffic and the cookout fragrance of the hot dogs and half-smokes wafting from the colorful vendors' carts and the bitter clouds of cigarette smoke trapped in the dead air above the maw of the building's entrance. Every busy courthouse must produce the same identifiable types—the cops in uniform, the rooster lawyers in their white shirts and yellow ties, the stricken-looking defendants in ill-fitting suits, the glum and serious and tight-lipped jurors, the loud-talking and used-to-it-all clerks, the bundled-up homeless muttering to themselves and intent upon whatever it is that keeps their souls attached to their ravaged bodies. Here in Washington these universal types come in a sprawl of styles and a global range of colors, and there were women in full African regalia and men in turbans and slick clerks with processed hair and young guys with dreadlocks or dew rags and Latino groups who stuck together like bunches of grapes and blond women in tailored suits and running shoes, and altogether such a shifting, dizzying, kaleidoscopic display of differences that you wonder—I did, anyway—how it is possible to bring people together in any kind of agreement at all.

Ian got out of his cab a few minutes before eleven, when the arraignment court came to order. He had on a dark summer suit, a white shirt, and a red tie, and he looked fresh and crisp despite the heat. We didn't have much time, but he went to one of the vendors' stands, bought a half-smoke, and gobbled it down before we went into the courthouse. "I have a weakness for these street dogs," he said. "It's the grease. You want one? My treat."

I would have gagged. On the way into the courthouse, standing in the line that formed at the metal detectors, he reminded me that I didn't have to say a word. He reassured me that the arraignment was a formality, a nonevent. The judge would read the charge, Ian would say I wasn't guilty—everybody pleads not guilty at an arraignment—the judge would set a trial date, and we'd be out of there. He didn't expect Briggs, the AUSA, to say much of anything. He tried to get me to laugh at the amount Vandenberg had asked for in his civil suit (I'd faxed him and Brian a copy), but I was too tight to be amused by anything.

He knew exactly where we were going—courtroom C10, down in the bowels of the building, a courtroom at the end of a maze of hallways, and I kept thinking, *This can't be happening. This can't be happening to me.* Somewhere I've read that, as dreaded events go, a jail term ranks with death and divorce, and I was afraid I would start shaking.

The courtroom looked like a chapel with its pewlike benches angled toward the pulpit of the magistrate. But it was not a pulpit; it was the judge's bench, a raised podium of blondish veneer behind which sat Judge Clarence A. Turner in his robes. He was black, bald, and bearded, and his bench loomed high above a curved counter of similar veneer where four clerks sat, only their heads visible. They reminded me of groundhogs peering out of their burrows. There were flags on either side of Judge Turner, an American flag and the red-and-white banner of the District of Columbia, and the quiet in the room was not a reverential hush but the result of industrial design, of the sound-deadening rubberized flooring, the acoustic tiles on the ceiling, and the multipaneled glass partition—bullet-proof, no doubt—that divided the room and separated the judge on his throne from those of us who waited. The six benches on either side of the room were arranged herringbone fashion, and they contained knots and clusters of people, lawyers and clients sitting together, sometimes flanked by a few supporters and sympathizers. The hard cases, the guys who arrived in handcuffs, were brought in through a side entrance and sat in a box with marshals in blue jumpsuits standing on either side.

Judge Turner and his main marshal, an enormous guy—also black and also bald, wearing a shiny green suit and a glistening gold vest with a matching tie—ran a tight courtroom, glowering at people who talked or failed to remove their hats, but I was surprised at the workaday atmosphere of the place, the comings and goings of what seemed like dozens of court officials, marshals and bailiffs and clerks, not to mention the lawyers and the prosecutor, John Briggs, the AUSA whose case files were spread out on a table behind the partition. He was short and clean-cut, probably in his early thirties, and his brown hair was neat and precisely combed. He had the build of a college wrestler and strutted about with his arms held out from his sides, barely glancing at the defendants who came forward as their cases were called, moving about with distaste and officiousness.

I could see that Ian was watching Briggs closely. They hadn't met, though they'd talked on the phone, and I knew that Briggs had dismissed the suggestion that there could be any plea bargaining in my case. I was trying to understand what was going on in that room, but the sounds were so muted and muffled that I had to strain to hear what was being said as the defendants stood before the judge, and I was surprised when Ian elbowed me and nodded at a man who'd sat down on the far side of the courtroom.

"Vandenberg," he whispered.

Vandenberg. The skin pulled tight across my shoulders. By then I'd seen pictures of Richard Vandenberg in the file that Ian and Brian had put together, and I recognized him, but there was no way I could have been prepared for the look I saw. Vandenberg's face was shiny with sunburn and his hair was gray, but in truth I hardly saw the man. I *felt* him. I don't know how it is that people radiate emotions, but I felt the hatred coming off him like heat off a griddle.

I couldn't meet his look. My nerves did strange, fluttering things. Vandenberg. He was brick-faced and overweight, and we were in a courtroom full of bailiffs and marshals, but I half expected him to leap from his seat and attack me.

"Guess he couldn't wait to meet you," Ian said.

He whispered, but that big marshal paced to the barrier and glared at us.

Vandenberg. For weeks I'd been dreading this moment, trying to convince myself that I wasn't afraid of him or of this whole legal process, that no matter what I had done, I could be certain that I had never meant to harm his son. I wouldn't let myself think that I was *guilty*, not in a legal sense, or that I really could end up behind bars. For weeks I'd been carrying on with my normal activities, a free man, and this moment had seemed not only far-off but unreal—but here it was. Here I was in a courtroom, and there was Richard Vandenberg, and all the fear I had been trying to stave off settled in my bones. I already felt like a prisoner.

"In the matter of the United States versus William Tucker Jones, case number M63719. Is there a William Jones present?"

I didn't recognize my own name until Ian nudged me and stood up.

We walked forward. Briggs also came to the bench. From what seemed a great distance, I heard the judge announce that I was charged with simple assault and Ian say that I was not guilty. I was aware of Vandenberg's eyes on me. I was grateful for Ian's smooth, sonorous voice.

The judge opened the case file—he was seeing it for the first time—and Briggs spoke up. He sounded pained as he said that in the opinion of the United States Attorney, this case had been mishandled from the start. The report of the investigating officer had been filed within hours of the crime, and it was woefully incomplete. The officer had spoken to two witnesses and to me, the accused, and filed a report that treated the incident as a backyard scuffle. "This was no scuffle," Briggs said. "If the officer had waited long enough to get the medical report, he would have realized that this is a serious felony. The victim of this attack, a juvenile, was attacked with a shovel. He had his eye put out."

Judge Turner glanced down at Briggs. At me.

"I have nothing here but the original report," he said.

"We have the medical records," Briggs said. With a jerk of his head toward Ian, he added, "Counsel is aware that we're going to take this case to the grand jury to get an indictment for assault with a deadly weapon. At this time, Your Honor, we respectfully request that the court set bail at a hundred thousand dollars."

Beside me Ian flinched.

In his pained, droning voice, Briggs said, "This case has been treated as if nothing of consequence happened, but the victim suffered severe injuries. He was in surgery for five hours while they tried to save his eye, and he's had to have extensive reconstructive surgery—and this is a sixteen-year-old we're talking about. There's no way this is simple assault. We feel that the bond should reflect the gravity of the offense that has been committed."

"That's an unusually large sum," the judge said. Then, to Ian: "Is there any reason why the court shouldn't set bond?"

Ian was smiling—a puzzled smile, and he spoke to the judge as though he was trying very hard to understand how Briggs could think that such a bond was reasonable. "Mr. Jones isn't going anywhere. He was released on his own recognizance a month ago and here he is today, in court. He has roots here in the District. He's a single parent and both his children go to school here. He runs a business that employs fifty people. He's not going to run off and put fifty people out of work."

"No need to editorialize," the judge said. "This is not an employment agency."

"Sorry, Your Honor. I'd simply like to add that, as you can see from the file, Mr. Jones has no criminal record. He's here today and he'll be here on whatever trial date is set. He wants to keep his record clear. If there was ever a situation where bond was requested purely for its nuisance value, this seems to be it."

Briggs's head swiveled around at that, though Ian's tone and manner hadn't changed at all. The judge's face showed nothing. He said to Briggs, "You say you have medical records?"

"Yes, we do."

Judge Turner closed the file and handed it down to one of the clerks. "I'm not going to ask the defendant to post bond. Mr. Briggs, I have no reason to doubt a word you say, but in the future it would be helpful, if you want this court to regard a case in a different light, to present the additional evidence you want us to consider."

"We'll present this evidence when we take the case to the grand jury," Briggs said.

"I understand that," the judge said, "but this is not the grand jury. This is the humble court of arraignment."

Briggs was fuming, I could see, as Judge Turner looked at his calendar and set a date for a trial and a status report. He told me in a boilerplate voice, delivering a warning that he had delivered thousands of times, that I was being released without bail and that if I failed to appear for my court date, the bench would issue a warrant for my arrest.

And that was it. There was no banging of a gavel to signal that the arraignment was over, and Ian had to nudge me again. I had the absurd impulse to thank the judge before I turned away.

Ian stopped where we'd been sitting to pick up his briefcase, and when we left the courtroom, when we entered the hallway, we were face-to-face with Richard Vandenberg.

"You turd," he said to me, and he was a big man with the kind of deep voice that seems to rise up from the bowels. He leaned so close that I thought he was going to spit. His mouth was working in a pursed, puckering way.

"Turd," he repeated, as though he had thought long and hard to come up with exactly the right word to describe me.

To Ian he said, backing away and drawing himself up to his full height, "Don't expect to plead this case. Don't even think about it. This turd is going to be put away."

"Have we met?" Ian asked in a tone that could have been mistaken as genuinely polite and collegial. "I'm Ian Bricker, of Crocker, Collinsworth, and deSantis."

He held out his hand but Vandenberg wasn't going to shake. He turned his back on us, and as he departed in a crushing, clump-footed walk, Ian said, "What a command of language. I guess that's why he makes the big bucks."

Outside the courthouse, we talked for a few minutes about Briggs and Vandenberg—one young, pint sized, and arrogant, the other middle aged, supersized, and arrogant—before Ian caught a cab and I took the Metro back uptown to Friendship Heights Station, where I'd parked the Jimmy. I didn't check my messages until I walked out of the Metro stop. In addition to the usual calls from clients and vendors and the office, there were two messages from Lily, phoning from the Adirondacks. *Where are you?* she demanded in both of them. The calls had been placed that morning, only twenty minutes apart, and her voice was full of urgency and distress. I returned her call immediately, and I was standing on a shady residential street when her sister-in-law picked up.

"Lily's already on her way back to Washington," she told me. "They all are. Her father died."

REAR ADMIRAL (ret.) Robert Sherwood Hastings was buried with full military honors in Arlington National Cemetery on August 7th, 1998.

Lily's father was eighty-one years old, a certified hero of World War II, a recipient of the Distinguished Flying Cross, a former captain of the USS *Farragut*, an aircraft carrier, and a bluff, vigorous, unregenerate old warrior who thought the country was going to hell in a handbasket. He died unexpectedly on his boat, a fifty-six-foot shrimp trawler that he had converted into a comfortable, seaworthy vessel and docked at a marina in Jacksonville, Florida. He was married to Elena, the handsome, capable woman in her late fifties who owned the marina and had enough backbone to stand up to him.

I went to the funeral, of course. I had met the Admiral on his visits to Washington, and even though he was a relic, though he was full of prejudice and pigheaded opinions, though his hands trembled and he'd had a couple of skin cancers removed from his face, leaving his skin mottled and his nose as misshapen as a boxer's, the old man had never lost his authority. I had tried, and tried again when I heard of his death, to imagine what he must have felt as a young pilot on his first combat mission over the Pacific, watching the Japanese fleet come into view at Midway. As he streaked through the sky over the vast stretch of blue water, as the dark specks upon the sea began to take the shape of destroyers and battleships and carriers, the enemy's fleet, the might of a nation, as he saw the Japanese planes, the Zeroes, catapulted into the sky to join in the battle, he must have had his moment of truth. He had to know that he could die that day. He had to realize that he was one of those who can look straight at death, without terror. I'd never heard the Admiral talk about Midway, but he'd told Lily that it was the great day of his life, the pivotal day, the day that marked him forever.

He'd been given his part in history, and as I stood at the grave site on that humid, drenching summer afternoon, in the hush of the National Cemetery, my mind reeled with the effort to grasp the essence of a life so different from my own. For sure the Admiral had earned his place here where the white grave markers stitched across the low hills, this land that had belonged to the Lee family until it was confiscated to use as the burial ground for the Union soldiers who died by the thousands in the makeshift hospitals in Washington, just across the Potomac. This place was imbued with grief.

Those of us at the grave site—there were probably a hundred people, mostly friends of Lily's, with a sprinkling of far-flung relatives and old friends of the Admiral—stirred and straightened when the caisson came into view. It emerged like an apparition from a line of trees. The caisson was drawn by a gray horse and the coffin was covered with a flag. Lily walked directly behind it, Lily in black, with a scarf of black lace covering her hair, Lily flanked on one side by her brother Rick and on the other by Elena. Rick was gray and heavy and looked old enough to be Lily's father; he was the brother who'd done too many drugs. Lily's other brother, her oldest brother, Bobby, had become a navy pilot and died in a mission over Vietnam. The other Moorefields, Tony and the three children, walked in a line just behind Lily.

The afternoon was utterly silent except for the fall of the horse's hooves and the creaking of wheels and harness. The procession was stark and solemn and the mourners at graveside, in the shade of a pavilion tent, stood as one when the caisson appeared and moved slowly, slowly until it neared the open grave and stopped. The honor guard stepped forward, and the young sailors in their blinding whites lifted the coffin, carried it to the grave, and placed it carefully on the straps that spanned the opening into the earth. When the honor guard stood aside, Lily and the other followers took their places at the foot of the coffin, in the sunlight. I saw Tony touch her shoulder in a gesture of comfort, but she did not need or want it and she stood away from him. She was the Admiral's daughter and this was not the time to falter. It was a time for pride. From where I stood among the mourners, I saw how staunchly Lily and Elena held themselves, straight and erect, and how Rick fidgeted and rolled his neck as though his collar was too tight. A navy chaplain spoke for a few minutes, but I cannot remember what he said, for when he was finished, he stood aside and the sailors at the bottom of the slope—they'd been standing at parade rest—fired the cannons in a final salute to the Admiral so that the air shook and filled with the blue smoke and smell of gunpowder.

Then the jets flew over. I hadn't expected this—hadn't been prepared for any of it, really—and I cannot tell you why a formation of three jets, flying at low altitude through a hazy, humid sky, seeming to shake the earth with their thunderous roar, expressed the majesty and solemnity of this man's death, but they did. When the shadow of the lead plane swept directly over the casket and the open grave, flicked over it, I had to catch my breath, so strong was the sensation that this was a chariot swinging low, as in the gospel song, coming to carry him home, and that his soul had been skimmed away to be set free in the great reaches of the sky. I was awestruck and proud that I had known the Admiral. Lily stepped forward as soon as the jets passed and stood alone at her father's coffin.

She stood there by herself when the six young sailors of the honor guard took hold of the edges of the flag and snapped it off—snapped it, with a pop. They folded it into a tight, precise triangle, and the officer took it from them, spun, and presented it to Lily. He saluted. We all heard Lily say in her clear, bold voice, "Thank you," and she remained where she stood, all alone, while the bugler played taps.

Day is done. Gone the sun. The mournful notes lingered in the air, the coffin was lowered into the earth, and the ceremony was over, but no one moved until Lily turned and faced us, clutching the Stars and

Stripes against her black dress, her gaze moving over us as if she wanted to make sure that we all understood who she was.

AFTER THE funeral there was a reception at the Moorefields' house, and Lily—her scarf removed, her smile now in place—stood at the door with Elena to greet the guests. She was animated. She was radiant. She kissed me, she kissed everyone that day, and asked me to make sure to sign the register. "Daddy liked you so much," she said. "He never stopped talking about that tennis match you played, god, years ago."

I remembered it, too, a doubles match against Tony and Jay back when we all still lived in Georgetown. The Admiral must have been a terrific player in his day, and he was still spry, but he was at least seventy years old at the time of that match and we shouldn't have had a chance against Tony and Jay. Somehow we got a few games ahead, and they started to press, and the old man took me aside to say he wanted to win. "OK," I said. "No," he said, "I don't think you understand. We are not going to let them win. This is important." He was holding on to my arm, squeezing it hard, and looking straight into my eyes and he was dead serious. I understood that this was an order. The Admiral was still giving commands. For the rest of the match, I flew all over the court and the Admiral returned everything he could reach, and we won two sets in a row in one of the damnedest displays of the will to win that I had ever witnessed. The Admiral simply was not going to lose. He shook my hand and growled, "Way to go, partner." He didn't let me—or Tony—forget that match, and whenever I saw him after that, he'd always greet me as *partner*.

I signed the register and then went into the living room and looked for a time at the photographs Lily had put out, not in any particularly organized way, but there were enough of them to tell her father's story. She must have spent hours pulling this exhibition together, selecting the grainy photos from old scrapbooks. There he was—the Admiral as a boy in short pants; as an ensign leading his bride through a tunnel of officers with raised sabers; as a young lieutenant on a flight deck, leaning against his Hellcat; as a father with his two young sons standing at the wheel of a sailboat; as a dashing captain in dress whites, dancing with his wife; as a fisherman standing beside a monster bill-fish; as an admiral shaking hands with JFK; as a rugged old goat with a spark in his eye as he married Elena, his younger wife; as a weather-beaten skipper on his converted trawler, holding up the Norwich terrier he doted on. There must have been twenty photos, all of them enlarged and placed in simple Lucite frames, standing on the tables and the piano, sharing the space with the wreathes and bouquets that filled the house with color and the green fragrance of cut flowers. Elena had brought the Admiral's medals up from Florida, and they were displayed in their shadow boxes, alongside the triangulated flag.

"Tony!" said a tiny white-haired man with arthritic hands and watery eyes. He turned out to be Willy Western, the Admiral's oldest buddy, known in the family as Wild Uncle Willy, a combat ace who'd shot down six Zeroes. I expected him to be a giant but he barely came up to my nose. With his bad eyes he had mistaken me for Tony, and we are roughly the same size and shape, though it's pretty hard to confuse us, Tony with his dark hair and me with my head of gray. "I can't see a goddamn thing anymore," Willy said when I corrected him, and his voice was still strong even if the rest of him was failing.

"I've heard of you," I said. "Wild Uncle Willy."

"What?" He leaned close to hear.

"Wild Uncle Willy."

"Oh, yeah, yeah," he said. "Who are you again?"

"Just a friend of Lily's. But I knew the Admiral."

"You fly?" he asked.

"No."

"Bobby was the best damn pilot you ever saw," he said.

Tony came up to us and threw his arm over Willy's shoulders—"Great that you could come, Willy, great to have you here"—and urged us to get another drink. It's what the Admiral would have wanted, he said, no long faces. "Didn't that just blow you away when the jets flew over? The old man would have loved that. Hell, he would have brought them in at fifty feet just to shake everybody up."

Tony does not permit anyone to mope. He is an ebullient, energetic host, and he steered Uncle Willy away so that other guests could make a fuss over him. It was still midafternoon, an odd time of day for any reception, and it was too hot, even inside, for anyone to feel festive. A few waiters in white jackets were moving around to keep the glasses filled, and there was a big spread on the table in the dining room. I hadn't intended to stay for long, but I had a surprising conversation with Abby—she came right up to me as though there'd never been any problem between us. She had on a black skirt and a white sleeveless blouse that buttoned at the throat and she kept tucking her hair back when she said that she wished Kat had been able to make it. "She told you about that day, didn't she, the day we went out on the boat with Grandy"—her name for her grandfather—"and he made us bring it into the marina? I thought he was like kidding, but we were at the wheel and he just sat there. That boat is *huge*."

I remembered. The girls couldn't have been older than ten or eleven when they went down to Florida for a spring break, and I understood that Abby was trying to repair the damage between us as she told her story. She was full of darting looks (it struck me again that afternoon, after seeing all the pictures of the Admiral as a young man, that both Lily and Abby resembled him with their broad cheekbones and wide-spaced blue eyes), and she was flirtatious in the involuntary way of a teenage girl talking to an older man, flirtatious because her instinct to please was so tied to an awareness of her physical appeal. She was in constant motion—hands in the hair, fleeting smiles, stray laughs—as she acted out how it felt to be at the bridge as an eleven-year-old, easing the throttle down, peering over the wheel to maneuver the giant boat in the close quarters of the harbor. "We were totally wigging," Abby said, "totally."

She told me she was really glad that Kat was going to stay in D.C., and then I found myself talking to Rick, the brother who'd flown in from California. He was toasted by the time we spoke, a round-faced man with long, lank gray hair. He was the brother who'd gone on a drug spree and now lived in Los Angeles, where he owned a kennel/dog-grooming establishment called Doggie Style. From Lily I knew that he'd been estranged from his father for years, and he told me that he almost hadn't come. "I thought it might help put some of this shit to rest," he said, "and maybe it did. I don't know. I can't get stuff out of my mind. Like the sharks. Here's a pretty picture for you—the

Admiral and his family on vacation, on a cruise, a fucking pleasure cruise, nice big stinkpot gliding along with a couple of half-dead sharks dragging along in the wake. He'd troll for them everywhere. He saw one of his buddies try to bring in a plane that was all shot up, but he couldn't land it, so he ditched. He ditched and the sharks were all over him in a flash. My father saw it from the flight deck, and that's when he decided to do his own *Jaws* thing. Whenever he was in shark waters, he trolled with a wire rig and hooks as big as horseshoes, and when he caught a shark, he'd drag it in the wake till it drowned. There was just one other little feature to this whole routine, the sea urchins. He'd dump sea urchins in the water so the sharks would stuff themselves—it was like feeding them nails. 'they wouldn't give us a break,' he said, 'so they don't get any breaks.' He was not your every-day dad."

After that conversation I was ready to leave, but when I tried to say good-bye to Lily, she put a hand on my arm. "No, stay. I haven't made my toast. My eulogy, or whatever it is. I need all the support I can get. You can't leave."

Soon she was tapping on a wineglass to get our attention, and when that didn't bring everyone into the living room, she gave a loud, piercing imitation of a ship's whistle. She was standing at her piano at the front of the living room, and her hair was loose and a little unruly as she thanked everyone for coming, singling out those who'd come the farthest.

Then she paused and gathered herself.

"I'm petrified," she said, "even though I know that you're all family and friends of Daddy's. After that ceremony I'm afraid that anything I say can only take away from this day. So I hope you'll forgive me if what I say is just personal. I hope you'll forgive me," she said, looking up, seeming to speak to her absent father.

"I have the strongest sense he's still here," she said as people crowded into the living room and the hallway, settling down, listening. "I can't believe he's gone."

She gave off a small helpless laugh, still trying to settle herself down, unsure where to rest her eyes until she finally fixed them on her children.

"This is hard," she said. "I didn't think it would be so hard. I've had so many thoughts and memories the last few days, but the one I want to tell you about goes back to my childhood, way back. I must have been about six or seven, and it's one of my first memories of my father. I think it's the day I realized who he was, and what he was to me.

"He'd been at sea on the *Farragut*. I don't know how long he'd been gone—forever, it seemed, and we'd been counting the days till he returned. My mother told me that we'd go down to the harbor to see him return, and I remember getting all dressed up with Momma— she put on her hat and white gloves, and I had a new dress and a brand new pair of patent leather shoes.

"She must have told me that there'd be a ceremony, but I wasn't prepared for the spectacle of it—the band and flags and the crowd. The return of the fleet. Everything seemed so immense that day. I don't think I'd ever seen the *Farragut* before, and I couldn't believe how huge it was as it came into the harbor. To me it looked like a whole city coming toward us, with the planes and the entire crew out on the flight deck, four thousand sailors in formation. The officers were standing in front of them in their whites, and out in front of them all, standing by himself—there was my father.

"Every little girl thinks her father is a great man, and when I saw Daddy standing there—I thought he was the greatest man in the whole wide world. Momma had told me that we were going aboard, and my heart was in my throat while they secured the ship and positioned the gangplank. It seemed to take forever, but they finally piped us aboard. 'the captain's daughter is now boarding—ten-hup!' I was so excited I let go of Momma's hand and ran up the gangplank, and when I got to the flight deck and saw all those thousands of sailors . . . klutzy Lily, I fell. Those slippery new shoes. Four thousand sailors saw my panties. My father scooped me up. This great man just scooped me up and held me in his arms. He said, 'Don't worry, sweetheart. Daddy's got you.'

"I felt so safe. I felt rescued. When I thought of Daddy, when I thought of what I wanted to say today, I realized that that's what he gave me, that feeling of safety. All my life I've believed that if I fell, my father would be there to catch me."

Lily struggled a little with those last sentences, but she wasn't going to let herself break down. She took a breath and looked directly, searchingly, at her children as she said, "Maybe that's the most important thing a parent can give."

Then to the rest of us she said, "I know all the navy people here know 'Eternal Father.' Please join in. Abby, you and Sophy come up here. Elena, stand beside me."

Without accompaniment, with her arm slipped through Elena's, she began to sing. Even though I could tell that she was holding back, her voice easily filled the room, with the girls' quieter, less confident voices amplifying the words of the hymn.

> *Eternal father, strong to save,*
> *Whose arm hath bound the restless wave,*
> *Who bidd'st the mighty ocean deep*
> *Its own appointed limits keep;*

Then several voices joined in for the refrain:

> *Oh, hear us when we cry to Thee*
> *For those in peril on the sea!*

The next verse was about guarding the men who fly, and Uncle Willy stepped forward and sang with the women in a cracked voice:

> *Be with them always in the air,*
> *In darkening storms or sunlight fair;*
> *Oh, hear us when we lift our prayer*
> *For those in peril in the air.*

Beside me stood Rick Hastings, who sang with tears running down his cheeks.

Two DAYS after the funeral, on a Sunday morning, Lily called me at the Hut and said, "If we're really friends, you're going to play tennis with me this afternoon. Singles."

"I thought we were friends."

"Real friends," she said, and a small self-conscious laugh tumbled out when she said, "I feel like opening a can of whoop-ass."

Whoop-ass? That is not the kind of thing Lily says. She was just
wound tight, I suppose, pent up after all the stresses and emotions of
the funeral, and she was completely amped when we met at the St.
Albans courts late that afternoon. She kissed me on the cheek, then
did a foot-flashing Ali shuffle and punched me on the shoulder. "You
call yourself Tucker but you're mine, you sucker," she said. Where did
that come from? She was bursting out of her skin, and on the way out
to the court she positively bounced, her thick ponytail bobbing with
its own life. Lily has always had enormous physical vitality, a dancer's
spring and energy, and she has never stopped taking dancing classes of
one kind or another, and that day, when we reached our court, she put
one foot up on the top of the net as though it were the barre in a studio and stretched her torso upon it. A standard dancer's exercise, I
know, but as a warm-up exercise on a tennis court it was exotic and eye
popping. People on the adjacent courts turned to look, and Lily, with
her face on her knee, grinned up at me and said, "Let's see you do *this*,
Mr. Jones."

She took all that stirred-up energy onto the court with her on that
late summer afternoon. Lily has always played tennis as if the point
was not simply to hit the ball between the lines but to do so with style
and exuberance. When she awaits a serve, for instance, she doesn't just
shift her weight from one foot to another. She gets into it. She rocks
her shoulders and moves her whole body to a music that only she
hears, and she plays the game with a leaping, swirling, bounding,
slightly over-the-top balletic fluidity which, that Sunday, was accompanied by all sorts of looks and gestures—a triumphant narrowing of
the eyes when she won a point, sticking her tongue out at me if I won
one—that amounted to a complete performance. I can't say exactly
what she was acting out, but I watched her with fascination, wondering what she'd do next, what movements she'd find to give expression
to the feelings of grief and deliverance that possessed her that day.

We played three sets of tennis—three and a half, to be exact, since
the last set ended when we could no longer see the ball. We were the
last ones on the courts, both of us giddy by then, and we made a darkness rule that the ball had to be lobbed on every shot, hit high enough
to rise against the sky. Otherwise it was impossible to see it, and I

remember watching Lily in that twilight, flitting around in her whites like a ghost, hearing the *thwock* of the ball, laughing as though we were just a couple of kids, just playing, unwilling to call it a day and go home, squeezing every drop of joy out of those last sweet moments of light. Of course Lily had feigned hurt feelings when I kept winning (she is a good player, having been groomed to play doubles with the Admiral, but she can't beat me and she knows it, and the whole question of our playing singles is loaded with history, going back to our Georgetown days when Lily and I first started playing singles and also played as a mixed-doubles team, since Trish wasn't a strong enough player and Tony wouldn't play mixed doubles for the same reason that he refused to play singles with his wife, namely, that there was no point in playing if you had to hold back), but we played into the darkness and when we finally called an end to it, we shook hands across the net and Lily pushed her racket against my chest and said, "You rat. You owe me dinner."

"For what?"

"For snatching victory from me."

And so, since it was already late, we went back to Lily's house and showered. We were going to eat at one of the bistros down on Connecticut Avenue and it would have taken awhile for me to go back to clean up at the Hut. Lily's house sitter was there, a clean-cut young man, a college student who was interning that summer in Tony's office. He was staying at the Moorefields' for the month of August, but everyone else—everyone who'd come for the funeral—was already gone. Tony and the children had flown back up to the Adirondacks, and the last of the out-of-town guests had left that morning. Lily had stayed behind in Washington to see everyone off and because she wasn't ready to go back to Tupper, not just yet. She wanted a day or two to herself. A day or two to be a Hastings, she said, before she went back to Club Moorefield. Having been to Tupper, I knew the scene and the pace of the place, the nonstop activity and the scads of kids that had to be fed and the complete lack of privacy. Nevertheless, there was a bite to Lily's voice when she said *Club Moorefield,* and though it wasn't the first time I had showered at her house, in the bathroom off the guest room, I have to say that with the young house sitter looking dubious, I felt a kind of impropriety about being there, particularly when I put on the clean clothes Lily laid out for me. They were Tony's clothes, his shirt and pants. He's a little taller than I am and a little leaner, but the pants fit at the waist since I'd lost weight after July 13th. I couldn't bring myself to wear his boxers. The house sitter said sternly that he was going to a late movie with friends but he'd be back at midnight.

"Our chaperone," Lily laughed. "He doesn't realize he's dealing with the original Miss Goody Two-Shoes." We were at Greenwood, in a booth, and she hadn't had time to dry her hair or put on any makeup. She was still brimming with that manic energy when she ordered a drink called a stinger. "He's dealing with Daddy's girl," she said, "but tonight Daddy's girl is going to have Daddy's drink. Do you think I've been *too* good? Is that why I can't understand my daughter?"

"What's a stinger?"

"It was one of Daddy's favorite drinks, brandy and white crème de menthe. I knew how to make them by the time I was ten. It was just one of the many ways I amused the Admiral and his cronies. You know, I did my tap dance routines"—she tapped her fingers on the table—"and mixed them all drinks. Stingers. I was the perfect daughter. You know that, Tucker. I've told you all those stories."

It was true that I'd known Lily long enough to have absorbed by hearsay much of her childhood, and I sometimes felt that I had known her as a child. I knew, for instance, that the theme song of her childhood was "Happy Talk," a ditty from *South Pacific*, which of course was regarded as the ultimate work of genius in her naval household, the one musical of which her father wholeheartedly approved. As we sat in the booth and waited for our stingers, Lily sang those pidgin words the way she once sang them, and though she mugged like a child, she has such a wonderful voice that she can't help giving any song, even a ditty, a sparkle and flourish. *Happy talk, keep talking happy talk, / Talk about things you like to do, / You got to have a dream, if you don't have a dream, / How you gonna have a dream come true?*

Her past was pouring through her that night, and I had never heard her stories quite the way I heard them as we dined on lobster and stingers, and it had never been so clear to me how much unhappiness she tried to overcome, how aware she'd been of her role as the family talisman. She was not only the baby of the family but the Baby Oops, fifteen years younger than her oldest brother, Bobby, the brother who followed in the Admiral's footsteps and became a navy pilot, the brother who was killed in 1969 on a mission over Vietnam. The Admiral was hard on both the boys—he woke them up in the morning as though they were on a ship at sea, bellowing, "Drop your cocks and grab your socks"—but he doted on Lily, who even knew that she had been conceived in Hawaii after a fancy luau. The Admiral joked that she'd turned out as a dancer because he was still thinking of those hula girls.

Both her parents were drinkers, perhaps alcoholics, though they belonged to a generation and a class that would have scoffed at the idea. Booze was one of the givens of their way of life, and the cocktail hour was its central ceremony. "Sun's over the yardarm" meant that the bottles came out, and the Filipino houseboys with their white gloves and silver trays showed up with the martinis—unless the Admiral wanted to see his little girl with the tray. That night, sitting across from me in the booth, Lily leaned back and recited the names of drinks as though they were magical incantations. "Martini," she said mystically, "sidecar. Manhattan. Whiskey sour—that's always pronounced *withkey thour*, as though you've just bitten into a lemon. Scotch and soda, mud in your eye. Hickory dickory daiquiri, the mouse has left the factory. Stinger. I can't remember what they said about stingers. They taste like mouthwash, but I don't feel a thing. Do you?"

She was buzzed. I can't say when she got there, since she started on such a high, but she didn't have any intention of slowing down. She was ripping. Lily is a social drinker and I'd seen her tipsy, but this was different. I was feeling the stingers, too, and just listening to Lily. Her childhood came back to her in the names of the drinks and in all the songs she'd learned, all the routines she'd rehearsed on naval bases all over the world, the Baby Oops who felt she had to be happy to lighten the gloom of the household, who had to perform to keep her parents from quarreling, the child who had to entertain to keep the anger away. She could remember her mother walking the halls at night and crying, just crying, and sometimes Lily heard her say, "Aye, aye, Captain," and she later realized that this was what her mother said during sex. "Oh god," Lily laughed, "can you imagine? 'Aye, aye, Captain'"— she put some passion into her voice, and then tried out the words as they might sound at orgasm —*Aye, aye, oh god, aye, aye, Captain, aye, aye, yes, Captain, aye, oh, aye, aye, YES!*

The waitress looked at her strangely, and who could blame her? The restaurant was almost empty by then, and Lily obviously didn't care, and didn't even notice, that anyone was paying attention to her. I didn't care, either, though a voice in my head did remind me from time to time that I had better stay sober enough to make sure that we got home that night. "I'm not sure Momma ever had an orgasm," Lily said. "She must have, don't you think? She had her secrets. I think she should have told me, but no. We did not talk about sex in the Admiral's house. Did I tell you I was a virgin when I went to New York? My daddy would have done the same thing you did if he got that phone call, except he probably would have killed the boys. So I was *good.* You should have seen me when I arrived in the Big Apple, ready for Broadway. I had my Tally-Ho sweaters and Villager skirts and three pairs of Pappagallos—three. My favorites were the blue ones, the ones with the little red lines and the little red bow. Abso-fucking-lutely classic."

Lily was laughing so hard that she had to keep running her fingertips under her eyelashes to flick away the tears. To remember herself as a twenty-year-old virgin in 1977, the Admiral's daughter who could do all of Shirley Temple's tap dance routines and thought she was ready for Broadway after her experience in musicals on naval bases, filled her with wild hilarity. She hadn't finished college ("if you could call Mount Vernon a college—it was a finishing school") but her mother had died. In Washington, as it happened, when her father was on a tour of duty at the Pentagon, his final tour. Helen Hastings died of uterine cancer, but that was the doctor's explanation, Lily said. She believed that her mother never got over Bobby's death and died of a broken heart. They lived in Alexandria and Lily took care of her mother, grooming her because she still wanted to look good for the Admiral even though she could hardly stand to be in the same room with him, or maybe she wanted to look good just for herself—anyway, that's what Lily did for six months; she did her momma's nails and hair; she bought her lingerie; she did her makeup. "That's when she told me," Lily said. "It was right at the end. About 'aye, aye, Captain,' I mean. She told me and we'd laugh about it when Daddy would come in and start to order her around, you know, like, 'Why aren't you eating what you're supposed to, why are you still drinking'—I made her martinis—and she'd say, 'Aye, aye, Captain.' And he knew, too. He knew I knew and he'd get red in the face. She was dying but she wasn't supposed to question his authority and god knows she wasn't supposed to make fun of him. Aye, aye, Captain. I made the martinis because she was so miserable, but you know what? That might have been the happiest I ever saw her. God, we laughed all the time. *She* laughed about how ridiculous she looked, all wasted away—she had every kind of wicked chemo. I did that, too, took her for the chemo and radiation. Took her to the wig store. I remember once I got her a black nightie, all sheer, and then I made her up and she looked in the mirror and couldn't stop laughing. She had this black wig on and she said, 'I'm Morticia,' and she was a dead ringer for Morticia."

Lily flicked at her tears. "Trust me, it was funny. But goddamn it I can't forgive my dad—I just can't. Every time I think of him, I think of Bobby, and I think of Rick, and I think of Momma, and he made every one of them miserable. Well, not Bobby. I don't think he was miserable. He was mad to fly... You know the first conversation I had when I got to New York? I lived in that hotel, the Dormer House, the young women's residence hotel. Daddy thought it would be all prim and proper. What a joke. The first night I was there, I got into a conversation with a girl from Texas who told me she was going to a group to get help with her orgasms. I felt sophisticated just to know what an orgasm was, and she was going to this group where they talked about it and the leader told them to use their hand mirrors and check out all the parts of their body and talk to them. 'What do you say?' I asked her. 'Ah jest look down there at my nubbin and say, *You don't know how great you are.*'"

This set her off again, and when the busboy came to clear away our plates, Lily said, "Aye, aye, Captain."

It was time to go. Past time, I suppose, and Lily mock-begged to have at least one more stinger. The chef in her white hat came up to our table and told us that it was time to leave. We were the last ones there, and I probably shouldn't have driven, but I did. I drove to Lily's house and walked her up the steps and she said, "You want to come in for a nightcap?"

Then she kissed me. The porch was dark—the house sitter had forgotten to turn on the porch light—and she put her arms around me and kissed me. She leaned back against the wall and drew me to her and cocked one leg up behind my legs and I responded to her kiss. I was wearing her husband's pants and I was aroused, and Lily felt it and, still standing on one leg, moved so that my erection was centered on her belly and whispered, "I just want to get comfortable."

I can't say what would have happened if we'd been able to get into the house. We tried, but the house sitter had locked the place and Lily, of course, didn't have a key. She thought one was hidden under one of the flowerpots, and we looked for a while, fumbling around until we finally found a key in one of those fake stones. Then we unlocked the door and set off a burglar alarm that was wake-the-dead loud.

Lily couldn't remember the code to turn it off. The siren went through cycle after deafening cycle, and my head was vibrating as I stood there trying to get her to remember and punching in the numbers she came up with. Lily didn't seem to mind the noise. She kept laughing at everything, even when a police car with lights flashing pulled up in front of the house.

Ellis, the officer who'd arrested me, came up the walk. What are the chances of that? I don't know, but it was Ellis. He recognized me, of course. "What's happening here?" he said. "This not your house, is it?"

"It's my house," Lily said. "It's my house but I don't know the numbers. I never turn the alarm on."

Ellis wanted to know her name.

She told him, and he asked for a picture ID. This, too, struck her as hilarious, and she kept saying, "Do I look like a burglar? Is that what you think? I look like a burglar?"

Ellis looked at me, a look I understood to mean that I had better do something quick to get this alarm turned off and put this woman to bed.

So, using Lily's cell phone, I called Tony up in the Adirondacks and got the code from him. It was Lily's birthday, as it turned out, and as soon as I punched it in, the siren went silent.

In the quiet Ellis looked at me, then at Lily, and shook his head. "You need to watch yourself," he said as he left.

The cell phone rang—Tony. I answered and he wanted to know what was going on. Lily took the phone away from me and said, "Hey, Tone, how is everybody? We almost got arrested. I have been *bad*. Stingers."

Then she handed the phone back to me. "It's always best to tell the truth," she said.

I got back on the phone and told Tony that his wife had overtrained. "She's a stem-winder," he said.

I helped Lily up the stairs. She grinned at me when she stood outside her door. She saluted and said, "Aye, aye, Captain," and for all I know, she went into her room and passed out laughing.

THE NEXT morning I awoke with a heavy head, a queasy stomach, and a mouth that felt as though a small rodent had gone there to die. It had been years since I'd had such a grisly hangover, and I cringed, as one does, remembering the reckless elations of the night before. My body retained the impression of Lily arranging herself against me, the sense of being enfolded with the light pressure of her touch on the back of my neck and her leg cocked behind mine. In the teasing echo of her voice—*I just want to get comfortable*—I seemed to understand the ease and sweet humor of her desire. The strongest memory, though, the one that clung to me like a dream I could not escape, was of the way she had lifted herself, standing on a single foot, rising on tiptoe so that her belly was pressed against me and she could take the full measure of my erection.

In all the years I had known Lily, and despite all the looks and touches that I had seen her exchange with Tony, I had never really imagined what kind of sexual companion she would be. I'd never attempted to. I cannot say that Lily had never figured in furtive, fleeting fantasies, but she was a friend's wife, absolutely off-limits, and I could no more indulge in a secret longing for her than I could for Abby.

Taboos are real, and in any case my own sexual fantasies seem to come to me mostly as memories, afterimages that remain hidden away like genies until the lamp is stroked and *abracadabra!* they emerge with all their power and magic.

I see what I have written, and I assure you that it is not my intention to compare my penis to a magic lamp. I will say, however, when I awoke that morning with a stiffy and saw Tony's pants on the floor near my bed, I groaned with lust and remorse and an awareness of the disorder that seemed ready to swallow me up.

If I'd had a hair shirt, I would have worn it to work that Monday morning, for I did get out of bed and go to work, and I was at my desk when Lily called me.

"I feel as though I should be in jail this morning," she said.

"We almost were," I said.

"What got into us?"

"Stingers," I said.

"At least I understand my father a little better now," she said. "Anyone who drinks stingers is going to undergo a personality change. Was I terrible?"

"You did have a personality change," I said.

She groaned. "You have to promise me you're going to forget *everything.* Was Tony mad? He sounded mad when I talked to him."

"I couldn't tell. He said you were a stem-winder."

"He did? A stem-winder? That's what he usually calls Abby. God, I feel like a criminal."

We both wanted, obviously, to get things back on a normal footing and to treat the desire that had arced between us as an aberration. "I don't trust myself to be alone," Lily said after she'd told me that she'd decided not to stay in Washington but to return to Tupper that afternoon. "And, besides, this is the month of getting to know Abby. I think these have been the strangest days of my life."

We talked a little then about our daughters, finding safety in the conversation that had linked us for years. She was glad that Kat had decided to go to Tandem, Lily told me, and she apologized for being so preoccupied these last few days that she'd hardly even asked about Kat. It had been such a strange, topsy-turvy time. "Nothing feels settled," she said. "Nothing feels permanent anymore. Maybe I'm just stunned to wake up every morning as an orphan. If you can call yourself an orphan at forty-one. I thought Daddy was immortal."

She sounded weepy but I could hear her trying to pull herself together. "I shouldn't have said all those things about him last night. I shouldn't have *thought* them. Promise me: you're going to forget *everything*."

I promised again, but of course the particulars of that night, the details of what was said and done and felt, were unforgettable, and for days I found myself sifting through them as I tried to shake off the sense that something was happening to me, something I couldn't control, something that stirred up emotions and desires that I hardly knew existed within me. I tried to forget, but I found myself wondering about Lily, and about Kat, too, and remembering how she'd said that maybe she wanted to get drunk. When she was at the Vandenbergs' putting down those vodka shots the way Lily and I put down the stingers, did she feel a growing exhilaration as each degree of restraint slipped away, imagining that her recklessness was leading to the discovery of something marvelous?

Here I should say that I'd had my own drinking experience, the standard experience that began in high school in Norfolk (beer) and took a quantum leap when I joined a fraternity at the University of Virginia (lethal punches) and settled into a groove when I moved to Washington as young single guy (Jay and I had an elaborate menu of drinks to suit many occasions, but our favorite was the black velvet, Guinness and champagne). It never occurred to me not to drink, for my father was a heavy boozer and my mother, in her pre-yoga days, could put down the martinis. I wasn't raised, as kids are today, with constant warnings about the dangers of drink. For those who went to college when I did, in the 1970s, alcohol was one of the milder, more conventional ways to get fucked up. There were plenty of other substances around, and the freewheeling consumption of those days did not feel jolly and innocent but went hand in hand with the national mood of disillusionment in the post-Nixon, post-Vietnam years, and I will say only that I tried most things that came my way and leave it at that. We were not saints, not the crowd that I knew.

Drink and sex. The chemistry is ancient, dangerous, and well documented, and I have the kind of story that just about everyone I ran with in those days, men and women both, could tell, the story of My Mistake. You go out, you meet someone, you have too much to drink, you wake up the next morning and see your clothes on the floor and try to remember how you ended up in the sack with a woman whose last name you have forgotten and couldn't pronounce anyway because it was Polish, a woman whose high-pitched, screeching laugh was what made you notice her in the first place. It cut right through the noise of the St. Patrick's Day party in the big brownstone on R Street, a run-down mansion not far from Dupont Circle that was occupied by a group of hell-raisers. Their parties were notorious meat markets. They always managed to get the word out all over D.C., attracting not just the usual uptown party crowd—a large loose-knit group of twenty-somethings like Jay and me, people who'd had our tickets punched by the right colleges and law schools, who had good jobs and expected to move ever onward and upward, though we were not in any great hurry to do so, not until our wild oats were sown, every last one of them—but all sorts of marginal characters, including young women who'd just arrived in town to take lousy government jobs and lived in cheap apartments out in Arlington.

I am speaking, of course, of Miriam. She was a secretary at the State Department, a GS-8, and she was twenty-six years old. She was from Chicago and she hadn't gone to college but to business school, which did not mean, to her, getting an MBA but learning stenography and typing. Her father was an elevator inspector and her mother was a semiprofessional hairstylist who did her friends' hair in her own house. She had one brother whose elevator, she said, didn't go to the top floor. He was a few years older than she was, still lived at home, went to every Cubs game, and did all the shopping and cooking for the family. I mention these things because they are almost the only things I know about Miriam, who talked about her brother not in a mean-spirited way but to let me know why she'd been so eager to leave home.

She had to yell to make herself heard over the din of the party, and she kept laughing—kept screeching—as though it was funny to have a slow brother whose pride was his pickles, the vats of pickles he made according to his secret recipe. Her laugh sounded forced, or at least unnatural, but Miriam had been drinking the green punch that was heavily spiked with grain alcohol. She was looped. Everything about her was wrong—wrong clothes (a shiny green party dress with a big bow just under her breasts), wrong accent (tough-gal Chicago), wrong hair (dark hair in a standard George Washington perm)—but none of that mattered. She was giving off the signals of availability, and I had just broken up with my on-again, off-again girlfriend for much of that period, Jenny Draper. I laughed hard at Miriam's jokes. I drank my share of green punch. For Miriam the party was an excursion into a world of glamorous debauchery that until then she'd only imagined; she'd come at the suggestion of a young foreign service officer who was there and had already hit on her, and even though Miriam screeched when she told me about him, I could tell that he'd made her feel cheap. "Hey," she said, "he oughtta know, you don't hump the help." She had nerved herself up to drive into the city alone and go to a party where she was virtually anonymous, and despite all her brashness and drunkenness, I understood how vulnerable she felt as she offered herself to me. She was afraid her offer would be rejected.

We walked back to my place, the place I shared with Jay. She started telling me about the friend who'd dared her to come to the party and just pick up some guy, the friend who was going to come with her but crapped out at the last minute. After we'd thrown off our clothes, Miriam took her pocketbook into the bathroom and stayed there so long I thought she might be sick. She wasn't, but she had a different look, a sad and chastened look, when she came back to the bed and told me that she hadn't had sex with anyone since she came to Washington, and I remember how she closed her eyes and bit her lip when I entered her. I could feel how much she wanted to respond, to express excitement, but she couldn't. Then she got a little teary and apologized—for the tears, for being such a putz, for everything. But she didn't leave. She'd come this far and she wasn't going home. We lay in the bed and snuggled for a while, and the next time we made love, I heard a different version of her high-pitched screech, this one ferocious and not forced, and after that it was Katy bar the door.

We had a couple of weeks of wild sex and take-out food. And booze. Miriam really wasn't a drinker, but she liked to have a bottle of vodka handy (the national beverage of Poland, she said). I wanted the vodka, too, for this wasn't my kind of affair. I suppose it was what in those days was called sport fucking. Miriam and I certainly had no future, and we both knew it. I was already wondering how I'd break it off when she told me that she was pregnant. It was a gorgeous May evening and we were sitting outside in the garden of a Georgetown saloon. She'd shredded her cocktail napkin to bits, but she always did that, and she laughed like a loon when she told me about taking the bunny test. One of my first thoughts, god forgive me, was that she wanted me to marry her, but she said quickly that she would take care of it. She'd already made an appointment at an abortion clinic.

"It was my fault," she said. "I was so drunk and nervous that first night I couldn't get my diaphragm to go in right. I mean, I had it, and I tried to put it in, but I kept crashing around in your bathroom— didn't you hear me? Anyway, I couldn't get it in and I figured it was probably because I'd shrunk down there for lack of use. And I never thought I'd get in trouble after such a long layoff."

She reached across the table and squeezed my hand, the only time she'd ever done anything like that in public. "We had great sex, didn't we? I mean, I think you have to, to get pregnant."

It seemed important to her to believe that. She went through with the abortion, and she didn't want me to accompany her, though she did let me pay for it and she allowed me to visit her that afternoon at her apartment in Arlington. The building was a midrise and the linoleum hallways smelled of laundry and ammonia and loneliness. I'd never been there before, and I will never forget how Miriam Kryszynsky, wearing pink jammies, opened the metal door of her apartment and kissed me. When I gave her the bouquet of white tulips I'd brought, she lowered her face to inhale the scent of the flowers and to conceal her tear-streaked eyes. Her apartment was on the fourth floor, and through the open window, we could hear kids playing basketball on the court below. She didn't have a single picture on her walls, but there was a crucifix in the tiny entryway where we'd kissed. She sniffled a little as we sat on her sofa. "It wasn't all that bad," she kept saying in her tough-gal Chicago accent so that *wasn't* came out as *wudden* and *bad* came out as *bed*, and when she saw that I was getting misty eyed, she got up and went into her galley kitchen, determined to find something to cheer us both up. "All right, here, you gotta try these," she said, taking a jar out of the fridge. "This is a new batch, but mature, you know, like the wine. We will sell no pickle before its time. OK, open up. You are about to have your first honest-to-god Polish dill."

She fed me one of her brother's pickles and cackled away. I left that apartment with a jar of the pickles and I did not see Miriam again, not for many years. We talked on the phone a couple of times, then months passed before she called to say that she had taken an overseas assignment, and she has been out of the country almost continuously since then. She has never married. Every couple of years when she comes through Washington, she phones to catch up on my news and fill me in on hers. We never, never make any reference to the child who was not born.

That is the secret I have never told anyone, and after my night out with Lily, I took it as a warning, and it also reminded me of why I'd been drawn to Trish, whom I met not long after Miriam. Insofar as I understand how these matters work, I believe that I fell for Trish because she seemed smart and purposeful and most of all disciplined, and I knew that my own crazy days had to come to an end. I chose a wife who seemed to have the very qualities I lacked. She was attractive and sexy enough, but she seemed to be the last person in the world to let desire get the best of her. Ha.

In any case, I tried to forget everything, as Lily had ordered me. I was ready for a vacation. I couldn't wait to get out of town.

MONTANA. Will and I flew to Great Falls in mid-August, and the high moment of the trip is captured in one of the best photographs I ever took, a shot of Will catching his giant brown trout. He's standing on the alder-lined bank of the Busthead River, a big, booming piece of water, and he looks absolutely transfixed as Jimi, our fishing guide, lifts that trout out of the foam-flecked water. The trout is so big that its boxy tail sticks out over the rim of the net, and the net's long, telescoping handle is bowed with its weight. Will is holding his rod tip high, and he's dressed like an updated, miniaturized version of the Compleat Angler, western edition, in his hip boots, many-pocketed vest, quick-drying fishing shirt (which he had to have after seeing Jimi's), and cowboy hat. In this late-in-the-day photograph, some trick of the light or the film makes both Will and Jimi seem lit with special clarity and brightness, like the subjects in Renaissance paintings who have been singled out to receive heavenly messages. They have a glow, at any rate, and Will's expression—his lips parted, his dark eyes brimming—has elements of wonder, triumph, and humility. He can't believe the size of that trout. He can't believe he caught it.

He is thrilled, but the trip didn't start that way. Will and I had been making these western trips, our boys-only August trips, since he was nine, and at the end of the summer, after Will's long stay with his mother on Long Island, it usually took a few days for us to readjust to each other. He likes the long, lazy days at the beach and the club, and I know that he gets a big kick out of all the luxuries and doodads that are a part of daily life up there. When he got home, his conversation was studded with references to Trish and Ray's fleet of cars (a yellow Kompressor convertible, a Mercedes 420S, a BMW 740i, a Toyota Land Cruiser fitted out with a couple of TVs and something called the Warner Brothers package, and the Ferrari that Ray liked to tool around in at night when there was no one else on the road), and he also had a lot to say about the entertainment center with its sixty-five-inch screen, the Bose sound system throughout the house, the broadband Internet access for the new flat-screen computers, and so on and so forth. He is up on technology and a master at video games. These games are his fairy tales, I suppose, and he seems to identify with the apparently helpless and clueless heroes who, confronted with impossible tasks, somehow find the right keys and open all the right doors, overcome all the obstacles and elude the fearsome monsters, and after many hair-raising and death-defying adventures secure the treasure, rescue the princess, take possession of the castle, and live happily ever after.

In his comments about his mother's house, I heard a put-down of the humble Hut, and in the few days that Will spent in Washington before we left for Montana, I often heard an edge in his voice that hadn't been there before. His droll, deadpan manner was now streaked with impatience. He'd shot up a couple of inches, though he was still no beanstalk, and he had to work to achieve an effect of awkward gangliness. Will has always been neatly proportioned and effortlessly agile, but now he slouched when he sat and shambled when he walked, dragging his untied shoes (he groaned if I reminded him to tie them) along the ground as though they weighed fifty pounds each. He kept experimenting with his voice, trying to drop it into the lower registers. He had his first pimples and he spent a lot of time in front of the mirror, picking at his spots or adjusting his Nike visor to precisely the right angle, all the while rattling his retainer against his teeth. He complained that all his friends were on vacation and spent hours lost in the alternate universe of GameBoy and PlayStation.

Will had hit puberty, and though I wanted to respect his new needs for independence and privacy, I couldn't make myself like the new attitude. We played tennis once so that he could show me the improvements in his game after weeks of lessons, and he had improved, but he made sneering comments about the surface of the St. Albans courts— way too soft, in his opinion—and actually expected to beat me. He sulked when he didn't win a game. Maybe I should have let him take a few, but I don't think fathers should just roll over for their kids.

Will was discouraged that night, and when we got back to the Hut, while we waited for a pizza delivery, he sat at the computer in the alcove, trying to locate a few buddies, griping that everyone was on vacation. I tried to talk to him. I didn't want to repeat the mistakes I'd made with Kat and let him drift too far.

But I didn't know how to start. I sat in the wing chair and made a couple of aimless remarks. I complimented him on his ground strokes, but he didn't turn around and the air seemed to have thinned as though he understood that I was leading up to a conversation he didn't want to have. I hadn't rehearsed it, and I finally said, straight out, "Things don't seem to be going so great. Can we talk for a few minutes?"

"About what?" He kept clicking away, eyes on the computer screen.

"About what's going on with you. About biological changes."

What a clunky way to put it. Will waited a beat, lifted his hand from the mouse, and turned slowly to face me. "You mean the extra head I'm growing? I didn't think you'd noticed."

He was so cool, so self-contained. I wish I'd been able to laugh, but he seemed to be putting me down, and I said, "You know what I mean. You're a teenager now. Your body's changing. We should talk about it."

"We talked about it in school," Will said, "about two years ago. About the *biological changes.*"

He was determined to keep me at a distance, and he sat there on the swivel chair, jiggling his knee and wearing an expression of blank boredom. No matter what he'd learned at school, I told him, he couldn't be prepared for all the confusion that was a part of growing up. Of maturing sexually, I said, and Will rolled his eyes. "Everybody makes mistakes," I said.

"Yeah, like Kat," he muttered.

"Kat did make a mistake," I said. "We all make mistakes. Your mother said she'd talked to you about Kat."

"So has everybody else."

"What do you mean, everybody? You mean your friends talk about her?"

"Dad, everybody knows about it. It's not a secret."

"I hope you stand up for her," I said. "I hope you don't let people bad-mouth her."

"I didn't say they bad-mouth her."

"What do they say?"

"They know what happened, that's all."

I didn't believe him. He spoke with such uncharacteristic defensiveness that I thought he'd probably heard plenty of cracks about his sister, maybe even made some himself. I said, "A lot of people think they know what happened. I don't want to hear you making remarks about your sister."

"I didn't, OK?"

"Have you talked to her? Have you supported her?"

"Is this all about Kat?" Will said. "Just because she screwed up doesn't mean everybody does. It doesn't mean I'm going to."

"What would you have done at that party?" I asked him. "Suppose you saw a girl getting drunk."

"I don't drink. I don't go to parties where people drink."

"You will, soon. Kat didn't go to those parties a year ago."

"So you want to lock me up?"

"Don't be flip. I'm asking you to think about it because something will happen. Something will happen and you'll need to know where you stand. You can't make it up as you go."

"I'll think for myself, OK? Rule number two. I got it, Dad. Check."

Romeo sniffed then and stood up—he'd detected the arrival of the pizza before the doorbell rang. Will said, with a thuglike finality he must have seen on TV, "Are we done here?"

We were. It has always been one of my failings as a parent that I let these matters drop, but we had days ahead of us in Montana, and I thought we could complete this conversation at a time when both of us were in a better frame of mind.

Didn't happen. We spent the first few days of the trip touring, following the Lewis and Clark Trail above Great Falls, but Will did his best to ignore everything I said. He was unable to conceal his disdain for the car I had rented, a Taurus. At night in our shared motel room, he watched TV and guarded his privacy.

By then our western trips had acquired a pattern: a few days of touring, followed by a longer stay at a dude ranch chosen not for its scenic beauty but for its fishing. When we made the first trip, to Colorado, we were both fascinated by fly-fishing and it turned out that Will had a precocious gift for it. He's always had excellent hand-eye skills (I like to think he gets them from me), and it took him no time at all to learn how to handle a fly rod, to cast a long, accurate line and drop a fly on the water as softly as a snowflake. Because he was so small, and because he insisted on the right gear—the vest, the hat, the polarized sunglasses—he was a bit of a curiosity, and other fishermen would stop to watch the little dude at work, carving out precise portions of the big sky with his tight casts. He wasn't all show, either. He concentrated in the same rapt way that he concentrated on his video games, he caught plenty of trout, and he had a kid's sense of the importance of numbers, keeping track of how many fish he'd landed and exulting when his tally was higher than mine.

That summer, at the Copper Kettle Ranch on the Busthead, once

Will met Jimi, he forgot about numbers and concentrated on size. "The Busthead is a big fish river," Jimi said the first day he took us out, "and we are gonna catch some of those big old uncle daddies." Right from the start Will was under Jimi's spell, and I could see why—Jimi not only had the gravelly, nicotine-enriched drawl and leathery, lived-in face of a cowboy but he also had the gift of self-dramatization. He smoked Marlboros and stroked the handlebars of his mustache and carried a sawed-off shotgun in his saddle holster ("the grizzlies run from it, but tell you the god's truth, I'm more worried about the painters"), and after the first day on the river, when Jimi hauled in one of the aforementioned uncle daddies—a glistening brown trout that weighted five pounds eleven ounces on Jimi's brass pocket scale (any fish over five pounds qualified as an uncle daddy)—every other sentence that came out of Will's mouth began with the words *Jimi says*. In that part of Montana, not far from Yellowstone, I don't think that there were many grizzlies or painters—panthers, to us city slickers—but Jimi liked to ratchet up the sense of danger. At Jimi's suggestion, Will traded in his visor for a sweat-stained cowboy hat and fished almost exclusively with dry flies. I hadn't intended to hire a guide for the entire week that we were at the Copper Kettle, but Jimi managed to convince Will—and me, too, since I was glad to see Will coming out of his sulk—that we should make our stay into a quest for those big old uncle daddies, the famous brown trout of the Busthead.

Every day we'd ride out, just the three of us, to parts of the river accessible only by horseback. We needed a guide to find our way to the fishable stretches of water, and Jimi didn't mind reminding us that without him we'd be up shit creek. Will laughed at all his raunchy, corny jokes, and Jimi gladly took Will under his wing. From a guide's point of view, it had to be a stroke of good fortune to spend a week with a kid who not only had some talent with a fly rod—with most dudes, Jimi told us, he spent his time getting the lines untangled—but who also worshiped him. Once we'd tethered the horses, I'd wander off to fish by myself, not too far from Will and Jimi, and I'd watch the two of them plotting out their plan of attack, Jimi wreathed in a cloud of cigarette smoke, Will hanging on his every word.

Then I caught an uncle daddy. Dumb luck. I was fishing a deep stretch of water with a bead-headed nymph and a big sculpin, a fly that looked like a small skunk. The sculpin wasn't a fly at all, Jimi had said scornfully when he saw me tie it on, but everyone else fishing the Busthead used them. "I'm not saying you won't catch fish with that thing," Jimi said, "but it ain't but one step up from the garden fly." The garden fly was a worm. After that I was bound and determined to use the sculpin, even though it was so heavy that I had to lob it in a high arc, and it splashed into the current like a cannonball. The virtue of the sculpin was that it was heavy enough to get down to the bottom of the Busthead, and it had been bouncing along the rocks when I felt it stop and twitched the rod, not wanting to get snagged.

A trout was on—a big one, I knew at once from the bend it put in my rod. I did have the presence of mind not to try to stop it on its first run, and I played it well enough to get a couple of grudging compliments from Jimi, who'd come upstream to coach me and stand by with his folding net. Will also came to watch, and I could see how crestfallen he was when Jimi slipped the hook of his pocket scales through the brownie's gills and announced that he weighed five pounds three ounces. An uncle daddy. "You caught him on a sculpin," Will said dismissively, and turned his back on me, walking downstream where I could see the furious energy he put into his casting.

The blowup came that night. When the twenty or so guests at the Copper Kettle gathered in the main house for dinner, in a room with the heads of elk and buffalo looking down from the walls, the owner of the place announced that I'd caught a big fish and rattled on about the brownies in the five-pound-plus category. There were other groups of fishermen staying there, including a fellow from Dallas with his two sons, young men in their twenties who needled Will about having to bear down now. He wasn't going to let me catch the biggest fish, was he? He had to show me who was chief. "He caught it on a sculpin," Will said, as though I hadn't played fair. Later, I heard him tell one of the girls from Louisville—the whole family was staying there, the parents and three daughters, the oldest one about Will's age—about all the fun stuff at his mother's house on Long Island. I tried not to listen, but I heard him say, "Yeah, I live with my dad now, but I don't know. I might like to live with my mom."

When we went back to our cabin after dinner, I called him on it. I asked him if he'd talked to Trish about living with her.

"No," he said. He'd just switched on the TV and he was channel surfing. "There's never anything to watch out here."

"Why don't you turn it off? We should talk about this."

"About what?"

"About what you said."

"What that I said?" His eyes were glued to the TV.

"That you might like to live with your mom."

No answer.

"Turn the TV off."

He did and glared at the dark screen.

"Is that the way you feel? Tell me what's on your mind."

"Nothing."

"Come on, Will. Let's put this behind us. We're going to have to talk about this sooner or later. This stuff doesn't just go away."

He finally looked at me, his eyes coal black and bitter. He has rarely shown as much emotion as he showed then. "How come Kat gets to choose and I don't?"

I hesitated long enough to make myself reply quietly. "Because she's older. That was always in the agreement I made with your mother. When you're sixteen, you can decide for yourself."

"She's not sixteen."

"She's older than you are."

"A year older," he said.

"A year and a half older."

"Big difference," he muttered.

"Will," I said, "you know what happened. It's been a rough summer for everybody, but especially for Kat. She made a mistake. It seemed like the right time to reevaluate."

"Yeah, a big mistake. It's like the only thing anybody can think about."

"Hey," I said, wanting to tone down his anger. "She's your sister. If it's hard on anybody, it's hard on Kat."

"She's always the one," Will said.

"What does that mean?"

"It's always about Kat."

"Not now it isn't," I said. "Right now she's a couple thousand miles away. I want to know about you, Will. Something's not right, and I want to know what it is. I've never seen you so angry at Kat."

"It's not just Kat."

"What is it, then?"

"You," he said.

You. The word tumbled out in his boy-man voice, and the retainer clacked against his teeth.

"What do you know about me?" I asked.

"Everything."

"All right, tell me," I said. "Are you angry? Embarrassed?"

"Just because you smashed some guy in the head with a shovel? That's totally normal, Dad, totally."

The sarcasm was as fierce as he could make it. "Hold on," I said. "Just hold on here. I don't know what you know, what you think you know, but you have to get this straight: I never hit Jed with the shovel."

He watched me skeptically.

"I didn't. I don't know what you've heard, but you have to understand that I didn't hit him. He fell when he tried to hit me, OK? I had the shovel but I held it up like this"—I made a blocking gesture— "and one of the other kids pushed me. I went forward, and Jed slipped and fell against the table. I just bumped into him. I did not hit him. That's the way it happened."

"Why were you even there?" Will said, and I could hear the disappointment in his voice, the disappointment and the hope that I could answer his question.

"I went there to get Kat," I said. "I wanted to help her."

"Yeah, you really helped," Will said.

"I'm sorry about it," I said. "I made a mistake, a huge mistake. I wish I could tell you how sorry I am."

"Everybody makes mistakes," he said with his smart-aleck sarcasm.

"Except you, right? You're way too smart to make a mistake," I said.

What a look we exchanged then. I didn't say another word, didn't trust myself to, but went outside into the night, shaking. How could it come to this? Shouting at my son, who was ashamed of me. Stars filled the sky, stars that I don't notice in Washington, but out there in Montana they were real stars, bright and fierce, not just pinpricks competing with the street lamps. The eternal silence of infinite spaces. My son was a hundred feet away, and I cannot describe how small and stupid I felt when I saw the light go out in our cabin.

I went back inside and stood for a moment, trying to let my eyes adjust to the darkness, breathing in the smell of wood and wool, trying to make out the shape of Will in his bunk, trying to hear him. I called his name.

No answer.

"Will?"

No answer. Moving more by feel than sight, I crossed the space to his bunk. I could just make out the shape of his dark head on the pillow, and I sat down beside him. I put my hand on his shoulder. "You're my life," I said, "you and Kat."

He stirred a little, and I could make out the shine of his eyes.

"I didn't realize how hard everything's been for you. I just didn't realize."

He made a sniffling noise and said in his deepest voice, "It's OK, Dad."

I don't kiss Will often but I leaned over and kissed him then, on his hair. I said, "There are six billion people on the planet but I have only one son."

He turned his face to look up at me. "This is getting a little weird," he said.

I recognized a familiar tone, though, and knew he'd let me get as close as he could. Over the next few days, after I'd switched to a dry fly, we fished as a team, in a friendly rivalry, trading off on the first cast at rising fish. Jimi was openly rooting for Will, who was easily more skilled and stylish than I was with a fly rod. He landed plenty of two- and three-pounders, but there was no more talk of an uncle daddy. Our time on the Busthead was running out, and Jimi seemed to have run out of secret holes where the uncle daddies lurked.

Then, late on our next-to-last day on the Busthead, there was a big rise under the alders, a rise that sent bulging ripples across the surface of the river. "Whoa," said Jimi, "that is one bad boy over there." The fish was in an eddy at the tail of a pool, a place where the current reversed itself to circle back upstream. The water was deep and dark and foam flecked, and Will talked to Jimi for several minutes about how to put the fly over the fish. They were both standing in the river, watching the trout feed. "You're not gonna have but one chance with that old man," Jimi said, "so you got to make it count."

Will did. He edged out into the current as far as he dared, and then leaned out still farther, stretching his casting arm across the front of his body so that he had the best possible angle to cast back toward the undercut bank. Somehow, from that awkward position, he managed to cast the line so that he dropped a perfect half-loop in the faster water and the fly could drift naturally, without drag, on the slower backward current where the big fish was feeding.

Gulp. The jolt goes right up your spine when a big fish takes a dry fly just as though—I'm quoting Jimi here—somebody popped a pair of battery cables on your tailbone.

"Never ever saw an uncle daddy tail-walk like that," Jimi said afterward, and it was amazing to see that fish—the size of it, the flash of it, the power of it—standing straight up on the water of the Busthead, skidding along on its tail as it tried to shake the hook. It did the tail walk seven times, Jimi claimed, before it settled down in the center of the river and fought from the deep. Will played the fish perfectly, with poise and restraint, walking slowly out of the river to gain the leverage of the bank, and when Jimi finally lifted that uncle daddy from the net and hoisted him on the scales, he weighed a whopping, glistening, majestic six pounds eleven ounces.

"You want to keep him?" Jimi asked Will. "Get this bad boy mounted and he'd look awesome on a wall back in Washington."

We'd been releasing all our trout, but regulations allowed a fisherman to keep one trophy fish.

"Nah," Will said. "I don't want to kill him."

I have another picture of Will holding his uncle daddy for the camera before he lowered him into the current, letting him swing with the gliding movement of the water, fanning his fins to stabilize himself. Then, flick! The brownie twitched his tail and he was gone.

I do not pretend to understand fully the magic of big fish or the emotions of my son, but I saw how happy he was at that moment, and how he gloried in the talk back at the ranch that night. Jimi ate with us, the only time he ate in the main dining room, and a bunch of us lingered late to listen to his fishing tales. I couldn't help liking the guy even if he was a brass band of bullshit, even though I understood that he was the first of many mentors that my son would have, and need, as he grew away from me and into manhood. On the flight back to Washington, after we'd gained altitude and he could see the whole sweep of the Rockies from his window seat on the plane, Will sat back and said, "I think that was our best trip so far. We're coming back to the Busthead, right?"

He added, "I'm gonna kick your butt again."

Then he leaned hard against my shoulder, gave me a big grin, and fired up his GameBoy.

6

On a late, lovely October afternoon, I was at a work site in Potomac, one of Washington's richest suburbs, standing on a slate patio behind an empty, almost-finished stone house, yet another hooha McMansion, looking out over the turf the crew had just finished putting down. Instant lawn! The irrigation system was sending up a fine spray, the darkness was gathering in the nearby woods, and there was a chill in the air, along with the fragrance of the grass and moist earth and the sharp pungency of the pine bark mulch that had been shaped into neat cones under the newly planted ornamentals, the dogwoods and Japanese maples that stood wired and staked at intervals in that green carpet. I was watching the bullbats slice through the air, listening to their keening, high-pitched calls, when a dark form sped toward me, passing so close overhead that I instinctively ducked. There was a sickening thump on the glass doors behind me, and when I turned around I saw a magnificent bird, a grouse, its wings outspread and its tail fanned open, the black ruff around its neck puffed up in display, resplendent as it tottered around and then lowered its head and sank down into itself, into death.

Romeo had heard the thump and arrived at the scene so swiftly that the bird's display could have been intended to signal its willingness to defend itself against this noisy dog, who seemed eager to take credit for the kill and made short, fearful, threatening dashes toward the grouse. I shoved him away with my foot—I don't think I'd ever done that before, disciplined him with my boot—and I was flooded with dismay when I felt the warm weight, the dead weight, of the bird in my hands. It was a large bird, as big as a football, and I could hardly believe that the life had gone so suddenly out of it. I wanted it to lift its head, fill its lungs with breath, and fly out of my hands. But it was dead, and I didn't know what to do except to take it to the edge of the woods, where I kicked aside a few leaves and made a shallow depression in the ground to bury it.

I couldn't get that bird out of my mind. The sound of its wings beating, the feeling of its dark speed as it passed over me, the rush and whistle of the air, the warm weight when I held it in my hands, the intricacy of its plumage, the absolute beauty of its coloration in patterns of black and gray and brown—in the landscape business, we often have to deal with dead critters of one kind or another, but I was shaken by that grouse, and I mentioned the incident to my head doctor, Joe Jarvis.

"The angel of death passes by," said Joe, a thickset, sleepy-looking man, probably close to sixty, who sees patients in the office—a sunporch, really—in his house in Wesley Heights. It's a nice house (either Joe or his wife must have money), and Twill takes care of the lawn and garden. I like the way Joe fusses about in his garden, the thoughtful way he *looks* at his plants, as though he is trying to divine their secrets. He has hundreds of species in his beds and is always planting new ones, and it is his wife, not Joe, who calls to schedule the maintenance visits and cleanups. Joe doesn't trust anyone else in the garden, and he is always standing fretfully by when the crews are at work, afraid that they will destroy some favorite specimen.

All summer I'd been thinking of going to talk to him, and when the kids started back to school in September, I finally asked for an appointment. He didn't seem at all surprised, perhaps because he'd noticed how I'd been sizing him up. Shrinks must see that all the time, people who are trying to decide whether or not to trust them. Joe hadn't heard a thing about Kat or Jed. He rubbed his own sleepy eyes when I told him about my headaches and insomnia, paused to think deep thoughts, then asked—he is a master of the pause—if I wanted sleeping pills. I almost laughed. To get myself into that room, to have that first conversation, I'd had to overcome all my inner resistance to asking for help, and he offered me sleeping pills? But I realized, even then, that his style was not simply laidback but calculated to make me articulate and admit the depth of my troubles. When he offered me pills, he waited for me to tell him why I'd really come.

I had to tell him that I was scared.

I was scared. I was talking to myself, I was obsessing about Richard Vandenberg, I was worried about Kat and Will, I was sick with guilt about Jed, I was afraid of what was going to happen in court. I told Joe Jarvis all this, told him that I was afraid I was falling apart, but I also found myself trying to describe the moments when that fall, the fall of 1998, seemed almost miraculous. Something had shifted inside me that evening when Kat and I had our dance, and that feeling of connection, that longing for connection, hadn't left me. I don't mean to give the impression that I was in some kind of heightened state of awareness, but some moments just lifted themselves right out of time. All would be familiar, even routine, and yet—this is what I tried to explain to Joe Jarvis—at unexpected moments, and for no predictable reason, something would strike me and I would feel stirrings of wonder.

Joe Jarvis said it was natural to take special notice when we are afraid of losing what we treasure, and for sure I was relieved to have my children at home again, under my roof. The most ordinary glimpses of them—of Kat taking her long strides as she slipped into the stream of other kids arriving at Tandem on a school-day morning, of Will looking for me on the sidelines after he'd made a good play in one of his soccer games, wanting to catch my eye—seemed extraordinary, and I would have the sense of them, the two of them, as worlds unto themselves, carrying about their hopes and fears and dreams. And the same sort of thing could happen elsewhere, with other people. I remember one day I happened to be at a site where the men were eating lunch in the shade, and a sly smile suddenly flew from one to another, and then all of us—four Latinos and I—broke into laughter without a word being spoken.

Maybe we were just intoxicated by the beauty of that fall. The Washington spring is famous for its cherry blossoms and its lush abundance, but I have always preferred the fiery brilliance of the fall and the succession of clear, still days when the beautiful light, October light, seems not so much to fall upon things as to light them from within, giving them a depth and richness of luster, a radiance, that they have at no other time of the year. That fall, in any case, I'd catch myself looking at the turning trees or at the deep sky as though I had never seen such things before. And when it came to music, I was still helplessly listening to Eva Cassidy (her CDs, as the kids often told me, were *seriously* overplayed at our house and in the car), and the songs we played at band practice seemed to be wired directly into my nervous system. After taking most of the summer off, the Make Believes were practicing again every Tuesday night, and the music sometimes struck me as it had years ago, when I first heard it, and every now and then, as we practiced, big emotions blew through me like high clouds sailing across the sky.

"What's going on with me?" I asked Joe. "Am I reverting back to adolescence? Am I one of these Peter Pans who wants to live on the planet of the Lost Boys?"

"Tinker Bell," Joe said, grinning. "If you believe in magic, clap your hands."

Wasn't I supposed to be the one who did the free-associating? But Joe's odd response set me off about the article I'd read on the popularity of middle-aged rock bands, the so-called Boomer Bands. The article made it out to be a nationwide trend, and as I sat there on the sunporch—Joe had filled it with plants, too, and he often gazed up toward the ceiling, where he had trained a vigorous ivy in a swirling green spiral—I ranted about David Crosby and Mick Jagger and the other rock icons who refused to hang it up, trying to draw some difference between a group of amateurs like the Make Believes and the stubborn old geezers who were no longer even shadows of themselves. "We know we're old," I said. "That's the point. That's what makes it fun. That's what makes it funny."

"Is it funny?" Joe asked. "Is that the point?"

I couldn't answer right away. There was a silence and Joe nodded. He didn't make me admit that I wanted to conceal how much the music meant to me. He asked, "Is there a particular song that keeps

going through your mind? That's often a good clue. I had a teacher
who used to say that it's the subconscious that hums the tunes. Of
course I don't know a thing about music."

The moment Joe asked it, I knew the song I'd have to mention,
and I didn't want to. I thought of lying to him.

"Take your time," he said.

"That's a direct hit," I said. "Look at me—I don't want to tell you
about this. About a song."

He nodded. Waited.

"It's just another love song," I said, "like practically every other
damn song in the world. It's like they always say. The sad songs are the
ones that keep the jukebox playing."

Joe furrowed his brow. He kept waiting.

"There's a song we're practicing, a Clapton song—it's been bug-
ging me for years, this song. There're a couple of lines I just can't get
out of my head. Jesus, this is embarrassing."

"What are they?"

"I hate feeling sorry for myself," I said.

"Do you?" Joe asked, and kept waiting.

"The song's called 'Running on Faith,' I told him, and hummed
the first bars. He shook his head to indicate that he didn't know it. So
I spoke the first words, *"Lately I've been running on faith, / What else can
a poor boy do...?"*

"'A poor boy.' Those are the lines that bother you?"

"No."

Joe rubbed his eyes. He has a round face and short blondish bangs,
and with his glasses on, he is a dead ringer for Elton John. The longer
I hesitated, the more embarrassed and vulnerable I felt, and I could
feel the thickening in my throat when I finally said, "There's a verse in
the middle of the song where he sings, *'Seems like by now / I'd find a love
who cares just for me.'"*

Joe took his glasses off and rubbed his eyes slowly. "If Eric Clapton isn't embarrassed to sing it, I wouldn't be embarrassed to feel it.
It's just loneliness."

Loneliness. He spoke offhandedly, but he might as well have struck
a gong. He seemed to have named my condition exactly, the state I'd

been in for years. Perhaps this had been obvious to everyone around me, but it hadn't been to me, not until that moment when I confessed to Joe, and I cannot describe how alien the idea was, how utterly opposed to the way that I usually thought of myself. I was El Jefe, the self-reliant one, the boss, not some lovelorn loser. For days, for weeks afterward, I found myself arguing with his diagnosis, but I knew that he was right. I knew that somehow this loneliness was linked to all my other fears and worries and premonitions and to my sense, that fall, of the terrible fragility of everything around me.

And to that grouse. My grouse conversation with Joe took place at a different session from the one I have just described, but in memory they are connected. I'd tried to laugh when he said the angel of death. It sounded so far-fetched. Joe had been listening to me carry on about the reading I'd done about grouse and their "crazy flight," a phenomenon that ornithologists couldn't explain. It seemed that the grouse, and especially the males, often grew disoriented with the coming of autumn, and they'd abandon their familiar territory and set out on mysterious journeys—crazy flights—that ended when they crashed into trees or houses. Or found new territory.

"I think the bird that flew over me saw the light through the house. He probably thought he could sail right through, right on out the other side."

"You identify with this bird," Joe said.

"I guess so," I said.

"With its search?" he asked. "Or with its death?"

When I didn't answer, he made one of the longest speeches he'd ever made. We all see symbols around us, he said, and try to interpret them, and I had found a symbol in this bird. "You are afraid of death," he said. "We all are, but I think you see yourself as particularly vulnerable right now—to death, I mean. To all the fears associated with death. You're feeling vulnerable because you are in your prime, or maybe I should say you're in full flight, just as that grouse was. You feel yourself speeding ahead, but you don't know where you're going, only that you want it to be someplace different from where you've been. You're looking for new territory and you know it's a dangerous journey—the grouse crashed and died. The most frightening thing about your situation is that your daughter has reminded you not only of your age but of what's missing in your life, and the fact that you don't know how to get it. Maybe you were so upset about Kat because you think she's like you. She wants love but doesn't know how to go about it, and of course you haven't been able to show her. But she has time, much more time than you have, to find the way. You feel an urgency about it that you've never felt before. You're afraid that you're in your own crazy flight. I think you are."

He glanced at the clock hidden among the spider plants and ivy, the signal that our session was over.

"That's it?" I said. I was suddenly pissed off. "You tell me I'm in crazy flight and show me the door?"

"You're not a grouse," he said.

"But I don't know where the fuck I'm going."

"Toward the light," Joe said.

"That's helpful."

"Be patient," he said. "It's always frightening to feel time the way you're feeling it now. Just remember that time is what gives the intensity to so many of the moments you tell me about. They're there for a second, and then they're gone. *Poof!* Gone, forever. Death is the mother of beauty, as they say. That's why I like to putter around in the garden, I think. Because everything keeps changing."

He got to his feet and smiled. "Time's up," he said.

ONCE AGAIN I have jumped ahead of the story in my attempt to describe the mood of that fall, and I've slighted the importance of the practical, daily adjustments that we were all trying to make as a new school year got under way. Kat was in the ninth grade that fall, Will in the eighth, and in our household there was definitely a feeling of change. Though we rarely mentioned the events of July 13th, it was understood that the legal uncertainties were still hanging over us, that we were perceived differently as a family, and that we had to make adjustments.

In Kat I sometimes saw a hopefulness, but most often a determination, as she shaped herself to the environment of a new school. She had a seriousness about her, and Will seemed to feel it, too, and they had mostly put their sibling rivalry aside. There was less teasing, though Will would occasionally ask Kat when she was going to dye her hair or get her nose ring—piercings were in fashion at Tandem, along with radical hairstyles—and she'd pretend to moisten the tip of her pinky and smooth down her eyebrows, her way of doing a dumb blond. I thought that Will now saw Kat as having crossed over some line, the line that divides innocence from experience, and he treated her as he treated me or any adult—that is, as one who inhabited an entirely different universe. Despite Will's own changes, despite his new status as a teenager, and despite the fact that he'd started going to dances and that girls were now calling him on the phone, Will still hadn't crossed the divide. He wouldn't admit it, but he got keyed up before the dances and the phone conversations often drove him straight to his PlayStation, where he could release his tensions by destroying the hordes of intergalactic invaders. A couple of times that fall, Will mentioned that his schoolmates had asked about me or Kat, and I'd tried to reassure him that I wouldn't be going to the slammer any time soon. Nevertheless, I noted that he didn't invite his friends to the Hut as often as he used to but, instead, spent a lot of time at their houses.

When I urged Kat to spend time with her friends, she always said she was too busy. She still kept up with Abby, mostly by phone, and she made one new Tandem friend, Jamie, a small, slight, chatty, wispy girl who lived nearby, used black nail polish and lipstick, and derived her personal style from the Woody Allen movies that she and Kat rented and watched on the weekends. Jamie seemed to amuse Kat, but neither of them was much interested in social activities involving boys. Now and then they'd mention a party, but on Saturday nights they were either at the Hut or at Jamie's house, watching Woody Allen. I didn't even ask about the movies' ratings. I wasn't about to deprive Kat of the one social event in her week because the movies might be too racy.

Jamie was quick and knowing, and, rightly or wrongly, I came to regard her wan disillusionment as the standard attitude at Tandem, where the school uniform seemed to be jeans and low-cut black Converse basketball shoes. The main school building was a retrofitted four-story former office building on Wisconsin Avenue, and the students clearly thought of themselves as city kids, urban and intellectual, way too smart and hip to get hung up on the usual teenage stuff. Many of them had a strong artistic bent—at the parents' meetings I'd heard about the talented artists and musicians and actors—and the politics at the school ran toward environmentalism and social activism, causes that appealed to Kat. The place wasn't cheap (Trish paid the kids' tuitions), but it was the only private school I'd ever seen where there wasn't a single whiff of money—no fancy offices or reception rooms, no parking lot where kids could show off their snazzy wheels.

Tandem didn't have a gym or any playing fields, though various aerobic, dance, and yoga classes were offered in the building still called the Giant, for it had housed the grocery store of that name before the school leased it and converted it into a performance space and art studio.

Frankly, the Tandem kids spooked me a little, and saddened me, too, for they seemed to have gone directly from childhood to a jaded world-weariness. They didn't strike me as problem kids, as Trish had thought, but simply as kids who already knew that they weren't mainstreamers. From the amount of time the school had spent informing new parents about its drug and alcohol policies (not zero tolerance but a program of counseling and rehabilitation), I gathered that Kat would be exposed to drugs and talked to her about them. This was a family conversation, with Will, and when I asked them if they knew what drugs looked like, if they'd ever seen marijuana, they glanced at each other with big eyes. Will said, "I saw some kids smoking, but they didn't inhale, I swear."

So he'd learned something from our president.

They both assured me that they'd never been tempted, and I believed them, even though that look that had passed between them reminded me, again, that I was way behind the curve. They knew so many things that I hadn't suspected, and that fall I realized that I had taken to watching them with a new concern and intensity. I didn't want them to catch me taking note, but sometimes I felt almost as though I was spying on them, on Kat in particular, for she was in such a big transition. She'd bought her black basketball shoes, and she did her hair differently, in a style that had long sweeps coming down like curtains on either side of her forehead, hiding most it, for she wanted to fit in at her new school. My daughter's struggle seemed as complicated and poignant as it had when she was just a little girl, and I'd watch to see how she was going to make her way, how she would organize and interpret it, how she'd find the looks and gestures and words that enabled her to take her place in the world as she found it.

Now she was in a different world and I thought that she was trying to reinvent herself. There was often a firmness in Kat, a resolution that revealed itself in her voice, her eyes, and even the way she walked and dressed and wore her hair, in those curtains or sometimes simply brushed out and pinned up in a no-nonsense, too-busy-to-bother high ponytail. She didn't try so hard to please, and she wanted to rid herself of the signs and traits of girlishness, to be accepted by her new schoolmates as someone to be reckoned with and respected. In her room she'd taken down the posters of Marilyn Monroe and Glacier National Park, replacing them with a Save the Rain Forest poster and a print of the Magritte painting of a man in a derby whose face is entirely hidden by a green apple, presumably the apple from the Tree of Knowledge. This surreal image, called *The Son of Man*, was right beside the calendar showing the women climbers, but Kat declined an invitation to go with some of the Rockrapids counselors on a weekend climbing trip to Seneca Rocks, a trip I'd heard about several times that summer. Abby was going, but—this came across as the kind of explanation that doesn't reveal the whole truth—Kat wanted to make sure that she got off to a good start at Tandem and she had too much to do to blow off a weekend on a climbing trip.

I know Kat discussed July 13th with her therapist, and most of the Tandem kids knew what had happened. "They feel sorry for me," she told me once, one of the few times she made any reference to that night. I think we were both trying hard to prove to ourselves, and to each other, that we could overcome the mistakes we'd made and keep moving forward. I sometimes helped Kat with her homework, and encouraged her in every way I could, and tried to keep alive the tenderness between us, but sometimes I could feel her shutting down. There were plenty of days when she just walled herself off from me, and I came to think of her as a kind of construction site, one of those sites protected by chain-link fence and sheets of plywood so that you only get a glimpse, through a crack, of what is going on inside. She was a woman under construction, or a soul under construction, and she wasn't ready to let anyone see how deep the excavation was or what shape the building was taking.

Maybe I should say that she wouldn't let *me* see. She had taken an instant liking to her therapist, Bonnie Weaver, and she always seemed to be talking with Gladys Ochoa, our housekeeper, who came to the Hut every weekday afternoon except Friday. There were afternoons when I'd come home and find the two of them together in the kitchen, and they'd glance as me as though I was an interloper. They'd always been close, as I have said, and Kat, growing up, had followed Gladys around the house for hours, chattering away in a mixture of English and Spanish. Now the two of them had become collaborators, for Kat had decided to do her first big school project on the Church of the Glorious Miracle. At Tandem all freshmen were required to partici- pate in a class called Our Town, where the major assignment was to learn about some local organization. Tandem is a school that encour- ages service, and most of the kids were doing their projects on soup kitchens or community centers, places where they could work as vol- unteers with the homeless or with disadvantaged kids, and prepare a report based on that experience.

Because of Gladys, Kat had decided to do her report on the Church of the Glorious Miracle. For years she'd been hearing about the church, and she knew that several of the men who worked for me also worshiped there (Gladys was married to Tomás, one of my best crew foremen). Now Gladys had introduced Kat to several other women, all church members, all of whom traveled from Silver Spring to do housework in our neighborhood. One day I'd came home to find half a dozen Hispanic women in the kitchen, being interviewed by Kat, who seemed flustered when I arrived, embarrassed by my pres- ence. I could tell that she was involved with Gladys and these women in a way that mattered to her, but that night, when I asked her about the project, she was monosyllabic. She wasn't ready to let me in on it.

She wasn't ready to talk about Bonnie Weaver, either, and I didn't pry. I knew Kat didn't like to talk about anything until she was good and ready, and I also knew that she regarded her sessions with Bonnie as absolutely private. She who never complained about her mother had griped that Trish kept asking her about Bonnie, and I wasn't going to make the same mistake. Trish attached great importance to therapy and was well informed about it, and she had flown down to Washington the week after Labor Day to accompany me to an initial meeting with Bonnie, a meeting that Kat did not attend. Trish's assistant, Sandra/Sondra, had arranged interviews for Trish and me with three of the city's top adolescent psychologists, though how she and Trish had determined that they were *top* psychologists wasn't clear to me. In any case, Trish regarded the selection of a therapist as far too important a matter to leave to chance, or to me, and she blocked off a day and took the early shuttle down from New York, meeting me at Bonnie's office near Dupont Circle.

My ex-wife talked more or less nonstop for the first thirty minutes. She wanted Bonnie Weaver to know that Kat was depressed, and why this was more serious than a situational depression, and to warn Bonnie that Kat would no doubt want to turn her into a surrogate mother, as she had done with Lily Moorefield and Gladys Ochoa. Trish sounded patronizing as she sat there and lectured Bonnie Weaver, a small woman who wore way too much makeup and dressed and did her hair in the wavy style of the 1950s. This seemed to be her strategy, not entirely successful, for trying to look normal. She even talked and acted like the mom in some antique TV sitcom, making broad facial gestures that conveyed SYMPATHY and WORRY and the other qualities she felt she should exhibit. But her eyes were a pale, pale blue, almost silver, and they shimmered like a pair of whirling pinwheels, and my impression was that she had the disconcerting gift of looking straight into other psyches and went to lengths to conceal it. Whenever I tried to interrupt Trish and get a word in, Bonnie turned those eyes on me and I saw a reflection of the useless hostility that Trish and I kept alive between us.

When Trish finally got to the end of her monologue, Bonnie said, "Gosh, this must be PAINFUL for you both."

"It has been," Trish said, "very. Kat doesn't trust me. That's been one price of our divorce. She's attached herself to other role models, but not to me."

Bonnie said that in a situation like ours, where the parents had different lifestyles and lived so far apart, youngsters sometimes kept things in separate compartments. Now that Kat was older, she might be able to begin to put the pieces together. "When the picture is big enough," she said, "they can find a way to place both parents in it. And, gosh, you two are such strong personalities that Kat probably needs a BIG frame."

She was the first therapist we saw that day, and Trish seemed downcast and dubious at the end of our session when Bonnie described her attitude toward antidepressants, explaining that she preferred not to prescribe them as long as a youngster was able to manage without them. "Medication sometimes undermines their own efforts," she said. "Not always, but I like them to believe that the magic comes from within, not from a bottle of pills."

"The magic?" Trish asked.

"Oh, I think it's magic, don't you? It's certainly not a SCIENCE. There's no FORMULA for getting them through. I think that each one of them has her own NORTH STAR, and that's what I try to help her find. They reach adolescence and suddenly they feel as though they've been in a SHIPWRECK, and now they're out there on the open sea, bobbing around in a LIFEBOAT, with no idea of where to go. Find your NORTH STAR, I tell them, and STEER toward that."

Bonnie Weaver was sitting straight in her chair, as she had throughout the interview, her hands folded in her lap and her legs turned to the side in that old-fashioned ladylike posture. She seemed to know that what she was saying was almost comically dramatic, and yet, clearly, she not only believed in this approach but was confident that it worked.

When we left her office, I asked Trish, "Should we cancel our other meetings? Is she the one?"

"You liked her?"

"I thought she'd be great with Kat."

We'd reached my car in the parking lot. Trish said, "You liked the part about the magic within? I wouldn't have thought that was your style."

"She seems intuitive," I said, "and that's the only way to get to Kat. The frontal approach doesn't work with her."

"We've scheduled other meetings," Trish said, but she didn't seem to want to put up the usual fight.

"I don't really see the point," I said, "and I'm not even sure that we should be trying to pick out someone for Kat. She'll have her own ideas."

"Of course she will."

"I'm saying it might be a strike against any therapist if we go to Kat and say, all right, we've checked out these three and here's the one we've decided on. She wants to make her own decisions."

Trish looked off toward the street. She takes excellent care of herself, but she seemed tired that day, and there was a pinkness around her bloodshot blue eyes. Perhaps she was thinking that she didn't want to have to go through the whole story again, or maybe she was just unwilling to agree with me. I don't know what sadness had stolen over her, but I saw her try to shake it off, forcing her face into a smile and almost getting me to smile with her, the overscheduled bi-city traveler, when she said, "So what am I supposed to do now? If we cancel those appointments, what am I going to do with an *open* afternoon?"

Her plan had been to spend the day in Washington, pick the kids up after school, take them to dinner, and catch a late shuttle back to New York, but she got on the cell phone and canceled the other appointments.

We ate lunch at an inexpensive Thai restaurant, the first time we'd eaten together in years, and we were both nervous. We'd been sparring with each other for so long that we didn't seem to know how to put aside our gloves, and Trish, looking for a neutral subject, steered the conversation to gardens and landscaping. She'd thought I was a fool to give up my career at Time-Life, but she said that Twill seemed to suit me. It kept me tan, anyway, she said. I said it kept me from having to buy new clothes. Trish drank a cup of tea and I ordered my usual diet Coke. "You don't need any caffeine," she said, and I agreed, admitting that I was still having trouble getting to sleep.

There was an awkward moment of silence, and then Trish quizzed me about the business. I complimented her on the landscape work around her Long Island house.

"Some days I think more about the gardens there than anything else," she told me. "I consider those good days. Plants don't talk back."

"Plants don't, but clients do."

"Children do," Trish said, "or even if they don't, they let you know what they think of you. This has been hard for me, Tucker. I mean Kat's decision to go to Tandem. Her decision not to come to New York even though everything is so up in the air here."

"This is where she's always lived," I said. "I wouldn't take it so personally."

"It couldn't have been any more personal."

By then our food had come, soft shell crabs for me and a salad for Trish, and, again, we didn't know how to continue. She'd confessed her unhappiness, I knew, and I couldn't help thinking how I would have felt had the situation been reversed and I'd been sitting there knowing that Kat was going to Trish. "She chose a place, not a parent," I said. "She has two parents, and she needs both of them. Can we agree that we'll try to keep our differences to ourselves?"

"I always try," Trish said.

"We have to do a better job of it."

"Yes, we do," she said, screwing up her mouth tightly. I think she was on the verge of tears, but damned if she was going to let me see them. She poked with her fork at the leaves of lettuce. "Iceberg," she said with distaste, and then, in some detail, she described the garden she was planning with a landscape architect's help, a garden inspired by Japanese principles of design, and she couldn't help implying that she was engaged in creating a work of art while my activities at Twill were more plodding and plebian. She and her brilliant designer had already spent weeks trying to select and place the rocks in the garden. They'd found an excellent source for rocks, she told me, and she went on and on about the supplier who sold rocks of extraordinary quality, simply extraordinary.

I was tempted to ask how much these extraordinary rocks were costing her, but I didn't want to risk the tiny truce we seemed to have achieved.

ROCKS. I remembered that conversation when I came home one evening and found Kat in the alcove reading *Sylvester and the Magic Pebble.* She'd had a session with Bonnie that afternoon, and I knew she wanted me to notice the book, a picture book, once her favorite book. "That's not a schoolbook, is it?" I asked.

Faint smile.

"What made you decide to read it again?"

"I wanted to look at it, that's all. I was talking about it with Bonnie."

The story is about Sylvester, a dear little donkey who finds a magic pebble that will grant him a single wish, but before he can decide what to wish for, he is attacked by a lion. In a panic, to protect himself, he wishes to be turned to stone. The wish, alas, comes instantly true. The seasons pass over him as he suffers silently, knowing now that the wish of his whole heart is to be restored to life and reunited with his parents. The book ends when the grieving parents discover the pebble and wish for his return, and the last picture shows the family united in an embrace, two big donkeys and a little one happily curled up together.

"I read this book a thousand times," Kat said, taking me in with her dark eyes, evaluating me, deciding just how much to confide in me.

"A thousand and one now," I said. "Was it different this time?"

"I must have felt like a stone," Kat said. "I remember how much I wanted you and Mom to get back together. I know it's never going to happen, but can I ask you something?"

"Sure."

"Were you and Mom ever in love?"

Why was I caught off guard? That was a crucial question, a necessary and inevitable question, but I was completely unprepared for it, and I made a stupid gulping cluck.

"I didn't think so," Kat said.

"Wait, Kat, give me a second. That's not an easy question."

"Why not?"

"It's not easy after so much has happened."

"OK," Kat said, "what about Christine and the others? Were you in love with them?"

"The others? You make it sound as though there've been hundreds."

"What about Christine?"

"No."

"Why not?"

"I don't know. Who ever knows? Wrong time, wrong place."

"So did you guys break up, you and Christine?"

"We broke up."

"Just wondering," Kat said in a voice that was elaborately indifferent, rising from the wing chair. She was headed for the hallway and staircase when I reached for her, but she permitted our hands to link in the thumb war position, and our thumbs circled warily as Kat gazed up through her dark lashes. Then Kat swept her left hand across mine, instantly pinning my thumb with her hand. She'd never done that before, and I said, "Not fair."

"I win," she said. "Had to happen sometime."

Her expression was strangely artificial and she was clearly giving me a brush-off, shutting off the glimpse she had just given me of something deeper, something that mattered to her. She was testing me in some way, I felt, and I never seemed to pass, though god knows I kept trying. Every time she initiated a conversation, I heard myself carrying on like a schoolteacher, saying more than I should to keep the silence from falling between us. On the subject of the Glorious Miracle, I was positively unstoppable, explaining at length the way the church united its members into a community, how it functioned not just as a church but as a neighborhood, how it was a beachhead for Latinos in a strange country, how it helped them find jobs and get medical care, how they pooled information and organized themselves to deal with the INS and the banks and the schools, how they bartered services with each other to save cash, and how lucky I felt that Twill had always been hooked into the Glorious Miracle network. "We've never had to go out and recruit," I said. "There's always a cousin or a friend who needs work."

"That's all the practical stuff," Kat said one afternoon as we were heading home in the Jimmy. She'd had a late afternoon at school, late enough for me to pick her up. "It's a church. I mean, they believe in something. They didn't join the church to get a job."

"Maybe not, but it's an incentive."

"They all have those decals all over their cars, even the guys who work for you. They don't say Twill Landscaping. They say *Jesús es maravilloso*. The job is like way secondary."

"OK," I said. "I see where I stand."

"Have you ever been there? To the church?"

I hadn't been.

"I'm going to go with Gladys next Sunday," she said. "I have to go for the project but I'm really interested, too, you know? I asked Gladys how she felt at church and she said, 'Happy.' 'Everybody happy,' she said."

She was quiet for a moment, then asked, "Did you ever believe in God?"

"I still do," I said.

"You do?"

"There had to be some prime mover," I said. "You can't make something out of nothing. So there had to be a moment when matter was created, and I guess God did it. He must have done it. How else could it have started?"

"That's it? That's what you believe? You used to take me to church."

"I think church is a good place to leave your troubles. The Mary Carter approach. Of course that was before she took up yoga. What do you believe?"

She looked straight ahead through the windshield, and again I had the feeling that she was deciding how much to trust me. "I don't know," she said finally, "but I know I'm envious of Gladys. If I did belong to a church, I'd want to belong to one that made me happy, not one where it was a duty to go."

"Are you a Christian?" I asked.

"Well, I'm not a Buddhist," Kat said, "or a Muslim. What a weird conversation this is."

I smiled, but I could feel a tingling at the nape of my neck, and I knew that what was being said mattered.

I asked Kat, "Do you pray?"

"Yeah. A lot, actually."

"When did this start?"

"I've always prayed—well, sometimes more than others. But Mary Carter wrote me that letter, remember? She's not just into her yoga. She said she was praying for me, and that made me want to start praying myself. It just seemed like a good idea."

We were on Macarthur Boulevard, near the Hut, and Kat decided that she wanted to give me another glimpse into the construction site she usually guarded from me. "I pray for all kinds of things," she said, suddenly sounding chatty and lighthearted. "I pray for Mom, I pray for you, I pray for Mary Carter, sort of like I did when I was little. You remember how we did God Bless every night? I even pray for people I don't want to pray for—for Phyllis, for instance. I don't want to go around being angry at her, so when I feel that, when I feel bitter, I just say a prayer."

She glanced at me for just a second. "It makes me feel better, you know? Bonnie says prayer is OK because we all need to believe in something greater than ourselves."

"You talk about this with Bonnie?"

"Yeah, she's really spiritual. You know how she looks at you with those whammy eyes. 'there is DEFINITELY something greater than we are, oh golly, there's a MUCH greater power out there.'" By then we were parked in the driveway of the Hut, and Kat was looking at me, wide eyed, doing an imitation of Bonnie.

She can make me laugh whenever she feels like it, and I asked if I could go along when she went to the Church of the Glorious Miracle.

THE CHURCH of the Glorious Miracle is on Colesville Road in a dreary area of Silver Spring that consists of several major arteries, parking lots, discount stores, and sad-looking strip malls. There is a busy car wash nearby, and a carpet warehouse, and an auto parts store, and a couple of used car lots, and the church itself was once an automobile dealership. The former showroom is now a foyer, and the garage is the room of assembly and worship. A plain sign out in front identifies the place, in both Spanish and English, as the Church of the Glorious

Miracle. At the bottom of the sign, in smaller italic letters, is the declaration *Nos Somos Una Iglesia de Fe Pentecostale.* We are a church of Pentecostal faith.

Need I state the reasons why I shouldn't have been there? I was a religious skeptic, I was an Anglo, I was the employer of several church members, I was horning in on my daughter's project, and on top of everything else, I was made uneasy by public demonstrations of strong feeling except at sporting events. Yet I was there, dressed in my dark suit, and already feeling the warmth of the late September afternoon when Kat and I got out of the car and walked toward the clusters of people standing in front of the church, in the shade of a few gingkoes and willow oaks that had somehow survived in those acres of soot and pavement.

The service was to begin at five, and little kids were running about, all dressed up but eager to play after their Bible study class. Most of the men were in stiff, shiny suits, standing to eat chicken and rice off paper plates. Several of them who worked for Twill came up to shake hands, carefully wiping their fingers on paper napkins, welcoming us with gravity and formality. Children stared at us frankly, and why not? We were strangers there, and Kat's blonde hair stood out like a banner. This was their territory, and I could see that the men set aside their comfort and ease when they stepped forward to greet us.

Gladys and Tomás had seen us through the plate-glass windows and came out to lead us back into the foyer where the churchwomen, serving the supper, managed to notice without noticing. The room was hot and many of the women were fanning themselves with paper plates, yet there was an air of calm and contentment, a Sunday peacefulness. Gladys was full of smiles and kept pressing us to eat, but Tomás, I thought, looked stern and disapproving as Gladys—her hair pulled back and glossy, wearing a magenta jacket with a yellow flower—chattered in her accented English. "Is different here, yes? Not like your church. No pictures, no statues. We don't believe in that. The faith here," she said, touching her jacket near the yellow flower, "inside. Not in pictures."

She introduced us to the minister, José María, a short slab of a man with a broad face and neatly parted hair. I had the feeling that he'd

been standing by to meet us. "God bless you," he said, speaking first
to Kat, then to me. "I have heard about you. El Jefe. But here you cannot be the boss, eh?" He smiled, holding my hand in both of his, looking at me with unsettling directness. "I hope you will find what you are
seeking."

What did he think I was seeking? I wondered what Gladys had said
about our visit, for it was clear enough that she'd let it be known we
were coming. Her friends circled about us, respectful and reserved in
their manner toward me, more forthcoming with Kat. My Spanish is
limited, but I heard them referring to Kat's school project, volunteer-
ing to tell her everything she wanted to know. Gladys hovered protectively at her side, and her daughter Carolina—a twelve-year-old
who'd always seemed to look up to Kat, all dolled up in a pink dress,
her hair in a complicated do that must have taken hours to achieve—
also positioned herself near Kat. We were an event, it seemed, and Kat
has never liked to be the center of attention. I could see that she had
butterflies in her stomach. Her hands were moving and the color ran
in her cheeks as she whispered, "*Gracias, gracias.*"

"God bless you," said young Tomás when the service was announced, and we moved into the large room, recognizable as a place of
worship only because it had pews. Tomás was seventeen, the oldest
child in the Ochoa family, a nice-looking boy with black eyes, shiny
hair, and sparkling teeth. He came down from the platform at the
front of the room to greet us. "He is one of the singers," Gladys said
proudly, and he nodded, smiling, shaking my hand, shaking Kat's. Another singer, a woman named Lourdes, also stepped down from the
platform to hug Gladys and to welcome us, beaming as she called
upon God to bless us. Call me an infidel, but these blessings were beginning to sound like the sentiments on greeting cards.

The congregation was filing in slowly, not in any hurry. Gladys led
us to a pew near the front, and she and her husband took their places
behind us as I tried to take in my surroundings. To anyone accustomed to rich, elaborate shrines like the National Cathedral, with its
stained glass and gilded altarpieces and carvings and tapestries, with
images everywhere of the life and death of Christ, this place looked as

bare as a bingo hall. The walls were white, the floor was linoleum, the ceiling was acoustic tile. Up front there was that elevated platform, with a stand for a speaker—not a true pulpit but a plain all-purpose podium—and a couple of chandeliers overhead, but otherwise the lighting was bright and fluorescent. The platform was occupied by a three-piece band of guitar, keyboard, drums, and there were three singers—Tomás and Lourdes and another woman with a great head of curly gray hair, all of them standing behind floor mikes. A pair of heavy, wheezing floor fans were laboring to circulate the warm air, and the kitchen must have been in an adjoining room, for the aroma was that of roasting poultry.

It was Lourdes who first came forward and began to speak, standing at the pulpit, holding the mike close to her lips, talking with great animation though the church was still stirring, settling down, as people found their places. She spoke in Spanish, of course, with one of her arms extended, open palm facing upward, her eyes fixed on a point overhead.

"She is saying how she think she know everything about the Lord," Gladys said from behind us, translating, not exactly whispering, "but every time she think that, He make a surprise for her. He remind her that she don't know so much. She say she think it is like driving at night because you don't see so far, only as far the lights shine, and maybe the road is twisting sometimes, but what you see is enough if you have faith and keep driving. You keep driving and you will get to the end of the road."

"Is she a minister?" I asked Gladys. Lourdes was talking with great rapidity and assurance and apparent amusement.

"No, she is just a person," Gladys said.

Kat was listening intently, but when I asked her if she could understand, she shook her head. I could pick out a few words—*el camino, la luz*—but Lourdes was going much too fast for me. Of course I had never seen anything remotely like this, a woman standing before a congregation of three hundred people and speaking with vivacity, with intimacy, of her experience of her Lord. That word—el Señor—was laced through her testimony and spoken with a friendly regard, even when she was scolded, or scolded herself, for thinking she understood everything. She wagged her forefinger and her expression changed to show a momentary disapproval, but she couldn't suppress her smile.

Then she moved effortlessly from speech to song. "Hallelujah," she said, not with an exclamation but quite naturally, savoring the word, pronouncing that *j*, lifting the congregation to its feet with her open palm. "Hallelujah," she repeated, and there was some clapping, some calls of hallelujah from those in the pews. The man at the keyboard played a few chords, and Lourdes began a hymn, a song that had the simple beat of one of those children's songs that Raffi sings. In fact, as the music began, I was reminded of a Raffi concert I had attended with Kat and Will years ago, for there was the same childlike eagerness to take part, the same murmuring undertone, the same innocent sense of uplift. I could see men and women raising their arms as they sang, but Kat's fingers gripped the top of the pew in front of us. Some members of the congregation had brought tambourines and metal noisemakers that looked like cheese graters, and these gave a Latin sound to the music that already had a samba beat. I was watching when young Tomás closed his eyes, lifting his arms to receive the spirit.

How is one to act in the presence of a strong, simple faith? I didn't know, but I could certainly feel the energies rippling through that room of believers. They weren't loud or showy, and there were no seizures and no talking in tongues, but the air in the room was electric. My cheeks were flushed and I could feel the sweat beading along my hairline when the minister took the pulpit and introduced us publicly, "Kathryn Jones *y su padre*, Tucker Jones." Gladys nudged my shoulder and told us to stand, and the congregation laughed and then clapped for us. "José María say you talk two languages when you leave today," Gladys said. My Spanish is not good but I understood him to continue with this theme, saying that everyone needed to know two languages, the language they spoke and the language of the heart. *La palabra de corazón.*

José María made other announcements in the same fashion, moving from the mundane to the serious without hesitation, without insistence, and apparently without design, though it was apparent that he was a practiced, artful speaker. He stood straight, a short man in a blue suit, proud in his bearing and demeanor, conscious of his power, I thought, and completely aware of the effect of his smallest inflection and the sudden, chopping gestures he made, bringing the edge of one hand down into the palm of the other as though splitting open something with a tomahawk. I couldn't have said exactly when the sermon proper began if young Tomás hadn't come down from the platform to sit with us. Or, to be accurate, to sit beside Kat. He slipped past me and sat on the far side of Kat, and then the woman, Lourdes, also came to our pew, and we all squeezed close to make room for her.

"I do a little of everything," she said in perfect English, "and I'll translate for you, if that's all right. That way Gladys can listen."

She was leaning against me, her shoulder touching mine, her voice low, her lips only inches from my ear, and her fragrance—heavy, like roses—filled the pew. On the other side of me, Tomás Ochoa was leaning against Kat, whispering his translation into her ear. My heart was pounding, for it was profoundly intimate to be pressed against this woman who had come to speak to me alone of the mysteries of the soul. "It might help you understand better," she said, her breath tickling my neck. "I can only tell you the idea, though. José María speaks too quickly for me to keep up."

I nodded and listened, and Lourdes leaned close and translated, "I know you are probably wondering, why should you love Christ? What was so special about Him, this man who was born in an unimportant country far away from the center of power? He was a minority, too, and He had very little education. He came from working people, simple people, and His public ministry was among simple people, fishermen, carpenters, people like that. He didn't care if they were rich or poor, and they didn't have to be educated to understand Him. His teachings were so clear that everyone could understand them."

She gave me a nudge. "Oh, he goes so fast. I have to leave some things out, but he's saying that it is still the same, His teachings are still clear, and it doesn't matter whether you are rich or poor, or educated or not, everybody can still understand them and if you do understand them, and accept Christ, you will have a purpose in life. He wants you to have a purpose. You are worthy of that. Everyone is worthy of that, even though so many people think they are not. They think they are worthless and they can't accept themselves. You should hear the things he hears, José María hears, all the things people tell him about how worthless they feel, like they are horses or pigs, but he doesn't think anyone here today is a pig. OK, now he is saying, 'Am I right? Am I right? Good, no one here is a horse or pig,' and he says we should tell each other that we are not, so I will tell you. I am not a horse or a pig." She shook my hand as she said this, and throughout the congregation there was laughter as people told their neighbors that they were not horses or pigs.

"Are you going to tell me?" she asked, leaving her hand in mine, smiling.

"I am not a horse or pig," I said.

"Good," she said, patting my wrist.

I saw Tomás holding Kat's hand.

I was acutely aware of my daughter beside me, and I could feel her struggle as José María urged the members of his congregation to accept themselves, and to accept forgiveness for their sins. He could not forgive anyone, he said, but the Lord could forgive. The Lord wanted to forgive, and He was there that evening, He was there and He was waiting, he wanted us all to be different people when we left that church, our hearts opened and our sins washed away. Lourdes kept murmuring the words of that interminable sermon, and every time José María built to a crescendo of guilt and longing and did his tomahawk chop, bringing moans and cries from the congregation, Kat squeezed more tightly against my side as though she wanted to disappear into my pocket. Of course she wanted forgiveness. Who doesn't? Who doesn't want to have her sins washed away? Who doesn't want infinite grace and eternal salvation?

"It is not so difficult," Lourdes whispered. "It is only difficult because you are too proud to accept it. Are you so proud? Here is the Lord with a gift, a great gift, and are you going to say, 'No, I don't want it'? He doesn't say, 'Do this or do that and I will love you.' He doesn't say that you must have money or a nice car or a nice dress. He doesn't set any condition. He just says, 'My love is here. Accept it.' It is like He is at the door and all you have to do is open the door. Don't be afraid. He does not want to come in to steal from you. He does not want to come in to eat your food. Maybe you only have some leftover chicken and rice anyway, so He doesn't need that. All you have to do is let Him in and you will be richer, not poorer. Accept His love and you will have love of your own. You will have love for yourself and love you can give to those who need it."

Our eyes met then, mine and the eyes of this woman who still held my hand in hers. "There is enough love for you," she said evenly, and I don't think she was translating, "if you will accept it."

The keyboards had started again, mercifully, signaling that we were coming to the end of the sermon, and José María spoke soothingly, in the lulling voice of a hypnotist. Lourdes whispered, "He wants you to come to him. He is waiting for you. He will always be waiting, but He says, 'Come now if you need me. Open your heart now. I am here today. I have come here because of you. Please, do not leave here without me. My arms are open. My heart is open. You see? Can you see? I am waiting. If you want to come to me, come now. Do not leave here without me. Take me. I want to be in your life. I want to love you. I want you to know that I love you. Please.'"

Her grip tightened on my hand. "You want to go?"

I shook my head.

"To the front," she said, "to receive the Spirit. I would go with you. I would take you there. You want to, I think."

I sat still, and what I felt was not the call of el Señor but the discomfort of my daughter beside me. Her head was bowed and her hands were in her lap when she suddenly reached for my hand and caught hold of it as if to keep herself from being swept away. Tomás was whispering to her, and she was shaking her head slightly from side to side. He seemed to be pleading with her, and I could feel the pressure of her grip.

Lourdes said, "I have to go now to sing. He is waiting."

The man at the keyboards had been laying down a series of repeated chords, and Lourdes touched my arm one final time as she rose to make her way back to the platform. Tomás, taking his cue from her, left the pew at the other end. The whole church now had the buzz of a hive, and four people did go forward—stumbled forward, really, blind with tears as they moved toward the front of the church, where they knelt before José María. The music had started but the noise of clapping and shouting washed over it, and Kat's hand tightened around my wrist. She whispered, "I have to go. I have to leave now."

"It's almost over," I said.

I did not want to offend, and Kat held herself together for the last few minutes of the service, but she was barely able to mutter a good-bye, another *gracias*, to Gladys, and she didn't say a word as we walked to the car, nor did she turn her head to look at the people leaving the church as we drove past.

For several blocks she didn't trust herself to speak. Then she said, "They had that all planned," the words breaking from her in a burst. "They planned every bit of it like I was some kind of idiot and wouldn't realize. I think Gladys should have told me what they were going to do. She should have said they were going to put us on the spot like that."

"Like what?"

"Like everything. Like introducing us. Like having Tomás and that woman come to sit with us. Like having the whole sermon directed at us."

I said the sermon seemed to apply to a lot of people.

"Why did they come and sit with us, then? What was that all about if it wasn't supposed to get through to us? How come we got our own personal translators? Then he wouldn't let go at the end. He wouldn't just let me say no. He was like one of those phone salesmen who won't let you say no. Why couldn't they just let us be there?"

"I'm not sure how much they planned," I said, "but I'm sure they thought they were doing us a favor. They tried to welcome us."

"That woman was practically in your lap," Kat said.

For a few minutes we drove in silence past the dangerous, boarded-up, and barricaded storefronts along Georgia Avenue. "I thought I was just going to observe," Kat said, "not to get converted or anything. I'm writing a report. Gladys knows that."

"Maybe it will be a better report since it got to you. It sounds like it did get to you."

"It was so personal," Kat said, "the way Tomás translated it right in my ear. Did she do that to you, too?"

"Lourdes. Yes. It was personal."

"He wanted me to go up there. He just wouldn't let me say no."

"Why didn't you go?"

Kat looked out the window. "It's not my church. It's theirs. It would have been disrespectful to go up there when I don't really believe what they do. Why couldn't they just let me make up my own mind?"

She didn't like to feel pushed into anything, but I thought her disappointment went deeper than that. What she was saying, I thought, was that she'd wanted her own glorious miracle to occur, and it hadn't.

KAT SEEMED to contract into herself after that Sunday. I knew that she felt she'd let Gladys down, but it took me several days to realize how upsetting the experience had been for her, and how much it took out of her. Perhaps she didn't know herself, not immediately, for she has some of my stubbornness about keeping herself in motion, refusing to yield to the temptation to curl up and pull the covers over her head.

Yet that is exactly what she did later that week. On Tuesday afternoon she came home from a session with Bonnie complaining of a headache, and on Wednesday morning she made a halfhearted effort to get dressed before collapsing back into her bed. She felt flu-ey, she told me when I came upstairs to hurry her along, and her eyes did look muddy. So I let her stay home and indulged her, bringing her a tray with English muffins, orange juice, the newspaper, and a couple of St. Joseph aspirin. The following morning she did manage to get dressed, but she complained that her head still ached and her stomach hurt. She did not have a fever, and when I offered to take her to the doctor, she said crossly that if she was going to waste the morning, she might as well waste it at school.

I gave her my standard pep talk, and, as I say, I did not connect her desire to stay home to anything that had happened at the Glorious Miracle. I thought that she'd probably gotten tired of hearing things at school, for it seemed impossible to get through a single day with being reminded of the rumors and suspicions and judgments that were spreading through the small world of private school families in the upper Northwest neighborhoods of the District. With

both investigators at work (Corinne Savino had gone back to George
Washington for her final year of law school but continued to work on
my case), the kids who'd been at the Vandenbergs' that night were
being interrogated, as were some parents, and people were taking
sides. Some kids refused to talk to Corinne, or Vandenberg's investigator, or to talk at all. I gathered from Jay and Lily, who always filled
me in at our band practices, that there were those who saw me as a
criminal and those who saw my actions as the forgivable panic of a father whose child had been molested. At social functions and in school
hallways, Jed Vandenberg and I were a topic of conversation.

And so was Kat. Usually, according to Lily, Kat was seen as a victim no matter what people thought of me, and the story of my divorce
from Trish was thoroughly rehashed. The gossips were in hog heaven.
I wanted to protect Kat from all the talk but knew I couldn't, and Lily
would try to calm me down by telling me that most of the parents who
talked about us were just worried about their own kids. "Everybody's
afraid of getting that phone call," she'd say, "and it could have been
worse, you know. It could have been a lot worse." Her tone reminded
me that she still had her problems with Abby, though Abby had settled
down a bit now that she and Jed were back in school. Puppy love, Lily
called their relationship, though I didn't think there was anything
puppyish about either Abby or Jed. Whenever our conversation about
the girls edged too close to their sexual behavior, I got uneasy, and I
think Lily did, too, for the memory of the night of the stingers still
hovered about us no matter how much we wanted to forget it.

Lily did tell me that, according to Abby, most of the kids could not
fathom why I'd gone after Jed instead of the boys who'd been in the
pool house. Everybody knew who they were, evidently, and Abby had
heard that Danny Owens and Matt Wyckoff and Luke Childs had all
talked to lawyers. This Abby had reported to Lily, with indignation,
wanting to know why I was dragging so many people into this mess.
Her view was that I was responsible for the continuing investigations
and the way the case kept growing.

Apparently, this was Jed's view, too, though Lily hedged everything
she said about him, caught in her conflict of loyalties. He was "upset"
that some of his friends might have to take an oath and testify about

what had happened on July 13th. In the Vandenberg household, they were obviously preparing themselves for legal action.

And it seemed more and more inevitable that there would be a trial. On October 7th, a grand jury listened to John Briggs for a few minutes and agreed that my behavior warranted a charge more serious than a misdemeanor. The fact that I had been carrying a shovel and the severity of Jed Vandenberg's injuries were all that the grand jury needed to hear to rubber-stamp Briggs's recommendation.

Assault with a deadly weapon. The trial date was set in early January.

I hadn't been present at the grand jury, nor had Ian or Brian, but they knew exactly what had happened, and I'd certainly seen plenty of them. Almost every week I went down to their office to discuss the case with the lawyers and read the interviews that Corinne had conducted.

The more I learned, the clearer it became that Jed Vandenberg had tried to orchestrate a cover-up.

That's why he'd sent Abby off to get Kat sobered up. He'd made everybody leave as soon as he realized that Alexa had fled, and he arranged for someone sober to take care of everyone who'd had too much to drink. He'd told everybody at his house that night that if Alexa Fogarty talked about what had taken place, they were supposed to deny it. Some of the kids, as I say, had refused to talk to Corinne, but two of them, one girl and one boy, had described in detail the way that Jed had instructed them to say that Alexa was the one who got drunk and hysterical and that they hadn't seen anything more than skinny-dipping. Alexa hadn't been in the pool house, Jed had told them, so how could she prove anything? Alexa Fogarty had too much to drink, wigged out, and ran home. That was the story Jed wanted them to tell, and he assured them that if they all stuck together, nobody would ever know about Kat.

Brazen behavior, but I didn't want Lily to know how Jed had acted that night and, besides, I was trying to give him the benefit of every doubt. When he was sending Abby off to take care of Kat, he didn't know that I was going to show up looking for my daughter. Even when he told me that he didn't know where Kat was, he might have been telling a technical truth in that he didn't know the exact address of the apartment. In any case, it seemed natural enough for a sixteen-year-old kid to want to hide misbehavior from all parents. In his misguided way, he probably thought that he was protecting Kat.

But he hadn't told me *anything*. It made me shudder every time I thought of how differently that night might have turned out if only he'd been more forthcoming.

I didn't tell Lily about Jed, and I didn't tell her all that I'd read about Abby in the transcript of the interviews. Maybe I should have, but I didn't want to be a John Fogarty (who'd told Corinne that I'd sounded "unstable" on the phone that night). Nor did I tell Lily that I'd asked Corinne not to interview Abby. The lawyers weren't happy about this request, for Abby could be a key witness in our case, the one who could tell us the most about Jed and his plans. But I insisted. She could be interviewed later if necessary, closer to the date of the trial, but for now I didn't want to do anything that would add to her grievance against me.

I didn't want to do anything that might turn her against Kat.

IN A GRIM WAY, it was actually comforting to go down to the offices of Crocker, Collinsworth, and deSantis to confer with the lawyers and to realize that they were *doing* something about it. My team of lawyers, I sometimes thought, since Brian and Ian, and sometimes Corinne, were all present at the meetings where we devised a strategy and the billable hours kept piling up. (I hate to whine about money but I am not a rich man, and by October I could see that, no matter how this case went, I was going to have a second mortgage on the Hut, and I couldn't even begin to get my mind around the millions that Vandenberg was asking for in the civil suit.)

In the criminal trial, Ian would be at the table with me, and he'd conduct the defense by calling witnesses like Alexa Fogarty to paint a graphic picture of what had taken place at the Vandenbergs' pool. He did not want to leave anything to a jury's imagination. He'd elicit every detail of the drinking, the skinny-dipping, and the pressure that had been put on Kat to go into the pool house. He intended to call the three boys to the stand, and to call other kids who could testify to the way Jed had orchestrated a cover-up. The key to our defense was that Jed's lie had triggered the violence.

I would be portrayed as the frantic, distraught parent who only wanted to rescue his daughter. When Jed refused to tell me where she was, I snapped. This was nothing more than a crime-of-passion defense, which, as Ian pointed out, was not a legal defense at all but an admission that a crime has been committed. The goal was to convince a jury that the circumstances were so extreme, and that Jed's lie so outrageous, that my actions were justified.

The story they wanted to tell wasn't false, nor was it entirely true. For instance, I had not been sure that Jed was lying that night. He seemed to be, but I couldn't possibly have known for sure. When I mentioned this, Ian looked at me over his wire-framed glasses as though I was smudging the careful tale he and Brian had been constructing on my behalf. "What we have to get across is that he lied," he said. "He's going to be sitting there with his glass eye, and we're in trouble if the jury feels too sorry for him."

It was a messy case, Brian said, and I had to get used to the idea that there was going to be blood on the walls. He and Ian even talked about calling Jed as a witness for the defense, putting him in the position of admitting his lie to me or perjuring himself. Every now and then, Ian or Brian would make a quiet reference to Kat, but this was a sore point, for I didn't want her to be involved in any of these legal matters. At my request, Corinne had not interviewed her, and Vandenberg's investigator hadn't attempted to contact her, either. If there was a trial, I wouldn't be able to keep her out of it, but for now I wanted her to be spared.

If there was a trial. Brian and Ian still wanted to avoid it. They kept warning me that trials were dangerous and costly and unpredictable, and they didn't conceal their concerns about this specific trial. They were worried. Despite Richard Vandenberg's declaration that there would be no plea bargain, they kept discussing ways to make him change his mind (they assumed that Briggs would do whatever Vandenberg asked him to do). Several times they brought up the possibility of filing countercharges, and at one of our meetings, Brian said, "We can't keep tiptoeing around this, Tucker. I know you want to set limits and keep everything neat and contained, but if we don't fight back, if we're not even *prepared* to fight back, they're going to walk all over us."

Ian seemed to agree. We were in his office, much smaller than Brian's, its walls covered with photos of his wife and two young daughters. His bright blue eyes looked like parrot fish behind the thick lenses of his glasses, and he nodded with unusual vigor as he picked up a copy of the District Code that lay open on his messy desk. He and Brian had obviously scripted this conversation.

"What they did constitutes rape," he said. "You realize that, don't you? It's rape. Here."

He shoved the book toward me, but I was too startled by his tone and manner to reach for it.

"Of course it's not called rape in the District. For reasons that elude me, the statute has been rewritten as sexual abuse, but it comes to the same thing." He was talking fast, and he pulled the book back toward him and started to read the list of sexual acts, his voice as pitilessly neutral as he could make it. Penetration of the vagina by the penis. Penetration of the anus by the penis. Penetration of any orifice by other portions of the anatomy, including the finger or tongue. Penetration of any orifice by other instrumentalities, whether or not such instrumentalities were intended for such use. Contact between the mouth and penis.

He repeated that. Contact between the mouth and penis.

He turned a few pages. "This is sexual abuse," he said, "when . . . Let me read this. It's sexual abuse when quote 'the person knows or has reason to know that the other person is either, A, incapable of appraising the nature of the conduct or, B, incapable of declining participation in that sexual act.' End quote. That's the law. Those are the conditions for second-degree sexual abuse, and conviction carries a prison term of up to twenty years. It's a serious offense."

There was a silence, and Ian said, "I think that's exactly what they did, Tucker. They got Kat drunk and they took her into that pool house. They knew that her judgment was impaired. I think they committed a crime."

Brian said, "I'm sorry we have to bring this up, but we have enough information right now to file a complaint, more than enough."

I said, "I don't want to send anyone to prison."

"You feel guilty," Brian said, "and I understand that. A boy was hurt. But your daughter was hurt, too."

I said, "I just can't sit here and try to figure out how to send three teenagers to prison for twenty years."

"You're saying you're willing to overlook what they did? Just let it go?"

"Let it go," I mumbled. Brian was looking at me as though he was disappointed and pissed off, and in truth I didn't know until that moment that I did not want to punish them. Maybe I will never be able to get the image of that pool house out of my head, but I didn't want revenge. I didn't know Luke or Matt or Danny, and didn't want to know them, but I didn't want to take their lives away from them.

In a conciliatory way, Brian said, "Can we back off for minute? We're not talking about pressing charges or locking anyone up. Right now all we're talking about is whether or not there are credible counter-charges in this case. That's all. The objective right now is to find a way to keep you from going to trial, because if you do, and if you are convicted, if you're sentenced to any time... Well, you won't be able to be much of a father to your children if you're in jail. I don't have to spell it out."

Brian spoke regretfully and exchanged a look with Ian. Then both of them seemed to wait for me to give some indication that I could regard my situation rationally.

I said, "So you think that unless we threaten the boys, I'm going to jail?"

"You have a melodramatic imagination," Brian said. "Try to turn off the fast-forward for a moment, and just think of where we are right now. We want to sit down at a table with Briggs and Vandenberg and talk to them about reducing the charge against you from a felony to a misdemeanor. So far they have expressed no interest in having such a meeting, and I don't expect them to change their minds until we have something to bargain with. What we're doing is attempting to find something that will give us some leverage."

By this time I knew that Brian saw himself as a psychologist, for he liked to say, letting his hands flutter, that 80 percent of the practice of law was in the fingertips. His hands were well shaped and his fingers looked as sensitive as a surgeon's or a safecracker's. As he talked that day, he gave me his analysis of Richard Vandenberg and all the reasons why we had to "arm ourselves for bear" if we expected to negotiate with him. Frankly, Brian seemed fascinated by Vandenberg, and even seemed to relish the chance to go up against a big shot who liked to throw his weight around. He'd certainly done his due diligence on the man, a graduate of Yale Law School, a partner at Devens and Shackleford, where he'd made his name representing the son in a high-profile case in which the son was trying to oust his father and take control of the family empire (the son won and the father died a week later). He was also an avid sailor, a self-styled gourmet and an in-vestor in restaurants as well as tech firms, a member of several corpo-rate boards and blue-ribbon committees. He had donated enough money to Republican causes to feel that he deserved an ambassador-ship and lobbied hard for one, but when he was offered the embassy in Ecuador, he turned it down. Too puny. He was a member of the Burn-ing Tree Club, a hacker on the golf course (Brian relished this fact), and a die-hard opponent of admitting women to membership. His wife, Valerie, was a manic-depressive with a complicated history of medications, and she spent a lot of time at spas, and their daughter, Vanessa, now a sophomore at Connecticut College, had been in a couple of drug scrapes while at Byrd-Adams.

Brian had dug up most of this information about Richard Vanden-berg the old-fashioned way—that is, by asking around. That day in Ian's office, Brian had a new Vandenberg story for me, a story that involved Jed. It turned out that a fellow attorney had a son Jed's age, and the boy had been on Jed's soccer team in middle school. Richard Vandenberg didn't attend many of the games, but when he did, he was the sort of father who spouted advice and criticism. At one point, Jed had turned to him and yelled, "Shut up, Dad. You don't know what you're talking about."

Brian had taken this scrap of information and put it together with the impressions of Jed that he'd heard from me, thirdhand impressions since they had gone from Abby to Lily to me. But Jed didn't sound as though he was eager to see his friends called to testify in a trial, and

Brian wondered what he'd think if he knew that they could be charged with sexual abuse.

The problem was to bypass the father and get this message to Jed.

"It's the long way around," Brian said, "but I really don't think we're going to be able to negotiate with Vandenberg unless we can somehow get the boy to listen to reason. The father won't. But maybe we can divide and conquer here—divide the son from the father. Is there any way you can get to him?"

"To Jed? I don't think so."

"What about talking to his girlfriend?"

Of course he knew that Abby and Kat were friends, and I realized that we'd gone through this entire exercise to get to the point where I would be assigned a mission.

"I could try to talk to Abby," I said, "but she won't be thrilled about it."

"Think it over," Brian said. "I don't want to be an alarmist, but this is going be a goddamn mess if we go to trial. One thing to consider is that if there is a trial, and this story gets into the papers, it might not be possible to keep this case from spawning other lawsuits. If that happens, it's not going to be up to you to charge those boys with sexual abuse. That's the United States attorney's call, and if the facts started coming out, he could be perceived as failing to do his job if he didn't prosecute them."

He gave me his boyish grin and said, "Think about it. It might be worth a shot."

That word *shot* triggered a nerve, and he made a smooth swing with an imaginary golf club.

"WHAT'S THIS? An ambush?" Abby asked when I walked into the back room of the Moorefields' house, the TV room with the beat-up black couches. She was lying on one of them with a pile of textbooks on the coffee table beside her. Lily had phoned, as I had asked, to let me know that Abby was at home. I'd told Lily why I wanted to talk to her daughter, and she was beside me when I entered the TV room. It took Abby no time at all to put two and two together. "You set this up, didn't you?" she said to her mother. "You told him I was here."

"I asked her to," I said. "I didn't know how else to talk to you when there wasn't anyone else around."

"Like Jed, you mean."

Abby was in jeans and a zip-up sweatshirt, and she hadn't risen from the couch, but her voice was enough to mark off her territory and set us at odds.

"There's a lot at stake," Lily said to her. "I wouldn't have told Tucker you were here if I didn't think it was important."

"You could have warned me," Abby said, but she didn't move from the couch.

Shaking her head as if to clear it of unwelcome images, Lily said, "I'm going to leave you two."

I walked around the couch, the empty couch, and thought about sitting down, but didn't right away. Abby was watching me with her hard, unblinking look. "Do you mind?" I asked.

She shrugged and I sat.

"I probably should have warned you," I said, "but I didn't want you to feel disloyal to Jed."

"So this is about him."

"It's about the trial. The lawsuit."

Abby just waited. One of the black-and-white cats came up and rubbed itself against her ankle. As she flicked it away, she looked down and said, "Die."

The house was quiet, and we heard Lily humming as she scampered up the back stairs, making a little extra noise so that we'd know we were alone.

"I'm sure you know what's going on," I said. "I've been charged with assaulting Jed with a deadly weapon. The trial date has been set."

"I know."

"Do you know that Richard Vandenberg has also filed a suit against me for seven and a half million dollars?"

She nodded.

"I don't have seven and a half million dollars," I said, "and I don't want to go to jail."

She waited a beat. "I'm supposed to take that message to Jed?"

"There's more to it, but yes, I want you to take Jed a message. I've been reading the investigator's reports and I've been talking to my lawyers, and I want you to tell Jed what could happen if we have a trial."

"Am I supposed to take notes?" she asked sarcastically.

I sat there in the TV room and tried to explain, as calmly and factually as possible, that many of the people who'd been at the party that night, her friends and Jed's, would be called to testify. I said, "I know that it's already unpleasant to have the investigators poking around, but it's going to be more unpleasant in the courtroom. Believe me, much more unpleasant. The whole story's going to come out, all of it. There could be other charges, sexual abuse charges, against Luke and Danny and Matt. Rape charges, basically."

Abby shifted and for the first time looked away from me.

"To get someone drunk and force them to perform oral sex is rape. Legally, that's what it is. I didn't know that, either. It's been hard for me to take all this in, Abs. I didn't want to come here to talk to you about it."

"Why did you?"

"Because I want to keep it from getting any worse than it already is. I'm still trying to keep Kat out of it. She doesn't need this trial."

"So you're going to charge Luke and Danny and Matt with rape?"

"I'm saying that could happen. It could happen."

"You'd charge them?"

"Not me, Abby. The United States attorney would charge them. This case could turn into a couple of other cases that would drag on for a long time, and a lot of people would get sucked in. It could be a horror show, and Kat doesn't need that."

"She's going to be all right," Abby said.

"Is she? I wish I knew that."

Abby put her hands in her biscuit-colored hair, a gesture that gave it more volume and left it swirled about her face as though she meant to hide behind it. I had promised myself to remain unemotional, but I had to interlace my fingers to keep my hands from shaking. I said, "A trial could hurt her. It could change a lot of lives."

Her eyes switched toward me and away again, and in that quick glance she betrayed fears of her own.

"I've read all these interviews," I said, "and I know some things that happened that night. I know that Jed tried to cover up. That's going to come out. It already has in the investigation. At the trial it's going to come out that he lied to me. When I asked him where Kat was, he said he didn't know. But he did know, and it's going to come out."

"He didn't know where we were going."

"You mean he didn't know the address. But he knew whose apartment it was. He could have told me that, but he told me nothing. Nothing at all."

She didn't deny it.

"What about you?" I asked her. "What are you going to say on the witness stand?"

She was listening, looking away, and I spoke as carefully as I could. "I know that you were in the house with Jed. I don't know when you went inside, or what you were doing, but I know what people thought you were doing. I know that Alexa Fogarty went in and knocked on the door and you didn't answer. She told you what was happening with Kat, and you didn't answer."

"She didn't say anything about Kat," Abby said. "We couldn't tell what she said, just that something was wrong. We went out right after that."

Her voice was defiant, and I had to collect myself. I said, "I wasn't there. I don't know what she said, or how long it took you to leave the house, but I've played this over and over in my mind. I'm not saying you could have prevented anything if you'd gone out right away. Maybe it was already too late. But, Abby—god, Abby, I've known you since you were yea-high—I have to tell you that I think you let Kat down that night. She counts on you. You're like her big sister. She was at that party because you wanted to be there with Jed. I wish you'd looked out for her. You two used to work on the buddy system. Remember that? Remember when you first started climbing together? You always look out for your partner."

Abby said, "It all happened so fast. It just happened so fast."

We were silent in that dusky room, and there was a moment when she looked vulnerable, a moment before she decided that I had accused her, and her face once more took on its hard set. "This is what you want me to tell Jed?"

"Tell him he could stop this right now," I said. "Tell him that if he wants to stop it, he should talk to his father. We've tried—the lawyers, I mean, and we can't talk to him. Tell Jed that if this case goes to trial..."

I was conscious of waving my hand as I stood up, and standing there awkwardly, not knowing how to take leave of this girl I once would have hugged.

KAT STARTED locking her door.

The first time was on a school day as we were getting ready to leave the house. She said she'd left a book in her room and went upstairs to get it. At breakfast she'd complained mildly of a headache and taken an Advil with her orange juice but hadn't even asked to stay home from school. It was a morning when I was scheduled to drive, and Will had shouldered his backpack and lugged it out to the Jimmy. The morning was crisp and brilliant, and the air seemed tinged by the orangy red of the turning maples that lined our block. I stood in the open doorway and called up to Kat and heard the soft *thunk* of her latch hitting the strike plate.

She did not answer me. For a few seconds I didn't move, but then I called again and walked up the stairs to make sure I wasn't imagining things. Her door was closed. I called her name a third time and she still did not answer. I knocked. I tried to turn the knob of her door. Locked.

Unbelievable.

"Kat? What's this about? Answer me."

The policy in our house is that doors may be closed but not locked. There is no policy about answering when called because there has never been a need for one. But Kat did not answer. She did not make a sound.

I will not attempt to describe my thoughts over the next few minutes as I knocked and waited, heard nothing, knocked again, waited, banged on the door and shook it and threatened to take it off its hinges even though I couldn't possibly have done so. The hinges were on the inside. I raised my voice and told my daughter in various ways that this was not acceptable, and even though I knew she *had* to be in that room—there was no porch roof or gutter of tree outside the window for her to slide down—I fantasized that she had escaped like the Birdman of Alcatraz.

She pushed a note under the door. It was written on a lined piece of paper torn from a notebook. It said, in block letters, GO AWAY AND LEAVE ME ALONE.

But I didn't. I did go downstairs, where I called a neighbor, another member of the carpool, and arranged a last-minute swap so that Will could get a ride to school. He had wandered back into the house, and I said, "Your sister has the vapors." The vapors? That was something Mary Carter used to say, and Will looked blank. I told him Kat was sick again and wouldn't be going to school, and he didn't ask any questions.

As soon as he was picked up, I called Bonnie Weaver. She didn't answer but she had to be in her office. Her patients were mostly teen-agers and she scheduled before-school sessions every morning. While waiting for her to return the call, I cleaned up the breakfast dishes and tried to talk myself out of the panicky fears that kept asserting them-selves, especially the fear that Kat was suicidal. I didn't believe she was, but parents are not rational about their children, and I'd had to fill out a form for Bonnie that asked whether she had "suicidal ideation," and I had never gotten that remark of hers, the remark about Eva Cassidy and her early death, out of my head, and in those books I was reading about adolescent girls they always cautioned parents not to dismiss the threat of suicide. My fears weren't so different, really, from those I'd had when Kat was a baby and I'd imagine that her next breath could be her last, breath seemed such a fragile, delicate thing—ridiculous. Ridiculous. Standing at the sink, I kept telling myself that I was over-reacting and Kat wasn't going to hurt herself, but I was so uncertain of my daughter that in truth I didn't know what she might do. That fall I had started keeping a mental list of things she would *not* do, a list I recited when I wanted to reassure myself that she was going to pull through. She was not going to get a tongue bolt or a tattoo, she wasn't going to obliterate herself with drugs or alcohol, she was not going to spread her legs for every boy who looked at her, she wasn't going to run away. She wasn't going to rebel in any of the obvious ways, at least not now. Her battle was silent, more inward and elusive, mostly hidden, but furious nevertheless. Her battle was within herself.

And with me. That's what Bonnie Weaver said when she called about half an hour later. Kat was prepared to act out with me, she said, and she urged me to take that as a positive sign. Youngsters always act out where they feel safest, not where they feel threatened. "Kat carries so much PAIN," Bonnie said, "and she doesn't have anywhere to put it down. Maybe you can help her get rid of it."

"How? She's not talking to me. She's behind a locked door."

"Be patient," Bonnie said. "She can't stay in there forever."

"Should I be worried that she'll hurt herself?" I asked.

Bonnie hesitated before saying that she didn't think so. She added, "Not as long as she thinks you love her."

"She doubts that?"

"We all wonder about it, don't we? I'd try to be patient, Mr. Jones, and TALK to her. I think she might be afraid that you AVOID talking to her because you have a low opinion of her."

I started to tell Bonnie that she was wrong, and Bonnie said politely, after listening to me for a minute or so, that this might be what I should be trying to tell Kat.

"All right," I said, for I'd heard impatience in her voice. She probably had another patient waiting to see her, and she wanted to get off the phone. "One last thing—will you talk to Kat? I think she'd talk to you."

"If she wants to call me, I'll talk to her. But I think you should regard this as YOUR chance, Mr. Jones. It's YOU that she really wants to talk to."

So I was on my own.

I made some business calls that morning, from the kitchen, where I listened for sounds overhead—a footstep, music playing, anything that would signal that Kat was stirring. On my yellow pad I tried to write a letter to her and tore off several pages before I composed a short message. *I'll be downstairs when you're ready to talk. Love, Dad.* This I slid beneath her door, and I made enough noise doing so, and then walking away, that she had to have heard me. On the staircase I stopped and waited silently.

She picked it up. After several minutes I heard the rustle of bedclothes and faint footsteps as she came to the door to pick up the note.

A short while later the door opened and she went into the bathroom. She wasn't trying to be quiet, and when she left the bathroom, I heard her footsteps pause for a moment at the top of the stairs before she decided to skip down. She breezed into the kitchen and said, only slightly remorseful, "Sorry I wigged out like that. I just couldn't face school today."

She walked to the refrigerator, opened the door, and peered in, acting as though it was entirely normal for the two of us to be at home at nine o'clock on a weekday morning.

"How's the headache?" I asked.

"Better."

"Are you ready to go to school? What's going on, Kat?"

"I think I want some coffee."

"Coffee? Since when do you drink coffee?"

"We go to that bagel place all the time, the one across from school."

She was in stocking feet, wearing a pair of black jeans and a sweater, and when she looked at me, she pulled a face as though she'd just bitten into a lemon. "So now you're going to tell me I shouldn't drink coffee?"

I said, "I called Bonnie. You scared me, Kat."

"You called Bonnie? Why? I told you I had a headache."

"You wouldn't talk to me. You closed your door and you wouldn't answer when I knocked."

"I said I was sorry, OK? You didn't have to call Bonnie. Can't I do anything without you freaking about it?"

"You just have to tell me what you're doing, that's all."

"Did you tell her I was depressed?"

"I told her you locked yourself in your room. Are you depressed?"

"Yes, yes, YES," she said angrily. "Is that acceptable? Why don't you just call up Mom and then you can argue about it for a while and decide what to do about me. Let me know when you do, OK?"

She grabbed a big bottle of diet Coke and she was gone. I heard the door lock click again, but at least she had the Coke. She wouldn't go thirsty.

FOR THE next few weeks, that's how it went. I couldn't say on any given morning whether Kat would come out of her room (except on the mornings that she was scheduled to see Bonnie—she always pulled herself together on those days). I didn't know when she'd close herself behind that locked door, nor could I guess at her mood when she did decide to emerge. Several times I was ready to take a screwdriver and remove the lock altogether, but I never did because it seemed important to grant her this power. Kat was pleased, I sensed, that she was able to keep me, a stickler for going to work, at home, and once she knew that she'd disrupted my day, that I'd changed my plans to accommodate her, she'd come downstairs. We'd gotten beyond the point where she pretended to have headaches, and to keep her from running back to her room whenever she didn't like a turn in the conversation, we'd walk up to Macarthur Boulevard and have coffee at Starbucks or the Greek deli. On good mornings, we'd go down to the Potomac—the river was only a few minutes away—and walk along the towpath or the narrow trails made by the fishermen and hikers. The parenting manuals wouldn't have approved of these walks taken during school hours, and I never stopped nagging Kat about all these days of hooky, but these seemed to be the conditions under which we could attempt to approach one another.

I did try to talk to her. Or TALK, I should say, since it had never been difficult to chat with my daughter, but we both struggled to give voice to the things that mattered to us now. The morning I asked her about the Glorious Miracle, she said, "Why do you care about that? You didn't want me to believe that sermon. You didn't want me to go up there at the end. You don't believe any of that stuff."

"That doesn't mean I don't want you to believe it."

We were walking along the towpath and she made a sound of annoyance. "I know you've always been drawn to religion," I said. "I remember how you used to read your Holocaust books. I remember how you used to put a towel over your head when you watched the *Sound of Music.* Sister Kat, my little nun."

"Those are totally different things, Dad."

"You're right," I said. "I just don't want to discourage you."

I saw her sideways look, the glance that came when she was trying to decide how much she could trust me. It took her several steps to make up her mind. Then she said, "I used to feel holy sometimes— you know, like there was nothing wrong with me. Like there was nothing wrong in the whole world. I can remember that. And when I went to Beauvoir, I remember how it felt to go to the Children's Chapel. That was after you and Mom split up, but I felt safe in there. I believed somebody cared how I felt. God cared, that's how it felt."

"You never told me this."

She shrugged, closing down.

"What happened?"

"It changed, that's all. It started to feel weird, like I wasn't supposed to believe it, not really. It seemed like it was OK to go to church now and then, but to believe it—oh, no, that was way uncool."

"Did I make you feel that way?"

"Not just you, everybody. It's just the way it is, right? Nobody believes, nobody we know—except Gladys. At the Glorious Miracle they all believe and they're not ashamed of it. You were there. You saw how they are in church. If anybody acted like that in the Cathedral, they'd get arrested. It's like this is the CATHEDRAL, so just shut up and be impressed. Just sit still and be polite. At the Glorious Miracle, that was the first time I ever saw people act like it meant something to be in church."

I asked her if she'd felt anything.

"I felt like I'd lost something, you know? Like I used to believe something and now I just wish I did."

"I'm proud of you," I said.

"Proud? How can you be proud?"

"I'm proud of you for making up your own mind."

"You're proud I don't believe?"

"I'm proud you didn't pretend to be something you're not."

She'd stopped walking and turned to face me. "I don't want to be an atheist or agnostic or whatever you call yourself. I don't want to be somebody who doesn't know what matters to them, and I don't know what matters to you. You're my dad and I don't have a clue what matters to you. I want to know—what's important to *you*? Do you ever think about who we are and what we're supposed to do with our lives? Who made us and why? You and Mom are always worried about whether or not I'm happy, but you never talk about this. Mom wants me to take some pill. You want me to follow the rules. But this whole huge part is just left out, like nobody knows what to say about it so they just ignore it. God? Oh, that's just something for those Latinos who work for you. We have better things for you—but what things, Dad? What things? Hanging out with guys at some stupid party? Is that what you think I'm supposed to do? Is that what you *want* me to do? Tell me. What do *you* want me to do?"

Those amber glints were flashing deep in her eyes and she expected an answer. She waited for a second or two, and when I didn't answer, she said, "Don't tell me, *Be happy*. That's too lame. I want to know what you think matters."

"This," I said. "This is what matters. What's happening right now."

"What? Standing here arguing with each other?"

"This isn't an argument."

"What is it? What do you call it?"

"This is the way people talk when they love each other and they're trying to figure things out. When they're trying to figure each other out."

"Love," she said with disgust. "What do you know about that?"

She took off running before I could answer her, speeding along the orange gravel of the towpath, headed in the direction of home. She was there when I arrived, and her door was locked.

I DIDN'T tell Trish how much school Kat was missing, and Kat didn't tell her, either, not because I had asked her to keep anything from her mother, but because we both seemed to sense that this drama of locked doors, and volatile moods, and walks along the river, and café lattes, and fierce conversations was between the two of us—our struggle and our secret, more or less, though plenty of others knew about it. Gladys knew, and Jamie, Kat's Tandem friend knew, for she was the one Kat called to get her homework assignments, and she occasionally stopped by the Hut to drop off work sheets or other handouts. And Will did his best to ignore what was going on, though he did ask one morning when I took him to school, "Is she going to be all right?"

"I think so," I told him, but I could hear that the question was real and that he was worried about his sister. I was, too, though I had gotten so that I could leave Kat at home for short periods without dreading what I'd find when I returned to the Hut. I had called Bonnie again, to ask about medication. Kat was resistant, she told me, and Bonnie's inclination was to wait for a few more weeks to see whether she leveled out. In her perky voice, Bonnie said it was natural to have a letdown after starting a new school, and maybe Kat was just trying to catch her second wind. She urged me to try to get Kat to school, but as long as she was going most of the time—she never missed more than two days in a row—and keeping up with her work, she wouldn't push the panic button. Bonnie had treated hundreds of girls, I told myself, though I didn't see how it could be healthy for a fourteen-year-old girl to lock her door and sleep till noon and spend hours reading the Tintin comic books that she'd first devoured when she was in the third grade.

And yet I couldn't make myself force Kat out of her room. Rightly or wrongly, I believed that something essential was playing out between the two of us and that it had to run its course.

That's what I told Lily the day we took the girls to see Riverdance at the Kennedy Center on a perfect Sunday in late October. The Moorefields had planned to go as a family, but at the last minute Tony was offered a pair of Redskins tickets, and he decided to take Rafe to the football game. Lily invited us to take their seats. She was going to try to get a ticket for Will, too, but he declined. He said he'd like to see Riverdance but not in this lifetime.

So Lily and I took the three girls—Kat, Abby, and Sophy. When we made our plans, Lily said she wanted to get Abby and Kat together since they were seeing so much less of each other, but I'm sure it was also her way of helping me get Kat out of the house, for I'd told her about the locked door. Kat also seemed to suspect that the afternoon was arranged to lure her out, and she seemed sullen as we were getting ready.

On the way over to the Moorefields', I could see that she wanted to shake it off, and I was glad to see her break into a grin when we got to Lowell Street. A Lily moment was in progress. Music was pouring out through the open doors, a Celtic jig with flute, fiddle, drums, and accordion, and Lily and her girls were in the front hall with the rugs pushed aside, working on their Irish step dancing on the oak floor, their hair loose and their faces rosy with exertion.

"You have to try this," Lily said to Kat as soon as she saw us coming up the steps. She was wearing black stirrup pants, and she'd kicked her shoes off. "The thing is, you have to keep your upper body completely still," she said, high stepping with her hands on her hips, bare feet flying as she gave us a demonstration. Kat was hesitant, but Lily wasn't taking no for an answer. She showed Kat how to stand, how to hold her arms, how to point her toes, and soon she had her leaping about with Sophy and Abby, the gang of them filling that hallway with motion and laughter as Lily swept them up in her own exuberance.

She tried to get me to join in. She looked gravity-free when she danced over and asked, "Aren't you going to try this? Come on, Tucker. It's all from the waist down. You're a good dancer."

"My step dancing is rusty," I said. "Nonexistent, actually."

"Killjoy," Lily said, but she was winding down and stopped after one last turn with the girls. She pretended to clear the sweat from her brow with her fingertips and to check her underarms for perspiration. Abby said, as she and Kat stopped dancing, "Ladies don't perspire, Mom. They *dew*." She'd learned that from Lily, of course, and she was just giving it back to her, but she was obviously ready to enjoy herself that day, and she pretended to be dazzled as Sophy kept springing about in the hallway. Sophy is Lily's second child, a tall, leggy girl with her father's features, build, and dark coloring, though she seems to have inherited Lily's temperament, in particular her playfulness and delight in movement. Sophy has been taking ballet classes since kindergarten, and some spirit of dance is so ingrained in her that it is next to impossible for her to walk in ordinary steps, or even to stand normally. She is always doing something with her feet or body or posture, and I wouldn't be surprised if she sleeps in some variation of the turnout.

"Show-off," Abby said to her sister, good-naturedly, as Sophy added balletic arm motions to the step dancing.

Lily looked on approvingly and tried to hurry the girls along when they insisted that they needed time to fix their faces. "You'll have to do it in the car," Lily told them, and she raked out her own thick hair with a broad-toothed comb on the ride down to the Kennedy Center.

In the backseat of the Cherokee, the girls were relaxed and chatty, passing around a mirror as they kidded Lily about running late, and then, somehow, they got off on a jag about the music our band played, all the slow, soulful, heartbreak stuff. Abby did an imitation of her mother singing "Time after Time," slowing the song down to a dirge. We needed something with more pizzazz, they agreed, and as if they'd been rehearsing it, they started swaying and jiving in their seat belts, pointing their fingers toward us, singing, *"Play that funky music, white boy."*

They thought they were hilarious, and none of them—not the girls, not Lily—betrayed the slightest awareness of the ways that the lives and friendships in that car had grown complicated over the last few months. They acted as though July 13th had never happened. Even Kat had let her guard down, for she was ripping right along with Abby and Sophy, and when we pulled into the underground garage at the Kennedy Center, she got out of the car and did a little shoulder shimmy, aimed at me, the white boy, that set them off on a new wave of merriment.

My daughter, beaming. How long had it been since I saw that?

Lily told them to settle down as we traveled up on the escalators, but the girls separated themselves, as kids will, and scooted ahead of us into the great hall where the giant chandeliers sparkled overhead and the light poured in through the enormous west-facing windows. "Why can't they be like this all the time?" Lily asked me, still patting at the hair she had pinned into place in the car and on the escalator.

"Do I look all right? Oh, don't tell me. We'll be in the dark in a moment and nobody will care."

It felt natural to be there that afternoon with Lily, seated beside her as the lights dimmed in the theater and Riverdance opened with its explosion of color and sound. The show is a spectacle, extravagantly produced and shamelessly commercial, but so what? When those fifty dancers soared onto the stage, I got goose bumps. Lily nudged me and turned so that we could laugh together at the sheer, soaring, triumphant energy.

On that afternoon, with the girls so enthralled on the other side of her, I felt as relaxed as I had been for weeks, and at the intermission, when we went outside onto the terrace that juts out over the river, I said so. I said, "I need to do this more often. Every day would be all right."

We were standing near the railing, and the girls were near the fountain, striking poses and laughing.

"Kat seems to be enjoying it," Lily said.

"This is the best day she's had in weeks."

"I'm glad." Looking away at the girls, she said, "You wouldn't think they had a care in the world, would you?"

"Maybe you should just keep Kat with you," I said. I told her that I was starting to feel like the boy in The Black Stallion—a movie that all our children had loved about a boy who gets shipwrecked on an is-land with a black stallion. At first the stallion rears and snorts and gallops off every time the boy tries to come near, but little by little, by offering him food, the boy calms the horse, and eventually he has the stallion eating out of his hand.

"That's an optimistic story," Lily said.

"I'd like to get her to trust me," I said. "I wish it was as simple as holding out food. Right now we seem to be at the stage when she'll come close enough to take a sniff, and then she snorts and takes off again."

"It sounds like a lovers' quarrel," Lily said, then seemed to want to correct herself. "I mean, you obviously adore her. She knows that."

"Sometimes I'm not sure how I feel about her. Sometimes I'd like to go in there and wring her neck."

"It's not easy to look deeply and bravely at your life," she said as though it was a natural conversational response, and then there was a hitch, a silence that was broken only when Lily giggled. She added, as though it amounted to an explanation, "I feel strange these days, ever since Daddy died."

She might have said more, but the crowd had started to drift back into the building, and Sophy came hopping over to us, where she made a curtsy intended to move us along.

The October sun was low in the sky when the show ended, and it was almost dark by the time we made it back to the Moorefields'. Lily insisted that we come in for a moment, and she made hot chocolate for the girls, and I think Kat would have gladly stayed for hours. But it was a school night and I had to go pick up Will, and I felt the letdown in Kat when we said our good-byes at the blue house and climbed into our own car. Her silence was heavy. So was mine, I suppose. I asked her if she'd had a good time, a question parents know they should avoid but rarely do.

"Yeah, it was fun," she said dutifully.

"How was it to see Abby? You two looked as though you were getting along."

"We always *get along*," she answered, letting me hear her annoyance with those repeated words.

"You don't see her that often," I said. "I'm curious about how you feel, OK? This isn't an interrogation."

"Why does it feel like one, then?"

"That's for you to figure out," I said in a flash of temper. "You're fine with other people, but I ask one simple question and you're in a snit."

Kat looked out the window.

I said, "It would be nice to get through one day without your moping."

"I'll work on it," Kat said. "Thanks so much for pointing it out."

When we reached the Hut, it looked dark and empty in the deep shadows of the trees, and I tried to catch hold of Kat as she unfastened her seat belt, but she was having nothing to do with me.

Ah fuck.

The Make Believes had begun to practice in September. I could never bring myself to say that we were rehearsing, though we had put ourselves up as an item in the Byrd-Adams auction and we'd been bought by a man named Rick Wolfe, who ran the bid for our services up to seventeen hundred dollars and wanted us to play a set at his wife's fortieth birthday party in November. I hadn't been at the auction (I never went because so many of the items, the cruises and weekend getaways, were geared to couples, and it was an evening for wealthy husbands and wives to bask in their own prosperity), and seventeen hundred seemed like a hefty price to pay for a garage band that had performed only once, but this was 1998, the stock market was red-hot, and people sprayed money around as though it came out of a fire hose. The school made over half a million bucks at that auction, and this same Rick Wolfe, I was told, had bought a weekend in Paris for twenty-five thousand.

I mention all this because I had considered canceling the gig, buying it back from Rick Wolfe or getting someone else to play the drums. I wasn't eager to perform in front of an audience of Byrd-Adams parents that could include the Owenses and the Wyckoffs and, for all I knew, the Vandenbergs. I didn't really know Rick Wolfe or his wife and had no idea who'd be invited to the party. But Jay knew Rick well enough to inquire about the guest list, and Rick assured him that none of those people would be present, and I was relieved. The Make Believes was my band, and I looked forward to our Tuesday night practices every week and didn't want to have to hide my face.

My band, I say, and I was the organizer and manager by default since I was the drummer and also owned the sound equipment and the soundproof garage. The Make Believes practiced at the Hut, but all five members of the band—Lily, Evan, Jay, Nancy, and I—had been talking about it since we were young parents in Georgetown. Those first conversations took place around Lily's piano, at the sing-alongs she started whenever there were a few people in her house, and Lily took a certain amount of good-natured needling for her old-fashioned musical tastes. She knew the standards, the show tunes and torch songs that had been her parents' music, the sprightly, sophisticated music of Cole Porter and Irving Berlin and Rodgers and Hammerstein, music that evoked an era when well-dressed couples smoked cigarettes and glided across the dance floor and made glittering eyes at each other in the booths of zebra-striped nightclubs. The music that had mattered so much to the rest of us, the music of our high school and college years, had passed right over her. We teased Lily because she couldn't, or wouldn't, play any song that was composed after 1960.

We'd stand around in her tiny Georgetown living room where the Baldwin baby grand took up half the space and sing "Anything Goes" and "I Get a Kick Out of You" and crank up our own voices until Lily really got into a song. Her voice was sleek and silken, and she usually kept it well in check so as not to overshadow and discourage the rest of us. When she felt like it, though, she could effortlessly enlarge her sound. It wasn't a matter of increasing the volume; it was like walking through a bright doorway out into the full sunlight. Suddenly that voice was all around you, bathing you in its shimmering, shining notes. That is a flowery description, I know, but when Lily decided to cut loose—well, all the kidding around stopped, all the clumsy efforts to harmonize or sing scat or bounce funny lyrics off the melody, all that came to a halt. She had a real set of pipes.

In those Georgetown days, when our children were still infants and toddlers, our band talk was just that—talk. Nobody had the time for a band. We were just starting our grown-up lives and I think our talk was a kind of nostalgia, a desire to keep alive a part of our past that seemed to be slipping away, to hang on to the big, chaotic emotions expressed in the music we'd loved and to the exciting, elusory sense of possibility that was being eaten away by careers and mortgages and diapers. We teased Lily because she seemed to have missed out on an entire musical era, our era, but we all realized that if we were to start a band, we wanted Lily to be the heart of it.

Then—jumping years ahead—Lily discovered Eric Clapton. By this time she had moved to the blue house on Lowell Street and the rest of us had been through our own changes and the idea of a band had been set aside and all but forgotten. I remember the afternoon that I stopped by the Moorefields' to pick up Kat and found Lily with eyes as glossy and purple as a pair of baby eggplants. She'd been listening to Clapton all day, weeping. "You have to tell me about this man," she said. "I can't stop listening to this song. I tell myself, 'Enough, enough, stop it,' but I can't stop. I play it again and start crying again—god, I am such a mess." The song was "Tears in Heaven," the song in which Clapton imagines meeting up with his son in heaven, the child who died when he fell from an apartment window in Manhattan, a song that evoked grief in millions of listeners, not just those who, like Lily, had lost a child of their own. "Have you heard it? I don't know how anyone can stand it. I feel like I'm dying every time I hear it and I just can't stop. I heard it on the radio and went straight to Tower to buy the CD, and I haven't stopped crying all day long. I've had a total meltdown. Look at this"—she indicated the disorder in her kitchen—"I've spent the day crying and trying to make a stupid crème caramel and I can't do it. I can't make custard."

The kitchen did have the bittersweet smell of burnt sugar and the counters were a blizzard of broken eggshells. "I knew there was a reason I shouldn't listen to this kind of music," she said. "I can't handle it."

Over the next weeks and months, I heard a lot about Clapton. She was discovering him, listening—for the first time really listening—to people like Clapton and dozens of others, and hearing a range of emotions that hadn't made it into the Cole Porter songbook. She was always borrowing CDs from me, and buying CDs of her own, and reading books about Clapton and Van Morrison and other performers whose music moved her, and it was only a matter of time before we started the Make Believes.

There is no point in describing the kidding we took. We'd explain that we weren't heavy metal, we weren't punk, we were just playing old songs, we were a country-rock-pop-blues kind of band, a golden oldies middle-aged white baby boomer garage band, but we ran into plenty of condescension. I heard Tony say, "It's all right with me as long as you don't embarrass yourselves in public," and I remember that remark because Lily bristled. She replied, "I didn't ask for your permission, and don't worry. We'll try hard not to embarrass *you*." That was one of the only times I'd ever heard her snarl at Tony, though this issue of respectability was a minor theme of their marriage, and Tony was always more concerned than Lily with the need to keep up appearances, to establish and maintain the right sort of social profile.

There is no point, either, in recounting the missteps and hard feelings as the Make Believes settled into a permanent configuration as a five-piece band, with Lily on the keyboards, Evan McSorley—who really did think Clapton was a god—on lead guitar, Nancy Sugarmaker on rhythm guitar, Jay on bass guitar, and yours truly sitting behind everyone, sitting back there on the throne and banging the drums. We started out playing just for the fun of it, with no intention of performing, but it is hard to keep practicing unless you are practicing for something, aiming toward some event. So we worked on a repertory of a few songs and, after about a year, invited a few friends over for a garage concert, and when that seemed to go over well enough—without embarrassing anybody—we decided to throw a Valentine's Day party at the Boat House, an old party haunt on the Potomac. To do the real work of the evening and get everyone dancing, we hired a professional band, the Mystery Band, but we'd put together a short set to do as a warm-up act, and we were all tight as ticks. We spent an absurd amount of time trying to figure out what to wear, and we must have rearranged our set a hundred times, but we started out with Lily singing "Heat Wave," a rouser, and before it was over we laid down a kick-ass version of "Mustang Sally," with Evan all over the vocals and Lily and Nancy leaning into the backup until they had the whole crowd of a hundred people screaming, *"Ride, Sally, ride,"* and the Boat House was jumping.

That was our big finale, but the audience had been friends and family—the kids were there, wide eyed and dubious, not at all sure they liked seeing their parents act this way—and our success at the Boat House in front of a handpicked crowd certainly didn't mean that we were ready for prime time. Nevertheless, we had decided back in the spring to offer ourselves in the school auction, and that fall, as we practiced for the Wolfe party, the lines of dissent were stretched tight. Evan—a tall, lanky guy with a puffy face and soulful eyes, the son of a prominent doctor and a Princeton graduate, a man who divorced after a brief marriage, didn't have to work, and spent his time playing guitar, getting high, and writing tough-guy screenplays that did not get bought—seemed to regard the gig as a major event, and he was unable to disguise his impatience with poor musicianship, especially Nancy's. She played rhythm guitar, and she lost the beat every time Evan held a chord or Lily stretched a note. Evan was on her case, and mine, too. He'd sometimes call me Ringo, a crack that didn't have even a trace of humor but was his way of reminding me that I didn't belong in a band with anyone of his class.

He was a Clapton freak, as I have mentioned, and he wanted us to load our set with Clapton numbers—all of which he would sing, of course. We wrangled about the selection of songs, but the underlying argument turned on his jealousy of Lily. Evan wanted to be the star, but in musicianship, he was nowhere close to Lily. The man could play the guitar, and he had a decent, gritty voice, though every number he did sounded like an imitation. Lily, on the other hand, couldn't have imitated anyone even if she tried and couldn't even sing a song the same way twice. She was always tinkering with the timing and phrasing of a song, plucking out syllables, lingering on some and barely touching others, sliding out one word, then another, with a sureness and delicacy that compelled you to *listen*.

In any case, Evan wanted equal billing with Lily. Every time we'd decide on a song for her, Evan would insist on having a number for himself. If she got a ballad, he had to have a ballad, and one of the slow songs Evan wanted to perform was "Running on Faith." We had rehearsed it throughout the fall. Evan didn't do a bad job with it, and it was clear when he sang it that he thought that the words applied to him, just as I imagined they applied to me. There had never even been a suggestion that Lily might sing it, but one October night Evan came to practice with a bad cold and a scratchy voice. He couldn't sing a note. We practiced Lily's songs, and then Nancy said, "What about 'Running on Faith'? We need work on that."

Evan looked at her scornfully.

"What?" Nancy said. She is not one to back down.

"Are you going to sing it?" he asked.

"Lily can sing it," Nancy said, and looked to Lily for support. Those two had been great friends back in Georgetown, and Lily had remained loyal to Nancy when she went through her divorce. Jay sometimes called her Nancy of the Large Complaint, and it was true that she was quick to find fault, especially when men were involved.

"I know all the words," Lily said. "I could probably get us through if everybody wants to try it."

Nancy said, "Let's go for it."

"Only if Evan's OK with it," Lily said.

"We can't transpose it to another key," Evan muttered, "and what would be the point, anyway?"

"We don't have to transpose it," Lily said, "The range isn't too low. '*Lately I been runnin' on faith*' . . . I think I can sing that. It's all in a pretty comfortable range."

"You sing backup on that song," Evan said bluntly.

Lily shrugged, and she seemed ready to let the matter drop, but Nancy said, "What's the deal here? Is this like a sacred guy thing? No women allowed to sing one of the great Clapton's songs?"

"It's OK," Lily said.

"We should work on it," Nancy said. "I can't believe we're into some territorial fight here just because you want to sing one song. In practice. Come on, Evan. Get over it."

Jay, I could see, wasn't going to say a word, and Evan looked at me—for support, I suppose, but I was tired of his me-first attitude and I said, "We need to tighten up on this song. Let's try it."

For a second I thought Evan might unplug his Stratocaster and walk out, but he didn't. He just fumed and snorted and jerked his head to the side, tossing the boyish flap of hair off his forehead. But he stayed. He settled down to play, and Lily sent me a guarded smile, winked as she puffed into her mike, did her little standing-in-place shuffle, and said, "This one's going out for the drummer." She was just thanking me, I think, acknowledging the fact that I'd come down on her side, but I saw Nancy's startled expression and also how Jay glanced up from his bass.

I was the one who started us off with a count, "One, two, three, four," and Evan glided into that opening riff with fierce concentration, laying it down as a challenge for Lily, playing those chords as if to say, *All right, measure up to that.* Lily was right with him on the keyboards, and I kicked in with the slow beat, heavy on the toms, and then Lily opened with a throatiness I had seldom heard in her voice, letting the rough side drag as she knocked out the first lines. She was at the keyboard, her mouth all over the globe of the mike, and even though she didn't have anything like that up-from-the-depths sound of Clapton, she gave the song a sorrowful dreaminess. As usual, the words had a sharp clarity—she just couldn't forget all the lessons she'd had about enunciation—and the phrasing was her own, just enough different from Clapton's, and Evan's, to make the words shimmer.

> *Lately I been runnin' on faith*
> *What else can a poor girl do?*
> *But my world will be right*
> *When love comes over you...*

I was behind her, of course, watching as she moved at the keyboard, the slow wheeling of her shoulders as she let her body slip into the melody, and perhaps it is futile to attempt, ever, to describe the way that a piece of music enters you, but when we got to the bridge and Lily glanced over her shoulder at me, swinging her hair so that I could see the smile on her face—an uncertain smile, an expression that asked, *Am I doing this right?*—I felt a kind of click, as though all the emotions that had been swirling within me that fall had suddenly locked into a pattern.

Love comes over you. That's what the song says, and that's what I sang with Nancy, backing Lily up, repeating those words as we tried to fade out. We were rough and choppy, not that it mattered. I was sitting there behind the drums trying keep my face from betraying what had just happened.

"Whoa," Nancy said, the first to speak in the silence that followed. "You go, girl."

And Jay said, "Where did that come from?"

So I wasn't the only one who'd heard something different in Lily, but she said, "What is this? Am I usually such a dud?"

But she knew. In a band you always know when the music has come alive, and we didn't run through the song again. We went back to one of Lily's regular songs, but everyone seemed a little dazed and disconcerted. Soon we called it a night, and Lily was the first one out the door, though she often stayed long enough for a leisurely winding down, sometimes playing for fun a few songs on the upright piano. Everyone took off quickly, and Jay, the last to leave, said, "All right, you don't have to tell me, but I hope nothing is going on between you and Lily."

"Nothing that isn't right out in the open," I said.

He looked at me carefully. "So what was that about? 'this one's going out for the drummer.'"

"I don't know. No one ever knows what's going to come out of her mouth next. I don't think Lily knows. She nailed it, though, didn't she?"

"Yeah, she nailed it," Jay said, zipping up his gig bag. "Watch yourself, amigo. The drummer should never fall for the singer. Old story, bad ending."

Then he was gone, and I stayed by myself in the music room, straightening up, letting the quiet settle around me, wondering if this could really be it, the way love would come to me—in a song, with a face that I had been looking at for years.

Lily. I was terrified.

I'M NOT PROUD of what I did next. I called Christine, a booty call, and we went out for dinner at Otello's, a place where we'd once been regulars. My plan was to woo her over a candlelit meal and then to proceed the few blocks down Connecticut Avenue to the Mayflower, the hotel where, needing privacy on short notice, we'd often taken a room. Behind the closed door she'd take the pins from her hair and press her familiar length against me as we kissed, and we would tear into each other.

Didn't happen, and I knew it wouldn't the moment Christine entered the restaurant, tall and poised, her dark hair cut shorter than I'd ever seen it, wearing a navy blue pantsuit with a tunic jacket and a white scarf at her throat. The fit and line of the suit showed off her height and the haircut revealed the slender length of her neck. This Christine was not the woman I had been imagining, though she looked exactly like what she was, an intelligent and stylish Washington professional woman who held down a serious job, a woman who took care of herself and kept her vulnerabilities well out of sight. I was at the bar, and it must have been apparent that I was taken aback. In her direct way, in a voice that went back to her sensible upbringing, she said, "Oh, for Pete's sake, my haircut can't be that bad."

"It's great," I said, standing and leaning forward into a sort of hug. Her cheek grazed mine, coolly, and there was the faint, elusive scent of Chanel. I'd already ordered Christine a *kir*, and right away she told me that I looked thinner, but mostly she talked, nervously, about chopping her hair off. She'd always worn it long, and it had taken several trips to the salon to work up the nerve to lop it off—to go whole hog, she said—but she'd gotten tired of people telling her she looked like a schoolteacher. "I loved your hair long," I blurted out, exactly the wrong thing to say, but she managed to smile and pat my arm. "I see you haven't forgotten how to sweet-talk a woman," she said.

By then we were seated at our table, and I cringed inwardly since my intention that night was to do nothing but sweet-talk. Perhaps Christine wasn't so different from what she'd always been, but my image of her didn't match up with the woman across the table. She was so *collected*. How could I have forgotten the way she held a glass, suspended on the tips of her long, slender fingers, or the way her smile flickered and then, as though it hadn't quite caught, left her face? When she removed the scarf of raw silk and carefully folded it, I saw that it had a few small dashed spots of crimson that stood out like drops of blood on the snow. I didn't say that. Neither of us knew what to say, really, even though we knew the menu at Otello's by heart, and even though we'd had a number of conversations over the last few weeks. She'd left a few things at my house, and I had some belongings at hers, and she wanted to start paying for the Twill crew that maintained her lawn, and so on. There are always things to talk about, and I wonder if anyone ever breaks off a relationship cleanly, with a single slice. Lovers are bound to each other by hundreds of ties and each one of them must be pulled off and, so far as I know, the task is never completed.

And then there is the memory of sexual intimacy that is no damn vine but flutters about such a meeting like a frantic moth dying to get through the windowpane.

I cannot deny that as guilty and awkward as I felt, I still desired this woman across the table from me, and after the first glass of Barolo, after the antipasto and the arugula salad with roasted, slivered almonds, after I'd begun to settle down, I realized that Christine must have desires of her own. Inevitably, we'd begun to talk about our children, and she told me the kinds of stories that reminded me of how much she cared for them, and let me into the sphere of her most confident emotions. Little by little it sank in that she had come to Otello's believing that I must want to renew our relationship—why else would I have invited her to a place so saturated with memories? She'd accepted, and for all her composure, I saw that she had decided to give it a chance. The soft look in her eyes was consent.

"Are you holding up all right?" she asked me. "I was afraid you'd be—I don't know, devastated. Exhausted. It has to be terrible to live with all these problems so unresolved."

"My hair went gray the last time," I said, meaning that it had turned when Trish left me, which was more or less true (my sister and I got the graying gene from Mary Carter). "Sometimes I'm afraid I'm getting used to the fact that I've been indicted for a felony. It's hard to remember when I didn't think about lawsuits ninety percent of the time."

"I hope you're taking care of yourself," Christine said. "You throw yourself at things."

I admitted that I had started seeing Joe Jarvis. I even got one of her unsteady smiles when I acted out the story of the grouse, or rather the way that Romeo had puffed himself up when the grouse dropped, and when I imitated Joe gazing up at the mandala swirl of ivy on his ceiling. I told her about crazy flight, leaving out the interpretation that had me searching for love. It was already bad enough to be seducing Christine without playing the trump card of desperation.

In truth, I no longer wanted this evening to be a seduction, and again and again I found myself looking for ways to lighten out conversation. I described Tandem in terms of Will's joke (How many Tandem students does it take to change a lightbulb? Answer: Five. One to write a letter protesting the conditions of the workers who made the bulb, one to paint a picture of the dead bulb, one to write a play about it, one to make it into a piece of jewelry, and one to call the janitor). Will knew all the jokes, I said, steering away from any discussion of Kat, and somehow I started talking about the band.

"How's Lily?" Christine asked, a question that set off all the inner alarms.

"Fine," I said, "fine. Well, maybe not fine. She's had her problems with Abby—you remember her, Lily's oldest."

"Kat's friend. Of course I remember her."

"She's still going out with Jed."

"That has to be awkward," Christine said.

"It has been, but there doesn't seem to be much we can do about it. Anyway, Lily is carrying the band, the way she always did—and her father died this summer, the Admiral? Did I ever tell you about him?"

I'm not sure why I added that remark except that I felt jittery. I'd always felt that Christine was jealous of Lily, and now she picked up her glass and looked thoughtfully down at her wine.

"You know a lot about her, don't you?"

"I can't help knowing a lot about her. We've been thrown together so much, first with the girls and then with the band."

Christine tucked her lips together in the gesture I'd seen so often. "I'm glad you have someone," she said. "Everyone has to have someone, don't they? Someone to tell their story to. I'm not surprised that it's Lily."

"It's not what you seem to think," I said, aware of the telltale sound of denial.

Christine glanced directly at me, the shadows from the candlelight flickering across the planes of her face. "Why did you ask me here tonight?"

I was unable to admit the truth. I said, "Loneliness. Crazy flight. I don't know, Christine. I don't seem to know anything for sure right now."

"The Lonely Hearts Club," Christine said. "I feel like a charter member, but I haven't gotten to the point where I'm writing personals yet." She was seeing a new therapist, she told me, a woman who was trying to get her to trust herself again. She couldn't believe she'd spent all those years going to see male therapists, she said, but this new woman had told her she'd lost touch with her instincts. She'd been so blind with Robert, her ex, and it was such a huge thing to miss. For years he had deceived her in the most intimate relationship of her life, and she'd never suspected a thing. "I thought I was damaged goods," Christine told me that night at Otello's, "the one woman on earth who wasn't equipped with intuition. If I couldn't see that my husband was gay, I couldn't see anything. And it was the same with you—how did I ever get myself to believe that we were a couple?"

"Not exactly the same," I said.

"No, but I kept missing the signs. I guess I just didn't want to see them. Even tonight—I came here with the same old hopes. I thought you wouldn't have called unless you'd really had a change of heart."

She must have seen the dismay on my face, for she patted my hand and said, "Don't worry. I'm not going to walk out on you this time."

"I'm so sorry," I said. "I just didn't think. I wanted—comfort, I guess. Company."

"Did I ever really comfort you?"

"Of course you did. Amish night was the best, and it wasn't just Amish night. It was all those late night conversations, checking in with you. We didn't miss many nights. You were the one I talked to."

She nodded. "We talked," she said, "but I've been trying to figure out how you always kept me at a distance. I was so mad at you for not letting me close."

She rolled the last of the wine in the glass and let her gray eyes meet mine. "You know what I think? You're carrying a torch for Lily.

That's what my rusty intuition is picking up. There's this electricity whenever you mention her name, as though you're afraid something's going to slip out."

"She's just an old friend," I said. "Maybe now, with the band practicing and all the stuff going on with the girls, we've gotten more tangled up than ever, but she's married, for god's sake. She's married to a good friend. You really do need to have your intuition checked."

Christine patted my hand as though it belonged to a child. "Listen to yourself. *She's married.* That never stopped anyone from falling in love. Is that what's happening?"

"God, no. Get real, Christine."

But she wasn't backing away. "This is too rich, isn't it? The irony. All this time I wanted to be closer to you. I wanted to know your secrets, the things you keep private, and finally I come to find out that your secret is you love another woman."

I denied it once more, and Christine told me not to worry. The secret was safe with her.

"THE DESIRES of the heart are crooked as corkscrews," Joe Jarvis said at our first session after my dinner with Christine. I'd been telling him how our conversation at the restaurant had veered onto the subject of Lily. I'd been insisting that Christine was wrong, that Lily and I had been friends for years and could never be anything else. When I said that she'd been like a sister to me and a mother to Kat, Joe interrupted. He rarely interrupted, but he said, "It sounds as though she's been like a wife to you."

"We've always talked about the kids," I said.

"Like a wife," Joe said. "Lily has been your companion in life."

"She's Tony's wife," I said.

Joe nodded agreeably. "That's true, too," he said.

"She's been more like a sister," I insisted. "Why do you say a wife?"

"You haven't had one," Joe said, "and I think you want one. A safe one, not one who's going to hurt you the way Trish did. Who could be safer than Lily? She's married to a friend and absolutely off-limits."

"She is off-limits," I said.

"Good," Joe said, and then added, "Keep it that way."

I spent the next half hour explaining to him why it could never be any other way, starting with the fact that Lily and Tony had more than a solid marriage. They had chemistry. Back in our Georgetown days, when we were all newlyweds, there'd been the usual undercurrent of bedroom talk when we got together, but the attraction between those two came at you like a storm front, with a lowering of atmospheric pressure and an invigorating reversal of ions. Trish and I had once been at their house for drinks on a day that Lily had bought a bathing suit, her first bikini, and somehow or other she had been induced to model it. When she stepped out onto the small patio and lowered the towel she'd wrapped around herself, Tony looked at his wife and said, "Mr. and Mrs. Jones, I think you'd better be leaving now." And we did. We went home and made love ourselves, and that was not the only time that a spark between the Moorefields ignited something between me and Trish.

I told Joe about that day. I told him how Tony and Lily had been the magnet couple of our Georgetown crowd, the glamorous, golden ones, the ones with everything—looks, money, health, charm, pedigrees, energy. They had the wonderful glow of physical vitality. They could easily have drifted into the ranks of the socialites (and they were eventually listed in the Green Book, and joined the Chevy Chase Club, and attended a fair number of gala charity events), but they never lorded it over anyone and always seemed as fully caught up as the rest of us in the ordinary challenges of getting started. There is a newness and excitement to that time of life—there was even for me, even though I was trekking out to Alexandria to work for Time-Life Books and scheming to achieve a promotion to senior editor. We all believed that life was still in front of us, and that great things were in store.

In those days we were all schemers, schemers and dreamers, and Lily hadn't given up her musical ambitions even though she'd already had Abby and Sophy. Whenever Lily told her version of the How We Met story, she'd mention her time in New York, describing herself as a wide-eyed wanna-be, a frequent performer in hopeless workshop productions, the no-lights, no-costumes, no-props, no-future productions that were staged in the hope of finding backers but never did. In one of these productions she was cast as the penniless princess of a small European country who came to America and got lost in Central Park, where, luckily, she was befriended by a wise horse and a handsome injured squirrel to whom she sang the haunting ballad "I'll Bring You Nuts," whereupon the squirrel revealed his true identity as a billionaire real estate developer. It so happened that she was working on this role on the night she met Tony at the bowling alley on Amsterdam Avenue. They were with different groups, but they were on adjoining lanes, and Lily's pals kept teasing her about the princess and the squirrel. She and Tony had already noticed each other, and Lily allowed herself to be persuaded to give an impromptu performance right there at the bowling alley in the hope of attracting his attention. "And that's how I hooked him," Lily would say. "I stood there in the bowling alley and serenaded him. I sang 'I'll Bring You Nuts,' and that did the trick."

And Tony would say, "Who could resist?"

I must have heard that story a dozen times, and even though it was probably embellished slightly (could the ballad really have been about *nuts*?), I repeated it for Joe Jarvis, wanting him to hear how the story linked Lily to Tony, not to me. I told him how she'd pursued Tony, dating him for months before she was finally invited out to Connecticut to meet his mother, Dotty, though he drove out nearly every Sunday for the family brunch at the baronial house in Greenwich. Dotty required the regular attendance of all her children. She was the despot of the Moorefield family, the beautiful girl from a blue-collar background who had succeeded in marrying old, old American money (the Moorefields were Connecticut gentry, and Tony's great-grandfather, an avid outdoorsman who'd bought up large chunks of the Adirondacks, was a founder of Moorefield Mossman, the investment banking house). Dotty's first words to Lily were, "Oh, you're the *showgirl* Tony's been talking about."

Dotty Moorefield was mindful of status, and Tony's siblings—two brothers and a sister—also seemed stuck on themselves. Tony, the baby of the family, the caboose, was the most accepting, welcoming one of the bunch, though it galled him that he hadn't been accepted at Yale. His brothers were both Yalies, and Moorefield men had gone

there for generations. The year he applied, Tony claimed, was the year
Yale decided not to accept any legacies. He would add that it was the
best thing that could have happened, for he ended up going to Georgetown and acquiring a taste for Washington. He loved this town, he
often said, even though he was a beggar compared to his brothers,
who'd both made BIG money on Wall Street. Tony had done well,
too, having started his own lobbying and PR firm. He'd made good
investments (who didn't in 1998?), but he always said he wasn't cut out
for finance. During the period that he'd lived in New York, the time
when he met Lily, he worked for a big brokerage house and fooled
around with the various illegal substances that were in fashion around
1980.

In any case, he met Lily and took her out to Greenwich, and she
liked what she saw—not the money, since she'd grown up surrounded
by all the trappings of privilege, but the sense of clan and permanence.
Her own family was already fragmented, but here were these active,
competitive, charged-up Moorefields, proficient in every sport under
the sun, involved in each other's lives, and surrounded by a whole set
of cousins and aunts and uncles. They had a history and a set of big
houses, and Lily—the military brat who'd gone from base to base,
who'd never lived in a house that wasn't owned by the government—
wanted to be a part of it. She wasn't afraid of Dotty—after growing
up in the Admiral's house, she was used to tyrants—and she adored
the old man, Arthur Moorefield, Tony's father, a fond old fellow who
kept himself busy with high-minded efforts to preserve the Adiron-
dack National Forest.

Lily wanted to be a part of it, but Tony didn't ask her to marry him
until he'd moved back to Washington to take a job in the lobbying
firm that represented the New York Stock Exchange. When he pro-
posed, Tony told Lily straight out that he wanted children and that
he expected her to give up her dreams of show business, and Lily
accepted. They had a big wedding—in Greenwich, since Lily really
didn't have any place to call home, and in short order they bought the
house in Georgetown and Lily gave birth to Abby and Sophy.

Dreams die hard, though, and Lily kept taking voice and dancing
lessons. Tony would sometimes, when he was miffed, or when she

pranced around on a tennis court or got too wound up at the piano, mutter about his *showgirl*, not without affection, but it was obviously a still-sore subject. Not long after Trish and I first met Lily, we were at the Moorefields' with a gang of other people, gathered around the piano, when somebody said Lily should sing professionally. "Well, I just might," Lily said. "I have an offer from the West End Café." This was news to Tony, and I think Lily broke it in company to disarm his reaction. Tony, by the way, has an excellent voice and a range of approximately three notes. Nancy Sugarmaker was there that night, and she was all in favor of Lily taking the gig. "Why wouldn't you do it? With your voice?" Lily listed the objections—it was at night, the kids needed her, the place was just another smoky joint.

"I'll tell you why she's not going to do it," Tony said. "Because she's my wife, that's why."

"Whoa," said Nancy. "*Excuse* me."

"I really shouldn't have brought it up," Lily said.

"You shouldn't have gone out behind my back looking for a singing job," Tony said. "We have an agreement."

"You're right. I'm sorry I brought it up."

But Tony was furious. It was the only time I'd seen him that way, and he wouldn't back off, and that night turned into one of those evenings where the fight just wouldn't go away. It kept breaking out in conversations not just about the Moorefields' marriage but marriage in general, and the roles of men and women, and the next day, a Sunday, Tony went around to the house of every woman who'd been there and presented her with a huge bouquet. The card read, "With apologies from the *new* Tony. The *old* Tony has been exiled to a rock where there are no women and no music and he has to eat pork rinds and watch televised football games for the rest of his life."

Nevertheless, Lily did not take the gig at the West End Café, and before long she was pregnant with her third child, Julia, the one who died, the one we all called the Bloomingdale baby because she was so perfect. She had fine features and long, slender hands and feet. She was one of the calmest babies imaginable, and even when she did cry, the sound was soft and delicate, as though she wished not to trouble anyone with her discomfort. And she had Lily's eyes and mouth, that broad mouth that hooked up at the corners as though designed to smile. When she took hold of your finger and gazed at you, she radiated a pleasure in the connection that was as pure as pure could be.

She was born March 5, 1987, a month premature, and the doctors reassured Lily that she had tested perfectly. She was a bit small for a newborn, but that's all. Lily nursed her, and she hired a full-time nanny—normally she got by with part-time help, which she preferred—to give her a hand with Abby and Sophy. By April Lily was going to a gym for a morning exercise class in order to get her figure back. Julia was healthy and growing and her habits were already quite predictable. She usually woke early, around six, for the morning nursing, and by eight o'clock, after a top-up, she was ready to sleep again. Lily's class was at nine o'clock at the gym on M Street, only a few blocks away, and she felt confident leaving both Sophy and the baby with Jo-Jo, the young Filipino nanny.

The morning of April 19th was glorious. After Tony left for work, Lily nursed Julia on the patio, listening to birdsong and to the bees already at work on the blossoms of purple wisteria that hung from the garden fence. Lily felt like singing, and the song she sang that morning, she had told me, was "Let's Do It," the breezy, bright, sophisticated song about the birds, the bees, and the educated fleas. They all do it, they all fall in love. That was the springtime tune in her mind when she sent Abby off to preschool with another mom, and it stayed there all morning. After her workout at the gym, she lingered with a couple of friends at a coffee shop, drinking a glass of orange juice. She was still humming that tune when she walked home on the brick sidewalks, breathing in the fragrance of spring, exulting in the day.

Her house was quiet when she entered. Jo-Jo was down on the floor playing with Sophy, who, unlike Abby, could put in hours at her dollhouse. It was almost eleven o'clock. Lily had been gone for just over two hours, and right away she knew that something was wrong. Perhaps she'd expected to see Julia awake, or perhaps there was, as she believes, the awful presence of death in the house. Her dog Posy (she was Rosa's predecessor), who ordinarily barked frantically when anyone entered the house, came up to her without a sound and licked her hand, then pushed against her as though attempting to comfort her.

Lily felt as though the marrow had been sucked out of her bones. She asked if the baby had been awake at all.

Jo-Jo said she had checked on her several times. "No wake," she said.

"She quiet," said Sophy, age two.

Sophy didn't look up from her dolls, and Lily knew why Sophy didn't say *She sleep.* She was rooted to the spot for a few seconds, unable to make herself climb the stairs to the tiny room that served as a nursery.

Julia was in the crib, motionless, and Lily knew at a glance that she was gone. She just knew. The life in a child is so apparent, so palpable, and it was gone. Her soul was gone, her spark. She must have died some time earlier, for she was already cool to the touch and the color was gone from her cheeks. The pulse in her fontanel was no longer showing, and Lily picked up and felt her chest. There was no heartbeat.

She wrapped Julia in a blanket and placed her in the carrier. Downstairs, she told Sophy and Jo-Jo that she was going to take Julia to the hospital. She spoke calmly because she didn't want to frighten Sophy and didn't want her to see her dead baby sister. She drove herself to Georgetown Hospital, only a few blocks away, instead of waiting for an ambulance. By the time she arrived, Julia's skin had a bluish cast, and the nurse in the emergency room took Julia away from her. Until that moment she had been intent on what she thought she needed to do, but when the nurse took the body she broke down. She couldn't stop sobbing. She couldn't bear knowing that she would never hold this child again.

I learned about Julia's death when I came back to my office after lunch. Someone had informed Trish, and she'd called to tell me. I left work and went straight to the Moorefields' house. Several people were already there, including Trish and Nancy, and Tony had come back from New York. He was out on the patio with Sophy. I think he must have just told her about Julia, for she had the grave, distant look that children get. I don't know how to describe Tony's face. He'd been crying, and he just shook his head back and forth, back and forth. He said, "Who would believe that life could be so sad?"

It took years for Tony and Lily to recover, though no one ever fully recovers from such a loss. I know that they went to counseling together after Julia's death, and that Tony soon wanted to have another child. He talked about it as the best way to move forward. It was an open secret that he'd always wanted a son, and he seemed to want this next child in order to set aside his sorrow, and Lily's, by the sheer force of his will. I think the loss struck terror into him, for it called into doubt his belief that his life was charmed and that he was exempt from the things that happened to other people. He was a man who needed to believe that he lived under a lucky star.

Their son, Rafe, was born in the summer of 1990, the same year that Trish left me for Blaine Baker. That was also the year the Moorefields sold the Georgetown house and moved to Lowell Street, to Big Blue—though it was a pearly gray when they bought it, before Lily transformed it. To most people, the Moorefields appeared to have regained their stride. They were still the golden couple, cruising ahead under full sail and with a brisk breeze at their backs. Their house remained the meeting place for their friends and the gathering place for their children's friends, and they still managed to magnetize people with their energy and gusto. But Julia's death changed them in some profound way, I thought. Sometimes I sensed that Tony's high spirits were manufactured, and that he had decided that if he could appear to be happy, he would succeed in being so. And in Lily there was a depth of emotion that simply wasn't there before. The smile was no longer as innocent as it was in the Georgetown days, but intricate and elusive. Its shadows were the shadows of loss and experience.

What they had been through, I told Joe Jarvis, had strengthened their marriage.

"That's possible," he said. "You know her well."

"Lily and I have always had the music in common, and the kids."

Joe's glasses had been pushed up over his short bangs, but he reached up with his hands, thick mitts, and lowered them to the bridge of his nose. He focused on me. He said, "Be careful. You're in the midst of a sea change."

"Nothing's going to happen with Lily."

"Good," he said, letting the word drop into a silent pause, glancing out the window before looking squarely at me again. "You haven't said much lately about your trial. I'm sure you realize that. When you first came here, that's what you wanted to talk about, but the subject has changed. Now you tell me about your daughter and Lily and Christine and sometimes your ex-wife. The women in your life."

Another pause, and I was unable to wait it out. "And?"

Joe sat forward on the edge of his wicker chair. "I want you to recognize the danger here," he said in a tone of unmistakable warning. "You love your daughter. You also love Lily."

He said that as a simple fact and waited, seeming to require a response. "It's not really any different from the way it's always been between us," I said.

"There's danger here," he repeated. "Don't underestimate the power of what you're feeling. You have a tendency to dismiss your emotions. You have too much faith in your ability to control them."

"Nothing's going to happen," I said. "I wouldn't let anything happen between us. I'm the one who got left, remember? I know what happens when a marriage breaks up. I'm not going through that again."

"Make sure you don't," Joe said.

"I said it's not going to happen."

Joe Jarvis heard the irritation in my voice and replied in kind. "Remind me, Tucker. What happened that night last summer when you went to pick up Kat?"

He waited a beat. "Get it?"

I got it.

WILL'S SCHOOL, St. Albans, is a series of stone buildings cleverly fitted into the hillside under the National Cathedral in a fashion reminiscent of a fortified medieval town. The playing fields are at the foot of the hill, and when I went to see Will's soccer games, I usually positioned myself on the grassy slope above the field rather than directly on the sidelines, where I would have had to mingle with other parents. This was a long-standing habit. Because I was a single dad, because I moved in less exalted orbits than most of the others, because the moms often

pestered me for landscape advice, I kept my distance, and that fall, I
have no doubt, people were relieved that I did. They still didn't know
what to say or even how to look at me.

Will could always find me on the hillside, and several times during
a game he'd make eye contact, sometimes making a gesture—a shoulder lift, a fist pump—to underscore a reaction. I'd always tried to get
to his games, and that fall I worked my schedule around St. Albans's
eighth-grade soccer team because I didn't want Will to feel over-
looked or in any way shortchanged. The fallout from July 13th had to
be affecting him more than he let on, and he was coping mostly by im-
mersing himself in his own social universe. He was quick-witted and a
little cocky, and I had to believe he was popular, for he had 130-some
names on his AOL buddy list, half of them girls. He'd organized his
buddy list as Girls 1, Girls 2, Girls 3, and Guys. I don't think I knew
the names of fifty girls when I was in the eighth grade, but Will assured me that everybody exchanged e-mail addresses these days and
the size of his list was nothing for me to worry about. His screen name
was coolhandwill.

I was glad he'd decided to play another season of soccer. He'd considered dropping it for fall tennis. All the boys his age were starting to
specialize, and there were several players on his team who did the
whole soccer deal—summer camps, select teams, indoor winter
leagues, the works. Will was a starter on his team, a fullback, but his
skills were somewhere in the middle range and he made the most of
them. He never lost his concentration. He wasn't a playmaker but he
was pesky. He persisted. He dogged his opponents, he played smart,
he always had a sense of the game, he knew where everyone else was,
he made crisp passes, and he wasn't afraid to mix it up with the bigger
kids. I'd never played soccer, but I have to say that Will reminded me
of myself when I played team sports—not a star but a grinder.

Will's team played on the small field, and when I turned out for
their game against Landon, a varsity soccer game was under way on
the main field. The St. Albans varsity was in blue and white, and the
other team, in red jerseys and black shorts, was Byrd-Adams. The tall
Byrd-Adams sweeper, one of the tallest kids on the field, the kid with
a patch over his left eye, was Jed Vandenberg.

Maybe it was the black pirate's patch that attracted my attention, or maybe it was his size, but once I'd singled him out, I could hardly follow Will's game. My gaze kept wheeling over to the main field. It was a cloudy, chilly November afternoon, damp and raw, and of course I scanned the bleachers for Richard Vandenberg. I didn't see him, but I did see Abby. There were about a hundred people in the bleachers or along the sidelines, and Abby was one of a group of girls that kept moving about, not really watching the game, but flitting here and there like a small flock of sparrows. She was wearing a boy's red-and-black jacket—Jed's, presumably—and to me it looked as though she was the queen, the one who decided when to move and where, and that the others fluttered to secure a place near her.

I don't think she saw me. I didn't really try to hide, but I wanted to watch the two of them in their own element. I got the attraction between them. I had always known that Abby was a leader, but that afternoon I saw how she identified herself as Jed's girl, and I saw how Jed dominated the game from his position as sweeper. They were an Alpha couple, high school version. For Byrd-Adams, which didn't have a football team, soccer was a major sport, and St. Albans was a major rival, and the Byrd-Adams team was less talented but more intense than the St. Albans team. Jed was all over the field. He played a reckless, physical game, using his size and power, and when he had a one-on-one, he just blew the other kid away. You could feel that he wanted to take charge of the game, and he completely frustrated the St. Albans striker, a shifty, speedy Hispanic boy who kept spreading his hands to ask for a penalty call. Whenever that kid was near the ball, Jed was all over him like stink on a monkey. Byrd-Adams took a 1–0 lead and hung on to it. The image that stays with me is of a St. Albans corner kick near the end of the game, when the ball was curling toward the striker and Jed Vandenberg, all muddy by then, launched himself and rose towering above everyone else on the field, meeting the ball with his head, timing his leap so perfectly that the ball sailed through the sky like a punt.

Byrd-Adams won, and they celebrated by doing what kids do—they dove into a big wiggling heap in the muddiest part of the field. By then Will's game was over and he was watching, with his teammates, from the sidelines. After the two varsity teams had lined up and shaken hands, Jed and Abby found each in the Byrd-Adams crowd, and even at my distance I could see the shine of happiness on their faces and the way they encountered the others, the players and girls and parents who wanted to congratulate Jed, as a couple. From my vantage point it seemed as though the crowd revolved around the two of them, the girl in the red jacket and the muddy boy with the patch on his eye.

I went back to the Jimmy, slinking up through the trees to the parking lot, to wait for Will. His team had won, and when he appeared, lugging a backpack, we talked at first about his game. Then he said, "Did you see the other game?"

I said I had.

He hesitated before asking, "So that's the guy, the one with the patch? He's the one you hit?"

"That's Jed Vandenberg," I said.

"He's a big dude," Will said. "That was awesome, that header. So does he take out his eye when he plays or what?"

"I guess he takes it out," I said.

Will shook his head and laughed at something private.

"What's funny?"

"I'm just thinking what would happen if some kid slammed his locker. I mean, it would be pretty weird when he sat down to check his loot. 'Let's see, hmmm, what have I got here—hey! An eyeball! Wonder if he'll miss it?'"

I laughed, too. Didn't want to, but I couldn't help it.

A FEW DAYS later, in his father's office, I saw Jed Vandenberg again.

The lawyers and I went there to meet with Richard Vandenberg and John Briggs, and we knew that Jed was going to be present, too. The meeting had been scheduled in the late afternoon to accommodate his school schedule, and we had to surmise, since Richard Vandenberg had been so adamant about not negotiating any plea, that it was Jed who wanted the meeting. I knew that Abby had spoken to him, for I'd called her after Richard Vandenberg's assistant phoned Ian to set up a time. I thanked her, and she said, yeah, she'd told him what I said, but if she knew what had gone on between Jed and his father, she didn't tell me.

Ian and Brian's plan was to try to appeal to Jed. Except for that, except to tell me that they hoped I wouldn't have to say anything, I had no idea what to expect and I was tense and cotton-mouthed as we sat in the conference room, a room with a glossy table of the same dark wood as the paneling and windows that opened onto the blue-black winter sky. Vandenberg kept us waiting for almost half an hour.

There were no apologies when he finally showed up, trailed by John Briggs and Jed, who was wearing that red school jacket with the black sleeves and who didn't look up at any of us as he slouched to a chair and took his seat. He was the only one who sat down right away. We'd all stood when they entered, and we kept standing, for Vandenberg didn't say a word. He stood there glaring. It was his turf and he couldn't bring himself to ask us to take a seat.

Ian broke the silence, thanking Vandenberg for meeting with us and Briggs for coming. Briggs, carefully groomed, moved his head about as though he had a crick in his neck, and even he seemed to feel the rudeness emanating from Vandenberg, whom he thanked for providing the room. Then Brian introduced himself to Briggs and introduced Corinne, and somehow, in the movement about the table, the shuffling of pads and papers, we all managed to get seated.

Richard Vandenberg was the last to sit down, taking the chair on the opposite side of the table from us, between Briggs and his son. He was wearing an expensive tailored suit and a striped shirt that had one of those English collars and probably also came from a tailor, but his clothes were tight on him. The collar seemed to bite into the flesh of his neck, and lines of tension radiated out from the button of his suit jacket. The summer sunburn was gone, but his face was still brick red and the arrogance, the hatred, came off him like a fume.

He hadn't met Brian, and when Brian explained that he'd tagged along because he'd be representing me in the civil suit, Vandenberg said in his bass voice, "We're not here to talk about the civil suit."

Ian agreed. In his affable, unruffled way, he explained that Crocker, Collinsworth, and deSantis was a small firm and that lines weren't

always as clear-cut as they probably were here at Devens and Shackleford. Brian had been looking over his shoulder, he said, and they were
working from the same investigative reports. He certainly hoped Vandenberg didn't mind Brian's being there.

"I do mind," Vandenberg said. "The sole reason we're here is to
discuss the developments that you claim have come to light in your investigation. What are these alleged developments?"

"Our thought," Ian said, "is that it's in everybody's best interest to
avoid a trial, and that's what we'd like to discuss. How to spare everyone the ordeal of a trial. Frankly, we believe that the right arena for
this case is a civil court, not a criminal court."

"Did I fail to make myself clear? We're not discussing the civil action, and we're not here to dismiss the case. He's been charged with
felony assault and a trial date has been set. There's not going to be a
plea."

Briggs piped up, "The grand jury didn't waste any time giving me
an indictment. Open-and-shut."

"We understand the indictment," Ian said, "and we acknowledge
the severity of Jed's injuries. It's been traumatic, we know that. But we
can all agree, can't we, that the injury took place under extreme circumstances? Tucker was living out a parent's nightmare when he went
to find his daughter that night."

"This is your defense?" Vandenberg snorted. "Extenuating circumstances? This is a waste of time. Unless you have something else
to say, this meeting is over."

"There is one strand of evidence that we feel compelled to mention. So much new information has come to the surface during the investigation that Corinne has been conducting. I know that you have
your own investigation under way—"

"At this point there is no evidence," Vandenberg said. "There are
various reports, but not evidence."

Ian fiddled with his glasses. He was able to smile faintly when he
said, "I stand corrected, but we do have *reports* that have materially altered our view of the case. To get right to the point, we know that Jed
wanted to conceal what happened at your house on the night of July
13th. He planned a cover-up. He instructed the others who were there

that night to deny what had happened to Kathryn Jones, and we have corroborating *reports* that confirm this."

Ian made it sound as though he regretted saying this, and Vandenberg didn't seem surprised. He was less belligerent when he said, "Jed's not on trial here."

"Of course not. No one's on trial here. But if our client goes to trial, we'd have to paint a complete picture of what happened that night. We'd have no choice but to call as many witnesses as needed to paint a full picture."

"This is bullshit," Vandenberg said. "No judge is going to allow you to turn this case into a circus. The issue isn't what Jed did or didn't plan. There's only one issue here, and that's what he"—he pointed at me—"did to Jed. Period."

"I take your point," Ian said, "but I think this is relevant. I've been trying criminal cases for ten years, and I'm quite certain this is relevant, as a matter of fact. What Jed said to Tucker that night at the pool—that's definitely relevant. That's the heart of this case. I have no doubt that a jury would find it relevant that he said he didn't know where Tucker's daughter was when, in fact, he did know. When he was the one who sent her there."

Jed was looking up now, and he kept rearranging his big frame in the banker's chair at the table. He drew a couple of breaths as if to speak, but didn't. His father said, "This is why you asked for this meeting? To threaten us?"

"We wanted you to know where our investigation is leading us."

Briggs said, "We don't have to put Jed on the stand."

Ian seemed to wonder for a moment what Briggs could possibly be thinking. He said, "We have no doubt that we could establish what was said with our own witnesses. But I suppose we could call Jed as a witness for the defense. In a pinch."

Briggs did the thing with his neck again, and in his mildest voice Brian spoke up. He asked if he could change the subject. He'd been trying to stay on top of the case, he said, and it wasn't so much the case itself as the emotional ramifications that he wanted to talk about. He chatted about his own kids who attended private schools in Maryland, and even out there the parents were talking about this case. It was on the grapevine, he said, and we were all lucky that the papers hadn't picked it up yet. In any town smaller than Washington, he thought it would have been all over the media.

"Are you now threatening to take this to the press?" Vandenberg asked.

"Not at all. God forbid that it should get into the papers—though it probably will if the case goes to trial. It would be hard to keep it out of the papers, and we all know what happens then. We know that the spotlight intensifies everything, and these are youngsters we're talking about."

"There's only one youngster, and that's my son. The victim of the assault."

"There are others," Brian said, shaking his head. "There are others, unfortunately. There's Tucker's daughter, Kat. The spotlight's going to be on her, too, and it's going to be on those boys who took her into the pool house. There could easily be other criminal charges filed. Frankly, I don't understand why the U.S. Attorney hasn't already charged those boys with sexual abuse."

Brian's voice is soft, and he has that choirboy face. He'd obviously startled Briggs, who said in his official voice, "I can't comment on any additional charges. That's outside the scope of our discussion."

"But if this case is tried, if it's publicized, do you really think it will be possible not to indict Owens and Wyckoff and—who's the third boy—Childs? You wouldn't have any choice, would you, once it's a matter of public record?"

Briggs said, "This is entirely a matter of speculation and I'm not going to comment on it."

"That's one way to describe what we're doing here," Brian said, and I saw that he was addressing himself to Jed. "We're speculating. We're trying to anticipate some of the results of a trial. We know that one possible outcome is that Tucker gets punished. He could be convicted and sent to prison, and, obviously, we want to avoid that. He's the only one, right now, who's been charged with a crime. But when you look at the potential damage of a trial . . . he might not be the only one at risk. That's what we're asking you today, to weigh all these risks carefully. That's what we've been doing, and if you do some soul searching, we think you'll come out where we do. We think you'll agree that it's best to try to contain the damage."

There was a pause and Richard Vandenberg said, "Nothing further? Is that it? No more threats and insults?"

"Dad," Jed Landenberg said, just that one word. *Dad.*

Then he didn't know what else to say and his gaze, the gaze of that single eye, traveled over the four of us seated across the table from him. The lid over the glass eye drooped down.

Brian said, "Did you have a question?"

"I wanted to know how it would work," Jed said. "I mean, if he gets off, there wouldn't be charges against Luke and Matt and Danny? Is that what you're saying?"

"That's not up to us," Brian said. "It's the U.S. Attorney who'd decide, but it sounds as though they'd be reluctant to indict. Correct me if I'm wrong," he said to Briggs, "but don't you rely heavily on the victim in sexual abuse cases? So it would depend on Kat's willingness to participate in a trial?"

"I really can't comment," Briggs said.

"I know Kat and Tucker don't want to pursue it," Brian said to Jed, "not if they can help it."

"So that would be it? If he gets off, there wouldn't be a trial and the investigation is over?"

Richard Vandenberg said, "There's a civil suit, Jed, and they'll pull this same stunt all over again. The investigation won't be over, and they'll threaten to bring civil actions. I've seen this ploy before."

"We could discuss the settlement of the civil suit if you'd like," Brian said.

Vandenberg, I swear, bared his teeth like a hyena.

Briggs pointed out that he was there to represent the U.S. Attorney, not to discuss a civil action.

"I thought that as long as we're all here, we might be able to kill two birds with one stone," Brian said.

"We haven't killed any birds," Vandenberg said. "The charge against him isn't going to be dropped or reduced. This whole scenario is full of holes you could drive a truck through. No judge is going to allow you to turn this into a mudslinging contest."

"I want it to stop," Jed said.

"You don't know what you're saying," his father said.

"I know what they're saying," Jed said. "I get it. It's coming through loud and clear, and I want it to stop."

"You're emotional right now."

"You're right," Jed said, standing up. "I'm emotional. I'm sick of this shit day in and day out. It's been going on for months and I want it to be over. Do I get to have an opinion? It's my eye, Dad. It's my fucking eye."

His voice was almost as deep as his father's, but it cracked and got away from him. He plunged his hands into his pockets and looked furiously at all of us, and Richard Vandenberg stood up as if to prevent him from leaving, but Jed walked right past him.

Vandenberg buttoned his suit jacket and attempted, oddly, to summon up a face of amused condescension, as though he could hardly believe he'd bothered talking to chumps like us. "There's no deal here," he said, "no deal, no deal."

When he was gone, Briggs rose to his feet uncertainly. He must have a windup tape inside him, and he punched the button that produced the message that he would take the matter under advisement and get back to us.

My lawyers and I left the building and ducked into the nearest bar, a dark place just beginning to fill with people getting off work. It was a Friday afternoon and the mood was festive. "Damage was *done*," Brian kept saying, and he ordered martinis for everyone but Ian, who downed a beer and left quickly to get home to his family. Brian and Corinne and I stayed for a while, drinking martinis that came in glasses the size of light fixtures. Corinne told Brian that he'd played Vandenberg like a violin, playing the air violin as she did so. They wanted to rehash all the details of the meeting, and they were confident that we'd gotten to Jed and that Richard Vandenberg was going to cave, but I didn't feel like gloating. It had been gruesome to sit in that room across from Jed Vandenberg. With that father, I thought, he was going to have more to overcome than a glass eye, and I admired the guts it must have taken to stand up to Richard Vandenberg.

In any case, I was the odd man out. Brian and his pretty young sidekick didn't need me to carry on with their celebration.

I DIDN'T mention that meeting to either of the kids. There were a few times when I felt like sitting them down and laying out the whole legal situation, but I don't think any of us had the stamina for any such discussion. After we went to daylight savings—the fall always seems to end on that day, and the world closes down—it seemed all we could do to drag ourselves through our daily routines, and Kat couldn't always do that. She was still locking her door and moping, and no one—not Will, not Gladys, and not I—knew what to do about it. Gladys had spoken to me a couple of times, worried, afraid that she was in some way responsible for Kat's despondency. She'd been watching Kat as closely as I had, noticing how little she ate, the paleness in her face, the emptiness in her voice. "She not right," Gladys said.

Maybe I should have told Trish, but Kat managed to do just enough to convince me, and perhaps herself, that she wasn't completely defeated. She still went to her sessions with Bonnie, and she went to school about as often as she stayed home. When I met with her teachers on conference day, they told me that she was keeping up with her work, but barely. I was inclined to give her one more chance to rally since there'd been one unavoidable setback—the AIDS test. During the summer she'd been tested for STDs, but she had to wait three months before taking the AIDS test, and of course she took it in New York, on a weekend visit to Trish. She tested negative, but the test itself had reawakened the shame and guilt she'd been trying to leave behind, or so I imagined. Of course she did not talk to me about it. I never stopped trying to get her to talk, but I often felt as though I was blowing on embers, trying to rekindle a fire. There wasn't much light in my daughter's beautiful eyes.

Something had to change, and I'd set a date—Abby's sixteenth birthday party in early November. It was the one thing that Kat looked forward to. After that, if the party didn't make a real difference, there had to be a new plan. I didn't know what the plan might be, but we couldn't go on like this. I took it as a promising sign that Kat liked the present she'd bought for Abby, an expensive silver cuff she'd picked out in New York. And she even managed to crack a joke, calling the party her coming-out. Not much of a joke, maybe, but it was an effort to laugh at her own nervousness. The party would be the first time that fall that she went to a large social event.

The party, I should mention, was not the kind of party Abby wanted to have. It was to be a Sunday brunch. For years these Sunday brunches had been a Moorefield tradition, the way the kids' birthdays and other family occasions were celebrated, with the blue house full of people of various ages and the birthday party itself one of many activities, not one of those ghastly, overproduced events featuring a clown or a puppeteer or a creepy magician and requiring the children to sit still and be appreciative. This year, however, Abby had told Lily she didn't want another random party. She wanted a blowout, a boys-and-girls party at a hotel or club, with a DJ and dancing, and she regarded this Sunday brunch celebration almost as a punishment.

Still, Kat was keyed up about going, and she took an unusually long time getting herself ready. When she finally came downstairs, she was wearing nice jeans and a dark green top, a baggy designer sweatshirt with the sleeves pushed up on her forearms. "You look *mahvelous,*" Will told her with impatience, showing off a jeering move he had just learned, a sharklike, sideways rolling of the head meant to emphasize his scorn, confident that he himself was perfectly attired in his visor and cargoes, with an oversize orange T-shirt that showed a large picture of a trout fly and read, *Flies with Attitude.*

It was a damp, drizzly Sunday and he groaned when I made him put on a jacket—"Like I'm gonna catch pneumonia on the way to the car"—and Kat had a stoic expression on her face as she pulled on her parka. She'd used makeup around her eyes, and she was wearing small earrings, little brown beads that matched her eyes. It had been months since I'd seen her wear earrings. Her hair was clean and plaited into a braid, and I hugged her as we were leaving the house. She was stiff as a rake.

"You have the best hair," Lily said when we arrived, running her fingers over Kat's braid, and it was impossible not to see how Kat soaked up her approval. The house was already full of people, but I think that Lily—who knew how Kat was feeling—must have been watching for us so that she could greet Kat right away. She tugged at Will's visor and hugged him, too, and I got my kiss, a social peck on the cheek, but it was Kat she fussed over, Kat she tried to cheer up. "Is this too silly? All these balloons? Did I overdo it? I lose control when I get to the party store. Abby said, 'Mom, I'm not six. I'm *sixteen.*'"

The house was festooned with balloons and colored streamers and glittery letters spelling out HAPPY BIRTHDAY and SWEET SIXTEEN, and there was a mound of brightly wrapped presents on the hall table, to which we added our own gifts (a Hudson Trail Outfitters gift certificate from me and Will, that cuff from Kat). Above that table, dominating the entrance hall, Lily had hung a poster-sized blowup of a picture of Abby climbing one of the rock walls in the Potomac Gorge, a photo taken from above and showing her smiling proudly, her eyes and teeth sparkling as she hung suspended over the river that looked far, far below.

"The girls are upstairs," she told Kat, giving her another encouraging pat on the arm as Kat headed for the stairs, her head ducked down as though she hoped no one would recognize her. Will had already made his way toward the back room, where the boys and most of the men were gathered in front of the big-screen TV to watch the Redskins play the Giants, and the women and smaller kids were in the front rooms. Fires were burning in both fireplaces, living room and dining room, and there were autumnal bouquets all over the place, bunches of dried sedum and hydrangea, as well as bright displays of yellow and purple chrysanthemums. Lily said, "She was brave to come, wasn't she? Don't you wonder sometimes how anyone ever makes it through high school?" She was smiling at me, and I got one of her encouraging pats. "You look like you could use a southsider," she said, guiding me to the dining-room sideboard where the bar was set up, "a nice stiff one. How are you holding up?"

When she squeezed my arm, I reminded myself that this was nothing more than the warmth that Lily radiated for everyone who came within her orbit. She'd been her old breezy self with me ever since that one band practice, and while we were standing there at the sideboard and I was pouring my southsider, Tony's trademark drink, a rum concoction with a wicked kick, Jay sauntered up to us and said, teasingly, "All right, kiddos, break it up. Band members have got to mingle today." Lily immediately let go of my arm and took hold of his, as easily demonstrative with him as she had been with me. I saw how Lily leaned against him and realized that she showered her affection on all who came near and that I was an idiot for having imagined anything otherwise.

I tried to act naturally that Sunday—a strange concept when you come to think of it, a contradiction in terms. If you're doing what's natural to you, you don't have to *act*. I have never had much reason to act, to attempt to be anything but myself, for I have never had much to hide. But that day I felt like an actor when I went into the back room and took my place among the men and fell into the usual banter with Tony. "Pony up," he said, holding out a cap full of bills. "Don't tell me—you like the Giants, 24–17, right? After your long and careful analysis."

I dug out my five bucks to put in the pool. This was another Sunday tradition, the football pool, and grown-ups had to wager five bucks each. Since I didn't know much about the National Football League, I always picked the same score, 24–17, and it irked Tony that I was frequently the winner, though I never pocketed the money. The kids put up a dollar each, and the pool usually amounted to thirty or forty bucks—and if an adult happened to win, Tony found some way to disqualify him so that the pot always went to a youngster. This was his way of providing the boys with early instruction in the pleasures of wagering. He is a sports junkie who likes to make real bets with his bookie, big bets, and even though the game was only in the first quarter, he was well into a rant about the Redskins coach and his loyalty to his dip-shit quarterback. Every time he said *dip-shit*, Rafe, age eight, looked around to see if everyone else was tickled to hear his father cuss.

The southsiders, the Redskins, the kids underfoot, the smell of wood smoke and Lily's chili, the hum and coziness of a full house—it was another Sunday at the Moorefields', and Tony, as usual, was holding forth, groaning about the hapless Redskins and predicting big trouble ahead for the Democratic Party. Dressed in corduroys and a soft sweater, wearing no socks and his at-home needlepoint slippers, an affectation for which he took a certain amount of grief, Tony bounced around making sure that everyone had a full glass and no one felt ignored. On that day, just after the midterm elections in which the Democrats had all scrambled to put distance between themselves and the disgraced president, there was a lot of political talk, and most of the men in the room—three lawyers, two lobbyists, a hotel owner, a banker, and me, a lawn guy—had some kind of insider information about candidates and races. They knew the back story, the gossip, the details that don't make it into the newspaper, and Tony saw to it that the discussion was conducted in a mood of friendly sparring. He jumped all over Jay when he described one congressman as a Boy Scout. "You should take a plane ride with him," Tony said, "like I did a couple of months ago. You would have thought the guy had never seen a Lear before. He was like a kid in his first limo. You wanna bet how long he stays in the House? I say he's gone at the end of this term if he can find a real job. He's tired of flying coach. He's a Boy Scout dying to turn into a fat cat."

Everybody but me seemed to have an opinion about the way the pay scale kept top people from running for Congress, but no subject lasted for too long with Tony. During the next commercial, he said, "So, drummer boy, how's the band sounding? You ready for the big performance? It's only a couple of weeks away."

"We're getting there," I said, "counting on Lily to pull us through."

"The Make Believes," he said. "I should have bid for you guys. I was tempted. I could have bought Lily at auction for what was it? Fifteen hundred bucks? She costs me a lot more than that."

There was the kind of uncomfortable laughter that follows a remark that everyone wishes had been funny.

"I do?" Lily asked. She'd materialized in the doorway and Tony hadn't known she was there. No one had. "How much do I cost you?"

She waited for a reply and the moment stretched into a silence that even the kids sensed. They were sitting on the floor close to the TV, and they probably hadn't caught the exchange, but they felt the snap in the air and craned around to see what was going on. The best way to describe Tony's expression would be shit-eating.

Lily, with a show of great deference, said, "I just came to announce that chili is being served," and she swept herself away with the kind of low, obsequious bow a courtier makes to the king.

"Whatever she costs," Jerry Goldfarb said, "I have a feeling the price just went up. A lot."

There was some relief and gratitude for the incorrigible Jerry, father of Rebecca and Ike, the gravelly voiced lawyer who referred to himself as our token Jew and could be counted on for remarks that, as he put it, cut the grease. Everyone in the room felt embarrassed for Tony, who hadn't intended to come off as mean-spirited, but even the *new* Tony just couldn't see why a woman with children and a big house, with a name and a position in the world, why his *wife* was so eager to perform in a garage band.

In the dining room, as we filled our plates with chili and salad and corn bread, Lily was flitting around, the busy hostess, urging the men to take their plates into the living room, to make the ultimate sacrifice and sit with the women, urging the girls, when they showed up, to stay downstairs and join the dreaded grown-ups, promising that we would not ask them how school was going. There must have been a dozen girls there, some younger than Abby, Sophy's friends, and I saw that Kat wasn't talking. She had her shoulders hunched and her head down when she went through the food line, putting only a few leaves of salad on her plate, looking around furtively, not certain where she should park herself to eat. Lily was watching the girls closely, and she went to stand at the foot of the stairs, blocking the way when Abby headed toward them, "It's going to be time for the cake soon," she said. "Why don't you eat down here?"

Abby was wearing a pair of ratty jeans with the top section, including the belt loops, cut off, and she kept pulling them up with one hand. "What," she said. "You afraid we're going to miss the sing-along?"

"It's your party," Lily said.

"Oh sure."

"Sweetie, please."

"Mom, there's no place to sit down here, OK?"

There was a standoff at the foot of the stairs, Lily not budging, Abby not turning away. I felt for Kat, who hovered at the edge of the gang of girls. The older ones, Abby's friends, all had the same disheveled, can't-be-bothered look, and poor Kat had taken such pains to pull herself together.

"People want to see you," Lily said, and she looked about for support.

Linda Goldfarb had also been watching this confrontation, and she chimed in, "Tell me about that fabulous picture. You look like such a pro up on that cliff. Who took that?"

Abby hiked at her jeans but they didn't cover her midriff. "A friend," she said, at first. Then she looked directly at me. "A guy named Jed Vandenberg."

"All right," Lily said, trying to prevent this moment from getting any worse, "I promise I won't sing. Now will you stay downstairs?"

But even as she said it, she was moving aside, and Abby and her cluster of pals headed up the stairs. Kat watched them go and then drifted into the living room, where some of the younger girls had taken places around the piano. Lily said to me, "I guess you're entitled to be touchy on your birthday, eh?"

But I saw the bars of anger shooting through her eyes.

I went into the living room and ate standing near Linda, watching for a chance to talk to Kat, who sat quietly on a little kid's chair, her legs folded up, not eating a bite. She wouldn't look at me, but she expected me to come to her when she stood and walked back into the dining room. "I want to get out of here," she whispered. "I knew we shouldn't have come."

"Let's wait for the cake, OK? It would be rude to leave before that."

She glared up at me for an instant. "Rude," she said, with a soft snort. "I want to go now. This is insane."

"Everybody will notice if we go now."

"Like I give a fuck," Kat whispered fiercely. "They already look at us like we're freaks."

It jolted me every time she used profanity. "OK, I'll get our jackets," I said, "and I'll tell Lily we're taking off. I'll let Will stay and come back for him later."

Lily wouldn't hear of it. She was in the kitchen putting the candles on the cake, and when I said we were leaving, she went instantly to

Kat. "You can help me," she said, "with these ridiculous candles. They're the kind that won't blow out—but I'm sure that's what Abby expects. You can't leave now, sweetie, and I'll tell you why—because if you leave, I'm leaving. Deal? You cannot be any more upset with Abby than I am. OK? Is that a deal?"

She stroked Kat's arm and we stayed. I wandered back into the TV room, wanting to get out of the way, wanting to let Lily soothe my daughter in a way that I couldn't. The Redskins were losing, the chili was being consumed, and the fart jokes were beginning, with Tony pretending to make a pool about which one of the boys was going to cut the first one. Ike Goldfarb, a kid with curly hair and a big infectious laugh, was already starting to quake. "Listen," Jerry said, "I have to tell you what my son thinks of me. Can I tell this, Ike?" Ike just writhed on the floor. "I get home the other night and Linda tells me Ike already thinks I'm there. You know why? He hears a bus go by and it lays this giant squelcher, a huge juicy one, and Ike perks right up. 'Hey, Mom,' he says. 'Dad's home!' I don't know, maybe I should be flattered. But do I really sound like a bus? Do I, Ike? A bus?"

Ike was roaring helplessly when Lily appeared in the doorway and told us that it was time for the cake.

Abby had come back downstairs and she stood, sourpussed, at the head of the dining-room table, flanked by her girlfriends, as everyone else pushed into the dining room and hallway to sing "Happy Birthday." Sophy carried the sheet cake in from the kitchen, candles blazing, and Tony was busily passing out flutes of champagne so that the grown-ups could toast his daughter. She was given a flute, too, and looked impatient with the folderol of pouring. Finally, when all the flutes were bubbling and all the young kids had a glass of something, Tony tapped a spoon against his glass to call for silence.

"We're here for Abby today, Abigail Helen Moorefield. I'm not going to say how quickly these years have passed, sixteen years, or how old it makes me feel. Sweet sixteen, when a girl becomes a woman, but I don't think that really applies to Abby. This daughter of mine has known her own mind since she's been five. Or two. The only difference now is that she climbs mountains, she skis like an angel, and she's turned into a beautiful woman. She still drives me crazy. I thought they broke the mold when they made my mother—most of you know Dotty, She Who Rules the World. Well, this daughter of mine got that same gene. So I say, Long May You Rule! We love you, Abs."

The glasses were raised then, and Abby said, "Thanks, I guess."

I was standing near the front of the crowd and I saw Kat sliding along the back edge, all the way back in the living room, keeping herself at a distance. Her expression said, *Enough.* It took me a couple of minutes to get our coats and extract myself, and Lily came onto the porch to see us off. Kat could hardly make herself say thank you, and she almost fled down the steps.

"God, it's rough," Lily said. "I hope she's all right. I can tell you this is the last one, the last birthday party. Sixteen is the cutoff. Did you notice that I didn't make the toast? I guess I don't have that ruler gene going for me."

There was bite in that remark, and Lily was still on the porch when we drove off, giving us a wave. That cold drizzle was coming down, and I didn't know what to say to Kat except that I was sorry it had gone so badly.

"I shouldn't have gone," she said. "Everything's different now."

"Not everything."

"Everything," she said flatly.

"What happened upstairs?" I asked. "Did something happen between you and Abby?"

"I don't want to talk about it, OK?"

The windshield wipers swept back and forth as the heat began to fill the chilly interior. "Abby wanted a different kind of party," I said. "She was in a lousy mood."

"She wanted to talk to Jed," Kat said. "That's what she did. She was on the phone with him the whole time."

We were on Chain Bridge Road, heading down the hill, and Kat was so close to breaking down that I pulled off in the entrance to Battery Kemble Park. I wanted to console her and I tried to tell her how sorry I was, how courageous she'd been to go to the party at all, but she cried, "Why are you stopping? Why are you stopping here? I don't want to stop here."

She sounded crazy with sorrow, and I thought she was going to jump out of the car. She did struggle with the door and opened it, but her seat belt was on and she was so distraught that she couldn't find the release. Her struggle had desperation in it, and then she leaned forward and cried as though she'd been storing up tears and sorrow for the whole of her short life. I rubbed her back and felt her shoulder blades jutting through her parka like a pair of ax blades.

When she could talk, she said, "I just want to go home."

BACK AT the Hut, Kat went straight to her room, and I took Romeo out for his walk. He senses my moods, I am convinced, and he was subdued that evening, unwilling to let me out of his sight, watching me as though my melancholy had seeped into him. I thought about Joe Jarvis and his notions of dog as therapist, but Romeo wasn't going to help me figure out how to come through in these situations with Kat. I wanted to know what to do, and I wanted someone to spell it out for me. I didn't want to be out walking my dog when my daughter was in her bedroom, deep down in her pillows, aching and alone. I would have gone up there if I'd thought she wanted me, but when I returned from my walk, I just called up the stairs to say that I was going back to the Moorefields' to pick up Will. My rain jacket was wet and my cap was soaked through. Kat's voice reached me faintly, and I was on the way out the door when the phone rang—Will, I thought, since the display showed the Moorefields' number.

But it was Lily who said in a shaky voice, "This isn't a call you want to get, Tucker, but let me say right out it's not as bad as you're going to think, OK? Will's not hurt. He got in a fight, and he's going to have a black eye, but he's not hurt, and neither is the other boy. He's right here and we have an ice pack on it, and he's going to be OK. There's no concussion, no bleeding, nothing like that. Just an old-fashioned black eye."

I asked all the predictable questions, breathing hard, watching Romeo watch me—he heard the urgency in my voice—but Lily didn't know all the answers, or didn't want to tell me over the phone. It started at the playground, she said, when the boys decided they wanted to go shoot a few baskets, and the other boy was somebody they'd run into at the basketball court. "Will is fine," she kept saying.

"We can talk about all this when you get here, but the main thing is he's fine. He's watching TV with Sophy and Rafe, and Tony's with them, too. He's clear as a bell."

"Will doesn't get into fights," I said.

"Well, he got in one tonight, but he's fine. We'll talk about when you get here."

When I hung up, I decided not to tell Kat because I expected her to think exactly what I was thinking—that the fight must have been about her. Will was too much in charge of himself to get drawn into a fight about a game.

All the guests had left the Moorefields' by the time I got there, and I found Will in the TV room with Rafe and Sophy, holding a blue ice pack to his left eye. He swiveled his head to give me a glum look from the couch. When Lily switched on the overhead lights, I saw that he had a scrape on his chin, but I had to ask him to lift the ice pack so that I could see.

His eye was swollen almost shut, and the bruise was not black yet. His clothes were soaking.

Tony had stood and come across the room to shake my hand. "Rafe, Sophy, out, OK? Time to hit the books."

"How's it feel?" I asked Will.

He squinted at me. "All right. Kinda numb, that's all."

"We gave him some Advil," Lily said.

I put my hand on his wet hair and said, "That's a beauty. What happened?"

Tony said, "I was telling him we should put a steak on that eye, draw the swelling out. Treat it the way Rocky would treat it." He made a couple of short punches, pow-pow, to illustrate his point, but I doubt Will had any idea who Rocky was.

"How'd it happen?" I asked, and saw him exchange a glance with Tony as if they'd rehearsed what he was going to say.

"Maybe we shouldn't have let them go over to the playground," Lily said. "It was late, but they'd been cooped up all day. It was barely raining. And we let Rafe and his friends go over there all the time by themselves. I'm really sorry, Tucker."

"It's OK, Lily. I'm not mad at anybody. I just want to know what happened."

"It was a fight, Dad, that's all. I just got pissed off at this guy."

"What guy?"

"The boy was Gus Howell," Tony said. "The girls see him over there all the time. Turns out Will knows him, too. Right? You've played soccer against him."

"He's an asshole, Dad."

"He's got a reputation, this kid," Tony said. "He likes to talk trash."

"What kind of trash?"

"Tucker, it was a playground fight," Tony said, "and it's over and done with. No great harm done."

"What's going on? Why can't you just tell me what happened?"

"We want to keep everything in perspective," Tony said.

Will said, "Dad, you don't have to do anything about it, OK? It was my fight, and I got the crap knocked out of me. End of story."

"Sometimes the parents should just stay out of these things," Tony said. "The kids know how to handle them. Jesus, I must have been in a dozen fights my parents never even knew about."

"Will's never been in any fight."

"I have, too," Will said.

Did Will really think that I was going to fly off the handle when I heard what happened? He must have, or he would have told me.

"So you were in a fight with a kid named Gus Howell," I said as calmly as I could. "Are you going to tell me how it got started?"

"He's an asshole, like I said. He goes to Sidwell and we should never have let him in the game. He was fouling and holding everybody and running his mouth, and I told him to shut up. I told him to play by the rules, OK?"

"That's all? Was he talking about Kat?"

Will looked around for support and finally let his gaze settle on the TV, where another football game was in progress.

"Was he?"

"Yeah, he said some stuff about Kat."

"What kind of stuff?"

In a mumbly voice: "Just stuff about what she did at that party."

Will was doing his best to seem interested in the football game, and Lily, who'd remained near the passageway to the kitchen, asked, "Does anybody want anything? Tucker, hot chocolate? I just made some for Sophy."

I did not want any hot chocolate. I wanted to know what Gus Howell had said to my son that would make him take a swing. I wanted to know why Will had found it easier to talk to Tony Moorefield than to talk to me. I said, "Come on, Will. We should be heading home now. Get you out of those wet clothes. Maybe we can stop on the way and buy a nice steak for that eye."

He glanced up in surprise, trying to read my voice. He said, "I think I'll just stay with the ice pack."

Lily told him to keep it, she had plenty of ice packs, and Tony put an arm over his shoulders, shaking him roughly as he made his way toward the hall. At the door Tony said, "All right, chief," and they high-fived as though they'd just scored on the opposition.

In the car Will was quiet, and I had to ask him all over again what had happened. He gave me another mumbly answer, but I heard the thickness in his voice, and I said, "This should come out, Will. What is it you're afraid to tell me?"

"Nothing. I just want it to be over and done with."

"You think I'm going to do something? You think I'm going to punish you?"

"I don't know. Are you?"

"I'd like to know what got to you, Will. Why you didn't walk away. Was it what he said about Kat?"

"He's an asshole," Will said with sudden vehemence, "a total asshole, and he takes cheap shots. He'd get in a fight in every soccer game if there wasn't a referee. You aren't going to do anything, are you?"

"What would I do?"

"I don't know. Call his parents. Go over to his house."

"What if I did call his parents? Why are you so worried about that?"

"I don't want it get worse, that's all. I mean, he already beat the shit out of me. Let's just leave it at that, OK? I don't want one of those phone calls where I have to get on and make some bogus apology. I'm not sorry. The guy is a fuck. I wish I'd slugged him."

Will was looking straight ahead through the windshield, and he still held the ice pack against his left cheek. I couldn't see his face, but his voice was rising and filling the cabin of the car with all his leftover anger and adrenaline.

"You didn't hit him?"

"I tried. I started it, OK? I took the first swing, and then he smacked me a couple of times. I went down. End of fight. I lost."

"What else did he say?"

Will turned to me then and lowered the ice pack. "He said you were fucked up and you should go to jail, OK? That's what he said. He said Kat was a slut and he said Mom was a rich bitch."

His voice cracked then, and I reached across the space to put my hand on his shoulder. He'd been trying so hard to hold it altogether, but now the emotions broke out of him in a few gulping sobs, and he leaned forward, resting his head against the dashboard, hiding his face. With my hand on his back, I could feel the heaving of his ribs and on Chain Bridge Road, at the entrance of Battery Kemble Park, I pulled off in the same place I had stopped earlier with Kat.

"This just sucks," Will said, sitting up, trying to get control of himself. "It totally sucks, hearing this stuff all the time."

"You don't hear it all the time, do you?"

He pulled in a deep breath and let it out in a woosh. "It's what everybody thinks," he said. "They don't all say it, but it's what they think."

"I'm proud of you," I said.

"What for? Getting the shit beat out of me?"

"For standing up for us. For yourself, too. But more than that, for taking everything the way you have, without complaining. You're the passenger on this ride, but it's been a rough ride, and I know it. But most of the time you handle it just fine, just fine."

He kept pushing at his nose with the back of his hand, a tears-and-snot moment, but he was thinking over what I'd said. "I am like the passenger," he said finally, "and sometimes I get sick of it."

"But you stood up for us."

"I couldn't walk away."

"Because other people were there?"

"Partly, but he just pissed me off, you know?"

"The red mist."

"The red mist? What's that?"

"It's what the detective books say when somebody gets mad. The red mist comes down over them and they don't know what they're doing anymore."

Will nodded a couple of times. "So that's what happened to you that night? The red mist?"

This was the first time he'd asked directly about July 13th.

"I guess. I certainly didn't know what I was doing."

"So what's going to happen now?" he wanted to know. "Are you going to jail?"

We stayed there at the park entrance, the motor running in the car, while I told him about the most recent meeting with the lawyers, and it seemed to settle us both down. I didn't want to give him any false hope, but I said that maybe, *maybe*, I'd end up getting off on a minor charge, without a trial and without any jail time.

"Woo-hoo," Will said, keeping his voice deep and measured.

WILL DIDN'T say anything to Kat when he went upstairs to shower and change, and he spent his usual half hour in the bathroom. He's the messy one in the family, despite his attention to the details of his appearance, and as I listened to the water running in the pipes, I reminded myself to get up there later and clean up after him. Will tries, but he doesn't see things like wet towels on the floor, or dirty clothes left out, or shampoo tubes dripping into the tub, or the flecks of Clearasil that he leaves to harden on the sink and mirror. Kat's not all that tidy, either, but she's less messy than her brother, and she's always after him about the way he leaves their shared bathroom.

She'd heard us return, but I didn't hear any voices upstairs while Will was dressing. He'd pulled on a pair of sweatpants and a sweatshirt, and the bruise on his cheekbone looked darker after the shower, still not black but a deep cordovan color that spread upward into his brow. The swelling wasn't too bad, not bad enough to keep him from going to the computer or spoiling his appetite. He was hungry, he told me, and asked for his favorite sandwich, a grilled cheese with tomato and bacon. When I started cooking the bacon, coolhandwill logged on and soon I heard the sound of that creaking door as the instant messages began to pour in. I wondered what he was telling Girls 1, 2, and 3 about the black eye.

Kat came downstairs when she smelled the bacon cooking. She must have taken a shower while I was gone, for she looked fresher than I expected, and her hair was combed out. "I don't know anybody else who still eats bacon," she said.

"You both love it," I said.

"I know, but Mom would have a fit."

She still had some of the sadness clinging to her, and I suppose she was thinking about making the evening call to her mother, wondering how to tell her about Abby's party. I was wondering how to tell Kat about Will's fight. She hadn't seen the black eye.

Kat said, "Anything happen after I left?"

She was standing in front of the open refrigerator, looking for a drink, but she might have been speaking to the old heads of lettuce and the Tupperware containers Gladys left for us. What she wanted to know, I thought, was whether anyone had commented on her departure.

"Something did happen," I said, "but I'm going to let Will tell you about it."

"Will?"

I told Will to log off, and of course he said, "Just a sec," in that vague tone that meant that my request had not registered. He'd tuned me out, and it took a couple more requests to get through to the functional part of his brain, but he did finally understand that his grilled cheese was ready. Kat was listening to this, pouring herself a glass of V8, and she reacted at once to his black eye.

"What's that?" she said.

"I walked into a door," Will said.

"You were in a fight," Kat said.

Will shrugged, and I saw a hint of a smile.

"What's this about?" Kat said. "Who'd you get in a fight with?"

"It's no big deal," Will said, sitting down at our small kitchen table, where I fixed his plate and his glass of milk.

Kat looked at me for an explanation. "Was this about me?" she said, still on her feet. "Was it?"

"It was about all of us," I said. "Sit down."

We don't say a real blessing before our meals, but when we eat together, even a kitchen meal, we wait until everyone is seated before we begin, and we lift our glasses. We all mutter *Blessing*, the single word, the way grown-ups say *Cheers*. This small ritual had been adopted at Kat's insistence years ago, and it had stuck.

"I'm waiting," Kat said as she set down her glass. "I don't want anybody fighting about me. Why can't people just forget about it?"

"Good idea," Will said. "Let's forget about it."

"Kat has a right to know," I said. "This affects all of us. This boy at the playground had things to say about all of us, Kat, and Will didn't want to hear them. I know you've both heard me say that fighting is a last resort, but sometimes there isn't a choice."

"Who was it?" Kat asked.

I tried to tell her what facts I knew—that it started at the playground, that Gus Howell simply happened to be there, that he started talking to Will.

"This is great," Kat said, "just great. Some guy I hardly know knows all about me."

"He doesn't know anything about you," I said, "nothing important. He knows rumors and gossip, but he doesn't know you, or Will, or me. All this is going to fade away, believe me, all this minor stuff, but the important stuff won't. That's our job now, to remember what's important."

"It's not so minor," Kat said. "You keep saying that, but it's what everybody thinks. It's what everybody knows about me. Shit. It's not minor."

"You ever heard of Gary Singer?" I asked, and of course they hadn't. He was a kid I had a fight with back in junior high in Norfolk. I don't completely understand how I got started telling them a story except that I wasn't sure what else to say, and I am as guilty as most parents of supposing that there is some parallel between my own past and my children's experience. And I suppose that I have always found it easier to tell stories than to make speeches to the kids.

And they listen to stories. They listened that night when I told them that I got in a fight about my sister, Emily. She was a grade ahead of me, just as Kat is a grade ahead of Will, and we went to the same schools when we were kids.

"You know Emily," I said. "She's particular about some things, but she doesn't care that much about how she looks or what people think of her. She doesn't get embarrassed easily. Not a bad trait, by the way. Nobody ever dies of embarrassment."

Kat looked at me skeptically, but she had picked up a half of her sandwich.

"One day on our way to school, after our mom had dropped us off, we were walking up to the door and her slip just came off. Fell off. I was walking behind her and suddenly there it was, around her ankles. What did Emily do? She stepped right out of it. There were a lot of other kids in front of the school, and they saw Emily step out of her slip, pick it up, and stuff it into her satchel—we didn't have backpacks in those days. We had these clunky little suitcase-like things we called satchels."

"Uh, excuse me," said Will, "but is a slip what I think it is?"

"You know what it is," Kat said.

"It's a slippery white garment women wear under their skirts," I said.

"Well, how would I know?" Will said, talking to Kat. "Nobody even wears skirts anymore."

"This was a big event in junior high, taking your slip off in front of the school, and I heard about it at lunchtime. Heard all about it. The whole school knew, including a guy named Gary Singer, a guy we all thought was the school jerk. I thought so, anyway. He was known for two things, his love of the Bible and his love of wrestling. Gary Singer walked around Marion Junior High School with a Bible in his hands and a pocket full of big spikes, challenging people to bend one. He'd seen some wrestler bend spikes, and he discovered he could do it, too, and somehow or other this was connected to his faith in the Bible."

"Jesus," said my irreverent son.

"You make this stuff up," Kat said, but she was eating.

"Only when I have to, and I don't have to with Gary Singer. It's all true, cross my heart and hope to die. He was one of a kind, Gary Singer, and we were outside at lunchtime, a whole bunch of us, when he started in on Emily. He said she was a sinner. A whore. Did I mention that he was a big kid? He was an eighth-grader and he was a lot bigger than I was, and I just sat there at first, and then, I don't know, it seems like I just flew at him. The red mist. I wasn't conscious of making a decision about it. I wanted to strangle the guy."

"What's the red mist?" Kat asked.

"Anger," I said. "People say you see red, and that's what it felt like. I jumped Gary Singer, but he had his wrestling moves, and I remember hitting the ground, hard. *Whumpf.* He pinned me in about three seconds, and then, I don't know how, I got loose and tried to box with him. I kept jabbing, and backing up, and jabbing, and backing up, and the next thing I knew I was looking up and there were kids leaning out every window, watching us fight. The school was three stories high, and there were kids hanging out every single window."

"Where was Emily in all of this?" Kat asked.

"I don't know. I didn't see her until I got hauled into the principal's office. I was sitting there with a handful of Kleenex and a bloody nose, and she came in and said, 'Don't ever do that again. You can't fight a lick.'"

The kids had polished off their sandwiches by then, and Will asked, "So what's the point? You trying to make me feel better about getting beat up?"

"The point is that Emily and I laugh about it now. Not often, but every now and then we do. She'll say, 'Remember that day my slip came off? Remember Gary Singer and those stupid spikes he carried around?' The point is that you two will remember this day for the rest of your lives. You'll be brother and sister for the rest of your lives, and one day Kat's going to say, 'Remember Abby Moorefield's sixteenth birthday? Remember that shiner you got? Remember those grilled cheese sandwiches we ate that night and that ridiculous story Dad told us about the guy with the spikes?'"

They smiled a little, but they must have been making their own associations, and they probably felt, as I did, that the story was less than a perfect fit. There was a big difference between Emily's slip and Kat's fall, but at least they had listened to me and eaten their supper, and they were interested enough, later that night, to want to call Emily, who confirmed every detail of my story and who happened to know that Gary Singer had joined the Special Forces after high school, but she hadn't heard of him since.

KAT DIDN'T get up the next morning. Rather, she got up long enough to come downstairs in her flannel pajamas and announce that she felt lousy. "Is she ever going back to school?" Will asked when I drove him to St. Albans. I asked Joe Jarvis the same question, for it was Monday morning and I went straight to his office, where I told him what had happened at the Moorefields' and afterward. I told him I was close to the end of patience and hope. "It does sound as though it's time to deal with it," he told me.

"You think I haven't been trying to deal with it?"

He spread his hands helplessly. Classic shrink. He didn't have any advice for me, and I went back to the Hut feeling that something *had* to change. Kat was asleep, but I banged on her door until I got an answer from her. I said we were going for a real walk. "It's a beautiful day," I said, "and you're not going to miss it. I'm taking you to the Billy Goat Trail."

"I don't feel like it," she said in a voice that barely penetrated the panels of the door. "I told you, I feel crummy."

"We're going," I said. "I'm not going to let you sleep through it. Can I come in?"

She hesitated before saying yes. She said the door wasn't locked.

The shades were drawn in her room and the air had a stuffy sickroom smell. Kat, almost lost in her bedding, squinted when I let the light in. "What's going on?"

"We're taking a walk." I told her I was going to run by the office for a while, and I'd pick up some sandwiches at the deli, but I wanted her ready to go when I got home.

"Do I have a choice?"

"Not today."

"Great," she muttered, placing a pillow over her face.

I did go by the office and bought sandwiches, and Kat was dressed when I got home, reading the paper and looking woebegone, but she didn't complain. She'd showered and her hair was shiny, hoisted up into a careless ponytail. I caught her glancing at me while I loaded up the small backpack, but she was mum when I reminded her how much she'd always loved the Billy Goat Trail. She wasn't going to give me one spark of enthusiasm.

She must have seen that I was half frantic, but she was quiet on the short drive up to Great Falls, and Romeo led the way when we got out of the car. At the trailhead below the falls, I let him off the leash. He went bounding ahead, thrilled and full of self-importance, pausing now and then to strike a pose atop a rock, head high and nose twitching as he busily sorted out the intoxicating aromas all about him. The Billy Goat Trail is crowded on the weekends, but on a weekday, in November, we were almost the only hikers on this rugged, spectacular walk that skirts the gorge of the Potomac. The sky was clear and the air was fresh, but we were alone. There weren't even any kayakers on the river, or climbers over on the Virginia side where the rock faces shear into the water.

Kat and I were both wearing jeans and fleece jackets, and I followed her, watching how easily she scampered along the rocky trail through the pines, watching the bounce of her high ponytail.

"He's pathetic," she said, referring to Romeo.

"He's just excited," I said.

"Seriously, he's got a twisted ego," she said. "Why'd you name him Romeo anyway?"

She turned briefly to talk over her shoulder but didn't slow down. I know I'd told her that Romeo came from an Amish farm and thought I'd also explained his name. "He's amorous," I said.

"Horny," Kat said, and then she stopped. We were at a place where the trail runs out from under the pines and onto the cliffs that must be a hundred feet high. The air was just cool enough to make vapor of her breath. "Bonnie told me I should mention this."

"What?"

"Romeo. You know, the way he climbs all over you."

"You talked about that with Bonnie?"

"Yeah."

She watched him press ahead with his short-legged trot.

"I didn't know it bothered you."

"Not Romeo. It's more the way you act, like it was hilarious. You're ready to laugh right now."

She was right. A grin was twitching on my face, but I said, "I always try to get him down when he starts that."

"Dad, he doesn't listen. It always makes me feel weird, OK? You yell at him but he just gets more excited. You treat it like a big joke."

"All right, I hear you. Tell me what you want me to do."

She gave me a searching look that had anger behind it. "Just don't say anything if he starts, OK? Let me handle it. Just don't make me feel creepy, like there's something wrong with me if I don't like a dog trying to hump my leg."

She didn't give me a chance to answer, and for the next few minutes I could barely keep pace with her. The trail forks in several places, offering an easier path through the woods and a more testing way that flirts with the edge of the cliffs, and Kat chose the cliff route every time. About half a mile into the trail, we reached the spot where the massive layers of granite have been twisted out of their horizontal plane into sharp angles, and you must hop from the upturned edge of one layer to the next. For a child of seven or eight, these hops are scary leaps, and Kat and Will had both spent hours here, jumping from one outcropping to another. Now my long-legged daughter made it appear as easy as walking on a level sidewalk.

"They don't look as big as they used to, do they?" I asked.

She shook her head.

"You remember coming here?"

"Sure," she said. "I remember seeing the climbers across the river. I thought it was the coolest thing ever."

"You were always a climber. That was your favorite game when we lived in Georgetown—you were like a lizard, moving all over the house without touching the floor. What's that on the wall? Oh, just the kid. The Kat. It's a good thing we didn't name you Elizabeth because then you would have ended up being called Lizard."

Kat had heard this a hundred times but she never minded hearing it again.

"So what's up with the climbing?" I asked her. "Have you sworn off?"

She was standing on a rock knob and there was a little color in her cheeks. We'd been moving quickly and I was feeling warm in my fleece, feeling the tug of the straps of the backpack that held our water and sandwiches.

"I don't know," she said. "I never climbed much during the school year anyway. That's more a summer thing."

"You didn't go on the trip this fall to Seneca Rocks."

Shrug.

"Was that about Abby?"

"Are you obsessed with Abby? You're always asking me about her. I just didn't feel like going."

"You don't feel like going most places."

"So I'm depressed? Is that what you brought me here to tell me? Yes, I'm depressed, OK. So are half the people I know. I've been depressed for about ten years. I don't feel like going anywhere. Satisfied?"

"We have to do something about it, Kat."

"Oh great. Here comes the pill talk."

"Maybe you should be taking medication."

"I'm already doing something about it, OK?"

"What?"

"What you always tell me to do. Suck it up and drive on, right?"

"Kat, please. That's not what I always want you to do, and it's not what you're doing. You're locking your door and sleeping sixteen hours a day."

"The door wasn't locked this morning. You didn't even check."

"That's not the point."

"What is, then?"

"The point is that you're in a bad place."

She rolled her eyes heavenward. "And you're in such a great place you can tell me about it?"

"This isn't the way to talk about this."

"Like you'd know."

"I mean standing here on these rocks."

Kat made a sound, surprised and disappointed, and shook her head. She was not amused, but we were awkwardly positioned for a conversation, perched on our separate outcroppings with a small chasm between us.

"I don't like heights," I said.

"This isn't high. Do you think you're funny?"

I looked around for a way to get down. Kat was right, it wasn't very high, but with the river so far below and the sharp drop of the cliffs, this section of the trail has a top-of-the-world feeling. Down between the rocks, in a kind of maze, Romeo was sniffing around and scrabbling to get up on top with us. I said it was time for a water break and Kat contemptuously sprang to the next ridge, showing me how easy it was.

I found a smooth sun-warmed place where we could sit and see the river running for a mile downstream. Kat took a sip from a water bottle and bit into an apple. She said she wished she'd brought her sunglasses, and the light did glint brightly on the pale rock all around us.

I said I'd seen Jed. "There was a meeting, a lawyers' meeting, but Jed was there. I think he was the one who asked for the meeting, as a matter of fact."

"Why would he? You're the one on trial."

I told her how my worried lawyers had suggested that I talk to Abby, and how she'd talked to Jed, and how he'd been treated by his father. I said, "Jed didn't want anyone to know what happened at that party. Maybe you're already aware of this, but he was lining everyone up to deny what went on."

"How would I know? You never tell me about this stuff."

"You could have heard it from Abby or someone else who was there."

"Who's going to talk to me? People look the other way when they see me coming. They treat me like you do, like I couldn't handle it, so they have to talk about stupid shit that doesn't mean anything."

I said, "I know a lot about what happened that night. I've been reading the interviews with the people who were there. One of the lawyers, Corinne, has been doing an investigation."

"How come she never talked to me?"

"I asked her not to."

"Why?"

"I wanted to keep you out of this part of it, the legal part."

"How could you keep me out of it? It's about me, what I did. You think I like knowing you're talking to Abby and going to all these meetings and I'm clueless the whole time? You think I couldn't handle it?"

"You have other things to think about."

"What things? School? That's what I'm supposed to be thinking about when nobody can look at me without going, 'Hey, she's the one. She's the one who went down on all those guys. She's the one whose dad put that guy's eye out with the shovel.' Why did you hit him? Why?"

She had risen to her feet and I thought she was going to stalk away. She did take a step toward the river, and she heaved her apple core so that it sailed out and over the edge of the cliff.

But she stayed there. She wanted an answer.

"I was in a rage," I told her. "I thought you'd been hurt—you *were* hurt, Kat. And I wanted to hurt the ones who did it."

"But it wasn't Jed."

Her breath was coming in quick bursts, and I asked her how much she remembered about that night.

"Enough," she said. "I've been talking to Bonnie about it, and I remember enough, OK? I lied when I said I totally blacked out—is that what you want to know? I lied."

"It wasn't your fault. I've read—"

"It *was* my fault. I knew they wanted to get me drunk, and I let them get me drunk. I knew they wanted blow jobs, and I gave them blow jobs. There. If anybody wants to know, that's what happened."

"You're fourteen—"

"I know how old I am. What has that got to do with it? You always say take responsibility for your actions. You are what you do, right? So that's what I did, and now you and Mom are both like, 'Oh my god, they took advantage of our poor innocent daughter.'"

"They did take advantage of you. You'd never even had a drink before."

"How do you know?"

"You made a mistake—"

"No kidding."

"You couldn't have known what you were doing that night."

"I knew I wanted to do something different, OK? I knew I didn't want to always be the one who tagged along behind Abby."

"I've read about her, too. I know she was in the house with Jed."

"She was in bed with him," Kat said.

"You knew that?"

"Yes, I knew that. Everybody knew that."

"And what did you think about it?"

"What did I think about it? What are you now? My shrink?"

I was on my feet by then, aware of the two of us, Kat and I, standing and shouting at each other, all alone in that landscape of rocks and river. "I'd like to know what goes on inside my daughter. How am I supposed to find out?"

"Your daughter wants someone to love her, OK? That's what goes on inside her. That's what she tells her real shrink."

"You think I don't love you?"

"Do you love anybody? You didn't even love Mom."

Tears suddenly filled her eyes, and she stamped her foot on the rock. "You were married and you didn't even love her."

Kat backed away when I stepped toward her, but she did let me catch hold of her hand. "I did," I said, leading her away from that cliff back to the place where we'd been sitting, a large slab of granite, tilted, big as a bed. She sat down cross-legged, and it was there that I told her how Trish had come to meet me, to surprise me, when I came home from a short business trip.

"She didn't ordinarily meet me at the airport, so I knew something was up. She'd stayed home from work, too, and she was in an old pair of jeans, with paint all over them. We'd just moved into the Georgetown house and she was excited—I'd never seen her so excited—but we were fixing the place up and I thought she was on a decorating high. Maybe I wouldn't have been so dense if the paint had been pink or blue, but I never guessed that she'd been painting your nursery. It was that color—"

"Celadon," Kat said.

"You remember that?"

"We lived there till I was six, Dad. And Mom still uses that color everywhere."

Kat had turned her face toward me to gather up every bit of this story, and I don't know why it was so hard to continue. I had to take a couple of breaths before I could say, "Anyway, your mom wasn't going to have a tacky nursery. Celadon. So I didn't guess what was going on until she led me upstairs and showed me how she'd been fixing up your room. It was tiny, and the only thing in it was the cradle—god, that little cradle with the rockers."

I had to stop again. Trish had been glowing that day, and perhaps I saw something of her in my daughter, but in any case I felt a wave pass though me, a shuddering, and I don't think I had cried like that since the night Trish left me. I just hung my head and bawled. I'd been going to say that I loved her but I couldn't get the words out.

"Dad? Are you all right?"

Kat looked frightened.

"I don't know why this gets to me," I said, trying to get control of myself, "thinking of that day. That cradle."

"I've never seen you cry like this," Kat said.

My nose was dripping like a faucet, and I dug around in the pack to find something to wipe it on. There was an old packet of Kleenex in there, and I snorted a couple of times to clear my passages. "I'm a pretty sight, huh?"

Kat dabbed at her eyes. She said, "But you loved her."

"Yes. Yes, I loved her."

Kat said, "That cradle is still in Mom's house. She used it for Cam and Lindsay."

She leaned forward to get onto her knees, and she placed her forehead against mine, her hands on my shoulders. Her breath smelled like apples.

When she leaned back on her heels, she looked at me with glittering eyes and giggled self-consciously, and I think that is the moment I believed she was going to make it. She was just a brown-eyed girl in a dark fleece, but she was going to make it. *We* were going to make it. I know that her sadness and confusion hadn't evaporated all at once,

and that the most difficult parts could be ahead of us, but a kind of relief flooded over me, and I said, "I love you, Kat," and she said, "I
know that," and I am almost embarrassed to remember how I started
to babble.

I could hardly shut up once I got on the subject of Joe Jarvis and
started telling her about my grouse and crazy flight. I told her how
scared I'd been that she was going to do something desperate. Kat had
pulled her legs up the way she does, monkey fashion, and she said, "I
knew you were worried, but I didn't know all this stuff was going on.
You didn't seem so different."

For some reason I was moved to speak in a ridiculous high-pitched
swami voice. "On the outside I wish to appear large and in charge,
while inside I am a disgustingly muddy river full of flotsam and
jetsam."

Maybe I do try to make a joke out of everything. Kat laughed,
thank god, and it was as if a fever had broken. I cannot account for this,
really, but after we'd eaten our sandwiches and left our stopping place,
Kat had a bounce in her step and I was humming "The Blue Danube."
Go figure. It was the wrong river and the Potomac was far from blue,
but I did feel like waltzing over the rocks. A giddiness had overtaken
both of us, and we cracked up when Romeo refused to climb the only
real slope on the trail, a place where the rock is pitched at about forty-
five degrees and you must scramble to the top. Romeo stood at the bottom and complained. We pretended to ignore him, and when we
reached the top and pressed on out of his sight—OK, I know this was
mean—he set up a tremendous wail but scrambled up the slope himself and then, when he caught up to us, he pretended to ignore us. Pretended to be out on a stroll by himself and deeply interested in some
invisible attraction in the undergrowth. Pretended that no one of his
dignity would deign to be associated with such a pair of twits.

One last thing I must report: we both climbed the Giant's Unkedunk. Let me explain. Just off the trail stands a rock formation con-
sisting of two bulging boulders with a crack in between them. It looks
like an unkedunk, exactly like an unkedunk—which is to say, like
somebody's backside (this particular word was a hand-me-down from
Mary Carter). On their childhood walks on the Billy Goat Trail, Will

and Kat had regarded the Giant's Unkedunk as a major landmark, and they'd always wanted to climb it. The formation is about two stories high, and of course it had always seemed far too daunting and dangerous.

Not that day. Kat took one look at it and veered off the path. "I'm going up," she said. "I remember how scary this used to look."

I asked her difficult it was. She said, "I don't know. It's probably not even a 5.1, not with that crack down the middle."

Up she went, hand over hand, rising as smoothly as liquid through a straw. Only at the very top, where the crack narrowed to a sliver, did she have to pause and cast about, feeling above her head for a hand-hold, tensing her body as she carefully entrusted her weight to that grip, then pulling herself slowly, inch by inch, to the summit. Two stories is not very high, but I felt that familiar lurch in my stomach. I don't like heights.

"Go for it, Dad," Kat said, looking down at me, beaming. It was more an invitation than a challenge. I don't even like being high up on a stepladder, and the only walls I've climbed have been indoors, the sport walls where you're safely belayed, but it seemed important—it seemed essential—to drag myself up there to where Kat stood. I can tell you that real rock is not at all like those sport walls, that it is greasy and unforgiving and smells like iron when you mash your face against it, and that you realize that your skull would crack like an eggshell if you fell. I can tell you that twenty feet feels as high and dizzy as a steeple and that when you come to an overhang at the top and start groping around, you are glad to feel your daughter's hand clamp onto yours and guide it to a small ridge, a handhold. I can tell you that you feel your heart racing like a hummingbird when you finally drag your-self to safety.

Up there on top of the Giant's Unkedunk, a peak that had once seemed sky-high, Kat and I glowed as though we'd scaled Everest.

CHAPTER

8

———

K at went back to school the day after that walk. She got up and ate her breakfast, washing down her bagel with a diet Coke, but she went to school that day, and the day after, and the day after. She bickered with Will about the mess he left in the bathroom, she teased him about his shiner—which had developed most of the colors of the rainbow—and she got down on the floor and roughhoused with Romeo. The mood in our house really did seem to lift. I didn't have a headache all week, and for the first time in months, it seemed, I slept through an entire night. At the office I was able to concentrate on my work, and I realized that the staff had been quietly taking care of tasks and problems that would normally have fallen to me. I also realized that Twill was having its best year ever. So much for El Jefe's indispensability.

"Did you swallow a Buddha?" Lily asked me one night after band practice, a session that had been full of rancor and quibbling. She meant that I had seemed serene, for our performance was just over a week away and we sounded hopelessly loose and sloppy. Evan asked Nancy if she could please, just once, stay on the goddamn beat, and Nancy got so rattled that she couldn't get through a song without breaking down. Lily tried to be the peacemaker, but even she had a tightness about her, and her voice sounded pinched when we worked on her numbers, throttled back.

"I need to unwind after that," Lily said. She was the last to leave, and she'd found, somewhere in the music room, a court jester's hat that I'd given Will years ago, one of those silly hats with three long prongs sticking out of it, each of them tipped with a tiny bell. She stood there and shook her head, making the bells tinkle, a rueful expression on her face. "I think we should all wear hats like this," she said, "to keep us from getting so serious about ourselves. What do you think? Can we pull it together? Or are we just going to make fools of ourselves?"

"We'll be OK," I said. I was straightening up, putting stuff away, and Lily sat down at the upright and began feeling out a song, playing chords that soon drifted into "But Not for Me," shaking her head in time, jingling her bells, trying to sound jaunty.

> They're writing songs of love—but not for me
> A lucky star's above—but not for me
> With love to lead the way I've found more clouds of gray
> Than any Russian play could guarantee.

She stopped, giving her head a good, hard shake as if to clear it. Tinkle, tinkle. "Good god, listen to me. What am I playing?"

"Cole Porter?"

"Gershwin," Lily said. "Maybe I should stick to that. Maybe we all should. Act our age. I mean, here we are, parents, pretending we're still a bunch of kids. Playing kids' music. And we can't even play it well."

"Not tonight we couldn't."

"What are we doing anyway?" she said. "Why do we put ourselves through this when it's not even any fun?"

There was a heaviness in her voice that she couldn't disguise or dispel, though she kept noodling at the piano, a battered old upright with yellowing keys and a wheezy, percussive sound. That night her hair was loose and she was wearing a red-and-green flannel shirt, a lumberjack shirt, and she sang meditatively, *I was a fool to fall and get that way...*

She turned on the stool to look at me when she asked, "You know what Abby would say about this? She'd say, 'God, Mom, what is it about that old stuff?' For her a song like this might as well be a madrigal or Gregorian chant. It's from another world that's dead and gone as far as she's concerned."

I was coiling an electric cord on my arm, and I suppose I had already guessed where Lily was headed with this conversation.

"She likes Clapton and some of the others we play, but this stuff is ancient. It was already ancient when I was a teenager. It was my mom's music, not mine. I'm the one out of sync, I guess."

In a cartoon Austrian accent, I asked, "So vat is vorrying you tonight?"

"Abby. Jed. Same old, same old. They're in love, you know."

Lily was trying to sound breezy, but she didn't. "She thinks it's something I couldn't possibly understand. It's *way* too deep for me. As far as she's concerned, I'm just an old relic who sings outdated songs but doesn't have a clue what they're really about. Maybe she's right. Maybe we don't connect with the music the way we should."

"With Gershwin? Or Clapton?"

She reached up and lifted the hat from her head, shaking out her hair. It swirled around her face in every direction. "I really don't want to make a fool of myself. Where'd this hat come from anyway?"

I told her I'd bought it for Will and said we'd get ourselves together for the Wolfes' party.

Lily wasn't ready to be reassured, though she tried to fetch up a smile as she changed the subject to Kat. I'd already mentioned our walk on the Billy Goat Trail, but she wanted to know more, and I tugged on the electric cord as though it were a rope. I said I had finally felt Kat at the other end.

"I'd like to feel Abby that way," Lily said. "Well, I do, sometimes, but she lets go whenever she feels like it, now that she's crazy about Jed. And she's dropped her end with everybody, not just me. I hate the way she's pulled away from Kat—remember the way they used to say BFF? Best Friends Forever?"

That came out like a lament, and I said, "You're in a strange mood tonight."

"I am? I would have said you were the one in a strange mood. All this has changed you, hasn't it?"

"All what?"

"You and Kat seem to be figuring it out, but Abby and I—she just keeps going the other way. She keeps dropping the rope. Who ever thought it would be so hard to have a relationship with your own child? Who knew she'd fall in love at sixteen? Sometimes I think I'm jealous—no, I *know* I'm jealous. How ridiculous is that? Her life is hell half the time, and I'm jealous of her."

"Why is her life hell?"

"She's in love, and when you're sixteen and in love, life is either heaven or hell. There's no in-between. It's all passion. That's it. That's what I have, passion envy. Abby's in love, how does it go? Madly, passionately, deeply. Everyday life, which includes me, is completely dull and boring and painful because it stands in the way of her passion."

By then my heart had begun to race, and that is just a fact. I understood what Lily was getting at and my heart was racing. She turned back to the keyboard and plinked out the melody one note at a time. "*'I was a fool to fall and get that way, / Heigh-ho, alas, and also lackaday'*... it's just another heartbreak song, isn't it? But you have to admit it's completely different from, oh, from drowning in a river of tears. There's not all that wallowing in self-pity."

She'd turned to face me again, the jester's cap in her lap, her palms spread as if to make a choice. "On the one hand, we have Gershwin, and alas and alack, a sophisticated kind of heartbreak. On the other, we have Clapton, drowning in a river of tears. Tell me, Mr. Jones, how do you like your heart broken?"

"I have to choose?"

"That's the way the cookie crumbles."

"What are you talking about?"

"I'm not making much sense, am I?" Her eyes suddenly misted over and she made a sound of frustration, of determination. "We have to talk about this, don't we? It's so thick all around us."

I stood there for a moment looking into Lily's wide-spaced, wet eyes. "Is *this* what I think?"

"Please," she said. "Please don't make me do this by myself. I promised myself that I was going to talk about it tonight. Don't tell me I've been imagining everything. I'm talking about us."

"Us?" The sound flew from me like a startled bird taking flight.

"You're not surprised, are you?" she asked.

"No. No," I said, but that was all I could say.

"So what do you think? How'd we get here? Are we sharing a midlife crisis?"

She wanted to sound jaunty again, but she couldn't, and the trembling smile wouldn't stick to her face. "We can't do this. We can't feel this way. That's why I decided I had to mention it tonight. Because I do feel this way and I can't do anything about it. I want to tell you so that it will go away."

"Is this going to make it go away?"

"It better," she said. "I'm drowning in a river of tears and I don't want to—not drowning, but sinking, and I don't want to drown. I don't want to drown, Tucker."

"When did you first know?" I asked her.

"After Daddy died," she said. "That tennis game. I was outrageous. I wanted you to know how I felt, even though I didn't know myself. And that kiss—that can't happen again. That's not right. It's just not right." She shook her head forcefully. She said, "I've never done anything like that, and I don't like it. I don't like feeling this way. I don't like feeling miserable wanting something I can't have. I'm saying we have to put this back in the box it came in." She made a series of small, sharp, shaping gestures with her hands as if she were compressing and folding up a large object and placing it in a small container.

I told her I loved her.

"Oh, don't say that," she said, lowering her head. "Don't, just don't."

"Why not? Isn't that what we're talking about?"

"We're talking about being attracted to each other, that's all." She looked up then the way Kat does, through her lashes. "We've always loved each other, haven't we? The right way, not like this. This is the wrong way with all this desire. It's wrong."

I agreed with her.

"So we're going to forget it, right? We can now that we've said it. I don't want to feel weird about it anymore. I don't want to feel guilty. It's not as if we've done anything—well, there was that kiss. But that's

it, absolutely it. I don't want to feel as though I'm always hiding something. It's back in the box now. Agreed?"

"Agreed," I said with reluctance.

"Was it right to say all this? I think it was. You have to lance the
boil—*psssst*. Let the pressure out."

Lily stood up then and spoke with a leave-taking brightness. "This
is better, isn't it? I feel better. I feel as though there's a weight off me.
Really, I've been feeling as though I'm going out of my mind. Now we
know, and we can forget it, right?"

To reach the door she had to walk past me, and she didn't make it.
I was thinking that if she made it to the door, if I let her go, this moment would never come again, and no power on earth could have prevented me from reaching out for her.

She stopped. She let me stop her. She gave me a look that meant
everything. She said, "There are a million reasons not to do this."

"I know."

I did know, and to this day I can hardly believe that we made love
on the plaid couch with the lights on and the children in the house a
few steps away. I cannot remember exactly how we made it to the
couch. I know that Lily rose up against me when we kissed, and that
we wobbled and almost lost our balance, and that she hopped around
as she pulled off her boots, and that she stamped on the tangle of her
jeans and panties as though she was afraid they might rise up off the
floor. I remember the goose bumps on her arms and shoulders and the
urgency as she guided me into her, as she folded her legs like bobby
pins in her eagerness to have me fully inside her. I remember the speed
and rush and the sense of being enveloped, the nudging of her heels
behind my thighs, the pressure of her fingertips on the small of my
back. I remember how quickly everything happened, and how Lily
widened her eyes when she started to laugh. She said, "So that's what
it feels like after ten years of foreplay. *Whoosh*. Shot from a cannon."

She took my face in both her hands and said, "And it's going to be
another ten before we do it again, right?"

But she didn't leave. She shivered a little, and I got up to lock the
door in case the kids wandered over. I got a couple of sleeping bags out
of the storage closet to cover her. I adjusted the acoustic panels over

the one window of the room so that no one could possibly see in. I turned out the lights, all except the lamp on the piano. By the time I got under the sleeping bags I was shivering, too, and Lily pressed her length against me, seemed to wrap herself about me, seeking warmth. Whenever I tried to say anything, she'd put her finger to my lips and say, *Shhh*, as though we were settling down to sleep. She kept moving against me, trying to get comfortable, and she closed her eyes. The sleeping bags were smooth, and I could feel the heat gathering, intensifying the scent that rose from Lily, from both of us, I suppose, a luxuriant, warm, hothouse scent. She seemed to be exploring me with her hands and feet, her breasts and belly and bush, and soon she said, "I want you. I just do. I can't help it. I already feel empty without you." This time we moved slowly, and at one point she said, "It's like being in the ocean, isn't it," and that is how I remember it, as though we were far out at sea, out of sight of any land, floating, riding currents that had traveled thousands of miles to rock us, holding on to each other as we drifted across the face of the deep.

EVEN NOW, at a distance of years, I hesitate to write what comes next. I am almost afraid to breathe on the memory of the days that followed November 17th, the days with Lily. There weren't that many days— weren't any days, in cold fact, only a few stolen hours that felt like days. They felt like a lifetime.

   Is it cheesy to say that Lily gave me the world? I told her that once. I must have uttered every stock phrase from every love song I'd ever heard. The words just tumbled out of me, but the redeeming feature of all these clichés was that they now applied to me. "You've given me the world," I said to Lily, and a few days later, looking for Christmas trinkets in a New Age shop, she noticed a bin full of large blue-and-green marbles, the blue representing the oceans and the green the continents. She bought one for me, and I have it still, a tiny globe that I keep in the original tissue in a fancy box, a gift that contains the essence of those days and cost $1.95, a sky-blue box that bears the shop's name, Transcendence Perfection Bliss.

   My tiny world. It makes me smile every time I take it out and roll it in the palm of my hand. It reminds me of how Lily made me laugh and how she kept trying to bring me back to earth. I was the one whose emotions were brimming, and she was the one who made the rules, starting the very morning after that first night in the music room. After getting her kids off to school, she called me on the cell phone and said she had to talk. We met at a busy Starbucks, where we ran into a chatty woman who knew Lily slightly, having taken gym classes with her. "How nice," she said, "having coffee with your husband."

Lily said, leaning close to me, "He's not my husband. He's my boyfriend—oh, I'm just kidding. He's just a pal. I'm sorry. It's still early." Then she introduced me to the confused woman, got a lid for her coffee, and whispered to me, "I have to get out of here."

Lily was in her gym clothes, wearing her leather bomber jacket and her sweatpants, and she made as if she was going to get in her Cherokee. "I didn't sleep a wink," she said. I expected her to tell me that she'd been overcome with remorse, but she said, "Can we go to your house? Is Gladys there? We have to talk."

We went to the Hut. Gladys came only in the afternoons. We went into the music room, where she said, "Kiss me, just kiss me, OK?" I felt her leg lift and cock itself behind me, drawing me close. "If we're going to do this, you have to promise me that it's our secret, absolutely our secret. We're not running away together, and we're not telling anyone, not a soul. Agreed? And we're not going to talk about Tony or Trish or anyone else. This is between us and it's separate from everything else. Just us. Promise?"

I promised.

Still clothed, we lay down on the couch and covered ourselves with the sleeping bags. This was Lily's idea. There was a transition problem, she said, and she curled up against me, closing her eyes as she had done the night before, as though she was going to sleep, making a journey to a dreamland, a faraway place where we could awaken only to each other.

We kissed, quietly, and soon she said, "I can't believe I'm doing this. I can't believe I'm such a wiggle worm."

She laughed a little. She really was squirming, and that phrase, *wiggle worm*, became a part of our language. She came up with names and phrases for most of the things that happened in the music room.

The language of sex was ugly, she thought, and if we were going to do this—it was always *if we're going to do this*—we needed the right way to talk about it. One day she reached down, touched my fly, and said, "Oh, ho. Freddy is ready. Hello, Fred." Before long Freddy had a play-mate named Davina and the orgasm would henceforth be known as the Yum-Yum, although there were variations called the Twister and the Thumper. These words came easily to Lily, and I think she used them in an attempt to keep our affair blithe and lighthearted, or at least to pretend to. She always looked alarmed when I told her I loved her, and she'd reach up and pinch my lips shut. "*Shhh,*" she'd say, "not that. We need another rule about that." She never told me she loved me. Wouldn't or couldn't tell me. Some scruple prevented her from using the words, though she would sometimes send the message in sign lan-guage—the raised little finger for *I,* the arms crossed quickly over the heart for *love,* the pointing forefinger for *you*—when she darted out the door after one of our meetings. The swift, silent gestures were more permissible, less compromising than the words would have been.

During the next few weeks we saw each other as often as we could, always in the music room at the Hut and always in the morning after we'd gotten the kids off to school. At that hour Lily was playing hooky from her dance class and there was no one to notice her absence, but I had to make excuses when I showed up late at the office. Christmas shopping, I'd say, or client meeting, but I'm not sure anyone believed me. "You're in an awful jolly mood for somebody who hates to shop," Dee said one morning, and I felt as though my joy must be written all over me.

Joy. It is strange to write that word, as strange as it was to feel it, for joy was so foreign to me as to be almost unrecognizable. I had operated mostly in the lesser realm of satisfaction, which is to joy as a drizzle is to a downpour. The heavens do not open for a drizzle. Exhilaration, ex-uberance, elation—all those feelings came to me on the plaid couch with Lily, came intensely, and I felt as though I'd been picked up and shaken hard like one of those glass wands that children like to shake, a wand full of bright particles that drift in a dreamlike glitter.

That is how I imagined this joy, as a swirl of incandescence mov-ing through me, even though I knew that Lily and I shouldn't have become lovers. I knew that she was married and that our affair was adulterous. I never forgot for long that we were both parents and the one time, the only time, Lily cried was when we were on the couch and Rafe tried to reach her on the cell phone. When she checked the message, we heard him say, *Mom, I forgot my math notebook and I really need it. Mom? Are you going to pick up? Where are you anyway?* Lily pulled her clothes on, crying and saying, "We can't do this, oh god, we just can't. This is what I can't stand, the lying. I have to lie to my son now and I can't keep doing this. I can't do it, Tucker."

We both had to lie, and we both kept doing it. We couldn't get enough of each other. At night I'd lie awake, conscious of the children sleeping in their beds, tormented by guilt, horrified by what I was doing, and I still couldn't stop. "This is all a dream," Lily once said, "and someday we'll have to wake up from it. It's not real life." And it was like a dream, with its own logic and fury, a dream that swept away every objection, every fear, every shame. I'd think of Trish, and all the damage she left in her wake, and still I would count the hours until I could see Lily again.

Lily and I did not have much time together. We had so little time, and I know that memory is imperfect, but so much remains. So much is still there. I can close my eyes right now and see Lily walking through the door of the music room, her cheeks flushed with color, her smile wavering. I can see her take off the red hat she wore that winter—a ski hat, a fuzzy thing in the shape of a big tam— and shake the cold out of her hair. I can hear her making that winter noise, *brrrrrr*, and shivering as she peels off her clothes. I can remember how her bare body felt against mine while we made our little journey, while we adjusted to each other under the sleeping bags. I can remember how it felt to be taken fully into her, not just to be joined but to be absorbed so that I had the sense almost of vanishing, of shedding my separate self. I can hear her saying, "I feel like we're in the ocean, in the big waves"—that force, sweeping us along. I can still see her stricken face when she suddenly reached down and felt her legs. "Whew. I haven't grown fins and scales. Not a mermaid yet. Still human."

She could make me laugh. She would not allow any moment to be solemnized, though she did give me a mermaid key chain. We both gave each other presents—small presents, but they all had stories. I had never known what to buy for a woman, but I always knew with Lily.

There was the prism, for instance. I was walking past a toy store when I knew I had to have a prism for her, for I had repeated to her these words of Neruda's: *"Juegas todos los días con la luz del universo."* "Every day you play with the light of the universe."

Yes, I quoted poetry, Neruda's poetry, even though I hadn't read poetry since college, even though Lily's Spanish was more limited than my own. Nevertheless, Neruda became our poet after the night I took Will and some of his pals to see a movie and decided, instead of going back home, to stay at the Cineplex and go to a movie myself. The only one running at the same time was an Italian flick, *Il Postino*, the story of a simple man who takes a job delivering mail to the exiled Chilean poet, Pablo Neruda, the poet of the people, the poet of love. The postman's soul takes wing as he gets to know Neruda. He writes his own poetry; he falls in love with a beautiful woman; he discovers his passion. (I should add that it kills him, for he is trampled to death at a demonstration on the day he is supposed to read his poems to a crowd.)

I believed that it was no accident that I happened to be sitting in that movie theater. I identified with the postman, I thought this movie was intended for me, and I immediately went out and bought a book of Neruda's poems. I carried it around in the Jimmy and I'd spend the day memorizing lines, feeling the weight of those words in my mouth. The words of Neruda, words in another tongue, expressed the magnificence that hovered about us, and Lily would close her eyes to take them in. *"Sutil visitadora, llegas en la flor y en el agua."* "Subtle visitor, you arrive in the flower and the water."

"I'm not that subtle," Lily said, but she was pleased. I could see that she liked knowing how she filled my horizon.

One line in particular became a kind of refrain for us: *"Oh poder celebrarte con todos las palabras de alegría."* "Oh to be able to celebrate you with all the words of joy." Lily thought that over for a moment, snuggled against me, and said, "There's a word I'd like to celebrate. It's a good one."

"What is it?"

"*Shag*," she said.

God, she made me laugh. She was carnal and exuberant and some-times, as we lay on the couch, she would kick aside the sleeping bag and lift her legs and dance with her feet aloft. She danced in the air. "*Niña morena y ágil, el sol que hace las frutas, / el que cuaja los trigos, el que tuerce las algas, / hizo tu cuerpo alegre.*" "Girl lithe and tawny, the sun that forms the fruits, / that plumps the grains, that curls seaweeds, / filled your body with joy."

"*Girl?*" Lily said. "I know love is blind, but *girl?*"

Poetry and nonsense. We had both, Lily and I, and sometimes we laughed until tears stood in our eyes. I cannot really account for that laughter since it bubbled up from a source I had never before tapped, never even discovered, and it brought back a memory of Trish, of our honeymoon. We went to Italy and stayed in a romantic hotel, and our room was adjacent to that of another pair of honeymooners. They were English, from York, a reserved couple, both a bit overweight, both with crooked teeth, both with that thick accent. By day they were shy and stuffy, but at night, through the thin walls, we heard them rattle the bed frame and roar with laughter. "It's not *that* hilarious," Trish said, and after two nights she requested a room change. The sound of their laughter stayed with me, and I must have always wanted to laugh like that, as I laughed with Lily. Sometimes I think that was the point of it all, the true consummation—not the sex but the inti-mate laughter that followed. Lily would dance in the air and I felt free within myself, free with her, and lifted up with laughter.

Free, I say, though we were free only within the four walls of the music room. Outside was the familiar world, the real world, where our dream had to be suspended, where we did our best to act as we always had, though I am not sure that we succeeded. At the last band prac-tices leading up to the party at the Wolfes', we got funny looks from the others. They didn't say anything, but I could feel them watching. Jay did comment on my playing, for I was suddenly *into* it. I'm no great shakes as a drummer, just another technician who can keep the beat, but my hands seemed to fly of their own accord. Back there on the throne, I did stuff that made even Evan look around with surprise.

As for Lily, she too had stopped holding back, and her musicality was so far beyond ours that, once she turned it loose, she made us all sound better. She could carry the whole band.

"Because I'm not afraid to trust it," she told me when we were alone, "and that's because of you. Because of us."

Us. It was strange to realize that there now was an *us*, a secret *us*, a dream *us*. How could it be real that Kat and Will and I went to the Moorefields' for Thanksgiving? But it was real. We did go. The kids always spent Thanksgiving with me since Trish got them at Christmas, and the last few years we had flown down to Isle of Palms to spend the holiday with Mary Carter and Larry. This year, with the performance scheduled just two days after Thanksgiving Day, we were staying in Washington, and Lily had invited us over to her house. The plan had been made long before Lily and I became lovers, and there was enough activity—a touch football game at the playground, the usual circles within circles of different age groups, so many people who came with hangers-on that Lily had to set an extra table in the front hall—that I only exchanged a few words with Tony.

I wanted to avoid him, but after the meal he sought me out. It was a warmish day and I had gone out into the garden where Will and Rafe and a couple of the other boys were tossing around a Nerf ball. Tony came out, fired up a cigar, and offered me one. "I'm stuffed," he said. "It'll take a week to work that meal off."

He is strict with himself on the subject of weight, and it is a point of pride with him that he weighs 196 pounds, exactly what he weighed when he graduated from college. He works out or plays squash at one of the downtown clubs almost every day.

"Great meal," I said.

"How's your girl doing?" he asked.

"Better," I said, "a lot better."

"And the legal stuff? That has to drag you down."

I said I was actually feeling hopeful about it.

"Good," he said, "good. This'll all be behind us soon. Abby has been on such a goddamn tear—Lily's probably told you. Whoever said girls were easy?"

Will and Rafe and the others were romping around in the small yard, dirty and happy, playing a game of keep-away.

"These guys are a breeze compared to Abby," he said. "Give 'em a ball and they'll play for hours. Abby's probably upstairs figuring out how to elope."

"It's a tough age."

"She reminds me of what a pain in the ass I was at that age. I couldn't think of anything but making out. Listen, how's the band sounding? You guys ready for Saturday?"

He probably wanted to reassure me that he was the new Tony, the one who didn't mind that his wife was in a garage band. I could sense his uneasiness, in any case, though it could hardly have been greater than my own. I had never attempted to converse with a man, a long-time friend, whose wife was now my lover. He blew cigar smoke out of the corner of his mouth like a gangster and said, "This is great for Lily, just great. She's a born performer. Without it she's a fish out of water. She's got a gift, and she should use it, right? Jesus, I hear her at night, humming the songs you guys are going to play. Last night she was in the shower singing that old Cyndi Lauper song 'time after Time.'" He grinned and puffed on the cigar. "I piled right in there. Hell, it's sexy hearing your wife sing in the shower."

He was letting me know he'd fucked her, and I could feel my heart pawing at my breastbone like a crazed, panicked dog. Was this what he'd come out to tell me? Was it blind intuition? Did he know about me and Lily? I couldn't say a word as he rattled on about how excited Lily was. How much he was looking forward to hearing us. "It's got to be good for you, too," he said. "Take your mind off all this crap with the Vandenbergs."

Then he seemed to feel he'd done his duty by me. Sometimes I think Tony must have an inner clock, a timer that starts to beep when he has spent five minutes talking to someone. It is his signal to move on, and he patted my shoulder in a show of sympathy. He left me choking down my guilt and shame and jealousy. I had not imagined that she would be faithful—*faithful!*—to me, but I certainly hadn't ex- pected to learn from Tony just how, when, and where they had fucked.

I don't think I would have been surprised if the earth had opened to swallow me up, but it didn't. It never does.

I didn't mention this conversation to Lily, but it was on my mind when I saw her on Saturday, the day of the party. We were at the Wolfes' house near Dupont Circle, one of those grand five-story townhouses with a ground floor designed for entertaining, a large, open space with a black-and-white marble floor in a checkerboard pattern, and I'd brought over all our equipment—the amps, the mikes, the drums, the keyboards. Cathy Wolfe was upstairs in the kitchen with the caterers, and Rick Wolfe had taken their kids to a Wizards game. Lily didn't know beans about setting up and she was there mostly to keep me company. "To get out of the house," she said. "I always hate the time before a performance, don't you?"

"I haven't done it often enough to know," I said. I was going to tell her what Tony had said. I was going to tell her that I couldn't keep doing this.

"I get so wound up," she said. "I don't have butterflies. I have big birds thumping around inside."

"Grouse?" I asked, and she smiled.

The big space was dim and Lily was in jeans, not yet dressed for the performance, watching me bolt the drums into place. She picked up a drumstick and tapped one of the cymbals, then another, then another, listening to the brassy vibration spread through the room. "Do you ever think that this was just to get us together? The band, I mean."

I waited for an explanation.

"Do you think it was just a ruse? I keep trying to figure out when this became inevitable, seriously, and sometimes I think it was the band. We were the ones who got it going after you got me started on Clapton."

"You discovered that yourself," I said.

"Tell me, really. Did you think this is where we were always headed?"

"I never know anything until it happens," I said.

"I think I know things in my body," Lily said. "I try to pretend I don't know them, but I do. I think I knew we were supposed to be together."

"Supposed to be? Do you believe in that?"

"I guess so. Is that mushy? Maybe I just don't want to take responsibility for it. The devil made me do it," she said, smiling, closing her eyes.

Then she opened them and tapped my head with the drumstick. "No. Nobody made me do it. I did it because I wanted to. I can't imagine my life now without this. Without you."

It was as close as she'd ever come to saying out loud that she loved me, and whatever thought I had of mentioning Tony, of jealousy and guilt, vanished. I couldn't imagine my life without her, either.

"You know that, don't you? Whatever happens, I want you to know that."

Then she stepped back, turned to face the empty room, threw open her arms. "So here it is, my destiny!" She glowered at me and wagged the drumstick in my face. "The day of destiny, drummer, and you better play your heart out for me. You've never heard me sing the way I'm going to sing tonight."

She was right. I hadn't heard her sing as she did that night. A performance always brings out something different in a singer, I knew that, but that night Lily was magic. The first number we did was Evan's, a hard-driving version of "Brown-Eyed Girl," something to loosen up the audience, some of them friends, most of them strangers who came downstairs because Rick Wolfe was ordering them to, and who listened skeptically, drinks in hand, settling into their places without much enthusiasm. These were well-off Washington people and I'm sure they wondered why they were being asked to listen to a garage band made up of people their own age.

Then Lily sang "Time after Time." The room got quiet. You could feel it, the quickening of attention, the surprise. A few people there had heard Lily at her own piano, but no one was prepared for what they heard that night, for the way she reached down into that song and plucked out the notes, building the song so that the whole of it seemed to hang shimmering in the air. I saw Tony in the crowd and saw the wondering expression on his face when he heard his wife, saw him turn and look about at the others to make sure they were hearing what he heard. Lily wasn't at the keyboards but standing, holding the mike, moving just enough so that you could see how the music rippled through her body, up through the fringed black skirt and the blue silk top, and when she sang that line *"the drum beats out of time,"* she cocked her head just enough for me to know that she meant to acknowledge me. Tony was out there in the crowd, but I thought, god help me, that this moment was ours, Lily's and mine. While she was up there singing and I was behind her on the drums, *we* were the couple. She was singing to me, and as she neared the end of the song, I could see her gathering herself, see her back rise and fall through the sheer of the blue silk, see how collected all the emotion she had released to concentrate it in those last bars, that pledge, *I WILL BE WAIT-ING*, followed by the final words, almost whispered, barely breathed, fading away.

There was a silence then, as though people didn't know what to make of what they'd just heard, or simply didn't know how to react to a woman, another parent, who could sing like that. It took a few seconds for the applause to begin, the clapping, the whistles, the hoots. Lily bowed once, and when she took her place at the keyboards—she winked at me as she turned—we dove right into an upbeat number, "Miles Away," and a couple of people in the audience started dancing. Frankly, we'd been afraid that people would just stand around politely while we performed, but once Lily put herself out there, she seemed to have given everyone permission to take part, and most of them did. Our pattern was to play a slow number followed by a faster one, a vocal number, sung by either Lily or Evan, and some people wouldn't stop dancing on the checkerboard floor. When we finally got to "Mustang Sally," our finale, the whole room was moving, Rick Wolfe was dancing a Cossack kick dance, five or six women had come up to stand with Lily and Nancy and belt out the chorus, Jay was hopping around with his bass like a man trying to cross a bed of hot coals, my shirt was soaked with sweat, and Evan did a moon-walk, first time ever.

Then it was over. The party moved back upstairs. Hugs, kisses, congratulations, drinks. Every time I looked at Lily, she was surrounded by a crowd, and I soon went back downstairs and started thinking about breaking all the equipment back down. I sat on the throne and sipped a beer and said good night to the people who were beginning to drift away. Tony clapped me on the shoulder and said, "Awesome. That was awesome." He and Lily had come in separate cars and he was going home to enforce curfew. Evan had carefully tucked his Stratocaster into his gig bag and he just wanted to hang around, soaking up the last of the excitement. By the time he left, I had most of the equipment ready to carry out to the van. There were a few strays still upstairs, including Lily.

When she came down the ceremonial staircase with a glass in her hand, I happened to be the only one in the room, and she couldn't help mugging for me, doing the Diva Making a Grand Entrance. I rose and bowed deep. She curtsied. I started to say something, but she put her finger to my lips, took my hand, and she led me into the small room just off the large one, an exercise room with weights and a bench and mirrors on the wall. Just a kiss, she said, and that's all it was, for we saw ourselves reflected in the full-length mirror.

"Uh-oh," Lily said, "that's us. I thought we were invisible, but look, Tuck. That's us. This is really happening."

The only person I told about Lily was Joe Jarvis, and I didn't tell him right away. Couldn't. I was afraid of what he'd say, and I mentioned it almost as an afterthought on a Monday morning in December. I had been talking about Christmas and how the kids would be in New York with Trish. I was going up to Croton-on-Hudson, to celebrate with my sister, Emily. The day after Christmas, Boxing Day, Kat and Will would come out from the city.

"I'm not dreading it quite so much this year," I said.

"Why is that?" Joe said.

"I'm just feeling different. Things are better with Kat, a lot better."

Joe waited and I blurted out, "Lily and I are lovers."

I got the delayed response. "Am I supposed to be surprised?"

He sounded disapproving. In fact, he got out of his chair and picked up a small brass vaporizer and started spraying the plants in his office. Beyond the windows of the sunporch the first snow, a few fine flakes, was just starting to come down.

"Have I offended you?" I asked.

"Interesting choice of words," he said. "Offended. Why do you think I'd be offended?"

"Because Lily's married."

"You're not the first to have an adulterous affair," Joe said.

He stayed busy with his little toy vaporizer. "Is that a judgment?" I said.

"You tell me."

"Yes. It feels like that. Yes."

"You don't expect me to congratulate you, do you?"

"Maybe not congratulate me, but I thought there might be a shred of understanding."

"It's not that hard to understand," he said.

"I'm not sure you do understand."

"Tell me what I'm missing."

"I'm in love with Lily," I said. "It's something I've never been able to accomplish."

"Oh. It's an accomplishment."

"I didn't mean it that way. I meant it hadn't happened to me."

"And this just happened?"

"No, it didn't just happen. You know how it happened. I've been talking about Lily for weeks."

Joe sighed, a sad sigh, and sat down heavily. "I'm sorry, Tucker." He waved the vaporizer in the air. "I saw this coming, and I was hoping it wouldn't. You don't need more problems."

"You think it's a problem?"

"I'm sure it is. It's an enormous problem. You know that. You've said so yourself, repeatedly. "

"I know," I admitted. "I keep telling myself it can't be, that we have to stop. But I can't."

Joe nodded in his sleepy way. He said. "Passion. What is a man but his passion?"

"Nothing," I said.

"That was rhetorical question," Joe said. "You have other passions—your children. Kat. Will. What would it do to them if they knew about this?"

"I know. I just can't make myself stop."

"Why not?" he asked.

A strange thing happened then, something that had never before happened to me. I hesitate to call it an out-of-body experience, but I did have the sensation of watching myself, watching from above, as I sought an answer to that question. I was aware of myself sitting in that plant-filled room with its heavy odor of humus and chlorophyll, aware of the snow falling silently outside the windows, aware of Joe holding his vaporizer as he sat deep in his wicker chair, aware of me, an ordinary gray-haired man adrift in the wide world, a man whose next words would stamp a meaning upon his life. From afar, it seemed, I heard my own voice say, "I think she loves me. She won't say it, but she does. Lily loves me."

How simple it was. It was what a boy says as he plucks the petals from a daisy. She loves me, she loves me not.

"She makes me feel alive," I said.

Joe was waiting.

"She makes me feel beloved," I said.

Yes, *beloved.* The word surprised me, and brought with it a sense of gratitude and fulfillment beyond anything I had imagined. I groped to express this to Joe Jarvis.

I said, "She makes me feel beloved in this life and on this earth."

Joe said, "I won't try to argue with that."

CHAPTER

9

———

When Lily asked me to meet her at Battery Kemble Park, I knew that something was wrong. Her voice was so tight, so distant. Her call didn't come until almost noon on a day when we'd planned to meet earlier at the Hut, where I had in fact waited most of the morning for her before giving up and going to the office. I'd tried her cell phone a couple of times, and I was already beside myself, trying to manage all my runaway fears, when she finally called me. "What is it?" I asked her, standing in my office, moving away from the door that stood open. "Are you all right?"

"I can't talk here," she said. "I'm on a pay phone. I forgot my cell. I only have a few minutes. Can you meet me there or not?"

I said I'd be there and got back into my jacket. I'd been at the office no more than thirty minutes, and I told Dee I'd be back after lunch. "Nothing wrong, I hope," she said.

And I said, "No, no. Will left something at home, that's all. I've got to get it to him at school."

We'd been found out, I thought. I couldn't imagine why else Lily would have selected Battery Kemble as the place to meet. The park was only five minutes away from my house, so whatever she had to tell me was something she couldn't say in the music room. What else could it be?

On that cold, clear December day, the park was empty. Lily had already arrived, and the red Cherokee was in the parking lot, the engine running, the exhaust rising in a heavy column. When she got out, I saw at once that her eyes were bloodshot, and she was wearing things I'd never seen her in—a blue parka, an orange ski hat, knit mittens— that she must have thrown on as she went out the door of her house. She looked stunned and sad and disoriented. She said, "I'm sorry I couldn't call earlier."

She kept her distance from me, shying away when I moved nearer to her. "I don't want to talk here," she said, looking around at the open space around us. "Let's walk for a minute."

I followed her to the path that skirts a small stream. Ice had formed along its edges, and the moving water made the sound of crystal. Lily didn't stop or turn until we'd left the parking lot well behind, and we scared up a few crows that went racketing loudly through the bare crowns of the trees. When she did turn to face me, she rubbed the back of the fuzzy mitten against her red, moist noise.

"She's pregnant. Abby's pregnant. And she wants to have an abortion. But that can't happen. It cannot happen."

The words came out in a rush, and Lily's voice rose unnaturally, filling the woods so that the gray stems of the trees seemed to ring with them. She was looking off into the winter distance and she didn't really seem to be talking to me. She was making a statement, her breath coming in small puffs of vapor, and she wobbled as though her legs were unsteady beneath her.

In a lower, grimmer voice, Lily repeated, "It can't happen. I told her that. I don't think I could bear it."

She tried to set her face with determination, but the muscles around her mouth trembled with the effort, and she seemed to lose her balance and stumble forward. "Hold me for a second, OK? Just hold me."

When she slipped into my arms, she felt like a different woman from the one I knew, and the orange ski hat bunched against my cheek. She did not try to fit herself against me but kept moving as if to detach herself. She backed away, saying, "I was so afraid of this. I've been such a bad mother. How could I let this happen?"

"You didn't let it happen," I said.

"I've been a terrible mother and a terrible wife. Don't say I haven't."

There was disgust in her voice, and she pushed back still farther, widening the space between us. She seemed to want to be able to see me whole. "I've been a terrible mother. It is what it is—isn't that what you say? I've been having an affair and my daughter is pregnant."

When I tried to speak, she held up a mittened hand. "You know what I thought when I found out? I thought, suppose I'd gotten pregnant, too? What if we were both knocked up? Tucker, what have we been doing? We've lost our minds."

I wanted to hold her again and moved toward her, but she leaned away. "What am I going to do? Tell me. What am I going to do?"

Her voice had risen again, frantic and beseeching, and she looked as though she was about to fly to pieces. I put my hands on her arms and she suddenly slumped against me. I think she would have fallen if I hadn't held her erect. "You're going to be all right," I said again and again, walking with her as one walks with an invalid, supporting her, moving slowly, measuring my short halting steps to conform to hers. She kept looking down at her black boots to see that she planted them securely on the path. My arm was around her back, and I could feel how she struggled to collect herself. She struggled to tell me what had happened that morning, trying to fit the details together.

"I found the package for one of those pregnancy tests on Abby's bureau, the box and the instructions. It was right there, right out in the open. I think she knew I'd find it. She must have known I'd see it."

She told me that this was a morning when Abby didn't have to be at school until nine o'clock. She'd let her sleep in and hadn't gone into her room to wake her until after eight. Tony had already left for the office and another mom had picked up Sophy and Rafe. "I don't snoop," Lily said. "I don't, but I saw the box on her bureau. I couldn't miss it. So I looked. Of course I looked. First Response, it said. The bunny test. I knew they were having sex. I should have gotten her on the pill. I knew they were having sex and didn't do anything about it because I was afraid to. How pathetic is that? I was afraid my daughter would be mad at me for intruding in her life, so I didn't talk to her.

I stuck my head in the sand. I figured they knew what they were doing. They've had classes about this since they were eight. Safe sex."

"You talked to her," I said. "You couldn't have prevented this."

"I didn't really talk to her, not the way I should have. Not the way a mother should. I was afraid of her. I was afraid of her this morning. When I woke her up, I said, 'Is this what I think it is?' I was trying to be polite, for god's sake. I was trying to pretend that nothing unusual had happened, nothing at all. Abby doesn't have that problem. She grabbed the box out of my hand and told me it was none of my business. I didn't even have to ask her about the result—I did ask, but I already knew. I knew here," Lily said, touching her heart. "She's been so, so impossible, and she's been taking forever in the bathroom in the morning. She has morning sickness but I was so preoccupied that I didn't put anything together. I knew she was hiding things from me, but I was so caught up in what I was hiding that I never suspected the worst. I'd be thinking about you, about going to see you. God, I can't believe this is happening."

She stopped. Tears were running from her eyes and she tried to rub them away with her mittens. "It's all coming apart, everything. I can't stop thinking of Julia and the way I felt when she died. I know this is different but all those feelings are still there. Every day, they're right there. I've been a terrible mother."

"This isn't your fault."

"I have to stop this crying. I have to think but I can't stop bawling. I've been crying all morning and I keep believing that there's got to be some magic solution, there's just got to be. I keep telling myself this can't be happening, but it is, and there's no solution."

"Is Abby sure? Those tests aren't reliable, are they?"

"This was the second one. Both positive. And she has all the signs. She's pregnant, but she's made up her mind that she wants an abortion. She doesn't see any other choice. 'It would ruin my life'—she kept saying that. 'It would ruin my life.' She can be so cold, but she's scared, too. She yelled at me but she cried her heart out—I shouldn't be telling you all this. It's Abby's secret, not just mine. What are we going to do? What?"

She was facing me again, and she'd caught hold of both my hands, looking at me as if I might hold the answer, but that *we* did not include me. She was talking about herself and Abby.

"I'm cold," she said, shivering. "I have to get back. I'm afraid if I'm not there—I don't know. I'm just afraid."

"Does Jed know?" I asked her.

She nodded, and the orange hat flopped over to one side. "He knows. He wants Abby to get the abortion. I can hardly make myself say that. Abortion. They've been talking about this for days now. Abby says they've made up their minds. She says it's their baby. They've already been making plans about how to get it done without anyone else finding out. Then she left that stuff out on the bureau."

"No one else knows?"

She shook her head. "No. Jed's parent don't know. Tony doesn't know, either, but I know where he'll stand on this. He'll be on her side. I really have to go now."

She took off the hat, shook her hair back, and then replaced the hat, drawing it low on her forehead. "I must look awful," she said. "I have to go."

Lily turned and we headed back toward the cars. She moved quickly, her hands tucked into her pockets, her shoulders hunched against the cold. At her car, she said, "I'm sorry. I'm so sorry to dump all this on you when it's not your problem. But I wanted to see you. I wanted you to know."

Her voice drifted off as she leaned against me, and then she was gone. The Cherokee climbed up the hill, leaving me alone in the parking lot, dazed and cold, looking at the turn in the narrow road where she disappeared. That was good-bye, I thought, she'd just said good-bye.

IT WOULD be three days before I saw her or heard from her, three days in which the minutes passed liked the water dripping from the gutters of the Hut. That's how I measured out those sleepless nights, by that *drip drip drip* outside my window. The house is surrounded by trees and I hadn't cleaned the leaves out of the gutter that fall—it was a job I always put off, hating to climb the ladder—and now, in December, in a spell of small, cold rains, the leaf mold was saturated and dripped steadily at the corner of the house, steadily and loudly.

Drip drip drip. I could do nothing but wait.

It was a weekend, and I couldn't call Lily. Saturday and Sunday were the days she belonged to her family. I could have called on some pretext, and invented several, but didn't call—what good would that have done? What good would it have done to ask her what Christmas present to buy for Rafe or Sophy? To talk about video games or gift certificates when I was knotted up with dread? When I couldn't stop imagining the scenes that had to be playing out in Lily's house? When every drip sounded to me as though time was running out and she was slipping away? For that is what I thought, that Lily was slipping away, that I was losing her, that I had already lost her.

I had a headache that felt like a hat of electric wires, but on Saturday I took Will and Kat to Georgetown Park to finish their Christmas shopping in that fancy triple-decker mall, with nonstop carols playing and all the usual decorations on display—the wreaths and bows and swags of red ribbon, the candy canes as big as light posts, the banks of red poinsettias, the raisin-eyed snowmen and red-nosed reindeer, the overstuffed and jolly Santas with entourages of sinister elves, the glittering synthetic trees wrapped with tinsel. I felt as though I had strayed into a place of delirium, and when Will settled in at his favorite store, the Sharper Image, where he could happily spend hours checking out the gadgets, I tagged along with Kat.

She had a long list. She has always taken the giving of presents seriously, and she had very particular ideas about what to buy for her stepbrother and stepsister, for new Tandem friends, for Abby, for Gladys and her children, for my sister, Emily, for Mary Carter, and of course for Trish and Ray. The mall was packed that day, and there were hundreds of couples, men tagging along with their wives, carrying the shopping bags, and we were the odd couple, Kat and I, a grizzled father following his daughter as she went from shop to shop, chatting about each person, testing her ideas on me, asking me if Emily already had refrigerator poetry, if I thought she'd like it, if it was too cheesy, and so on. She was so intent on making the right purchases, and she had such distinct ideas about all these people in her life, that she didn't seem to notice my mood, and in fact she brought me out of it.

She got me thinking about Trish. Kat was having a hard time, as she always did, deciding what to get for Trish and Ray, and we went through what had become an annual conversation—they had everything, it was silly to shop for them, she knew they didn't expect anything from her, she should probably just make a donation to Save the Rainforest in their name. But she wanted to give them something. So she got Ray what she usually got him, a funny video (I hardly knew Ray, but I did know that he loved the same goofy videos that Will liked, and I knew that when he spent time with the kids, they spent it in front of the big projection screen), and she wanted to buy Trish a garden book. She thought I could help her pick one out. "That's her big thing," she said, "that garden. She's been going out to Long Island a lot this fall."

"She must have hundreds of garden books."

"She does, but isn't there one that's not so known? Like the opposite of Martha Stewart?"

We were in the garden section of a bookstore when she said that, looking at a huge display of Martha Stewart books. It struck me, as Kat talked about her mother, that she sounded worried—Kat, worried about Trish. She knew that Trish's obsession with her garden reflected some discontent. At my suggestion, she finally selected a book I was pretty sure Trish wouldn't own, a book by my favorite garden writer, a cranky fellow who wrote under the name Earthman and who had feisty opinions about plants. "You really think she'll like it?" Kat wanted to know.

"I don't know," I said. "Maybe I should give it to her."

"You?"

"Why not?"

Kat's eyes were big. "You don't give Mom presents."

"Maybe I should. It won't kill me."

I bought the book. I can hardly trace all the thoughts that were tumbling through me, but I had such a sharp sense of Trish that day—of Trish as she must have felt when she was in love with Blaine Baker, and her life was in the balance, and she had to know that she was going to lose something that was precious to her. I bought the book, and Kat fretted about what to buy her mother and didn't make a decision until we were in a New Age shop where she was shopping for Mary Carter. There was a little Zen garden on display, a black-framed tray of white sand with pebbles in it. "Mom'll love this," Kat said, drawing patterns in the sand with the tiny rake, making the sand swirl around the pebbles.

"Magic pebbles," she said, with a look that went straight through me.

She bought two miniature gardens, one for Trish and one for Mary Carter.

We spent hours at the mall. Will was all excited when we joined up with him, having found several things he wanted for himself—that was part of our deal, that he got to pick out things for himself—and also exactly the right gift for me. I must have mentioned my headache, and in the Sharper Image he found a head massager, a sort of basket that fit on the head and sent out vibrations. He wanted me to try it right there. So I sat down and put the contraption on my skull and turned it on. "You look like you're in the electric chair," Will cackled. "How's it feel to be sitting in Old Sparky?"

It felt fantastic, as a matter of fact.

That's how I made it through that afternoon. That's how I was able to stop thinking for a minute about Lily and Abby, and that night I went to a Christmas party at the Walkers', half hoping that Lily would show up, though I knew she had other plans—Sophy, her ballerina, was in a dance concert that weekend. The Walkers' invitation had included the kids, but Will had another party that night and Kat was just going to watch a movie at Jamie's house. So I attended the party by myself and wandered through the noisy rooms until I found myself face-to-face with Christine. I hadn't expected to see her there and I tried not to betray any surprise. We'd only talked once, briefly, since our dinner, and she'd never told me about the man she was with, a huge guy with thinning hair and the most enormous pair of tassel loafers I have ever seen. I don't know why I noticed them. I don't how I could possibly have felt an odd jab of jealousy when he put his hand protectively on Christine's back, but I did. They'd obviously been seeing each other for a while, and he seemed to know that I was her ex-boyfriend. He said, in an earnest drawl, that he was working with Teddy Walker at the Interior but thought it might be time for him to reenter the private sector. Reenter the private sector. "This little lady has just about convinced me that it's time to make a move," he said.

Christine looked relieved when I removed myself.

Drip drip drip. I went home and wondered if I would ever hear from Lily.

The kids slept late on Sunday. When I went out front to pick up the newspaper, I slipped on the doorstep where a patch of ice had formed. There was another gutter leak directly above the door, and I must have spent an hour out there in front of the house, chipping away at that stubborn patch with a shovel, but the ice had bonded with the cracked concrete. The morning was cold and moist and heavy drops kept coming down as I worked. *Drip drip, chip chip.* I finally gave up without removing all of the ice, knowing that the patch would just keep re-forming until the gutter was fixed, and went inside to make the kids a breakfast of bacon and pancakes. I grabbed for the phone every time it rang. Mary Carter called. Trish called. Someone called for Kat—Lourdes, it turned out, arranging a time to pick up Kat that afternoon to take her to the Church of the Glorious Miracle. Kat didn't go to the service, but she had volunteered to baby-sit the young children so that their mothers, some of them no older than she was, could listen to José María. She'd worked on homework most of the day, and I drove her to the Friendship Heights Metro station to hand her over to Lourdes, who was waiting in her car with her two little boys and asked me if I wanted to come along. Her winter coat had a collar of fake black fur that surrounded her face like a ruff and she said, "OK, we'll pray for you. We just have to pray a little bit harder." This seemed to amuse her, and Kat, too.

I tried to watch TV while Kat was gone—the strongman competition, of all things. Enormous men grunting as they lugged boulders around and harnessed themselves with chains to pull railroad cars. Will wandered into the room and saw what I was watching and said,

"Have you lost your mind?" I switched to a football game, watched for a while, then went out to the music room to try to fool around on the piano, taking the cell phone just in case. I didn't feel like playing and I'd exhausted the Sunday paper. I ordered Chinese for dinner and picked it up on my way to get Kat. I helped Will with his homework, but at ten o'clock, when Will was going to bed, I could stand it no longer. "I'll be right back," I told Kat. "I'm going out to the CVS to try to find some sleeping pills. I can't take another night without sleeping."

"I thought sleeping pills made you feel funny," she said.

"They do," I said, "but funny is better than the way I feel now. I'll have the cell phone with me. I'll only be gone a few minutes."

I didn't go to the drugstore. I went over to Lowell Street, drove past Lily's house, and parked a few houses away. The fine mist that had been coming down most of the weekend was still coming down and the wet street looked oily. The streetlights had moist haloes around them. I wasn't sure what was going to happen but I knew I had to see Lily, and I got as far as the stone steps, where I looked up at the dark shape of the house, the white columns of the porch showing with a faint ghostly glow. The lights downstairs had been turned off, but the upstairs windows, the bedroom windows, were bulging with yellow light, and I looked up.

I looked up and saw Lily. She was in the corner room, in Abby's bedroom, and I knew the position of the furniture in that room well enough to know that they were both seated on a bed I could not see. Abby, in a robe, was turned away from Lily and her head was bent forward. Lily was brushing her hair. I saw Abby turn once to speak to her mother, and Lily leaned away and held up the brush and smiled, then resumed her work.

My heart seemed to crumple within me and I went back to the car. I drove home, told Kat that it was time for bed. I told her I'd be out in the music room. I put on *Songbird*, the copy that Kat had burned for me, having kept for herself the CD Lily had given to us. I kept the light low and listened to the music and then I picked up a pen and a pad of paper and started to write.

Dear Lily,

It's Sunday night and I am in the music room, our room, losing my mind. How many times have we said that to each other, that we must be out of our minds? It's a figure of speech, but this weekend it seems like nothing more than the simple truth. Less than an hour ago I drove to Lowell Street and parked and walked up to the steps of your house, imagining—imagining what? I hardly know. I didn't have a plan or thought beyond my need to see you, and yet I imagined that you would fly out of your house and into my arms and we would embark on a glorious, passionate life together—somehow, somehow.

Lunacy. Pure lunacy. Right now, sitting here in the music room, I know that there is no Hollywood ending. Never was, never will be. You know what I saw from the sidewalk? I looked up at those huge windows and saw you in Abby's room, sitting behind her, brushing out her hair. How many times have I seen you do that over the years? A mother and her daughter, a mother soothing her daughter at bedtime.

That's who you are, Lily. You're Abby's mother. You're other things, I know, but none of them means as much to you. You're Abby's mother, and Sophy's mother and Rafe's mother and Julia's mother, and nothing will ever be more important to you. You are a mother and a wife. During these last few days, as I've wondered what you must be going through, I've kept thinking that we are back in real life. Our dream has ended, as we knew it would. It's over. At the park the other day, you were already gone.

And yet. And yet. Here I am in the middle of the night, imagining the you that I know, that I have known in this room, recognizing that this is only more make-believe and that my emotions will have no bearing whatsoever on any real outcome. Why do they seem so important, these emotions? At this moment I am listening to music, to Eva Cassidy, as a matter of fact, who has just sung the line "We were like children laughing for hours." *Yes, we did laugh like children, and I feel my love filling this room, filling the night, filling the world—ha! Lunacy. I know that. I know that to anyone but me, my emotions are probably horrifying, but I can't let them go. On this night, as I feel you slipping away, I can't stop trying to hold on to you, to hold on to happiness. Remember that line of Neruda's?* "The way nets cannot hold water." *We talked about that, one of our oceanic talks. Our happiness felt so immense, but every time you got ready to leave, every time we had to haul in the nets, there were just a few bright drops glimmering on the cords. Which makes me think of another line:* "You are taken in the net of my music, my love, / and my nets of music are wide as the sky."

I have the book right here—yes, I have the book beside me and the music playing, and I am here in the music room, Lily, writing away, working away like some quack medium trying to conjure up another spirit, hoping to capture you in the net of my music, equipped with my props, our props, our music and poetry, to evoke you and make you real for another few minutes. It's over, but I don't want to let you go. It's over, and I know that it had to end, that we couldn't have kept on meeting, that we could never have decided to run off, and that we could never have had any life outside the walls of the music room. You have your children, and I have mine, and you could never have made the choice Trish made. I could never have made it.

But I don't want to let you go. I listen to Eva singing and her voice pierces me and I know that I hear all music differently because of you. Because of you the whole world has opened with a grandeur and beauty I couldn't see. I look at Neruda's words, the lines of poetry that once would have seemed utterly without meaning—before you, they would have seemed false and exaggerated and absurd—and I know just how my life has changed. Nets of music? Nets as wide as the sky? Yes, exactly. Yes. Right now Eva is singing "Somewhere Over the Rainbow" and I can hardly believe that I am sitting here with tears in my eyes, hearing something profound and majestic in a song about happy little bluebirds and troubles melting like lemon drops.

That's where I stopped. That song reminded me so much of Kat, and when I thought of her in her bed, asleep, it was too appalling to go on. I turned off the CD player, I put away the book, and I tore the pages off the lined pad, intending to destroy them. I went back to the house and searched the kitchen for a box of matches, intending to burn the letter in the fireplace—yes, burn them, like all the doomed lovers in bad movies.

I couldn't find a match. I rummaged through every cabinet and I was standing there, frantic, when Kat walked in, wearing flannel jammies. "Dad? Dad? What's going on? Are you OK?"

I tired to hide the letter, turning slowly so that Kat wouldn't see it in my hand. "It's just the headache," I said.

"Can't sleep? Did you get any pills?"

"I'll be all right," I said. "You go on back to bed."

"I was having this weird dream about you," Kat said, smiling a little. "We were at the beach and you were trying to show me how to ride the waves but you kept getting wiped out."

"Nice," I said.

"It wasn't that bad," she said. "I mean, you kept trying. Every time you got wiped out, you'd get back up and try again. You kept saying, 'No problem. No problem.' And you kept getting wiped out." Her smile got broader, and she said, "I just remembered what I was doing— I was on the beach watching you and I was building a castle, but it wasn't a sand castle. It was a real fairy-tale castle. Shining and everything. Flying banners. The works."

My daughter, building castles in her sleep. I said, "Keep building," and Kat padded off toward the stairs. I stood there with the pages of the letter balled up in my hand and listened to her overhead in the quiet house, settling down in her bed. As a child she always wanted a lullaby, and she still liked to drop off to sleep with music playing. The CD she put on was Eva Cassidy's *Songbird*.

Too much. It was too much for me to understand or deal with. I didn't know what to do with the letter in my hand or what to do about anything, so I walked upstairs and with no more purpose than a man in a trance, I placed the letter in the filing cabinet in my closet, in a file labeled Medical Records.

Then I went to bed and heard, faintly, the songs drifting out from Kat's room, the songs and the water dripping in the gutter at the corner of the house, *drip drip drip.*

"WHAT DO you want?" Joe Jarvis asked me when I went to my regular Monday appointment. I had told him everything. Everything.

"Want?"

"What do you want? It's a useful question. Until you know what you want, you won't know what to do."

"What difference does it make what I want? I have no control over what's happening now."

"It might make a difference to you," Joe said. "It might help you sort out this confusion."

"I want Lily," I said, "but I know that's over."

"Do you?" Joe asked in his enigmatic way, his expression hinting that he was aware of things hidden from me.

"All right, tell me," I said, flashing out. "What do I want, O wise one? You seem to know all about it."

"I think you want someone to tell you what to do," he said, a sharp reproach in his voice. "You want someone to get you out of this mess."

"Well, thank you," I said. "Are you that person?"

"It's your mess," he said. "You know the joke about the man who goes into a Chinese restaurant? He orders, but when he gets his meal, he calls the owner over. 'this is shit,' he says. 'It's what you order,' the owner tells him. 'Yes, but it's shit,' the man says. 'So sorry,' the owner says. 'You order shit, you eat shit.'"

The way Joe told it, it didn't sound like a joke. I was stunned, as a matter of fact, by the harshness of his manner, though he began immediately to backtrack. He apologized. He said it was a story that therapists told each other, because patients sometimes got themselves into situations that... his thick mitts fluttered above his lap and his voice trailed into vagueness.

He looked embarrassed and he said, "Let me try this again. I know you're in love with Lily, but the question is what you want *most*."

"I just said, it doesn't matter that I want Lily."

"Yes, but you were standing outside her house last night, and I don't think you had any more idea of what you were going to do than you had last summer when you went to that party to find Kat. Sometimes you act without thinking, Tucker. Everyone does. Right now you want to run away with Lily—"

"I know I can't run away."

"But you'd like to—you would. You'd like to, but you couldn't without leaving your children behind, could you? And you're not going to do that."

"Lily's not running away with me," I said.

"Maybe not," Joe said, "but it matters how you state the case. You can't let Lily make this decision for you. It's really your decision, Tucker, and I want you to be clear within yourself. Let me turn it around this way: What are you most afraid of? Are you more afraid of living without Lily than of living without Kat?"

I knew the answer but didn't say it.

Joe said it for me. "It comes down to that, doesn't it? You're more afraid of losing Kat," he said, "and you have to be clear about that, no matter what happens now."

I nodded, and Joe appraised me as if deciding whether his warning had been stern enough. He said, "This could take strange turns before it's over, and you have to get through them. Remember what you've decided before you do anything—will you do that? And if you want to talk, you'll call me, won't you? Call me anytime."

Even the unflappable Joe Jarvis was scared. He patted my shoulder as I left and wished me good luck. As soon as I was in the car, I turned on my cell phone and hit the speed-dial buttons that would connect me to Lily. By then it was after nine o'clock and she would have finished her morning chores.

No answer. At least I heard her voice on the message.

She didn't return the call until late in the morning. I was in the office, going over the numbers and squaring all the accounts. I was on the office phone with a deadbeat builder who owed Twill close to fifty thousand dollars, a man who always had a dozen complaints and excuses for not paying his bills, when the cell phone rang and I saw her name on the display. *Lily is calling on line 1.*

There was traffic noise on the phone and her voice broke into digital pieces, but I heard her say that she had just dropped Sophy at school. Abby was still at home.

"Are you all right?"

A pause. A faint roar. Then, "No. I'm not all right. We have to talk, but not now. I'm on my way back home."

"What's happening? God, I'm glad to hear your voice. These last three days have lasted forever."

"I really can't talk now," she said. "But I'll try to call you this afternoon, OK? Maybe we can meet somewhere before I have to pick up Rafe at three. I'll call you at two. I have to go now. I have to go."

Dead air. I'd put the builder on hold when I took Lily's call, and he'd clicked off, too, but I didn't call him back. It was almost eleven o'clock, so I had another three hours to wait, trying not to imagine what Lily and Abby were saying to each other, but imagining it anyway. Trying not imagine what Lily and Tony had said to each other, and imagining that, too. What did I want? Joe Jarvis was right: I wanted someone to get me out of this mess.

At noon the entire office staff drove into Bethesda for a long-planned celebratory lunch at an expensive Italian restaurant. This was our Christmas party, and Dee had spent weeks preparing us for it, discussing the menu items and circulating the restaurant reviews she'd downloaded. That morning she'd been strutting around the office in a new pantsuit, wearing a pair of four-inch heels, her hair done up in a full Dolly Parton, all waves and finger curls. Everyone was dressed for the occasion, including me, and we found our table set with a centerpiece that Dee had dreamed up, a toy truck with the red-and-green Twill Landscaping panel on the doors. The truck bed contained a beautiful bonsai tree, an evergreen not shaped like a Christmas tree but decorated like one, covered with tiny red and silver cloth ornaments. She'd gotten them from a dollhouse supplier, Dee said proudly. The tree was my Christmas present, and I must have looked stricken, or just sick, for they all kept asking me how I felt. Everyone was there, Dee and Jackie and Max, Barbara and Randy and Don, and they got their bonuses, three grand each, by far the biggest bonuses I'd ever been able to pay. Dee squealed and jumped up and down with excitement, and I couldn't think of anything except the minutes ticking away before Lily called.

I missed the call, as it turned out. It was almost two when we left the restaurant and I was able to check my messages. Hers was brief: *I can't make it. Abby has taken off with the car.* No answer when I tried to call her. I'd told everyone to take the rest of the afternoon off, and I went back to the office, planning to make a few more calls before I closed the place, but my head was splitting and I locked up and went home a little before three.

The red Cherokee was in the driveway in front of the music room, the Cherokee and Gladys Ochoa's small white car with its bright bumper stickers. Lily's car, I thought when I saw it, but Abby had taken it. Abby—what was she doing at the Hut? I tried to be prepared for anything when I let myself in, but there was no sign of Abby. Romeo was barking, Gladys was in the kitchen, and Carolina, Gladys's daughter, was watching a television show in the alcove.

I asked about Abby.

"She bring Kat home from school," Gladys said. "They just go out for a cup of coffee, just now. Worry, I think."

"Kat's worried?"

"Both," Gladys said. "They don't talk to me. So."

So it was serious, she was telling me. Otherwise Kat would have talked to her. Otherwise they wouldn't have found it necessary to leave the house to walk the few blocks up to the shops on Macarthur. Gladys watched me with her black eyes. The kitchen was spotless and I told her she could leave if she was done.

"You home early," she said. "You look bad."

"I have a headache, but I'm OK. Just tired. I can wait for Kat if you're ready to leave."

She seemed uncertain whether she should leave me alone, though Carolina had been listening and she was on her feet, ready to go.

When they left I called Lily again and, this time, reached her. I told her that Abby had evidently picked Kat up at school and brought her here, to the Hut. Lily said she'd borrow a car and be right over.

I heated water for a cup of coffee and stood in the kitchen watching the television show that Carolina had left on. A bald-headed man was explaining the mind-body connection and how stress pitched people into a state of adrenal arousal. The blood started pumping into the peripheries, he said. The stomach grew more acidic. Blood pressure increased. This was not some New Age bull, he said, but scientific fact.

Romeo, who'd been curled up in the wing chair, suddenly came alive and filled the house with his barking. Someone was coming—the girls, I thought, and I turned off the electric kettle and the TV and went to the front door to let them in.

It was not the girls. It was Jed Vandenberg.

His head was bare, his hands were jammed into the pockets of his red-and-black team jacket, and he was paused on the sidewalk near his canvas-topped Jeep, wary, listening to Romeo barking and studying the house, trying to figure out who was there. For a second I imagined, absurdly, that he'd come there to see me, but of course he hadn't. He was looking for Abby, and when he caught a glimpse of movement in the sidelights that frame the front door—when he caught a glimpse of me—he lifted his hands from his pockets and his face settled into the defensive, defiant look I'd seen so often.

I opened the door. I think I said his name. I know Romeo was barking and wrapping himself around my ankles. He barks at visitors but has learned not to dash at them, and he was raising a clamor as I stepped out of the house and onto the doorstep, onto that patch of ice. My foot slipped, and I fell right on my tailbone.

Right on my ass, I should say. Jed's face broke into a big grin. Volts of pain were shooting up my spine, I gasped and swore, Romeo kept braying, and Jed grinned as I sat splayed out on the cement doorstep. "Fuck you," I said.

He laughed out loud then, but he did take a few steps closer and tried to assume an expression of concern. I wanted to get up but couldn't. It hurt like hell when I attempted to bend my knees and get my legs under me.

"Is that dog going to bite me?"

"Shut up, Romeo," I said, and he backed himself toward the door as Jed advanced.

"Can you get up?" he asked cautiously.

The pain crackled and I said, "Sure, I can get up. I just like sitting here."

He grinned again, a grin that split his face. "Do you want me to help you? Or, I don't know, should I call somebody?"

I tried again to get up. My legs were straight out in front of me and I couldn't make myself bend my knees. I felt absolutely helpless, twitching like some injured insect in front of this boy who watched with his one good eye, the glass eye veering up and away. His face grew serious as he calculated the implications of touching me. He asked, "How bad is it?"

"I don't know," I said.

"Should I call the ambulance or anything?"

"God, no. I'll be all right once I get on my feet."

Jed stepped up onto the doorstep and walked around behind me. "Watch out for that patch of ice," I warned him. "You can hardly see it. That's what I slipped on."

"I see it. So you're sure about this? You want to get up? I can call somebody."

"Just help me up, OK?"

He slipped his hands under my arms and his fingers dug into the sides of my chest. "All right," he said, "I'm going to lift now. Ready?"

"Go ahead."

I could smell the damp wool of that jacket and feel the warmth of his breath on my neck as he lifted, considerately, and I tried to get my legs under me. My feet flapped about like an old man's. "These goddamn shoes," I remember saying, "these goddamn shoes." I wasn't wearing my usual winter boots but the leather-soled shoes I'd put on for the office lunch, and they felt slippery and useless. Jed was still supporting me lightly, his hands on my ribs. "It's OK," he said. "I've got you. I'll help you in."

When he looped his arm around my waist, we turned slowly and in tandem to face the house. I tried to breathe evenly as I lifted my foot to cross the threshold and took a few steps into the hall. "Where to?" Jed asked, and I said the kitchen. I wanted to get to the kitchen where I could support myself at the counter.

"OK, that's good. I can stand here."

He backed away. "You sure? You want to stand?"

"I'll stand for a while. I'm not ready to sit down again just yet."

He grinned again, and I saw his glance dart about. "Abby's not here," I said. "She and Kat went out to get some coffee."

"Yeah, well, that's why I came," he said, as though he felt he owed me an explanation. "Abby called me and said she was here. She wasn't

at school today. I mean, she left a message on my phone. I just got it."
He made a gesture with his hands, uncertain whether he should stay
or go.

"They should be back any minute," I said.

"I can wait outside," he said. He nodded his head toward the door,
and I could see the dismay coming back into his face. He had no idea,
of course, that I knew why Abby had stayed home from school and
why her call had been urgent enough to make him come to my house.

"Wait here if you want."

"You sure you don't want me to call anybody?" he asked. "It looks
like it hurts."

"It does hurt. I'll take something. I think that's all I can do,
anyway."

I sidestepped along the counter, making my way to the sink to fill a
glass with water, suddenly afflicted with thirst and with the need to
splash water in my face, to rinse the salt from my eyes. I must have
stood there gasping at the sink, for when I had gulped down a glass of
water and rinsed my face, drying it with a dish towel, Jed was watching me closely. It was still hard for me to get my breath, but I knew
there were things I had to say to him, things that needed to be said.

"I know what's happening," I said, unable to be more exact.

"You know? You know about Abby? Fuck. No one is supposed to
know about that. It was a mistake. Obviously, it was a mistake. Who
told you about this? Lily? Who else knows?"

"Lily and I talk about our children," I said.

The word *children* made him clench his jaw. "Jesus," he said. "Who
else knows?"

"I don't think she's told anyone else. I won't, either. I understand
that this is private."

"It was supposed to be private. It's between me and Abby, and now
the whole fucking world knows about it."

"I'm not the whole world. I don't think Lily has gone around
telling people."

"She's not the one pregnant," he said. "She acts like she is. Like it's
her child but it's not."

"Lily lost a child."

"That's different. Lily had a baby, and she was married. Look, I'm sixteen and there's no way I'm getting married and having kids now. We had a plan until Lily found out about it. We had the same plan that everybody else who gets into this situation has. That's what clinics are for. That's what laws are for. Christ, I can't believe I'm talking to you about this. Butt out, OK? This is not your problem."

He looked toward the door but he didn't leave.

"I'm not judging you," I said.

"Gee, thanks. That makes me feel better."

The sarcasm should have been familiar, but it stung me. I said, "You're not the only who's been in this spot."

"So what are you telling me? You're saying you know all about it?"

His voice hung somewhere between anger and astonishment, and I was astonished, too, realizing what I had just said. Even now, even after reconstructing this scene, I can hardly believe that I had admitted to Jed Vandenberg the secret I had always kept to myself. All I can say is that I was groping for some way to keep him there, some way to make a connection with him, a connection different from the one that linked us so with such distrust and bitterness. "It was a long time ago," I said, "but yes. I have some idea of what you're going through."

His nose twitched and he said, "So what am I supposed to do?" There was hostility in his voice, but it was a real question.

"I don't know, Jed. Be brave, be bold." I couldn't think of anything else to tell him.

"What?"

"That's a saying we have, me and the kids. It's a rule—Kat's rule. It's from a fairy tale. Be brave, be bold, let not your heart grow cold."

"A fairy tale. Great. This is no fucking fairy tale."

He shoved his hands back into his pockets. "Are we through here?" he said, but he still didn't leave.

"No," I said. "I want to talk about something else."

He swore, but stayed there.

"I want to talk about that night. July 13th."

"What now? Abby gave me your message. I was there the other day, at that meeting. I know your deal."

"You do? What is my deal?"

He shook his head as if he couldn't believe what I'd asked. As if he was sick to death of this conversation. "You want to get off."

"I do want to get off. I don't want to stand trial or go to jail. What do you want?"

"Want?"

"You want me in jail?"

Jed looked at me with his jaw clenched, then let his eye wander off. "Fuck. I don't know. I'm not a lawyer."

"There are no lawyers here," I said. "There's just you and me. I think about you every day. I'm going to think of you every day for the rest of my life. I'm going to remember that night, and so will you."

"Yeah," he said, the word coming out as a low growl.

"No matter what happens in a trial, I want you to know what I did. Sometimes when I read the reports the investigator is getting, I start to wonder if anybody is ever going to agree about what happened. Sometimes I start to doubt myself. But, Jed, listen. I go over and over it, and I didn't go in there to hurt anybody. Do you know that? Even when you stood up, I didn't swing at you. Maybe it didn't look like that, but I didn't swing that shovel at you."

"So what? You knocked me down. My eye is gone. You want me to say it's all just fine? You want me to feel sorry for you?"

"No," I said, although I did want him to forgive me. I couldn't say it. I wanted him to forgive me, but his suffering seemed to fill the house, his suffering and anger, and I could feel how impossible that was. He was so young. "I don't want you to go through life thinking I wanted to do this to you."

"So what am I supposed to think?"

"That I was trying to find my daughter. That I was crazy with worry about her."

Jed weighed what I'd said and glanced around as if searching for a way to escape. He took a couple of deep breaths before he said, "I should have told you where she was."

Then he started to nod his head. "Yeah, I should have told you. I didn't know where it was, Matt's brother's apartment, but I knew that's where Abby was going with her. I should have told you that."

"Why didn't you?"

That was asking too much. He'd admitted as much as he could, and he ignored the question. He said, the iron coming back into his voice, "Listen. If this legal stuff keeps going, is your lawyer going to do what he said? Bring charges against Matt and Danny? Or is that bullshit?"

I said I didn't know. I said I wasn't a lawyer, either.

"I know Kat," he said unexpectedly.

"I know you do."

"I hope she's going to be all right."

"Thank you," I said. "I hope so, too."

I don't know what he was thinking, but he had reached his limit. He said politely, "You said they went for coffee? I think I'll wait outside."

I didn't try to stop him when he left the Hut.

I WAS SO TIRED. I was in that impossible state when the body is exhausted but the mind is on fire. Meltdown. Coffee was the last thing I needed, but I turned the kettle back on and gimped over to the fridge, jarring my tailbone with every step, to get the coffee out of the freezer. Our fridge has the usual clutter on it—magnets in various shapes, snapshots of the kids, menus for carryout food, schedules for sports and school events—but I happened to notice the rules, the Big Rules and Little Rules, while I was standing there waiting for the water to boil. The rules had once occupied a place of prominence, but both sheets looked dingy and tattered and they had slid down lower on the door. The fact is we hadn't talked about them much during the fall, and on that day they just seemed to mock me. *It is what it is. Play hard, play fair. Finish what you start.*

It is what it is—but what *was* this? And I hadn't played fair. And I had no idea how I was to finish what I had started.

I splashed my face with water and made myself a strong cup of coffee. I took Advil. I had to move carefully, but I could hobble from place to place, and when Romeo leaped up from the wing chair and headed for the front door, barking again, I followed him, expecting to see the girls through the sidelights.

Lily. Lily was on the sidewalk. She and Jed were standing at the fender of his Jeep, and she was talking, her hands moving, almost flashing, like a boxer's. Jed's were shoved into his jacket pockets, and I saw him back away from her step by small step as she pressed in on him. She seemed to want to take hold of him and shake him. She was wearing a yellow rain slicker and rubber boots, and she occasionally pushed her damp hair back from her face, looping it over her ears, but she obviously wasn't aware that she was getting soaked by a December drizzle or that anyone might be watching her.

She wasn't aware of me. For three days I'd been counting the minutes until I could see her again, and now she was at my house, but she hadn't come for me. She didn't know I was watching. She was in another story now, not our story, and I was an onlooker, peeking out the window.

I tried to shush Romeo and simply watched as the drama in front of my house played out in silence. I couldn't hear a word, but I saw Jed remove his hand from his pocket and gesture up the street; I saw Lily turn; I saw the girls, just rounding the corner, stop in their tracks. Abby and Kat were both wearing parkas with the hoods up to cover their heads, and their faces seemed to recede into their garments. They looked like a pair of turtles slowly tucking in their heads, but after a pause they came forward, slowly, Abby a few steps ahead of Kat, angling right across the street. She had a paper coffee cup in one hand and she'd set her face to meet whatever awaited her. When she stepped up over the curb, nearing Lily and Jed, she reached up with her free hand and pushed the hood back. Lily had backed away from Jed and it looked as though Abby, who hesitated in the narrow grass strip between the sidewalk and street, deliberated while making a choice between them.

She chose Jed. She went to his side and he put his arm around her shoulders, lowering his face to kiss the damp crown of her head. Lily watched this, as did Kat, hanging a few steps back, still at the edge of the street, peering out of her hood. I think she was the first to see Tony's car, and she was certainly the first to move, stepping up on the grass as the silver BMW burned around the corner and slammed to a loud stop right behind Jed's Jeep. The scream of rubber was the first sound I'd heard, but after Tony had slammed his door, the volume went up and I heard voices—not words, but thick cords of sound that made Romeo whimper and paw at the base of the door. Tony, in his long black overcoat, had evidently come straight from his office, and he was the one who noticed me in the sidelights. He said something to the others, and when he headed for the door, I opened it. I had no idea what I'd do until I heard myself say, "Watch the ice. It's slippery."

Tony looked down. His black shoes were shined, and the collar of his white shirt and the knot of his red tie showed at his throat, in the neat V of his lapels. Even with his dark hair flattened by the drizzle and lying close to his skull, he looked groomed and elegant. His eyes flickered over the icy doorstep, and I have to admit here that I was re-lieved. It was clear to me, as he shifted from one foot to the other, stepping off the grass and onto the stones of the walk when he noticed the drops of moisture on his shoes, that Lily had told him nothing about us. "You're probably wondering what's going on," he said grimly. "Maybe Lily told you—told you why we're having this family meeting on your sidewalk." He gestured toward the others and made a strange noise, not a laugh. "We should get out of the rain. Do you mind? Do you mind if we go into your garage?"

The music room, he meant. It still looked like a garage, though the car doors had been sealed off and weatherproofed. "Of course not," I said.

"We might as well settle it now, now that we've tracked down the young lovers," he said. As though he disbelieved it himself and cer-tainly expected me to disbelieve it, he said, "She's pregnant. Abby has gone and gotten herself pregnant. With your boy."

My boy—that would be Jed. My boy. The phrase was so jarring that I didn't know what to say, and perhaps Tony was simply trying to avoid speaking Jed's name. Perhaps he was so dazed that he didn't know what he was saying. He stood there looking at the music room as though it were a walled fortress and he couldn't begin to figure out how to enter it.

"The side door should be open," I said, "the door facing the house."

Carefully, watching where he set his feet in the wet grass, he began to cross the lawn. "Come on," he said, gesturing curtly to the others.

For a second or two Lily's eyes met mine, taking notice as though she were looking through the window of a passing car.

Kat watched them straggle along behind Tony, then picked her way toward the house. I warned her about the ice, too, and stood back to let her in the door. Romeo greeted her joyfully. The shoulders of her green parka were soaked a darker green, and a few damp strands of hair were stuck to her forehead and cheeks. Her eyes seemed huge, widened by the enormity of what was happening all around her, and her wet lashes stuck together in spikes. She looked rapt, solemn, and alive.

"You should get out of those wet things," I said.

She unzipped her parka but couldn't decide what to say to me. I said, "I know what's happening. Tony just told me."

"He did? He told you?"

"He said Abby..." But I didn't finish the sentence. Kat was watching me, and I had a sense of her trembling already with her knowledge, containing it like a cup that has been overfilled. One shake and it would spill.

"Let me take your coat," I said, and I managed to turn her so that I could slip the wet parka from her shoulders. "Your shoes are soaked, too. Why don't you leave them here?"

I hung the parka on the hall tree and rubbed her cold hands between mine to warm them up. "She's pregnant," Kat said, letting the words spill out. "She gave herself the test, so she's sure. But she doesn't want to have it. The baby. She doesn't want to have the baby."

Kat was watching me as if I might know what to do.

"Take your shoes off," I said. "We don't need you getting sick."

Kat slipped off her shoes without even bending down, the athletic shoes she'd worn to school. They were saturated, and she hooked her socks off, too. "I'll get you a towel," I said, trying to walk naturally as I went into the bathroom.

Kat sat in the wing chair, sharing it with Romeo, using the towel to dry her face and warm her feet. We were both thinking of what was happening out in the music room. I asked, "How did you and Abby get together? I thought you'd still be at school."

"She called me. I checked my messages during break and she called."

"They let you go?"

"I just left. Dad, she said it was an emergency. I didn't hang around trying to get permission."

She sounded as though she expected me to scold her. I said, "I'm surprised, that's all. It is an emergency. Obviously."

I was trying to sound calm and trying not to say how surprised I was that Abby had called Kat when they'd been off balance with each other throughout the fall, but perhaps it made sense, as much sense as anything else. Perhaps this was a time when Abby would turn to her oldest friend. I could see, anyway, that Kat was filled with the sense of trust and intimacy that this friendship conferred. I told her that it was the right thing to do, leaving school. I asked her if this was the first she'd known about Abby.

"It was the first I heard about the baby. But I knew about her and Jed." She twisted a strand of hair, waiting to see how I would respond before adding, "A lot of people knew that he was her boyfriend, but nobody is supposed to know about this. About the baby. They want to keep it private." She spoke as though it remained private with her, as though she would naturally share any secret of Abby's. "They haven't decided what to do. I guess that's what they're doing right now."

"I thought Abby had decided."

"She doesn't want it," Kat said, and seemed to consider how much of the story to reveal to me. "She doesn't want it, but Lily does. Lily wants her to have it."

"She lost a baby," I said. "Julia."

Kat's eyes filled with tears then and she lifted the towel to her face to stop them. She took a deep breath when she lowered it and said, "I remember Julia—not Julia, really, but I remember the funeral they had for her. I remember the white roses."

"You do?"

Kat would have been three when Julia died, and there was a funeral in the small church in Georgetown that we all attended in those days. Everyone at Julia's funeral was given a white rose to hold.

"I still have my rose," Kat said.

"I have mine, too, somewhere."

Kat rubbed her face once more with the towel. "You think Abby will have the baby? She says she doesn't want it, but she hasn't really made up her mind. She doesn't know what she believes—about abortion, I mean. When they talked to us about this in school, they talked about the moment that life begins, but they didn't talk about souls or heaven or anything like that. They said some people believe in it, that's all. They said *some people*, like they had to be strange to believe in something like that. But I believe in it. I've always believed in it, ever since Julia died, and you're the one who told me about it. You said Julia was in heaven."

"I know."

"So why did you tell me that?"

"Because you were what? Three years old? Four? Because you already believed in it and maybe you were right. I didn't want to be the one to take it away from you."

"I think she should have it," Kat said, trying to keep her voice from crumbling. "She asked me and I said she should have it. She asked me what I'd do, and I said I'd have it."

My daughter fixed her dark eyes upon me and said, testing her statement, "I said I'd have it. I would. I'd have it."

She sniffed a couple of times and looked around for a box of tissues. The box was on the counter, and when I carried it over to her, she blew her nose loudly. "What a honker I am," she said.

"It would be strange not to cry," I said.

"Why does it have to be so sad?" she asked me. "What will she do with a baby? She has to go to school. I mean, they don't have child care at Byrd-Adams."

She blew her nose again, trying to stop the tears. "I get so afraid, Dad. What if it had been me? I keep thinking that—what would I do? I know I couldn't have an abortion. But what would I do? I'd be terrified."

"I'm sure Abby is."

"You really think she'll have it?"

"I don't know."

She held the towel over her shins and seemed to gather herself, looking at me as though what she was about to say was too terrible to express. "It could have been me. It could have been. Anything could have happened that night. Anything."

I knew what night she meant. "You don't have to talk about that."

"Anything could have happened. I was so out of it."

"But it didn't. That's behind you now."

My daughter held my gaze, wanting to believe me, and then she wrinkled her nose, suddenly noticing Romeo's smell. "*Eee-eww,*" she said to him, "you're a smelly dog. I reek, too. I have to change out of these clothes."

She stood up and arched her back, drawing her lungs full of air, and I could tell that she wanted to get away. Had to get away. She scampered up the stairs and soon I heard the shower running.

I lowered myself into the wing chair, still warm from her body, trying to find a way to sit without discomfort, trying to absorb what she had just told me, but it wasn't long before I heard an engine start outside the house—the Jeep. Standing, I was able to catch a glimpse of it through the front windows. Jed was leaving, and a few minutes later another engine started, and Tony left, too.

Then Lily came into the house through the side door, Lily and Abby. They both looked exhausted.

"I'm sorry about all this—this confusion," Lily said, "but you know what's been going on. You're the only ones who know, you and Kat."

Abby glared at me.

"I hope you'll keep it quiet," Lily said.

"It's nobody else's business," Abby said. "Where's Kat?"

Before I could answer, Kat was coming down in her bare feet, wearing sweats, drying her hair with a bath towel. Lily thanked her for being a good friend to Abby, and there was a silence as Kat waited, as I waited, to hear what they had decided.

Abby said, "It looks like I'm going to have it. It looks like I'm going to be a mom."

Tears ran down Abby's cheeks, but she didn't bawl or sob. She stood straight and she looked to me like a general handing over a sword, like one who has surrendered without giving up a shred of her pride. When the girls hugged, it was Abby who seemed to be comforting Kat. As for Lily, her eyes were frightening when she turned to me and said in a flat voice, "This has been hell, pure hell."

FOR THE next few days I hardly knew what to think or do. I was glad the kids were preoccupied with their exams and didn't pay much attention to me. I tried to help them study and at night I went to bed with a heating pad on my aching tailbone.

Then, on Thursday morning, Lily called. I remember that it was a Thursday because the next day, Friday, was the kids' last school day before Christmas break. We talked about that. "Once school's out," Lily said, "I won't have a minute to myself. Can you get away at all this afternoon?"

Her voice was quick, cheerful, light, slightly rushed—in short, normal. She managed to sound as though nothing special had taken place over the last few days. I said, "Are you asking me to take another walk in the park?"

"Ah, no," she replied, with husky undertones of suggestiveness. "I've booked a room, a room at the Tabard. I called 1-800-AFFAIR."

I was so taken aback by her attempt to joke that I didn't answer, and she added, slipping back into the breezy voice, "Today's the day I try to put myself back together. I'm on my way to the salon right now—my annual visit. But I do have a room. I should be there by two. I'm getting the whole works."

At two o'clock I was entering the Tabard Inn, a small, cozy hotel where a wood fire was burning in the lobby. There was no elevator. I climbed a staircase to the third floor and walked down a creaky hall, past doors with glass doorknobs that looked as though they might come off in your hand. When Lily opened the door to her room, she stood before me in a blue robe. "Come in, come in," she said, plucking at my sleeve. "I've been waiting for you."

The curtains were drawn, admitting one vertical bar of afternoon light that sliced through the velvet gloom, and Lily plucked at the sleeve of my jacket to draw me in, closing the door behind me. The room was dim, and she put her arms around me, but I caught a glimpse not only of the robe—sky-blue silk or satin, it was slippery against me—but of painted eyes, rouged cheeks, and hair shaped into sleek waves. Her mouth tasted of lipstick and her hair had that salon smell, a chemical smell. Though she cocked her leg behind mine, though I had longed to see her, though she squirmed in that way of hers to adjust her body to mine, I was disoriented, and she felt it.

"Do I look silly?" she asked, leaning away. "I always feel ridiculous after getting my hair done at that place."

Lily ordinarily used makeup in such a way that I simply didn't notice it. "I don't usually see you like this. So glamorous. So groomed."

"I look ridiculous," she said, suddenly tearful. "I *am* ridiculous."

She stepped back, holding on to my hands. "I knew this was a bad idea."

"Maybe you should tell me—what is the idea?"

"Don't look at me like that," she said, drawing me more deeply into the dimness of the room, passing through that wall of light. It glinted on the frame of a brass bed, showing the pillows piled high and the linens folded back, but Lily was leading me to a different part of the room where there was a glass-front bookcase, a writing desk, and a tile fireplace with a white mantel. In front of the fireplace, two pumpkin-colored love seats faced each other across a table on which stood a bouquet of red roses—florist's long-stemmed roses, not the kind of bouquet sold on the street.

"I felt ludicrous signing in with them," Lily said, following my eyes to the flowers, "the box of roses and my little overnight bag in the middle of the day. I was so afraid someone would recognize me I thought I'd faint. The girl at the registration counter had an amazing black eye, but she knew exactly why I was here. Who wouldn't? I don't think I'm cut out for this, for romantic trysts. I'm going to be a grandmother."

We stood there shyly, sadly, hand in hand. "Red for passion," Lily said. "I wanted this to be different, our last time—but it's too different, isn't it?"

"They're beautiful," I said vaguely, wanting to reassure her, but those words pierced me. *Our last time.*

"I've already ruined it, haven't I? I look like a tramp. I *feel* like a tramp."

Her voice had a catch in it, a sound almost of choking, and she slipped her hand from mine to pull the robe more closely to herself. "I don't know what I was thinking. I wanted this to be romantic and I feel like I'm at the doctor's office. You're looking at me like you're examining me. *Hmm, your pulse is a little fast. Have you been drinking coffee?* Yes, Doctor Jones, I've been drinking so much coffee I feel drunk." She looked about her, taking in the room. "Maybe I am drunk. I must have been to think that this was a good idea, to get a room. I thought it would be grown-up. That's what I told myself—this is what grown-ups do, they get a room. They don't pretend that it's just *happening*. That's what I've been doing this whole time, telling myself it was all just happening. All those times I met you in the music room, I always managed to convince myself that I hadn't really planned anything. To have a plan—that would have made it too deliberate. So today I had the salon appointment and I wanted to see you and I decided to make a plan, and here we are—oh god, here we are. I'm so sorry."

She shook her head slowly and crossed her arms tightly across her chest. Since entering the room, I had been studying her, trying to judge her mood, but this distraught woman who talked so quickly, in such a panicky voice, was hardly recognizable to me.

She could read my thoughts, though. She said, "Here we are and you don't even like me. How could you? I don't like myself. I don't even know who I'm supposed to be anymore."

"I'm trying to get used to you," I said, reaching for her. "So much has happened."

She stepped farther away, and my hand slid down the sleeve of that slick robe. "I've ruined this," she said quietly, "ruined it."

"I didn't expect you to call," I said. "Nothing is ruined."

"Don't say that. Don't talk to me as if I were a child." She glared at me then and found fierceness in her voice. "I'm such a fool. I had the idea that somehow I'd make you understand what all this had meant to me. What you've meant. How important it's been. This is it, the last act of my great love affair—how pitiful is that? You can't even look at me. This was going to be the last bright flicker before the flame goes out, *pffff*. It was all going to be romantic and tender and passionate—red roses. What was I thinking? I *am* a fool."

I reached out and again she stepped away, eluding my touch. "This has been a terrible week," I said.

"Has it? Has it? Have you had a terrible week? Poor thing."

"Don't, Lily. Don't do this."

"Do what?"

"Talk to me."

"What would you like to know?"

"Talk to me. Come sit down."

When I caught hold of her wrist, she tried to pull away but struggled only for a moment before giving in, not so much to me as to a sorrow that made her shudder as it raked through her. Somehow we ended up on the love seat, and she was curled against me, weeping, tugging at the opening of my jacket as if she wanted to crawl inside it. Her weeping came from down deep, with a croupy, rasping, rattling sound, and it went on and on. In all the years I'd known her, I'd seen her shed tears but not like this. She kept her displays of suffering private—the Admiral's training, I suppose—and these tears, this weeping, made me feel that some last privilege of intimacy had been granted, or so I realize now. At the time I stroked her sleeve and said soothing words, still a little frightened by her strangeness, feeling her warm weight sink into my chest and settle there, not knowing what to do except hold her.

When she finally lifted her head, her breath still coming in short snatches, her makeup was ruined. She tried to say something, tapping the damp spot on my jacket where her cheek had rested. *Wet*, I think she said, or *Wait*. She went into the bathroom and for several minutes I sat and waited, unable to grasp what was happening, listening to the sound of water running through pipes hidden in the walls, looking at the deep red roses, a dozen of them with a few sprigs of baby's breath threading through the stems, standing in a glass vase that was much too small. She'd bought me roses, red roses. I don't think any woman had ever given me red roses. *Red for passion*, she had said. *Our last time*, she had said. They were beautiful, beautiful roses.

"You're still here," Lily said when she came from the bathroom, approaching me cautiously. Her face was scrubbed clean. The lipstick was gone and her hair was damp, pushed straight back from her forehead, showing the lines of a broad-toothed comb. She stood close to me and allowed me to catch her hand. "I wouldn't blame you if you'd left. I haven't cried like that in years," she said, sitting down beside me, tucking her legs under her, tapping the damp spot on my jacket. "You caught it, didn't you? Lucky you."

She reached up and stroked my cheek. The last time, I thought, watching her hand with its netting of veins, looking at those wide-spaced eyes that even in the dim light appeared to be a deeper, more refined shade of blue, like the sky after a storm. She curled up against me, her head on my shoulder, and began to speak in a weary, wondering voice, as though she were telling a story she herself couldn't quite believe.

Abby was going to have the baby, she told me. Abby, a mother. The decision to keep the baby had been made in the music room, and the strange thing was that Tony was the one who forced it—Tony, who wanted a different outcome. But he had such a phobia about putting things off that he insisted on a decision. Still, Lily hadn't been convinced that Abby would actually have the child until yesterday, when she announced that she'd chosen a name for it. Ruby. "'What if it's not a girl?' I asked her, and she said, 'Mom, I know it's a girl.'"

So this child had a name, but the plans were still up in the air. The whole family was going out west right after Christmas for their annual ski trip, but she and Abby weren't coming back to Washington immediately. They were going to Jacksonville to stay with Elena. Lily wanted a little time alone with Abby, and she didn't want to be any place where there were Moorefields to sit in judgment on her. Maybe they'd just stay in Florida—could I imagine Abby here in Washington, pregnant, going to school? Going to Byrd-Adams? Maybe they'd just stay there in Jacksonville and work at the marina. They could scrub boats for six months. The baby was due in early June and they hadn't decided what they were going to tell people, or even whether they'd say that it was Abby's baby.

"We might just pretend it's mine."

"Yours?"

"Well, I'm going to be the one who raises it. I'm the only one who could. Abby thinks she can raise it and go to school at the same time. People do it all the time, she says, but I'm the one who has the time to spend. I could raise a child without changing everything—I'd just have to set up the nursery again. I'd tell people we were just continuing the Baby Oops tradition in the family, but I don't know if Abby would let me get away with it."

What had persuaded Abby not to have the abortion, she said, was the idea that she wouldn't have to go it alone. Or that's what she, Lily, had been saying when Abby made up her mind—who knew what really persuaded her? Maybe it was what she said, or what Kat said—Abby had been surprised by Kat's ideas—or the fact that Tony was pressing her. Maybe it was the way she felt about Jed, or the sheer challenge of having a child so young, or maybe her mothering instincts had kicked in. The real decision had to come from somewhere deep within Abby, didn't it? Didn't I think that all important decisions came from a place so deep within us that we never really understood them? We just made up stories to make ourselves think we understood.

Lily's head, that mass of damp hair, was against my chest, and she spoke as if in a reverie, stroking my chin and throat almost absentmindedly. Her words bubbled out of her in what seemed like a free flow of consciousness, words that weren't considered, simply released. "Maybe that's what I really wanted, another baby. Does that sound too strange? I've had such strange thoughts about all this. A baby. Maybe that's what I'm supposed to be—a mother. Or maybe I'm supposed to keep doing it until I get it right."

She said she'd never gotten it right with Abby, but maybe now she would, maybe this was her chance, maybe they really ought to stay down in Florida. Abby was almost the age she'd been when she spent so much time with her mother, those months when her mother was dying—and this was different, it was so different, but they'd be alone together, they'd be thrown together, they'd have to learn to get along and trust each other. Did I know that Abby's middle name was Helen? Helen, her mother's name. Wasn't it odd that she felt Elena was the one she could turn to now—Elena, her stepmother, though she'd been married by the time the Admiral met Elena, and she'd resented her at first. Wasn't it odd how people just entered your life? Like Jed. How could that happen? How could it happen that she would end up raising Jed Vandenberg's child?

I didn't interrupt her. I wanted her to keep talking, and I wanted to keep listening as she made up a future. If they stayed in Florida, she mused, she might be able to get away with telling people that she was sorting out her father's estate. That sounded plausible, didn't it? People sometimes went away for months to take care of their parent's estate. Of course there was usually a house to sell, stuff to go through, things to distribute, and Elena was still in the house, but it was plausible. It would be harder to explain why Abby wasn't in school, but who really cared? So what? That was Abby's attitude, and maybe she was too worried about what people might think. Whatever they did, they weren't going to do it to please other people. Maybe some people would assume that she'd taken Abby to Florida to get her away from Jed. Wouldn't that be old-fashioned? Like those rich people who sent their children on world tours to prevent them from marrying the wrong person. And maybe it wasn't Abby who was being sent away. Maybe she was sending herself away, to get away from me. Maybe she was feeling penitential—yes, she was feeling guilty and penitential. Why deny it? Those feelings were part of it; all her feelings were a part of it. She'd done things she shouldn't have done, we'd done things we shouldn't have done, but we'd been lucky in some ways, hadn't we? How could everything have gotten so mixed together, all the sorrows and all the joys? How could it be possible that she was going to be a grandmother? That this child's other grandparents would be Richard and Valerie Vandenberg? Tony had talked to them, but she hadn't, and of course they were horrified at the decision Abby had made. She didn't think Jed would be in the picture much longer.

Tony. He'd been great about it, really, once Abby had made up her mind. Lily's hand stopped moving for a moment as she considered how to speak about her husband. "I decided not to tell him about us," she said, lifting her head, wanting to see my face again, wanting me to feel what the words conveyed. "There were so many times that I was about to tell him about us, but I couldn't, not in the midst of every-thing that was going on around us. I just couldn't. Tony had an af-fair—did you know that?"

I didn't know, and I didn't know why she'd blurted it out.

"He had an affair, years ago, after we lost Julia. I found out about it, but this hasn't been about getting even with Tony."

"What was it about?"

Lily said in a dreamy voice, "I wish I knew, especially after all the hours I've thought about it. I wish I could explain why I did something I swore I'd never do—not just swore at the altar, but swore in my heart. Sometimes I think it was Daddy's death that unmoored me, or having Abby fall in love, or turning forty. Maybe it was about wishing I'd had a big talent when I only had a small one. It was about a thousand little disappointments and resentments. It was about all that, but mostly I think it was about us. It was about you and me and about all those years that piled up around us. Do you know that song "I Could Write a Book"? I've been humming it to myself for months."

"How does it go?"

She hummed a few bars but I still didn't recognize it. "I never let you hear it," she said. "I was afraid you'd know what I was thinking—it's such a giveaway. The last lines are about how the book ends. About the friends who become lovers. You know those lines."

She half sang the words, her breath on my neck. "I couldn't let you hear that, could I? Because that's not how it ends. I stay with Tony. That's something I realized—well, I've always known. We don't run off. That was the agreement, remember? The world doesn't discover anything, but we were lovers, weren't we? For a while we were lovers."

Were, I heard.

The room was still and quiet.

"Is this the ending?" I asked.

"It has to be," Lily said. She put my fingers to her lips, then placed them inside her gown, above her heart.

"It's the last time. Can you feel my heart racing? The last time."

She tugged at the sleeve of my jacket, tugged lightly with her thumb and forefinger, as if unsure how to take hold of me. She got to her feet, and when she had me standing beside her, she moved back just long enough to untie the sash of her robe and let it fall to the floor. Underneath she was wearing a white negligee, and she leaned against me, carefully, fitting herself against me as if using her body to make a mold. The last time. Through the film of the silk every sensation was magnified, and her head was bent slightly back so that she could watch my face, concentrating as though her movements required the most delicate precision. She never looked down when she unbuckled my belt, trusting her fingers more than her eyes, never looked down as she let that fabric glide against my flesh, rising on her tiptoes to do so. "I want to remember this," she said, "every bit of it."

The last time, the last time. I remember the sensation of her rising, and the straight, clear collarbones, the field of faint freckles at the top of her chest, the breasts trembling under the white silk, the shiver that passed through her like a visitation when she lifted the front of her negligee and permitted her flesh to touch against mine. She closed her eyes, and I understood that she was giving herself to me as completely as she could.

The last time. In that room, on that bed, I felt the fullness of that gift, and as I write now, I seem to remember her as though—oh, as though she was the great wave that had broken over me. She was like water, around me everywhere, not a mermaid but the sea itself, an element altogether foreign to the air in which I was accustomed to living. How could she seem at once so strange and so familiar, so beautiful and so ordinary, so present and so elusive? How could I have found her if there was no way to keep her? How could she, at the moment she was leaving, leaving, leaving, receding like surf on the sand, have whispered the words she had never before allowed herself to say?

She said them. She said, "I love you, Tucker Jones," and then she was gone.

The beautiful, beautiful roses.

CHAPTER 10

The final surprise came the next day. My lawyers called, both of them on the speakerphone. "We've got a Christmas miracle for you," Brian said in a voice joyful and triumphant. "I hope you're sitting down because this is the phone call you've been waiting for. Briggs is ready to cut a deal. The little fucker called this morning and he's ready to cut a deal."

"Santa's little elf," Ian said, "just trying to make us merry."

They told me that Briggs was willing to let me plead guilty to simple assault. This was a misdemeanor, and there'd be no trial. There'd be no jail time. Since I was a first-time offender, I'd be on probation for a year, but after that my record would be clean again.

"Best possible outcome," Brian said, "and there's more. Vandenberg has been busy. He must have decided that he never wants to hear your name again, because Briggs wanted me to call his other lawyer, the guy representing him in the civil action—and he wants to settle. You ready for this? He wants to settle for two hundred and fifty thousand."

I didn't respond right away, and Brian asked, "You there? I said 250K. I never thought I'd hear that number, not from Vandenberg. I didn't think he was going to back off until he'd ruined you."

That amount came close to ruining me, but I could raise it. With a second mortgage on the Hut and a big loan on the business, I could raise it. I'd be paying off the loans for the rest of my life.

"We got him down seven million—more than that, seven and a quarter million. You can go shopping with that. Son of a bitch, I never thought he'd throw in the towel."

This outcome was miraculous, I suppose, but I couldn't stop thinking of everything that had taken place over the last few days. The fact that Richard Vandenberg was going to be a grandparent, that Jed was going to be the father of a child—surely that stood behind this offer to settle. As Brian and Ian filled me in on the next steps, the paperwork and procedures needed to complete both lawsuits, I kept wondering about Jed and the scenes he must have gone through with his father. I will never know, of course, how it played out between them, or how it played out in his heart. Did he tell his father to back away from the charges because he wanted to protect his friends? Had our meeting at the Hut figured in his decision? Did he think this was a just outcome? Was he fed up with his father? Did the lawsuit simply not matter any longer now that Abby was carrying his child?

I think Lily was right: our most important decisions come from deep down, and we never understand them completely.

At any rate, I was not as jubilant as Brian thought I should have been. I was relieved, of course, but even as I sat there in my office and let the news sink in, I felt the magnitude of the changes that had taken place during that year—half a year, really—that had begun the night I left my house in search of Kat. Here's a last cheesy image: I was like a runner who has just staggered across the finish line, and it hits him all at once just how far he has gone and what that effort has taken out of him. I wasn't the same man I had been when I started, and even as Brian exulted in our victory, I knew that I would be trying to make sense of all that had happened for a long time to come.

None of us—not Jed, not Abby, not Lily, not Trish or Christine, not Kat—was going to be the same again. *This* story was over, and I seemed to feel the weight of it, all the guilt and sadness, as I sat in my office on that dreary December day. I knew better than anyone how many mistakes I'd made, how many rules I'd broken, how frightened and remorseful and ashamed I'd been. I'd done things for which I can never atone, and yet I have to say that I felt the stirrings of something else, something like gratitude.

Does that seem strange? It did to me, but as the days and weeks and months have passed, as all these events had receded further and further into the past, I've had to rely on my old rule: *It is what it is.* The gratitude and the remorse are twined together in strands that I cannot separate. I can and do wish that I hadn't harmed anyone, but I feel closer than ever to my children. I can and do wish that there'd been a future for me and Lily, but there wasn't. Sometimes when I look at Kat or Will, or when I hear a snatch of song that reminds me of Lily, love comes over me just like that, sudden and irrefutable, as real as breath. There's no arguing with it, as Joe Jarvis said. It's there, and it seems to have staying power.

And so, forgive me, I end up feeling blessed. Can you imagine?

THERE IS one last memory to write down.

It has to be the last one, the last memory of 1998. We were in the car, Will and Kat and I, driving northward across New Jersey on a starry winter night. "Oh, great," Will said sarcastically when I announced that I was going to tell a story, "that's just great." The kids had been bickering for miles, ever since Will started complaining about the tape I had selected, *A Christmas Carol,* and trying to imitate the voice of Tiny Tim, making up lines as though he were putting together a skit for Monty Python, whose humor he had just discovered, and he'd also discovered that he could rile his sister by locking into his Monty Python routines. The Dickens story was too sentimental for him, and by his count he'd seen the play a thousand times. His Tiny Tim said, "My leg? Oh, it's falling off, and I expect to die tonight, but pay no mind, pay no mind."

"That is so not funny," Kat said from the backseat. When we were all together, she usually rode in the back, letting Will win the battle for the front seat. But she didn't seem all that interested in hearing the rest of *A Christmas Carol,* either, and defended it more for the sake of quarreling with her brother. We were all grouchy, I suppose, for the drive from Washington to New York always takes longer during the holidays, and we'd been in heavy traffic the whole way. The trunk was filled with Christmas presents, for I was going to deliver the kids to

Trish's apartment in New York and continue northward to spend Christmas with my sister.

"You guys used to like to hear stories in the car," I said.

"We're not three years old anymore," Will said.

"I'm going to tell you a story anyway, your Christmas story."

Will groaned.

"Think of it as a tradition," I said. "You have to listen to it once a year."

He slipped down a bit in his seat, his face shadowed with the glow from the orange lights on the dash, and I could see the outline of Kat's head in the rearview mirror. "It'll help get us there," I said, "and what's so terrible about hearing a story about yourselves?"

"It's not like we're heroes in it," Will said.

"You want me to make you heroes?"

"What? You're going to give me crutches in the story?"

"You want crutches?"

"Sure."

"Dad," Kat said, "don't ruin it." She'd slid toward the center of the backseat so that she could make eye contact with me in the mirror.

"All right, then, no crutches. Maybe a few special effects, OK?"

They were silent and I began.

"Once upon a time there were two children, a brother and sister, who lived in a little white house with their father. Their names were Kat and Will, and they lived in a city where it didn't often snow. On this night, though, a night not long before Christmas, a perfect snow was falling, perfect fine flakes, covering the street and the sidewalk and the cars parked on the street. Their father had let them go out and play in the snow and when they went to bed, they were too excited to fall asleep. They kept going to the window to watch the snow coming down, falling silently, covering the whole wide world."

I didn't mention that this was our last Christmas in Georgetown, the only Christmas we spent there after Trish left.

"Well. When they finally drifted off to sleep, visions of sugarplums danced in their heads—no, not sugarplums. Visions of snowmen, the snowmen they were going to make the next day. The brother, Will, woke up in the middle of the night and looked out the window to make sure that it was still snowing. It was. The snow was piling up everywhere, and Will decided he should tell his father. But when he went into his father's room, the bed was empty. His father was nowhere to be found.

"So Will went to his sister's tiny bedroom and woke her up. She was a little older than he was, and he thought she would be able to find the father—but she couldn't. They looked upstairs and downstairs in that little house, but they couldn't find their father anywhere, and do you know what they decided?"

I let the question hang for a moment, and Will answered, "To go look for him."

"That's right. They decided to go look for him. They thought they had looked everywhere, but they hadn't gone down into the basement—and that's where the father was. He'd gone down there to build a fantastic car."

"That yellow Corvette," Will said.

I nodded. Will had loved that toy car. "Some assembly was required," I said. "Quite a lot of assembly, actually, and the father had decided to take a short rest on the bed down in the basement, but he fell fast asleep. Now here's one of the strange parts of the story—Will and Kat didn't cry. They were frightened when they couldn't find their father, but they didn't cry and scream. They were brave children and, besides, they both wanted to go out into the snow. So they decided they'd go look for their father. They thought they knew just where he'd be, at a friend's house nearby. They knew the way, and they put on their snowsuits to go look for him. That's another surprising part of the story—the father didn't know they could put on those snowsuits by themselves. He usually had to help them. But they put on everything— the snowsuits, boots, hats, gloves, everything they needed."

"I put his on for him," Kat said.

"How can you remember that?" Will said.

"I do," Kat said.

"Whoever put them on, they both got dressed for their expedition. They got dressed and they left the house and set out for that neigh-

bor's house. They were confident that they knew the way. They'd
been there many, many times, and it wasn't far away, not far at all. But
that night, with the snow falling, the world looked different. It wasn't
the same place at all. All the usual landmarks were covered up with
snow, and the children walked right by the neighbor's house without
recognizing it. The snow was up to their waists—"

"It wasn't that deep," Kat said.

"In the drifts, the snow was up to their waists, but they still weren't
frightened. The world looked new and beautiful and magical. Everyone else was snug in their beds, and they were all alone. Maybe they
were just a little bit frightened, but they kept walking until they came
to the bright lights in the heart of the city."

"Wisconsin Avenue," Will said.

"There were a few other people on the street, and now, for the first
time, the children realized they were lost. They realized that this
wasn't the way to the friends' house, and they decided to turn around
and go back home. Their plan was to follow their own footsteps
back—that was the sister's idea. She must have gotten it from a fairy
tale. She was a girl who liked fairy tales. But when they tried, they discovered that the snow had filled in their footsteps and they weren't
sure which way to go.

"There was nothing to do but push on. They were getting cold
now, and people stopped to talk to them. Of course they did. It was
after midnight and there they were, two children walking the streets
by themselves. A giant in a fur coat and a huge hat, a hat as big as an
umbrella, swooped them up in his arms and carried them away. He
took them to his castle where there was music and feasting and gave
them big steaming mugs of hot chocolate topped with mountains of
whipped cream."

"It was just Nathan's," Will said. We were nearing the end of the
New Jersey Turnpike, passing the Newark Airport, and he was looking
out the window at the planes lined up along the blue runway lights.

"The people in the castle treated them as though they were the
long-lost prince and princess. They helped them out of their snowsuits
and wrapped them in warm, dry clothes—since they were wearing

their jammies underneath, and they were wet, too—and sat them right up on the place of honor, the bar, and serenaded them with Christmas carols. The princess was wearing the giant's fur coat and the prince was covered up with a Redskins jacket, a royal garment."

"Was I really in a fur coat?" Kat asked. "Or did you just make that up?"

"It was a fur coat, and you know what I think? I think Kat and Will had such a good time that they forgot all about their father. They didn't know that they'd left the front door open when they left the house, and the cold air rushed in so that he woke up shivering. He woke up shivering, and when he came upstairs to see why the house had gotten so cold, when he saw that door standing open—well, he thought someone had broken in. He raced upstairs and saw that his children weren't in their beds. His dear children were gone, but he didn't think they'd gone looking for him. How could he imagine that they'd awakened in the middle of the night and stolen out of the house without a sound? No, someone must have come in and taken them away. Kidnapped them, that's what he thought. They'd been kidnapped.

"He was frantic. He immediately called the police, but he thought his heart would explode, it was beating so hard in his chest. It took him awhile to calm down enough to realize that if someone had come to steal his children, there would have to be footsteps in the snow. It took him awhile to look outside the door, and there, to his surprise, there were only two sets of footsteps, little ones, already filling up with snow. His children had run away! But he didn't think they'd go far, and he raced over to the neighbors' house and banged on their door."

"The Moorefields," said Will, my literal-minded son.

Kat was sitting forward now, listening, watching me steadily in the mirror as we entered the vortex of traffic that whirls around New York. There always seems to be a perceptible increase in volume, speed, and tension as you pass the airport and roll through the Meadowlands, as though you have entered the magnetic field of the city that lies just beyond the low lights of the Jersey horizon.

"He woke up the whole household, but he still couldn't decide what to do. Should he try to follow the tracks? Not a good idea, since he couldn't even see their tracks. Had the children decided to go out and play in the snow? He knew how excited they were. But why hadn't they told him? He talked this over with the neighbors and sent them out to look in the children's favorite places because he had just remembered the first rule. What is it?"

"Rules," Will groaned.

"Stay put when someone's lost. What good is it to have everyone lost? So the neighbors went out looking and the father went back home, and it's a good thing he did."

"Because the phone rang and the police arrived and the children were OK and everybody lived happily ever after," Will said.

"I can see you're going to be a real storyteller," I said.

"That is how it ends."

"A man from Nathan's did call me. The sister knew the phone number. She actually remembered it."

"My hero," Will said. "If it weren't for her, we'd probably still be at Nathan's."

"It's amazing that you two made it that far by yourselves. Seven blocks in the middle of that night, two kids in a snowstorm? It was your magnificent journey."

"Except we weren't going home," Kat said. "We were going in the other direction."

"Yeah," Will said, "so what is the moral?"

I could think of several, but I said, "Not every story has to have a moral. You made a journey. You left home and traveled through the dark and stormy night to reach a safe place. You stuck together, and when you got back home, I was waiting for you. The story is its own moral."

I hope they were satisfied. I think they were. They'd listened thoughtfully, in any case, to this retelling of their adventure. Even to them, especially to them, that night must have seemed long ago and far away, and for a few moments—before we reached the place where the roadway is elevated and the city comes into view all at once, before that astonishing skyline of lights suddenly appeared and Will announced, "There it is," before Kat slid over to peer out the window and I felt a shift in the air of the car, the quickening, the leap of excitement as they cast their wondering minds toward our destination, toward the future, toward the brilliant towers of light—we journeyed along in a nostalgic silence, my children and I, imagining a snowfall and a journey, imagining the search for each other, bound together by a family story that seemed to hold the clues to who we were.